The Scalp Hunters

by Mayne Reid

Jefferson Publication

ISBN-13: 978-1515171652

Printed in the United States of America

Contents

Chapter One.

The Wild West.

Unroll the world's map, and look upon the great northern continent of America. Away to the wild west, away toward the setting sun, away beyond many a far meridian, let your eyes wander. Rest them where golden rivers rise among peaks that carry the eternal snow. Rest them there.

You are looking upon a land whose features are un-furrowed by human hands, still bearing the marks of the Almighty mould, as upon the morning of creation; a region whose every object wears the impress of God's image. His ambient spirit lives in the silent grandeur of its mountains, and speaks in the roar of its mighty rivers: a region redolent of romance, rich in the reality of adventure.

Follow me, with the eye of your mind, through scenes of wild beauty, of savage sublimity.

I stand in an open plain. I turn my face to the north, to the south, to the east, and to the west; and on all sides behold the blue circle of the heavens girdling around me. Nor rock, nor tree, breaks the ring of the horizon. What covers the broad expanse between? Wood? water? grass? No; flowers. As far as my eye can range, it rests only on flowers, on beautiful flowers!

I am looking as on a tinted map, an enamelled picture brilliant with every hue of the prism.

Yonder is golden yellow, where the helianthus turns her dial-like face to the sun. Yonder, scarlet, where the malva erects its red banner. Here is a parterre of the purple monarda, there the euphorbia sheds its silver leaf. Yonder the orange predominates in the showy flowers of the asclepia; and beyond, the eye roams over the pink blossoms of the cleome.

The breeze stirs them. Millions of corollas are waving their gaudy standards. The tall stalks of the helianthus bend and rise in long undulations, like billows on a golden sea.

They are at rest again. The air is filled with odours sweet as the perfumes of Araby or Ind. Myriads of insects flap their gay wings: flowers of themselves. The bee-birds skirr around, glancing like stray sunbeams; or, poised on whirring wings, drink from the nectared cups; and the wild bee, with laden limbs, clings among the honeyed pistils, or leaves for his far hive with a song of joy.

Who planted these flowers? Who hath woven them into these pictured parterres? Nature. It is her richest mantle, richer in its hues than the scarfs of Cashmere.

This is the "weed prairie." It is misnamed. It is "the garden of God."

The scene is changed. I am in a plain as before, with the unbroken horizon circling around me. What do I behold? Flowers? No; there is not a flower in sight, but one vast expanse of living verdure. From north to south, from east to west, stretches the prairie meadow, green as an emerald, and smooth as the surface of a sleeping lake.

The wind is upon its bosom, sweeping the silken blades. They are in motion; and the verdure is dappled into lighter and darker shades, as the shadows of summer clouds flitting across the sun.

The eye wanders without resistance. Perchance it encounters the dark hirsute forms of the buffalo, or traces the tiny outlines of the antelope. Perchance it follows, in pleased wonder, the far-wild gallop of a snow-white steed.

This is the "grass prairie," the boundless pasture of the bison.

The scene changes. The earth is no longer level, but treeless and verdant as ever. Its surface exhibits a succession of parallel undulations, here and there swelling into smooth round hills. It is covered with a soft turf of brilliant greenness. These undulations remind one of the ocean after a mighty storm, when the crisped foam has died upon the waves, and the big swell comes bowling in. They look as though they had once been such waves, that by an omnipotent mandate had been transformed to earth and suddenly stood still.

This is the "rolling prairie."

Again the scene changes. I am among greenswards and bright flowers; but the view is broken by groves and clumps of copse-wood. The frondage is varied, its tints are vivid, its outlines soft and graceful. As I move forward, new landscapes open up continuously: views park-like and picturesque. Gangs of buffalo, herds of antelope, and droves of wild horses, mottle the far vistas. Turkeys run into the coppice, and pheasants whirr up from the path.

Where are the owners of these lands, of these flocks and fowls? Where are the houses, the palaces, that should appertain to these lordly parks? I look forward, expecting to see the turrets of tall mansions spring up over the groves. But no. For hundreds of miles around no chimney sends forth its smoke. Although with a cultivated aspect, this region is only trodden by the moccasined foot of the hunter, and his enemy, the Red Indian.

These are the *mottes*—the "islands" of the prairie sea.

I am in the deep forest. It is night, and the log fire throws out its vermilion glare, painting the objects that surround our bivouac. Huge trunks stand thickly around us; and massive limbs, grey and giant-like, stretch out and over. I notice the bark. It is cracked, and clings in broad scales crisping outward. Long snake-like parasites creep from tree to tree, coiling the trunks as though they were serpents, and would crush them! There are no leaves overhead. They have ripened and fallen; but the white Spanish moss, festooned along the branches, hangs weeping down like the drapery of a deathbed.

Prostrate trunks, yards in diameter and half-decayed, lie along the ground. Their ends exhibit vast cavities where the porcupine and opossum have taken shelter from the cold.

My comrades, wrapped in their blankets, and stretched upon the dead leaves, have gone to sleep. They lie with their feet to the fire, and their heads resting in the hollow of their saddles. The horses, standing around a tree, and tied to its lower branches, seem also to sleep. I am awake and listening. The wind is high up, whistling among the twigs and causing the long white streamers to oscillate. It utters a wild and melancholy music. There are few other sounds, for it is winter, and the tree-frog and cicada are silent. I hear the crackling knots in the fire, the rustling of dry leaves swirled up by a stray gust, the "coo-whoo-a" of the white owl, the bark of the raccoon, and, at intervals, the dismal howling of wolves. These are the nocturnal voices of the winter forest. They are savage sounds; yet there is a chord in my bosom that vibrates under their influence, and my spirit is tinged with romance as I lie and listen.

The forest in autumn; still bearing its full frondage. The leaves resemble flowers, so bright are their hues. They are red and yellow, and golden and brown. The woods are warm and glorious now, and the birds flutter among the laden branches. The eye wanders delighted down long vistas and over sunlit glades. It is caught by the flashing of gaudy plumage, the golden green of the paroquet, the blue of the jay, and the orange wing of the oriole. The red-bird flutters lower down in the coppice of green pawpaws, or amidst the amber leaflets of the beechen thicket. Hundreds of tiny wings flit through the openings, twinkling in the sun like the glancing of gems.

The air is filled with music: sweet sounds of love. The bark of the squirrel, the cooing of mated doves, the "rat-ta-ta" of the pecker, and the constant and measured chirrup of the cicada, are all ringing together. High up, on a topmost twig, the mocking-bird pours forth his mimic note, as though he would shame all other songsters into silence.

I am in a country of brown barren earth and broken outlines. There are rocks and clefts and patches of sterile soil. Strange vegetable forms grow in the clefts and hang over the rocks. Others are spheroidal in shape, resting upon the surface of the parched earth. Others rise vertically to a great height, like carved and fluted columns. Some throw out branches, crooked, shaggy branches, with hirsute oval leaves. Yet there is a homogeneousness about all these vegetable forms, in their colour, in their fruit and flowers, that proclaims them of one family. They are cacti. It is a forest of the Mexican nopal. Another singular plant is here. It throws out long, thorny leaves that curve downward. It is the agave, the far-famed mezcal-plant of Mexico. Here and there, mingling with the cacti, are trees of acacia and mezquite, the denizens of the desert-land. No bright object relieves the eye; no bird pours its melody into the ear. The lonely owl flaps away into the impassable thicket, the rattlesnake glides under its scanty shade, and the coyote skulks through its silent glades.

I have climbed mountain after mountain, and still I behold peaks soaring far above, crowned with the snow that never melts. I stand upon beetling cliffs, and look into chasms that yawn beneath, sleeping in the silence of desolation. Great fragments have fallen into them, and lie piled one upon another. Others hang threatening over, as if waiting for some concussion of the atmosphere to hurl them from their balance. Dark precipices frown me into fear, and my head reels with a dizzy faintness. I hold by the pine-tree shaft, or the angle of the firmer rock.

Above, and below, and around me, are mountains piled on mountains in chaotic confusion. Some are bald and bleak; others exhibit traces of vegetation in the dark needles of the pine and cedar, whose stunted forms half-grow, half-hang from the cliffs. Here, a cone-shaped peak soars up till it is lost in snow and clouds. There, a ridge elevates its sharp outline against the sky; while along its side, lie huge boulders of granite, as though they had been hurled from the hands of Titan giants!

A fearful monster, the grizzly bear, drags his body along the high ridges; the carcajou squats upon the projecting rock, waiting the elk that must pass to the water below; and the bighorn bounds from crag to crag in search of his shy mate. Along the pine branch the bald buzzard whets his filthy beak; and the war-eagle, soaring over all, cuts sharply against the blue field of the heavens.

These are the Rocky Mountains, the American Andes, the colossal vertebras of the continent!

Such are the aspects of the wild west; such is the scenery of our drama.

Let us raise the curtain, and bring on the characters.

Chapter Two.

The Prairie Merchants.

"New Orleans, *April 3rd*, 18—

"Dear Saint Vrain—Our young friend, Monsieur Henry Haller, goes to Saint Louis in 'search of the picturesque.' See that he be put through a 'regular course of sprouts.'

"Yours,—

"Luis Walton.

"Charles Saint Vrain, Esquire, Planters' Hotel, Saint Louis."

With this laconic epistle in my waistcoat pocket, I debarked at Saint Louis on the 10th of April, and drove to the "Planters'."

After getting my baggage stowed and my horse (a favourite I had brought with me) stabled, I put on a clean shirt, and, descending to the office, inquired for Monsieur Saint Vrain.

He was not there. He had gone up the Missouri river several days before.

This was a disappointment, as I had brought no other introduction to Saint Louis. But I endeavoured to wait with patience the return of Monsieur Saint Vrain. He was expected back in less than a week.

Day after day I mounted my horse, I rode up to the "Mounds" and out upon the prairies. I lounged about the hotel, and smoked my cigar in its fine piazza. I drank sherry cobblers in the saloon, and read the journals in the reading-room.

With these and such like occupations, I killed time for three whole days.

There was a party of gentlemen stopping at the hotel, who seemed to know each other well. I might call them a clique; but that is not a good word, and does not express what I mean. They appeared rather a band of friendly, jovial fellows. They strolled together through the streets, and sat side by side at the table-d'hôte, where they usually remained long after the regular diners had retired. I noticed that they drank the most expensive wines, and smoked the finest cigars the house afforded.

My attention was attracted to these men. I was struck with their peculiar bearing; their erect, Indian-like carriage in the streets, combined with a boyish gaiety, so characteristic of the western American.

They dressed nearly alike: in fine black cloth, white linen, satin waistcoats, and diamond pins. They wore the whisker full, but smoothly trimmed; and several of them sported moustaches. Their hair fell curling over their shoulders; and most of them wore their collars turned down, displaying healthy-looking, sun-tanned throats. I was struck with a resemblance in their physiognomy. Their faces did not resemble each other; but there was an unmistakable similarity in the expression of the eye; no doubt, the mark that had been made by like occupations and experience.

Were they sportsmen? No: the sportsman's hands are whiter; there is more jewellery on his fingers; his waistcoat is of a gayer pattern, and altogether his dress will be more gaudy and super-elegant. Moreover, the sportsman lacks that air of free-and-easy confidence. He dares not assume it. He may live in the hotel, but he must be quiet and unobtrusive. The sportsman is a bird of prey; hence, like all birds of prey, his habits are silent and solitary. They are not of his profession.

"Who are these gentlemen?" I inquired from a person who sat by me, indicating to him the men of whom I have spoken.

"The prairie men."

"The prairie men!"

"Yes; the Santa Fé traders."

"Traders!" I echoed, in some surprise, not being able to connect such "elegants" with any ideas of trade or the prairies.

"Yes," continued my informant. "That large, fine-looking man in the middle is Bent—Bill Bent, as he is called. The gentleman on his right is young Sublette; the other, standing on his left, is one of the Choteaus; and that is the sober Jerry Folger."

"These, then, are the celebrated prairie merchants?"

"Precisely so."

I sat eyeing them with increased curiosity. I observed that they were looking at me, and that I was the subject of their conversation.

Presently, one of them, a dashing-like young fellow, parted from the group, and walked up to me.

"Were you inquiring for Monsieur Saint Vrain?" he asked.

"I was."

"Charles?"

"Yes, that is the name."

"I am—"

I pulled out my note of introduction, and banded it to the gentleman, who glanced over its contents.

"My dear friend," said he, grasping me cordially, "very sorry I have not been here. I came down the river this morning. How stupid of Walton not to superscribe to Bill Bent! How long have you been up?"

"Three days. I arrived on the 10th."

"You are lost. Come, let me make you acquainted. Here, Bent! Bill! Jerry!"

And the next moment I had shaken hands with one and all of the traders, of which fraternity I found that my new friend, Saint Vrain, was a member.

"First gong that?" asked one, as the loud scream of a gong came through the gallery.

"Yes," replied Bent, consulting his watch. "Just time to 'licker.' Come along!"

Bent moved towards the saloon, and we all followed, *nemine dissentiente*.

The spring season was setting in, and the young mint had sprouted—a botanical fact with which my new acquaintances appeared to be familiar, as one and all of them ordered a mint julep. This beverage, in the mixing and drinking, occupied our time until the second scream of the gong summoned us to dinner.

"Sit with us, Mr Haller," said Bent; "I am sorry we didn't know you sooner. You have been lonely."

And so saying, he led the way into the dining-room, followed by his companions and myself.

I need not describe a dinner at the "Planters'," with its venison steaks, its buffalo tongues, its prairie chickens, and its delicious frog fixings from the Illinois "bottom." No; I would not describe the dinner, and what followed I am afraid I could not.

We sat until we had the table to ourselves. Then the cloth was removed, and we commenced smoking regalias and drinking madeira at twelve dollars a bottle! This was ordered in by someone, not in single bottles, but by the half-dozen. I remembered thus far well enough; and that, whenever I took up a wine-card, or a pencil, these articles were snatched out of my fingers.

I remember listening to stories of wild adventures among the Pawnees, and the Comanches, and the Blackfeet, until I was filled with interest, and became enthusiastic about prairie life. Then someone asked me, would I not like to join them in "a trip"? Upon this I made a speech, and proposed to accompany my new acquaintances on their next expedition: and then Saint Vrain said I was just the man for their life; and this pleased me highly. Then someone sang a Spanish song, with a guitar, I think, and someone else danced an Indian war-dance; and then we all rose to our feet, and chorused the "Star-spangled Banner"; and I remember nothing else after this, until next morning, when I remember well that I awoke with a splitting headache.

I had hardly time to reflect on my previous night's folly, when the door opened, and Saint Vrain, with half a dozen of my table companions, rushed into the room. They were followed by a waiter, who carried several large glasses topped with ice, and filled with a pale amber-coloured liquid.

"A sherry cobbler, Mr Haller," cried one; "best thing in the world for you: drain it, my boy. It'll cool you in a squirrel's jump."

I drank off the refreshing beverage as desired.

"Now, my dear friend," said Saint Vrain, "you feel a hundred per cent, better! But, tell me, were you in earnest when you spoke of going with us across the plains? We start in a week; I shall be sorry to part with you so soon."

"But I was in earnest. I am going with you, if you will only show me how I am to set about it."

"Nothing easier: buy yourself a horse."

"I have got one."

"Then a few coarse articles of dress, a rifle, a pair of pistols, a—"

"Stop, stop! I have all these things. That is not what I would be at, but this: You, gentlemen, carry goods to Santa Fé. You double or treble your money on them. Now, I have ten thousand dollars in a bank here. What should hinder me to combine profit with pleasure, and invest it as you do?"

"Nothing; nothing! A good idea," answered several.

"Well, then, if any of you will have the goodness to go with me, and show me what sort of merchandise I am to lay in for the Santa Fé market, I will pay his wine bill at dinner, and that's no small commission, I think."

The prairie men laughed loudly, declaring they would all go a-shopping with me; and, after breakfast, we started in a body, arm-in-arm.

Before dinner I had invested nearly all my disposable funds in printed calicoes, long knives, and looking-glasses, leaving just money enough to purchase mule-waggons and hire teamsters at Independence, our point of departure for the plains.

A few days after, with my new companions, I was steaming up the Missouri, on our way to the trackless prairies of the "Far West."

Chapter Three.

The Prairie Fever.

After a week spent in Independence buying mules and waggons, we took the route over the plains. There were a hundred waggons in the caravan, and nearly twice that number of teamsters and attendants. Two of the capacious vehicles contained all my "plunder;" and, to manage them, I had hired a couple of lathy, long-haired Missourians. I had also engaged a Canadian voyageur named Gode, as a sort of attendant or compagnon.

Where are the glossy gentlemen of the Planters' Hotel? One would suppose they had been left behind, as here are none but men in hunting-shirts and slouch hats. Yes; but under these hats we recognise their faces, and in these rude shirts we have the same jovial fellows as ever. The silky black and the diamonds have disappeared, for now the traders flourish under the prairie costume. I will endeavour to give an idea of the appearance of my companions by describing my own; for I am tricked out very much like themselves.

I wear a hunting-shirt of dressed deerskin. It is a garment more after the style of an ancient tunic than anything I can think of. It is of a light yellow colour, beautifully stitched and embroidered; and the cape, for it has a short cape, is fringed by tags cut out of the leather itself. The skirt is also bordered by a similar fringe, and hangs full and low. A pair of "savers" of scarlet cloth cover my limbs to the thigh; and under these are strong jean pantaloons, heavy boots, and big brass spurs. A coloured cotton shirt, a blue neck-tie, and a broad-brimmed Guayaquil hat, complete the articles of my everyday dress. Behind me, on the cantle of my saddle, may be observed a bright red object folded into a cylindrical form. That is my "Mackinaw," a great favourite, for it makes my bed by night and my greatcoat on other occasions. There is a small slit in the middle of it, through which I thrust my head in cold or rainy weather; and I am thus covered to the ankles.

As I have said, my *compagnons de voyage* are similarly attired. There may be a difference of colour in the blanket or the leggings, or the shirt may be of other materials; but that I have described may be taken as a character dress.

We are all somewhat similarly armed and equipped. For my part, I may say that I am "armed to the teeth." In my holsters I carry a pair of Colt's large-sized revolvers, six shots each. In my belt is another pair of the small size, with five shots each. In addition, I have a light rifle, making in all twenty-three shots, which I have learned to deliver in as many seconds of time. Failing with all these, I carry in my belt a long shining blade known as a "bowie knife." This last is my hunting knife, my dining knife, and, in short, my knife of all work. For accoutrements I have a pouch and a flask, both slung under the right arm. I have also a large gourd canteen and haversack for my rations. So have all my companions.

But we are differently mounted. Some ride saddle mules, others bestride mustangs, while a few have brought their favourite American horses. I am of this number. I ride a dark-brown stallion, with black legs, and muzzle like the withered fern. He is half-Arab, and of perfect proportions. He is called Moro, a Spanish name given him by the Louisiana planter from whom I bought him, but why I do not know. I have retained the name, and he answers to it readily. He is strong, fleet, and beautiful. Many of my friends fancy him on the route, and offer large prices for him; but these do not tempt me, for my Moro serves me well. Every day I grow more and more attached to him. My dog Alp, a Saint Bernard that I bought from a Swiss *émigré* in Saint Louis, hardly comes in for a tithe of my affections.

I find on referring to my note-book that for weeks we travelled over the prairies without any incident of unusual interest. To me the scenery was interest enough; and I do not remember a more striking picture than to see the long caravan of waggons, "the prairie ships," deployed over the plain, or crawling slowly up some gentle slope, their white tilts contrasting beautifully with the deep green of the earth. At night, too, the camp, with its corralled waggons, and horses picketed around, was equally a picture. The scenery was altogether new to me, and imbued me with impressions of a peculiar character. The streams were fringed with tall groves of cottonwood trees, whose column-like stems supported a thick frondage of silvery leaves. These groves meeting at different points, walled in the view, so dividing the prairies from one another, that we seemed to travel through vast fields fenced by colossal hedges.

We crossed many rivers, fording some, and floating our waggons over others that were deeper and wider. Occasionally we saw deer and antelope, and our hunters shot a few of these; but we had not yet reached the range of the buffalo. Once we stopped a day to recruit in a wooded bottom, where the grass was plentiful and the water pure. Now and then, too, we were halted to mend a broken tongue or an axle, or help a "stalled" waggon from its miry bed.

I had very little trouble with my particular division of the caravan. My Missourians turned out to be a pair of staunch hands, who could assist one another without making a desperate affair of every slight accident.

The grass had sprung up, and our mules and oxen, instead of thinning down, every day grew fatter upon it. Moro, therefore, came in for a better share of the maize that I had brought in my waggons, and which kept my favourite in fine travelling condition.

As we approached the Arkansas, we saw mounted Indians disappearing over the swells. They were Pawnees; and for several days clouds of these dusky warriors hung upon the skirts of the caravan. But they knew our strength, and kept at a wary distance from our long rifles.

To me every day brought something new, either in the incidents of the "voyage" or the features of the landscape.

Gode, who has been by turns a voyageur, a hunter, a trapper, and a *coureur du bois*, in our private dialogues had given me an insight into many an item of prairie-craft, thus enabling me to cut quite a respectable figure among my new comrades. Saint Vrain, too, whose frank, generous manner had already won my confidence, spared no pains to make the trip agreeable to me. What with gallops by day and the wilder tales by the night watch-fires, I became intoxicated with the romance of my new life. I had caught the "prairie-fever!"

So my companions told me, laughing. I did not understand them then. I knew what they meant afterwards. The prairie fever! Yes. I was just then in process of being inoculated by that strange disease. It grew upon me apace. The dreams of home began to die within me; and with these the illusory ideas of many a young and foolish ambition.

My strength increased, both physically and intellectually. I experienced a buoyancy of spirits and a vigour of body I had never known before. I felt a pleasure in action. My blood seemed to rush warmer and swifter through my veins, and I fancied that my eyes reached to a more distant vision. I could look boldly upon the sun without quivering in my glance.

Had I imbibed a portion of the divine essence that lives, and moves, and has its being in those vast solitudes? Who can answer this?

Chapter Four.

A Ride upon a Buffalo Bull.

We had been out about two weeks when we struck the Arkansas "bend," about six miles below the Plum Buttes. Here our waggons corralled and camped. So far we had seen but little of the buffalo; only a stray bull, or, at most, two or three together, and these shy. It was now the running season, but none of the great droves, love-maddened, had crossed us.

"Yonder!" cried Saint Vrain; "fresh hump for supper!"

We looked north-west, as indicated by our friend.

Along the escarpment of a low table, five dark objects broke the line of the horizon. A glance was enough: they were buffaloes.

As Saint Vrain spoke, we were about slipping off our saddles. Back went the girth buckles with a sneck, down came the stirrups, up went we, and off in the "twinkling of a goat's eye."

Half a score or so started; some, like myself, for the sport; while others, old hunters, had the "meat" in their eye.

We had made but a short day's march; our horses were still fresh, and in three times as many minutes, the three miles that lay between us and the game were reduced to one. Here, however, we were winded. Some of the party, like myself, green upon the prairies, disregarding advice, had ridden straight ahead; and the bulls snuffed us on the wind. When within a mile, one of them threw up his shaggy front, snorted, struck the ground with his hoof, rolled over, rose up again, and dashed off at full speed, followed by his four companions.

It remained to us now either to abandon the chase or put our horses to their mettle and catch up. The latter course was adopted, and we galloped forward. All at once we found ourselves riding up to what appeared to be a clay wall, six feet high. It was a stair between two tables, and ran right and left as far as the eye could reach, without the semblance of a gap.

This was an obstacle that caused us to rein up and reflect. Some wheeled their horses, and commenced riding back, while half a dozen of us, better mounted, among whom were Saint Vrain and my voyageur Gode, not wishing to give up the chase so easily, put to the spur, and cleared the scarp.

From this point it caused us a five miles' gallop, and our horses a white sweat, to come up with the hindmost, a young cow, which fell, bored by a bullet from every rifle in the party.

As the others had gained some distance ahead, and we had meat enough for all, we reined up, and, dismounting, set about "removing the hair." This operation was a short one under the skilful knives of the hunters. We had now leisure to look back, and calculate the distance we had ridden from camp.

"Eight miles, every inch!" cried one.

"We're close to the trail," said Saint Vrain, pointing to some old waggon tracks that marked the route of the Santa Fé traders.

"Well?"

"If we ride into camp, we shall have to ride back in the morning. It will be sixteen extra miles for our cattle."

"True."

"Let us stay here, then. Here's water and grass. There's buffalo meat; and yonder's a waggon load of 'chips.' We have our blankets; what more do we want?"

"I say, camp where we are."

"And I."

"And I."

In a minute the girth buckles flew open, our saddles were lifted off, and our panting horses were cropping the curly bunches of the prairie grass, within the circles of their *cabriestos*.

A crystal rivulet, the arroyo of the Spaniards, stole away southward to the Arkansas. On the bank of this rivulet, and under one of its bluffs, we chose a spot for our bivouac. The *bois de vache* was collected, a fire was kindled, and hump steaks, spitted on sticks, were soon sputtering in the blaze. Luckily, Saint Vrain and I had our flasks along; and as each of them contained a pint of pure Cognac, we managed to make a tolerable supper. The old hunters had their pipes and tobacco, my friend and I our cigars, and we sat round the ashes till a late hour, smoking and listening to wild tales of mountain adventure.

At length the watch was told off, the lariats were shortened, the picket-pins driven home, and my comrades, rolling themselves up in their blankets, rested their heads in the hollow of their saddles, and went to sleep.

There was a man named Hibbets in our party, who, from his habits of somnolency, had earned the sobriquet of "Sleepy-head." For this reason the first watch had been assigned to him, being the least dangerous, as Indians seldom made their attacks until the hour of soundest sleep—that before daybreak.

Hibbets had climbed to his post, the top of the bluff, where he could command a view of the surrounding prairie.

Before night had set in, I had noticed a very beautiful spot on the bank of the arroyo, about two hundred yards from where my comrades lay. A sudden fancy came into my head to sleep there; and taking up my rifle, robe, and blanket, at the same time calling to "Sleepy-head" to awake me in case of alarm, I proceeded thither.

The ground, shelving gradually down to the arroyo, was covered with soft buffalo grass, thick and dry—as good a bed as was ever pressed by sleepy mortal. On this I spread my robe, and, folding my blanket around me, lay down, cigar in mouth, to smoke myself asleep.

It was a lovely moonlight, so clear that I could easily distinguish the colours of the prairie flowers—the silver euphorbias, the golden sunflowers, and the scarlet malvas, that fringed the banks of the arroyo at my feet. There was an enchanting stillness in the air, broken only by an occasional whine from the prairie wolf, the distant snoring of my companions, and the "crop, crop" of our horses shortening the crisp grass.

I lay a good while awake, until my cigar burnt up to my lips (we smoke them close on the prairies); then, spitting out the stump, I turned over on my side, and was soon in the land of dreams.

I could not have been asleep many minutes when I felt sensible of a strange noise, like distant thunder, or the roaring of a waterfall. The ground seemed to tremble beneath me.

"We are going to have a dash of a thunder-shower," thought I, still half-dreaming, half-sensible to impressions from without; and I drew the folds of my blanket closer around me, and again slept.

I was awakened by a noise like thunder—indeed, like the trampling of a thousand hoofs, and the lowing of a thousand oxen! The earth echoed and trembled. I could hear the shouts of my comrades; the voices of Saint Vrain and Gode, the latter calling out—

"Sacr–r–ré! monsieur; prenez garde des buffles!"

I saw that they had drawn the horses, and were hurrying them under the bluff.

I sprang to my feet, flinging aside my blanket. A fearful spectacle was before me. Away to the west, as far as the eye could reach, the prairie seemed in motion. Black waves rolled over its undulating outlines, as though some burning mountain were pouring down its lava upon the plains. A thousand bright spots flashed and flitted along the moving surface like jets of fire. The ground shook, men shouted, horses reared upon their ropes, neighing wildly. My dog barked, and bowled, running around me!

For a moment I thought I was dreaming; but no, the scene was too real to be mistaken for a vision. I saw the border of a black wave within ten paces of me, and still approaching! Then, and not till then, did I recognise the shaggy crests and glaring eyeballs of the buffalo!

"Oh, God; I am in their track. I shall be trampled to death!"

It was too late to attempt an escape by running. I seized my rifle and fired at the foremost of the band. The effect of my shot was not perceptible. The water of the arroyo was dashed in my face. A huge bull, ahead of the rest, furious and snorting, plunged through the stream and up the slope. I was lifted and tossed high into the air. I was thrown rearwards, and fell upon a moving mass. I did not feel hurt or stunned. I felt myself carried onward upon the backs of several animals, that, in the dense drove, ran close together. These, frightened at their strange burden, bellowed loudly, and dashed on to the front. A sudden thought struck me, and, fixing on that which was most under me, I dropped my legs astride of him, embracing his hump, and clutching the long woolly hair that grew upon his neck. The animal "routed" with extreme terror, and, plunging forward, soon headed the band.

This was exactly what I wanted; and on we went over the prairie, the bull running at top speed, believing, no doubt, that he had a panther or a catamount between his shoulders.

I had no desire to disabuse him of this belief, and, lest he should deem me altogether harmless, and come to a halt, I slipped out my bowie, which happened to be handy, and pricked him up whenever he showed symptoms of lagging. At every fresh touch of the spur he roared out, and ran forward at a redoubled pace.

My danger was still extreme. The drove was coming on behind with the front of nearly a mile. I could not have cleared it had the bull stopped and left me on the prairie.

Nothwithstanding the peril I was in, I could not resist laughing at my ludicrous situation. I felt as one does when looking at a good comedy.

We struck through a village of prairie dogs. Here I fancied the animal was about to turn and run back. This brought my mirth to a sudden pause; but the buffalo usually runs in a bee-line, and fortunately mine made no exception to the law. On he went, sinking to the knees, kicking the dust from the conical hills, snorting and bellowing with rage and terror.

The Plum Buttes were directly in the line or our course. I had seen this from the start, and knew that if I could reach them I would be safe. They were nearly three miles from the bluff where we had bivouacked, but in my ride I fancied them ten.

A small one rose over the prairie, several hundred yards nearer than the main heights. Towards this I pricked the foaming bull in a last stretch, and he brought me cleverly within a hundred yards of its base.

It was now time to take leave of my dusky companion. I could have slaughtered him as I leaned over his back. My knife rested upon the most vulnerable part of his huge body. No! I could not have slain that buffalo for the Koh-i-noor.

Untwisting my fingers from his thick fleece, I slipped down over his tail, and without as much as saying "Goodnight!" ran with all my speed towards the knoll. I climbed up; and sitting down upon a loose boulder of rock, looked over the prairie.

The moon was still shining brightly. My late companion had halted not far from where I had left him, and stood glaring back with an air of extreme bewilderment. There was something so comical in the sight that I yelled with laughter as I sat securely on my perch.

I looked to the south-west. As far as the eye could see, the prairie was black, and moving. The living wave came rolling onward and toward me; but I could now observe it in safety. The myriads of glancing eyes, sparkling like phosphoric gleams, no longer flashed terror.

The drove was still half a mile distant. I thought I saw quick gleams, and heard the report of firearms away over its left border; but I could not be certain. I had begun to think of the fate of my comrades, and this gave me hopes that they were safe.

The buffaloes approached the butte on which I was seated; and, perceiving the obstacle, suddenly forked into two great belts, and swept right and left around it. What struck me at this moment as curious was, that my bull, my particular bull, instead of waiting till his comrades had come up, and falling in among the foremost, suddenly tossed up his head, and galloped off as if a pack of wolves had been after him. He ran towards the outside of the band. When he had reached a point that placed him fairly beyond the flank, I could see him closing in, and moving on with the rest.

This strange tactic of my late companion puzzled me at the time, but I afterwards learned that it was sound strategy on his part. Had he remained where I had parted with him, the foremost bulls coming up would have mistaken him for an individual of some other tribe, and would certainly have gored him to death.

I sat upon the rock for nearly two hours, silently watching the sable stream as it poured past. I was on an island in the midst of a black and glittering sea. At one time I fancied I was moving, that the butte was sailing onward, and the buffaloes were standing still. My head swam with dizziness, and I leaped to my feet to drive away the strange illusion.

The torrent rolled onward, and at length the hindmost went straggling past. I descended from the knoll, and commenced groping my way over the black, trodden earth. What was lately a green sward now presented the aspect of ground freshly ploughed, and trampled by droves of oxen.

A number of white animals, resembling a flock of sheep, passed near me. They were wolves hanging upon the skirts of the herd.

I pushed on, keeping to the southward. At length I heard voices; and, in the clear moonlight, could see several horsemen galloping in circles over the plain. I shouted "Hollo!" A voice answered mine, and one of the horsemen came galloping up; it was Saint Vrain.

"Why, bless me, Haller!" cried he, reining up, and bending from his saddle to get a better view of me, "is it you or your ghost? As I sit here, it's the man himself, and alive!"

"Never in better condition," I replied.

"But where did you come from? the clouds? the sky? where?" And his questions were echoed by the others, who at this moment were shaking me by the hand, as if they had not seen me for a twelvemonth.

Gode seemed to be the most perplexed man of the party.

"Mon Dieu! run over; tramp by von million buffles, et ne pas mort! 'Cr–r–ré matin!"

"We were hunting for your body, or rather, the fragments of it," said Saint Vrain. "We had searched every foot of the prairie for a mile round, and had almost come to the conclusion that the fierce brutes had eaten you up."

"Eat monsieur up! No! tre million buffles no him eat. Mon Dieu! Ha, Sleep-head!"

This exclamation of the Canadian was addressed to Hibbets, who had failed to warn my comrades of where I lay, and thus placed me in such a dangerous predicament.

"We saw you tossed in the air," continued Saint Vrain, "and fall right into the thick of them. Then, of course, we gave you up. But how, in Heaven's name, have you got clear?"

I related my adventure to my wondering comrades.

"Par Dieu!" cried Gode, "un garçon très bizarre: une aventure très merveilleuse!"

From that hour I was looked upon as a "captain" on the prairies.

My comrades had made good work of it, as a dozen dark objects that lay upon the plain testified. They had found my rifle and blankets, the latter trodden into the earth.

Saint Vrain had still a few drops in his flask; and after swallowing these, and again placing the guard, we returned to our prairie couches and slept out the night.

Chapter Five.

In a Bad Fix.

A few days afterwards, another adventure befell me; and I began to think that I was destined to become a hero among the "mountain men." A small party of the traders, myself among the number, had pushed forward ahead of the caravan. Our object was to arrive at Santa Fé a day or two before the waggons, in order to have everything arranged with the Governor for their entrance into that capital. We took the route by the Cimmaron.

Our road, for a hundred miles or so, lay through a barren desert, without game, and almost without water. The buffalo had already disappeared, and deer were equally scarce. We had to content ourselves with the dried meat which we had brought from the settlements. We were in the deserts of the artemisia. Now and then we could see a stray antelope bounding away before us, but keeping far out of range. They, too, seemed to be unusually shy.

On the third day after leaving the caravan, as we were riding near the Cimmaron, I thought I observed a pronged head disappearing behind a swell in the prairie. My companions were sceptical, and none of them would go with me; so, wheeling out of the trail, I started alone. One of the men, for Gode was behind, kept charge of my dog, as I did not choose to take him with me, lest he might alarm the antelopes. My horse was fresh and willing; and whether successful or not, I knew that I could easily overtake the party by camping-time.

I struck directly towards the spot where I had seen the object. It appeared to be only half a mile or so from the trail. It proved more distant—a common illusion in the crystal atmosphere of these upland regions.

A curiously-formed ridge, a *couteau des prairies* on a small scale, traversed the plain from east to west. A thicket of cactus covered part of its summit. Towards this thicket I directed myself.

I dismounted at the bottom of the slope, and leading my horse silently up among the cacti plants, tied him to one of their branches. I then crept cautiously through the thorny leaves towards the point where I fancied I had seen the game. To my joy, not one antelope, but a brace of those beautiful animals were quietly grazing beyond; but, alas! too far off for the range of my rifle. They were fully three hundred yards distant, upon a smooth, grassy slope. There was not even a sage bush to cover me, should I attempt to approach them. What was to be done?

I lay for several minutes, thinking over the different tricks known in hunter-craft for taking the antelope. Should I imitate their call? Should I hoist my handkerchief, and try to lure them up? I saw that they were too shy; for, at short intervals, they threw up their graceful heads and looked inquiringly around them. I remembered the red blanket on my saddle. I could display this upon the cactus bushes; perhaps it would attract them.

I had no alternative, and was turning to go back for the blanket, when, all at once, my eye rested upon a clay-coloured line running across the prairie beyond where the animals were feeding. It was a break in the surface of the plain, a buffalo road, or the channel of an arroyo; in either case the very cover I wanted, for the animals were not a hundred yards from it, and were getting still nearer to it as they fed.

Creeping back out of the thicket, I ran along the side of the slope towards a point where I had noticed that the ridge was depressed to the prairie level. Here, to my surprise, I found myself on the banks of a broad arroyo, whose water, clear and shallow, ran slowly over a bed of sand and gypsum.

The banks were low, not over three feet above the surface of the water, except where the ridge impinged upon the stream. Here there was a high bluff; and, hurrying round its base, I entered the channel, and commenced wading upward.

As I had anticipated, I soon came to a bend where the stream, after running parallel to the ridge, swept round and cañoned through it. At this place I stopped, and looked cautiously over the bank. The antelopes had approached within less than rifle range of the arroyo; but they were yet far above my position. They were still quietly feeding and unconscious of danger. I again bent down and waded on.

It was a difficult task proceeding in this way. The bed of the creek was soft and yielding, and I was compelled to tread slowly and silently lest I should alarm the game; but I was cheered in my exertions by the prospect of fresh venison for my supper.

After a weary drag of several hundred yards, I came opposite to a small clump of wormwood bushes growing out of the bank. "I may be high enough," thought I; "these will serve for cover."

I raised my body gradually until I could see through the leaves. I was in the right spot.

I brought my rifle to a level, sighted for the heart of the buck, and fired. The animal leaped from the ground, and fell back lifeless.

I was about to rush forward and secure my prize, when I observed the doe, instead of running off as I had expected, go up to her fallen partner and press her tapering nose to his body. She was not more than twenty yards from me; and I could plainly see that her look was one of inquiry and bewilderment. All at once she seemed to comprehend the fatal truth; and throwing back her head, commenced uttering the most piteous cries, at the same time running in circles around the body.

I stood wavering between two minds. My first impulse had been to reload and kill the doe; but her plaintive voice entered my heart, disarming me of all hostile intentions. Had I dreamt of witnessing this painful spectacle, I should not have left the trail. But the mischief was now done. "I have worse than killed her," thought I; "it will be better to despatch her at once."

Actuated by these principles of a common, but to her fatal, humanity, I rested the butt of my rifle and reloaded. With a faltering hand I again levelled the piece and fired.

My nerves were steady enough to do the work. When the smoke floated aside, I could see the little creature bleeding upon the grass, her head resting against the body of her murdered mate.

I shouldered my rifle, and was about to move forward, when to my astonishment, I found that I was caught by the feet. I was held firmly, as if my legs had been screwed in a vice!

I made an effort to extricate myself; another, more violent, and equally unsuccessful; and, with a third, I lost my balance, and fell back upon the water.

Half-suffocated, I regained my upright position, but only to find that I was held as fast as ever.

Again I struggled to free my limbs. I could neither move them backward nor forward, to the right nor to the left; and I became sensible that I was gradually going down. Then the fearful truth flashed upon me: I was sinking in a quicksand.

A feeling of horror came over me. I renewed my efforts with the energy of desperation. I leant to one side, then to the other, almost wrenching my knees from their sockets. My feet remained fast as ever. I could not move them an inch.

The soft, clinging sand already overtopped my horseskin boots, wedging them around my ankles, so that I was unable to draw them off; and I could feel that I was still sinking, slowly but surely, as though some subterranean monster were leisurely dragging me down! This very thought caused me a fresh thrill of horror, and I called aloud for help. To whom? There was no one within miles of me—no living thing. Yes! the neigh of my horse answered me from the hill, mocking my despair.

I bent forward as well as my constrained position would permit, and, with frenzied fingers, commenced tearing up the sand. I could barely reach the surface; and the little hollow I was able to make filled up almost as soon as it had been formed.

A thought occurred to me. My rifle might support me, placed horizontally. I looked around for it. It was not to be seen. It had sunk beneath the sand.

Could I throw my body flat, and prevent myself from sinking deeper? No. The water was two feet in depth. I should drown at once.

This last last hope left me as soon as formed. I could think of no plan to save myself. I could make no further effort. A strange stupor seized upon me. My very thoughts became paralysed. I knew that I was going mad. For a moment I was mad!

After an interval my senses returned. I made an effort to rouse my mind from its paralysis, in order that I might meet death, which I now believed to be certain, as a man should.

I stood erect. My eyes had sunk to the prairie level, and rested upon the still bleeding victims of my cruelty. My heart smote me at the sight. Was I suffering a retribution of God?

With humble and penitent thoughts I turned my face to heaven, almost dreading that some sign of omnipotent anger would scowl upon me from above. But no! The sun was shining as brightly as ever, and the blue canopy of the world was without a cloud.

I gazed upward, and prayed with an earnestness known only to the hearts of men in positions of peril like mine.

As I continued to look up, an object attracted my attention. Against the sky I distinguished the outlines of a large bird. I knew it to be the obscene bird of the plains, the buzzard vulture. Whence had it come? Who knows? Far beyond the reach of human eye it had seen or scented the slaughtered antelopes, and on broad, silent wing was now descending to the feast of death.

Presently another, and another, and many others, mottled the blue field of the heavens, curving and wheeling silently earthward. Then the foremost swooped down upon the bank, and after gazing around for a moment, flapped off towards its prey.

In a few seconds the prairie was black with filthy birds, which clambered over the dead antelopes, and beat their wings against each other, while they tore out the eyes of the quarry with their fetid beaks.

And now came gaunt wolves, sneaking and hungry, stealing out of the cactus thicket, and loping, coward-like, over the green swells of the prairie. These, after a battle, drove away the vultures, and tore up the prey, all the while growling and snapping vengefully at each other.

"Thank Heaven! I shall at least be saved from this!"

I was soon relieved from the sight. My eyes had sunk below the level of the bank. I had looked my last on the fair green earth. I could now see only the clayey walls that contained the river, and the water that ran unheeding by me.

Once more I fixed my gaze upon the sky, and with prayerful heart endeavoured to resign myself to my fate.

In spite of my efforts to be calm, the memories of earthly pleasures, and friends, and home came over me, causing me at intervals to break into wild paroxysms, and make fresh, though fruitless, struggles.

Again I was attracted by the neighing of my horse.

A thought entered my mind, filling me with fresh hopes. "Perhaps my horse—"

I lost not a moment. I raised my voice to its highest pitch, and called the animal by name. I knew that he would come at my call. I had tied him but slightly. The cactus limb would snap off. I called again, repeating words that were well known to him. I listened with a bounding heart. For a moment there was silence. Then I heard the quick sounds of his hoofs, as though the animal were rearing and struggling to free himself. Then I could distinguish the stroke of his heels in a measured and regular gallop.

Nearer came the sounds; nearer and clearer, until the gallant brute appeared upon the bank above me. There he halted, and, flinging back his tossed mane, uttered a shrill neigh. He was bewildered, and looked to every side, snorting loudly.

I knew that, having once seen me, he would not stop until he had pressed his nose against my cheek, for this was his usual custom. Holding out my hands, I again uttered the magic words.

Now glancing downward, he perceived me, and stretching himself, sprang out into the channel. The next moment I held him by the bridle.

There was no time to be lost. I was still going down; and my armpits were fast nearing the surface of the quicksand.

I caught the lariat, and, passing it under the saddle-girths, fastened it in a tight, firm knot. I then looped the trailing end, making it secure around my body. I had left enough of the rope, between the bit-ring and the girths, to enable me to check and guide the animal, in case the drag upon my body should be too painful.

All this while the dumb brute seemed to comprehend what I was about. He knew, too, the nature of the ground on which he stood, for during the operation he kept lifting his feet alternately to prevent himself from sinking.

My arrangements were at length completed; and with a feeling of terrible anxiety I gave my horse the signal to move forward. Instead of going off with a start, the intelligent animal stepped away slowly, as though he understood my situation. The lariat tightened, I felt my body moving, and the next moment experienced a wild delight, a feeling I cannot describe, as I found myself dragged out of the sand!

I sprang to my feet with a shout of joy. I rushed up to my steed, and throwing my arms around his neck, kissed him. He answered my embrace with a low whimper, that told me I was understood.

I looked for my rifle. Fortunately, it had not sunk deeply, and I soon found it. My boots were behind me, but I stayed not to look for them, being smitten with a wholesome dread of the place where I had left them.

It was sundown before I reached camp, where I was met by the inquiries of my wondering companions. "Did you come across the 'goats'?" "Where's your boots?" "Whether have you been hunting or fishing?"

I answered all these questions by relating my adventures; and that night I was again the hero of the camp-fire.

Chapter Six.

Santa Fé.

After a week's climbing through the Rocky Mountains, we descended into the Valley of the Del Norte, and arrived at the capital of New Mexico, the far-famed Santa Fé. Next day the caravan itself came in, for we had lost time on the southern route; and the waggons, travelling by the Raton Pass, had made a good journey of it.

We had no difficulty about their entrance into the country, with the proviso that we paid five hundred dollars of "Alcavala" tax upon each waggon. This was a greater extortion than usual; but the traders were compelled to accept the impost.

Santa Fé is the entrepôt of the province, and the chief seat of its trade. On reaching it we halted, camping without the walls.

Saint Vrain, several other *propriétaires*, and myself, took up our quarters at the Fonda, where we endeavoured, by means of the sparkling vintage of El Paso, to make ourselves oblivious of the hardships we had endured in the passage of the plains.

The night of our arrival was given to feasting and making merry.

Next morning I was awakened by the voice of my man Gode, who appeared to be in high spirits, singing a snatch of a Canadian boat-song.

"Ah, monsieur!" cried he, seeing me awake, "to-night—aujourd'hui—une grande fonction—one bal—vat le Mexicain he call fandango. Très bien, monsieur. You vill sure have grand plaisir to see un fandango Mexicain?"

"Not I, Gode. My countrymen are not so fond of dancing as yours."

"C'est vrai, monsieur; but von fandango is très curieux. You sall see ver many sort of de pas. Bolero, et valse, wis de Coona, and ver many more pas, all mix up in von puchero. Allons! monsieur, you vill see ver many pretty girl, avec les yeux très noir, and ver short—ah! ver short—vat you call em in Americaine?"

"I do not know what you allude to."

"Cela! Zis, monsieur," holding out the skirt of his hunting-shirt; "par Dieu! now I have him—petticoes; ver short petticoes. Ah! you sall see vat you sall see en un fandango Mexicaine.

"'Las niñas de Durango
Commigo bailandas,
Al cielo saltandas,
En el fandango—en el fan-dang—o.'

"Ah! here comes Monsieur Saint Vrain. Écoutez! He never go to fandango. Sacré! how monsieur dance! like un maître de ballet. Mais he be de sangre—blood Français. Écoutez!

"'Al cielo saltandas,
En el fandango—en el fan-dang—.'"

"Ha! Gode!"

"Monsieur?"

"Trot over to the cantina, and beg, borrow, buy, or steal, a bottle of the best Paso."

"Sall I try steal 'im, Monsieur Saint Vrain?" inquired Gode, with a knowing grin.

"No, you old Canadian thief! Pay for it. There's the money. Best Paso, do you hear?—cool and sparkling. Now, voya! Bon jour, my bold rider of buffalo bulls I still abed, I see."

"My head aches as if it would split."

"Ha, ha, ha! so does mine; but Gode's gone for medicine. Hair of the dog good for the bite. Come, jump up!"

"Wait till I get a dose of your medicine."

"True; you will feel better then. I say, city life don't agree with us, eh?"

"You call this a city, do you?"

"Ay, so it is styled in these parts: 'la ciudad de Santa Fé;' the famous city of Santa Fé; the capital of Nuevo Mexico; the metropolis of all prairiedom; the paradise of traders, trappers, and thieves!"

"And this is the progress of three hundred years! Why, these people have hardly passed the first stages of civilisation."

"Rather say they are passing the last stages of it. Here, on this fair oasis, you will find painting, poetry, dancing, theatres, and music, fêtes and fireworks, with all the little amorous arts that characterise a nation's decline. You will meet with numerous Don Quixotes, *soi-disant* knights-errant, Romeos without the heart, and ruffians without the courage. You will meet with many things before you encounter either virtue or honesty. Hola! muchacho!"

"Quc cs, señor?"

"Hay cafe?"

"Si, señor."

"Bring us a couple of tazas, then—dos tazas, do you hear? and quick—aprisa! aprisa!"

"Si, señor."

"Ah! here comes le voyageur Canadien. So, old Nor'-west! you've brought the wine?"

"Vin délicieux, Monsieur Saint Vrain! equal to ze vintage Français."

"He is right, Haller! Tsap—tsap! delicious you may say, good Gode. Tsap—tsap! Come, drink! it'll make you feel as strong as a buffalo. See! it seethes like a soda spring! like 'Fontaine-qui-bouille'; eh, Gode?"

"Oui, monsieur; ver like Fontaine-qui-bouille. Oui."

"Drink, man, drink! Don't fear it: it's the pure juice. Smell the flavour; taste the bouquet. What wine the Yankees will one day squeeze out of these New Mexican grapes!"

"Why? Do you think the Yankees have an eye to this quarter?"

"Think! I know it; and why not? What use are these manikins in creation? Only to cumber the earth. Well, mozo, you have brought the coffee?"

"Ya, esta, señor."

"Here! try some of this; it will help to set you on your feet. They can make coffee, and no mistake. It takes a Spaniard to do that."

"What is this fandango Gode has been telling me about?"

"Ah! true. We are to have a famous one to-night. You'll go, of course?"

"Out of curiosity."

"Very well, you will have your curiosity gratified. The blustering old grampus of a Governor is to honour the ball with his presence; and it is said, his pretty señora; that I don't believe."

"Why not?"

"He's too much afraid lest one of these wild Americanos might whip her off on the cantle of his saddle. Such things have been done in this very valley. By Saint Mary! she is good-looking," continued Saint Vrain, in a half-soliloquy, "and I knew a man—the cursed old tyrant! only think of it!"

"Of what?"

"The way he has bled us. Five hundred dollars a waggon, and a hundred of them at that; in all, fifty thousand dollars!"

"But will he pocket all this? Will not the Government—?"

"Government! no, every cent of it. He is the Government here; and, with the help of this instalment, he will rule these miserable wretches with an iron rod."

"And yet they hate him, do they not?"

"Him and his. And they have reason."

"It is strange they do not rebel."

"They have at times; but what can they do? Like all true tyrants, he has divided them, and makes them spend their heart's hatred on one another."

"But he seems not to have a very large army; no bodyguard—"

"Bodyguard!" cried Saint Vrain, interrupting me; "look out! there's his bodyguard!"

"Indios bravos! les Navajoes!" exclaimed Gode, at the same instant.

I looked forth into the street. Half a dozen tall savages, wrapped in striped serapes, were passing. Their wild, hungry looks, and slow, proud walk at once distinguished them from "Indios manzos," the water-drawing, wood-hewing pueblos.

"Are they Navajoes?" I asked.

"Oui, monsieur, oui!" replied Gode, apparently with some excitement. "Navajoes!"

"There's no mistaking them," added Saint Vrain.

"But the Navajoes are the notorious enemies of the New Mexicans! How come they to be here? Prisoners?"

"Do they look like prisoners?"

They certainly showed no signs of captivity in either look or gesture. They strode proudly up the street, occasionally glancing at the passers with an air of savage and lordly contempt.

"Why, then, are they here? Their country lies far to the west."

"That is one of the secrets of Nuevo Mexico, about which I will enlighten you some other time. They are now protected by a treaty of peace, which is only binding upon them so long as it may suit their convenience to recognise it. At present they are as free here as you or I; indeed, more so, when it comes to that. I wouldn't wonder it we were to meet them at the fandango to-night."

"I have heard that the Navajoes are cannibals."

"It is true. Look at them this minute! See how they gloat upon that chubby little fellow, who seems instinctively to fear them. Lucky for the urchin it's broad daylight, or he might get chucked under one of those striped blankets."

"Are you in earnest, Saint Vrain?"

"By my word, I am not jesting! If I mistake not, Gode's experience will confirm what I have said. Eh, voyageur?"

"C'est vrai, monsieur. I vas prisonnier in le nation; not Navagh, but l'Apache—mooh de same—pour trev mono. I have les sauvages seen manger—eat—one—deux—tree—tree enfants rotis, like hump rib of de buffles. C'est vrai, messieurs, c'est vrai."

"It is quite true; both Apaches and Navajoes carry off children from the valley, here, in their grand forays; and it is said by those who should know, that most of them are used in that way. Whether as a sacrifice to the fiery god Quetzalcoatl, or whether from a fondness lor human flesh, no one has yet been able to determine. In fact, with all their propinquity to this place, there is little known about them. Few who have visited their towns have had Gode's luck to get away again. No man of these parts ever ventures across the western Sierras."

"And how came you, Monsieur Gode, to save your scalp?"

"Pourquoi, monsieur, je n'ai pas. I not haves scalp-lock: vat de trappare Yankee call 'har,' mon scalp-lock is fabriqué of von barbier de Saint Louis. Voilà monsieur!"

So saying, the Canadian lifted his cap, and along with it what I had, up to this time, looked upon as a beautiful curling head of hair, but which now proved to be only a wig!

"Now, messieurs!" cried he, in good humour, "how les sauvages my scalp take? Indien no have cash hold. Sacr–r–r!"

Saint Vrain and I were unable to restrain our laughter at the altered and comical appearance of the Canadian.

"Come, Gode! the least you can do after that is to take a drink. Here, help yourself!"

"Très-oblige, Monsieur Saint Vrain. Je vous remercie." And the ever-thirsty voyageur quaffed off the nectar of El Paso, like so much fresh milk.

"Come, Haller! we must to the waggons. Business first, then pleasure; such as we may find here among these brick stacks. But we'll have some fun in Chihuahua."

"And you think we shall go there?"

"Certainly. They do not want the fourth part of our stuff here. We must carry it on to the head market. To the camp! Allons!"

Chapter Seven.

The Fandango.

In the evening I sat in my room waiting for Saint Vrain. His voice reached me from without—

"'Las niñas de Durango
Commigo bailandas,
Al cielo—!'

"Ha! Are you ready, my bold rider?"

"Not quite. Sit down a minute and wait."

"Hurry, then! the dancing's begun. I have just come that way. What! that your ball-dress? Ha! ha! ha!" screamed Saint Vrain, seeing me unpack a blue coat and a pair of dark pantaloons, in a tolerable state of preservation.

"Why, yes," replied I, looking up; "what fault do you find? But is that your ball-dress?"

No change had taken place in the ordinary raiment of my friend. The fringed hunting-shirt and leggings, the belt, the bowie, and the pistols, were all before me.

"Yes, my dandy; this is my ball-dress: it ain't anything shorter; and if you'll take my advice, you'll wear what you have got on your back. How will your long-tailed blue look, with a broad belt and bowie strapped round the skirts? Ha! ha! ha!"

"But why take either belt or bowie? You are surely not going into a ball-room with your pistols in that fashion?"

"And how else should I carry them? In my hands?"

"Leave them here."

"Ha! ha! that would be a green trick. No, no. Once bit, twice shy. You don't catch this 'coon going into any fandango in Santa Fé without his six-shooters. Come, keep on that shirt; let your leggings sweat where they are, and buckle this about you. That's the *costume du bal* in these parts."

"If you assure me that my dress will be *comme il faut*, I'm agreed."

"It won't be with the long-tailed blue, I promise you."

The long-tailed blue was restored forthwith to its nook in my portmanteau.

Saint Vrain was right. On arriving at the room, a large sala in the neighbourhood of the Plaza, we found it filled with hunters, trappers, traders, and teamsters, all swaggering about in their usual mountain rig. Mixed among them were some two or three score of the natives, with an equal number of señoritas, all of whom, by their style of dress, I recognise as poblanas, or persons of the lower class,—the only class, in fact, to be met with in Santa Fé.

As we entered, most of the men had thrown aside their serapes for the dance, and appeared in all the finery of embroidered velvet, stamped leather, and shining "castletops." The women looked not less picturesque in their bright naguas, snowy chemisettes, and small satin slippers. Some of them flounced it in polka jackets; for even to that remote region the famous dance had found its way.

"Have you heard of the electric telegraph?"

"No, señor."

"Can you tell me what a railroad is?"

"Quien sabe?"

"La polka?"

"Ah! señor, la polka, la polka! cosa buenita, tan graciosa! vaya!"

The ball-room was a long, oblong sala with a banquette running all round it. Upon this the dancers seated themselves, drew out their husk cigarettes, chatted, and smoked, during the intervals of the dance. In one corner half a dozen sons of Orpheus twanged away upon harp, guitar, and bandolin; occasionally helping out the music with a shrill half-Indian chant. In another angle of the apartment, puros, and Taos whisky were dealt out to the thirsty mountaineers, who made the sala ring with their wild ejaculations. There were scenes like the following:—

"Hyar, my little muchacha! vamos, vamos, ter dance! Mucho bueno! Mucho bueno? Will ye?"

This is from a great rough fellow of six feet and over, addressed to a trim little poblana.

"Mucho bueno, Señor Americano!" replies the lady.

"Hooraw for you! Come along! Let's licker fust! You're the gal for my beaver. What'll yer drink? Agwardent or vino?"

"Copitita de vino, señor." (A small glass of wine, sir.)

"Hyar, yer darned greaser! Set out yer vino in a squ'll's jump! Now, my little un', hyar's luck, and a good husband!"

"Gracias, Señor Americano!"

"What! you understand that? You intende, do yer?"

"Si, señor!"

"Hooraw, then! Look hyar, little 'un, kin yer go the b'ar dance?"

"No entiende."

"Yer don't understan' it! Hyar it is; thisa-way;" and the clumsy hunter began to show off before his partner, in an imitation of the grizzly bear.

"Hollo, Bill!" cries a comrade, "yer'll be trapped if yer don't look sharp."

"I'm dog-gone, Jim, if I don't feel queery about hyar," replies the hunter, spreading his great paw over the region of the heart.

"Don't be skeert, man; it's a nice gal, anyways."

"Hooray for old Missouri!" shouts a teamster.

"Come, boys! Let's show these yer greasers a Virginny break-down. 'Cl'ar the kitchen, old folks, young folks.'"

"Go it hoe and toe! 'Old Virginny nebir tire!'"

"Viva el Gobernador! Viva Armijo! Viva! viva!"

An arrival at this moment caused a sensation in the room. A stout, fat, priest-like man entered, accompanied by several others, it was the Governor and his suite, with a number of well-dressed citizens, who were no doubt the elite of New Mexican society. Some of the new-comers were militaires, dressed in gaudy and foolish-looking uniforms that were soon seen spinning round the room in the mazes of the waltz.

"Where is the Señora Armijo?" I whispered to Saint Vrain.

"I told you as much. She! she won't be out. Stay here; I am going for a short while. Help yourself to a partner, and see some tun. I will be back presently. *Au revoir*!"

Without any further explanation, Saint Vrain squeezed himself through the crowd and disappeared.

I had been seated on the banquette since entering the sala, Saint Vrain beside me, in a retired corner of the room. A man of peculiar appearance occupied the seat next to Saint Vrain, but farther into the shadow of a piece of furniture. I had noticed this man as we entered, and noticed, too, that Saint Vrain spoke to him; but I was not introduced, and the interposition of my friend prevented me from making any further observation of him until the latter had retired. We were now side by side; and I commenced a sort of angular reconnaissance of a face and figure that had somewhat strangely arrested my attention. He was not an American; that was evident from his dress; and yet the face was not Mexican. Its outlines were too bold for a Spanish face, though the complexion, from tan and exposure, was brown and swarth. His face was clean-shaven except his chin, which carried a pointed, darkish beard. The eye, if I saw it aright under the shadow of a slouched brim, was blue and mild; the hair brown and wavy, with here and there a strand of silver. These were not Spanish characteristics, much less Hispano-American; and I should have at once placed my neighbour elsewhere, but that his dress puzzled me. It was purely a Mexican costume, and consisted of a purple manga, with dark velvet embroidery around the vent and along the borders. As this garment covered the greater part of his person, I could only see that underneath was a pair of green velveteen calzoneros, with yellow buttons, and snow-white calzoncillos puffing out along the seams. The bottoms of the calzoneros were trimmed with stamped black leather; and under these were yellow boots, with a heavy steel spur upon the heel of each. The broad peaked strap that confined the spur, passing over the foot, gave to it that peculiar contour that we observe in the pictures of armed knights of the olden time. He wore a black, broad-brimmed sombrero, girdled by a thick band of gold bullion. A pair of tags of the same material stuck out from the sides: the fashion of the country.

The man kept his sombrero slouched towards the light, as I thought or suspected, for the concealment of his face. And yet it was not an ill-favoured one. On the contrary, it was open and pleasing; no doubt had been handsome beforetime, and whatever caused its melancholy expression had lined and clouded it. It was this expression that had struck me on first seeing the man.

Whilst I was making these observations, eyeing him cross-wise all the while, I discovered that he was eyeing me in a similar manner, and with an interest apparently equal to my own. This caused us to face round to each other, when the stranger drew from under his manga a small beaded cigarero, and, gracefully holding it out to me, said—

"Quiere a fumar, caballero?" (Would you smoke, sir?)

"Thank you, yes," I replied in Spanish, at the same time taking a cigar from the case.

We had hardly lit our cigarettes when the man again turned to me with the unexpected question—

"Will you sell your horse?"

"No."

"Not for a good price?"

"Not for any price."

"I would give five hundred dollars for him."

"I would not part with him for twice the amount."

"I will give twice the amount."

"I have become attached to him: money is no object."

"I am sorry to hear it. I have travelled two hundred miles to buy that horse."

I looked at my new acquaintance with astonishment, involuntarily repeating his last words.

"You must have followed us from the Arkansas, then?"

"No, I came from the Rio Abajo."

"The Rio Abajo! You mean from down the Del Norte?"

"Yes."

"Then, my dear sir, it is a mistake. You think you are talking to somebody else, and bidding for some other horse."

"Oh, no! He is yours. A black stallion with red nose and long full tail, half-bred Arabian. There is a small mark over the left eye."

This was certainly the description of Moro; and I began to feel a sort of superstitious awe in regard to my mysterious neighbour.

"True," replied I; "that is all correct; but I bought that stallion many months ago from a Louisiana planter. If you have just arrived from two hundred miles down the Rio Grande, how, may I ask, could you have known anything about me or my horse?"

"Dispensadme, caballero! I did not mean that. I came from below to meet the caravan, for the purpose of buying an American horse. Yours is the only one in the caballada I would buy, and, it seems, the only one that is not for sale!"

"I am sorry for that; but I have tested the qualities of this animal. We have become friends. No common motive would induce me to part with him."

"Ah, señor! it is not a common motive that makes me so eager to purchase him. If you knew that, perhaps—" he hesitated a moment; "but no, no, no!" and after muttering some half-coherent words, among which I could recognise the "Buenos noches, caballero!" the stranger rose up with the same mysterious air that had all along characterised him, and left me. I could hear the tinkling of the small bells upon the rowels of his spurs, as he slowly warped himself through the gay crowd, and disappeared into the night.

The vacated seat was soon occupied by a dusky manola, whose bright nagua, embroidered chemisette, brown ankles, and small blue slippers, drew my attention. This was all I could see of her, except the occasional flash of a very black eye through the loophole of the rebozo tapado. By degrees, the rebozo became more generous, the loophole expanded, and the outlines of a very pretty and very malicious little face were displayed before me. The end of the scarf was adroitly removed from the left shoulder; and a nude, plump arm, ending in a bunch of small jewelled fingers, hung carelessly down.

I am tolerably bashful; but at the sight of this tempting partner, I could hold in no longer, and bending towards her, I said in my best Spanish, "Do me the favour, miss, to waltz with me."

The wicked little manola first held down her head and blushed; then, raising the long fringes of her eyes, looked up again, and wits a voice as sweet as that of a canary-bird, replied—

"Con gusto, señor." (With pleasure, sir.)

"Nos vamos!" cried I, elated with my triumph; and pairing off with my brilliant partner, we were soon whirling about in the mazy.

We returned to our seats again, and after refreshing with a glass of Albuquerque, a sponge-cake, and a husk cigarette, again took the floor. This pleasurable programme we repeated some half-dozen times, only varying the dance from waltz to polka, for my manola danced the polka as if she had been a born Bohemian.

On one of my fingers was a fifty-dollar diamond, which my partner seemed to think was *muy buenito.* As her igneous eyes softened my heart, and the champagne was producing a similar effect upon my head, I began to speculate on the propriety of transferring the diamond from the smallest of my fingers to the largest of hers, which it would, no doubt, have fitted exactly. All at once I became conscious of being under the surveillance of a large and very fierce-looking lepero, a regular pelado, who followed us with his eyes, and sometimes *in persona*, to every part of the room. The expression of his swarth face was a mixture of jealousy and vengeance, which my partner noticed, but, as I thought, took no pains to soften down.

"Who is he?" I whispered, as the man swung past us in his chequered serape.

"Esta mi marido, señor," (It is my husband, sir), was the cool reply.

I pushed the ring close up to the root of my finger, shutting my hand upon it tight as a vice.

"Vamos a tomar otra copita!" (Let us take another glass of wine!) said I, resolving to bid my pretty poblana, as soon as possible, a good-night.

The Taos whisky had by this time produced its effect upon the dancers. The trappers and teamsters had become noisy and riotous. The leperos, who now half-filled the room, stimulated by wine, jealousy, old hatreds, and the dance, began to look more savage and sulky. The fringed hunting-shirts and brown homespun frocks found favour with the dark-eyed majas of Mexico, partly out of a respect for, and a fear of, courage, which is often at the bottom of a love like theirs.

Although the trading caravans supplied almost all the commerce of Santa Fé, and it was clearly the interest of its inhabitants to be on good terms with the traders, the two races, Anglo-American and Hispano-Indian, hated each other thoroughly; and that hate was now displaying itself on one side in bullying contempt, on the other in muttered *carrajos* and fierce looks of vengeance.

I was still chatting with my lively partner. We were seated on the banquette where I had introduced myself. On looking casually up, a bright object met my eyes. It appeared to be a naked knife in the hands of *su marido* who was just then lowering over us like the shadow of an evil spirit. I was favoured with only a slight glimpse of this dangerous meteor, and had made up my mind to "'ware steel," when someone plucked me by the sleeve, and turning, I beheld my quondam acquaintance of the purple magna.

"Dispensadme, señor," said he, nodding graciously, "I have just learned that the caravan is going on to Chihuahua."

"True, there is no market here for our goods."

"You go on then, of course?"

"Certainly, I must."

"Will you return this way, señor?"

"It is very likely; I have no other intention at present."

"Perhaps then you might be willing to part with your horse? You will find many as good in the great valley of the Mississippi."

"Neither is likely."

"But, señor, should you be inclined to do so, will you promise me the refusal of him?"

"Oh! that I will promise you, with all my heart."

Our conversation was here interrupted by a huge, gaunt, half-drunken Missourian, who, tramping rudely upon the stranger's toes, vociferated—

"Ye—up, old greaser! gi' mi a char."

"Y porque?" (And why?) demanded the Mexican, drawing in his feet, and looking up with astonished indignation.

"I'm tired jumpin'. I want a seat, that's it, old hoss."

There was something so bullying and brutal in the conduct of this man, that I felt called upon to interfere.

"Come!" said I, addressing him, "you have no right to deprive this gentleman of his seat, much less in such a fashion."

"Eh, mister? who asked you to open yer head? Ye—up, I say!" and at the word, he seized the Mexican by the corner of his manga, as if to drag him from his seat.

Before I had time to reply to this rude speech and gesture, the stranger leaped to his feet, and with a well-planted blow felled the bully upon the floor.

This seemed to act as a signal for bringing several other quarrels to a climax. There was a rush through all parts of the sala, drunken shouts mingled with yells of vengeance, knives glanced from their sheaths, women screamed, pistols flashed and cracked, filling the rooms with smoke and dust. The lights went out, fierce struggles could be heard in the darkness, the fall of heavy bodies amidst groans and curses, and for five minutes these were the only sounds.

Having no cause to be particularly *angry* with anybody, I stood where I had risen, without using either knife or pistol, my frightened *maja* all the while holding me by the hand. A painful sensation near my left shoulder caused me suddenly to drop my partner; and with that unaccountable weakness consequent upon the reception of a wound, I felt myself staggering towards the banquette. Here I dropped into a sitting posture, and remained till the struggle was over, conscious all the while that a stream of blood was oozing down my back, and saturating my undergarments.

I sat thus till the struggle had ended. A light was brought, and I could distinguish a number of men in hunting-shirts moving to-and-fro with violent gesticulations. Some of them were advocating the justice of the "spree," as they termed it; while others, the more respectable of the traders, were denouncing it. The leperos with the women, had all disappeared, and I could perceive that the Americanos had carried the day. Several dark objects lay along the floor: they were bodies of men dead or dying! One was an American, the Missourian who had been the immediate cause of the fracas; the others were pelodos. I could see nothing of my late acquaintance. My fandanguera, too—*con su marido*—had disappeared; and on glancing at my left hand, I came to the conclusion that so also had my diamond ring!

"Saint Vrain! Saint Vrain!" I called, seeing the figure of my friend enter at the door.

"Where are you, H., old boy. How is it with you? all right, eh?"

"Not quite, I tear."

"Good heavens! what's this? why, you're stabbed in the hump ribs! Not bad, I hope. Off with your shirt and let's see."

"First, let us to my room."

"Come, then, my dear boy, lean on me—so, so!"

The fandango was over.

Chapter Eight.

Seguin the Scalp-Hunter.

I have had the pleasure of being wounded in the field of battle. I say pleasure. Under certain circumstances, wounds are luxuries. How different were the feelings I experienced while smarting under wounds that came by the steel of the assassin!

My earliest anxiety was about the depth of my wound. Was it mortal? This is generally the first question a man puts to himself, after discovering that he has been shot or stabbed. A wounded man cannot always answer it either. One's life-blood may be spurting from an artery at each palpitation, while the actual pain felt is not worth the pricking of a pin.

On reaching the Fonda, I sank exhausted on my bed. Saint Vrain split my hunting-shirt from cape to skirt, and commenced examining my wound. I could not see my friend's face as he stood behind me, and I waited with impatience.

"Is it deep?" I asked.

"Not deep as a draw-well, nor wide as a waggon-track," was the reply. "You're quite safe, old fellow; thank God, and not the man who handled that knife, for the fellow plainly intended to do for you. It is the cut of a Spanish knife, and a devilish gash it is. Haller, it was a close shave. One inch more, and the spine, my boy! but you're safe, I say. Here, Gode! that sponge!"

"Sacré!" muttered Gode, with true Gallic aspirate, as he handed the wet rag.

I felt the cold application. Then a bunch of soft raw cotton, the best dressing it could have, was laid over the wound, and fastened by strips. The most skilful surgeon could have done no more.

"Close as a clamp," added Saint Vrain, as he fastened the last pin, and placed me in the easiest position. "But what started the row? and how came you to cut such a figure in it? I was out, thank God!"

"Did you observe a strange-looking man?"

"What! with the purple manga?"

"Yes."

"He sat beside us?"

"Yes."

"Ha! No wonder you say a strange-looking man; stranger than he looks, too. I saw him, I know him, and perhaps not another in the room could say that. Ay, there was another," continued Saint Vrain, with a peculiar smile; "but what could have brought him there is that which puzzles me. Armijo could not have seen him: but go on."

I related to Saint Vrain the whole of my conversation with the stranger, and the incidents that led to the breaking up of the fandango.

"It is odd—very odd! What could he want with your horse? Two hundred miles, and offers a thousand dollars!"

"Capitaine!" (Gode had called me captain ever since the ride upon the buffalo), "if monsieur come two hunred mile, and vill pay un mille thousan dollar, he Moro like ver, ver moch. Un grand passion pour le cheval. Pourquoi: vy he no like him ver sheep? vy he no steal 'im?"

I started at the suggestion, and looked towards Saint Vrain.

"Vith permiss of le capitaine, I vill le cheval cache," continued the Canadian, moving towards the door.

"You need not trouble yourself, old Nor'-west, as far as that gentleman is concerned. He'll not steal your horse; though that's no reason why you should not fulfil your intention, and 'cache' the animal. There are thieves enough in Santa Fé to steal the horses of a whole regiment. You had better fasten him by the door here."

Gode passed to the door and disappeared.

"Who is he?" I asked, "this man about whom there seems to be so much that is mysterious?"

"Ah! if you knew. I will tell you some queer passages by and by, but not to-night. You have no need of excitement. That is the famous Seguin—the Scalp-hunter."

"The Scalp-hunter!"

"Ay! you have heard of him, no doubt; at least you would, had you been much among the mountains."

"I have. The ruffian! the wholesale butcher of innocent—"

A dark waif danced against the wall: it was the shadow of a man. I looked up. Seguin was before me!

Saint Vrain on seeing him enter had turned away, and stood looking out of the window.

I was on the point of changing my tirade into the apostrophic form, and at the same time ordering the man out of my sight, when something in his look influenced me to remain silent. I could not tell whether he had heard or understood to whom my abusive epithets had been applied; but there was nothing in his manner that betrayed his having done so. I observed only the same look that had at first attracted me—the same expression of deep melancholy.

Could this man be the hardened and heartless villain I had heard of, the author of so many atrocities?

"Sir," said he, seeing that I remained silent, "I deeply regret what has happened to you. I was the involuntary cause of your mishap. Is your wound a severe one?"

"It is not," I replied, with a dryness of manner that seemed somewhat to disconcert him.

"I am glad of that," he continued, after a pause. "I came to thank you for your generous interference. I leave Santa Fé in ten minutes. I must bid you farewell."

He held forth his hand. I muttered the word "farewell," but without offering to exchange the salutation. The stories of cruel atrocity connected with the name of this man came into my mind at the moment, and I felt a loathing for him. His arm remained in its outstretched position, while a strange expression began to steal over his countenance, as he saw that I hesitated.

"I cannot take your hand," I said at length.

"And why?" he asked, in a mild tone.

"Why? It is red, red! Away, sir, away!"

He fixed his eyes upon me with a sorrowful look. There was not a spark of anger in them. He drew his hand within the folds of his manga, and uttering a deep sigh, turned and walked slowly out of the room.

Saint Vrain, who had wheeled round at the close of this scene, strode forward to the door, and stood looking after him. I could see the Mexican, from where I lay, as he crossed the quadrangular patio. He had shrugged himself closely in his manga, and was moving off in an

"Three human forms were moving along"

attitude that betokened the deepest dejection. In a moment he was out of sight, having passed through the saguan, and into the street.

"There is something truly mysterious about that man. Tell me, Saint Vrain—"

"Hush–sh! look yonder!" interrupted my friend, pointing through the open door.

I looked out into the moonlight. Three human forms were moving along the wall, towards the entrance of the patio. Their height, their peculiar attitudes, and the stealthy silence of their steps, convinced me they were Indians. The next moment they were lost under the dark shadows of the saguan.

"Who are they?" I inquired.

"Worse enemies to poor Seguin than you would be, if you knew him better. I pity him if these hungry hawks overtake him in the dark. But no; he's worth warning, and a hand to help him, if need be. He shall have it. Keep cool, Harry! I will be back in a jiffy."

So saying, Saint Vrain left me; and the moment after I could see his light form passing hastily out of the gate.

I lay reflecting on the strangeness of the incidents that seemed to be occurring around me. I was not without some painful reflections. I had wounded the feelings of one who had not injured me, and for whom my friend evidently entertained a high respect. A shod hoof sounded upon the stones outside; it was Gode with my horse; and the next moment I heard him hammering the picket-pin into the pavement.

Shortly after, Saint Vrain himself returned.

"Well," I inquired, "what happened you?"

"Nothing much. That's a weasel that never sleeps. He had mounted his horse before they came up with him, and was very soon out of their reach."

"But may they not follow him on horseback?"

"That is not likely. He has comrades not far from here, I warrant you. Armijo—and it was he sent those villains on his track—has no force that dare follow him when he gets upon the wild hills. No fear for him once he has cleared the houses."

"But, my dear Saint Vrain, tell me what you know of this singular man. I am wound up to a pitch of curiosity."

"Not to-night, Harry; not to-night. I do not wish to cause you further excitement; besides, I have reason to leave you now. To-morrow, then. Good-night! Good-night!"

And so saying, my mercurial friend left me to Gode and a night of restlessness.

Chapter Nine.

Left Behind.

On the third day after the fandango, it is announced that the caravan will move onward to Chihuahua. The day arrives, and I am unable to travel with it. My surgeon, a wretched leech of a Mexican, assures me that it will be certain death to attempt the journey. For want of any opposing evidence, I am constrained to believe him. I have no alternative but to adopt the joyless resolve to remain in Santa Fé until the return of the traders.

Chafing on a feverish bed, I take leave of my late companions. We part with many regrets; but, above all, I am pained at bidding adieu to Saint Vrain, whose light-hearted companionship has been my solace through three days of suffering. He has proved my friend; and has undertaken to take charge of my waggons, and dispose of my goods in the market of Chihuahua.

"Do not fret, man," says he, taking leave. "Kill time with the champagne of El Paso. We will be back in a squirrel's jump; and, trust me, I will bring you a mule-load of Mexican shiners. God bless you! Good-bye!"

I can sit up in my bed and, from the open window, see the white tilts of the waggons, as the train rolls over a neighbouring hill. I hear the cracking whips and the deep-toned "wo-ha" of the teamsters; I see the traders mount and gallop after; and I turn upon my couch with a feeling of loneliness and desertion.

For days I lay tossing and fretting, despite the consolatory influence of the champagne, and the rude but kindly attentions of my voyageur valet.

I rise at length, dress myself, and sit in my ventana. I have a good view of the plaza and the adjacent streets, with their rows of brown adobe houses, and dusty ways between.

I gaze, hour after hour, on what is passing without. The scene is not without novelty as well as variety. Swarthy, ill-favoured faces appear behind the folds of dingy rebozos. Fierce glances lower under the slouch of broad sombreros. Poplanas with short skirts and slippered feet pass my window; and groups of "tame" Indians, pueblos, crowd in from the neighbouring rancherias, belabouring their donkeys as they go. These bring baskets of fruit and vegetables. They squat down upon the dusty plaza, behind piles of prickly pears, or pyramids of tomatoes and chile. The women, light-hearted hucksters, laugh and sing and chatter continuously. The tortillera, kneeling by her metate, bruises the boiled maize, claps it into thin flakes, flings it on the heated stone, and then cries, "Tortillas! tortillas calientes!" The cocinera stirs the peppery stew of chile Colorado, lifts the red liquid in her wooden ladle, and invites her customers by the expressions: "Chile bueno! excellente!" "Carbon! carbon!" cries the charcoal-burner. "Agua! agua limpia!" shouts the aguadord. "Pan fino, pan bianco!" screams the baker; and other cries from the vendors of atole, huevos, and leche, are uttered in shrill, discordant voices. Such are the voices of a Mexican plaza.

They are at first interesting. They become monotonous, then disagreeable; until at length I am tortured, and listen to them with a feverish excitement.

After a few days I am able to walk, and go out with my faithful Gode. We stroll through the town. It reminds me of an extensive brick-field before the kilns have been set on fire.

We encounter the same brown adobes everywhere; the same villainous-looking leperos lounging at the corners; the same bare-legged, slippered wenches; the same strings of belaboured donkeys; the same shrill and detestable cries.

We pass by a ruinous-looking house in a remote quarter. Our ears are saluted by voices from within. We hear shouts of "Mueran los Yankies! Abajo los Americanos!" No doubt the pelado to whom I was indebted for my wound is among the ruffians who crowd into the windows; but I know the lawlessness of the place too well to apply for justice.

We hear the same shouts in another street; again in the plaza; and Gode and I re-enter the Fonda with a conviction that our appearance in public might be attended with danger. We resolve, therefore, to keep within doors.

In all my life I never suffered ennui as when cooped up in this semi-barbarous town, and almost confined within the walls of its filthy Fonda. I felt it the more that I had so lately enjoyed the company of such free, jovial spirits, and I could fancy them in their bivouacs on the banks of the Del Norte, carousing, laughing, or listening to some wild mountain story.

Gode shared my feelings, and became as desponding as myself. The light humour of the voyageur disappeared. The song of the Canadian boatman was heard no longer; but, in its place, the "sacré" and English exclamations were spluttered plentifully, and hurled at everything Mexican. I resolved at length to put an end to our sufferings.

"This life will never do, Gode," said I, addressing my compagnon.

"Ah! monsieur, nevare! nevare it vill do. Ah! ver doll. It is like von assemblee of le Quaker."

"I am determined to endure it no longer."

"But what can monsieur do? How, capitaine?"

"By leaving this accursed place, and that to-morrow."

"But is monsieur fort? strongs beau-coup? strongs to ride?"

"I will risk it, Gode. If I break down, there are other towns on the river where we can halt. Anywhere better than here."

"C'est vrai, capitaine. Beautiful village down the river. Albuquerque; Tome: ver many village. Mon Dieu! all better, Santa Fé is one camp of tief. Ver good for us go, monsieur; ver good."

"Good or not, Gode, I am going. So make your preparations to-night, for I will leave in the morning before sunrise."

"It will be von grand plaisir to makes ready." And the Canadian ran from the room, snapping his fingers with delight.

I had made up my mind to leave Santa Fé at any rate. Should my strength, yet but half restored, hold out, I would follow, and if possible overtake the caravan. I knew it could make but short journeys over the deep sand roads of the Del Norte. Should I not succeed in coming up with it, I could halt in Albuquerque or El Paso, either of which would offer me a residence at least as agreeable as the one I was leaving.

My surgeon endeavoured to dissuade me from setting out. He represented that I was in a most critical condition, my wound far from being cicatrised. He set forth in most eloquent terms the dangers of fever, of gangrene, of haemorrhage. He saw I was obstinate, and concluded his monitions by presenting his bill. It amounted to the modest sum of one hundred dollars! It was an extortion. What could I do? I stormed and protested. The Mexican threatened me with "Governor's" justice. Gode swore in French, Spanish, English, and Indian. It was all to no purpose. I saw that the bill would have to be paid, and I paid it, though with indifferent grace.

The leech disappeared, and the landlord came next. He, like the former, made earnest entreaty to prevent me from setting forth. He offered a variety of reasons to detain me.

"Do not go; for your life, señor, do not!"

"And why, good José?" I inquired.

"Oh, señor, los Indios bravos! los Navajoes! carambo!"

"But I am not going into the Indian country. I travel down the river, through the towns of New Mexico."

"Ah! señor! the towns! no hay seguridad. No, no; there is safety nowhere from the Navajo. Hay novedades: news this very day. Polvidera; pobre polvidera! It was attacked on Sunday last. On Sunday, señor, when they were all en la misa. Pues, señor, the robbers surrounded the church; and oh, carambo! they dragged out the poor people—men, women and children! Pues, señor; they kill the men: and the women: Dios de mi alma!"

"Well, and the women?"

"Oh, señor! they are all gone; they were carried to the mountains by the savages. Pobres mugeres!"

"It is a sad story, truly; but the Indians, I understand, only make these forays at long intervals. I am not likely to meet with them now. At all events, José, I have made up my mind to run the risk."

"But, señor," continued José, lowering his voice to a confidential tone, "there are other ladrones besides the Indians: white ones, muchos, muchissimos! Ay, indeed, mi amo, white robbers; blancos, blancos y muy feos, carrai!"

And José closed his fingers as if clutching some imaginary object.

This appeal to my fears was in vain. I answered it by pointing to my revolvers and rifle, and to the well-filled belt of my henchman Gode.

When the Mexican Boniface saw that I was determined to rob him of all the guests he had in his house, he retired sullenly, and shortly after returned with his bill. Like that of the medico, it was out of all proportion; but I could not help myself, and paid it.

By grey dawn I was in my saddle; and, followed by Gode and a couple of heavily packed mules, I rode out of the ill-favoured town, and took the road for the Rio Abajo.

Chapter Ten.

The Del Norte.

For days we journey down the Del Norte. We pass through numerous villages, many of them types of Santa Fé. We cross the zequias and irrigating canals, and pass along fields of bright green maize plants. We see vineyards and grand haciendas. These appear richer and more prosperous as we approach the southern part of the province, the Rio Abajo.

In the distance, both east and west, we descry dark mountains rolled up against the sky. These are the twin ranges of the Rocky Mountains. Long spurs trend towards the river, and in places appear to close up the valley. They add to the expression of many a beautiful landscape that opens before us as we move onward.

We see picturesque costumes in the villages and along the highways: men dressed in the chequered serape or the striped blankets of the Navajoes; conical sombreros with broad brims; calzoneros of velveteen, with their rows of shining "castletops" and fastened at the waist by the jaunty sash. We see mangas and tilmas, and men wearing the sandal, as in Eastern lands. On the women we observe the graceful rebozo, the short nagua, and the embroidered chemisette.

We see rude implements of husbandry: the creaking carreta, with its block wheels; the primitive plough of the forking tree-branch, scarcely scoring the soil; the horn-yoked oxen; the goad; the clumsy hoe in the hands of the peon serf: these are all objects that are new and curious to our eyes, and that indicate the lowest order of agricultural knowledge.

Along the roads we meet numerous atajos, in charge of their arrieros. We observe the mules, small, smooth, light-limbed, and vicious. We glance at the heavy alparejas and bright worsted apishamores. We notice the tight wiry mustangs, ridden by the arrieros; the high-peaked saddles and hair bridles; the swarth faces and pointed beards of the riders; the huge spurs that tinkle at every step; the exclamations, "Hola, mula! malraya! vaya!" We notice all these, and they tell us we are journeying in the land of the Hispano-American.

Under other circumstances these objects would have interested me. At that time, they appeared to me like the pictures of a panorama, or the changing scenes of a continuous dream. As such have they left their impressions on my memory. I was under the incipient delirium of fever.

It was as yet only incipient; nevertheless, it distorted the images around me, and rendered their impressions unnatural and wearisome. My wound began to pain me afresh, and the hot sun, and the dust, and the thirst, with the miserable accommodations of New Mexican posadas, vexed me to an excess of endurance.

On the fifth day after leaving Santa Fé, we entered the wretched little pueblo of Parida. It was my intention to have remained there all night, but it proved a ruffian sort of place, with meagre chances of comfort, and I moved on to Socorro. This is the last inhabited spot in New Mexico, as you approach the terrible desert, the Jornada del Muerte.

Gode had never made the journey, and at Parida I had obtained one thing that we stood in need of, a guide. He had volunteered; and as I learnt that it would be no easy task to procure one at Socorro, I was fain to take him along. He was a coarse, shaggy-looking customer, and I did not at all like his appearance; but I found, on reaching Socorro, that what I had heard was correct. No guide could be hired on any terms, so great was their dread of the Jornada and its occasional denizens, the Apaches.

Socorro was alive with Indian rumours, "novedades." The Indians had fallen upon an atajo near the crossing of Fra Cristobal, and murdered the arrieros to a man. The village was full of consternation at the news. The people dreaded an attack, and thought me mad, when I made known my intention of crossing the Jornada.

I began to fear they would frighten my guide from his engagement, but the fellow stood out staunchly, still expressing his willingness to accompany us.

Without the prospect of meeting the Apache savages, I was but ill prepared for the Jornada. The pain of my wound had increased, and I was fatigued and burning with fever.

But the caravan had passed through Socorro only three days before, and I was in hopes of overtaking my old companions before they could leave El Paso. This determined me to proceed in the morning, and I made arrangements for an early start.

Gode and I were awake before dawn. My attendant went out to summon the guide and saddle our animals. I remained in the house, making preparations for a cup of coffee before starting. I was assisted by the landlord of the posada, who had risen, and was stalking about in his serape.

While thus engaged I was startled by the voice of Gode calling from without, "Von maître! von maître! the rascal have him run vay!"

"What do you mean? Who has run away?"

"Oh, monsieur! la Mexicaine, with von mule, has robb, and run vay. Allons, monsieur, allons!"

I followed the Canadian to the stable with a feeling of anxiety. My horse—but no—thank Heaven, he was there! One of the mules, the macho, was gone. It was the one which the guide had ridden from Parida.

"Perhaps he is not off yet," I suggested. "He may still be in the town."

We sent and went in all directions to find him, but to no purpose. We were relieved at length from all doubts by the arrival of some early market men, who had met such a man as our guide far up the river, and riding a mule at full gallop.

What should we do? Follow him to Parida? No; that would be a journey for nothing. I knew that he would not be fool enough to go that way. Even if he did, it would have been a fool's errand to seek for justice there, so I determined on leaving it over until the return of the traders would enable me to find the thief, and demand his punishment from the authorities.

My regrets at the loss of my macho were not unmixed with a sort of gratitude to the fellow when I laid my hand upon the nose of my whimpering charger. What hindered him from taking the horse instead of the mule? It is a question I have never been able to answer to this day. I can only account for the fellow's preference for the mule on the score of downright honesty, or the most perverse stupidity.

I made overtures for another guide. I applied to the Boniface of Socorro, but without success. He knew no mozo who would undertake the journey.

"Los Apaches! los Apaches!"

I appealed to the peons and loiterers of the plaza.

"Los Apaches!"

Wherever I went, I was answered with "Los Apaches," and a shake of the forefinger in front of the nose—a negative sign over all Mexico.

"It is plain, Gode, we can get no guide. We must try this Jornada without one. What say you, voyageur?"

"I am agree, mon maître; allons!"

And, followed by my faithful compagnon, with our remaining pack-mule, I took the road that leads to the desert. That night we slept among the ruins of Valverde; and the next morning, after an early start, embarked upon the "Journey of Death."

Chapter Eleven.

The "Journey of Death."

In two hours we reached the crossing at Fra Cristobal. Here the road parts from the river, and strikes into the waterless desert. We plunge through the shallow ford, coming out on the eastern bank. We fill our "xuages" with care, and give our animals as much as they will drink. After a short halt to refresh ourselves, we ride onward.

We have not travelled far before we recognise the appropriate name of this terrible journey. Scattered along the path we see the bones of many animals. There are human bones too! That white spheroidal mass, with its grinning rows and serrated sutures, that is a human skull. It lies beside the skeleton of a horse. Horse and rider have fallen together. The wolves have stripped them at the same time. They have dropped down on their thirsty track, and perished in despair, although water, had they known it, was within reach of another effort!

We see the skeleton of a mule, with the alpareja still buckled around it, and an old blanket, flapped and tossed by many a whistling wind.

Other objects, that have been brought there by human aid, strike the eye as we proceed. A bruised canteen, the fragments of a glass bottle, an old hat, a piece of saddle-cloth, a stirrup red with rust, a broken strap, with many like symbols, are strewn along our path, speaking a melancholy language.

We are still only on the border of the desert. We are fresh. How when we have travelled over and neared the opposite side? Shall we leave such souvenirs?

We are filled with painful forebodings, as we look across the arid waste that stretches indefinitely before us. We do not dread the Apache. Nature herself is the enemy we fear.

Taking the waggon-tracks for our guide, we creep on. We grow silent, as if we were dumb. The mountains of Cristobal sink behind us, and we are almost "out of sight of land." We can see the ridges of the Sierra Blanca away to the eastward; but before us, to the south, the eye encounters no mark or limit.

We push forward without guide or any object to indicate our course. We are soon in the midst of bewilderment. A scene of seeming enchantment springs up around us. Vast towers of sand, borne up by the whirlblast, rise vertically to the sky. They move to and fro over the plain. They are yellow and luminous. The sun glistens among their floating crystals. They move slowly, but they are approaching us.

I behold them with feelings of awe. I have heard of travellers lifted in their whirling vortex, and dashed back again from fearful heights.

The pack-mule, frightened at the phenomenon, breaks the lasso and scampers away among the ridges. Gode has galloped in pursuit. I am alone.

Nine or ten gigantic columns now appear, stalking over the plain and circling gradually around me. There is something unearthly in the sight. They resemble creatures of a phantom world. They seem endowed with demon life.

Two of them approach each other. There is a short, ghastly struggle that ends in their mutual destruction. The sand is precipitated to the earth, and the dust floats off in dun, shapeless masses.

Several have shut me within a space, and are slowly closing upon me. My dog howls and barks. The horse cowers with affright, and shivers between my thighs, uttering terrified expressions.

My brain reels. Strange objects appear. The fever is upon me! The laden currents clash in their wild torsion. I am twisted around and torn from my saddle. My eyes, mouth, and ears are filled with dust. Sand, stones, and branches strike me spitefully in the face; and I am flung with violence to the earth!

I lay for a moment where I had fallen, half-buried and blind. I was neither stunned nor hurt; and I began to grope around me, for as yet I could see nothing. My eyes were full of sand, and pained me exceedingly. Throwing out my arms, I felt for my horse; I called him by name. A low whimper answered me. I staggered towards the spot, and laid my hands upon him; he was down upon his flank. I seized the bridle, and he sprang up; but I could feel that he was shivering like an aspen.

I stood by his head for nearly half an hour, rubbing the dust from my eyes; and waiting until the simoom might settle away. At length the atmosphere grew clearer, and I could see the sky; but the sand still drifted along the ridges, and I could not distinguish the surface of the plain. There were no signs of Gode.

I mounted and commenced riding over the plain in search of my comrade. I had no idea of what direction he had taken.

I made a circuit of a mile or so, still calling his name as I went. I received no reply, and could see no traces upon the ground. I rode for an hour, galloping from ridge to ridge, but still without meeting any signs of my comrade or the mules. I pulled up in despair. I had shouted until I was faint and hoarse. I could search no longer.

I was thirsty, and would drink. O God! my "xuages" are broken! The pack-mule has carried off the water-skin.

The crushed calabash still hung upon its thong; but the last drops it had contained were trickling down the flanks of my horse. I knew that I might be fifty miles from water!

You cannot understand the fearfulness of this situation. You live in a northern zone, in a land of pools and streams and limpid springs. How unlike the denizen of the desert, the voyageur of the prairie sea! Water is his chief care, his ever-present solicitude; water the divinity he worships. Without water, even in the midst of plenty, plenty of food, he must die. In the wild western desert it is the thirst that kills. No wonder I was filled with despair. I believed myself to be about the middle of the Jornada. I knew that I could never reach the other side without water. The yearning had already begun. My throat and tongue felt shrivelled and parched.

I had lost all knowledge of the course I should take. The mountains, hitherto my guide, seemed to trend in every direction. Their numerous spurs puzzled me.

I remembered hearing of a spring, the Ojo del Muerto, that was said to lie westward of the trail. Sometimes there was water in the spring. On other occasions travellers had reached it only to find the fountain dried up, and leave their bones upon its banks. So ran the tales in Socorro.

I headed my horse westward. I would seek the spring, and, should I fail to find it, push on to the river. This was turning out of my course; but I must reach the water and save my life.

I sat in my saddle, faint and choking, leaving my animal to go at will. I had lost the energy to guide him.

He went many miles westward, for the sun told me the course. I was suddenly roused from my stupor. A glad sight was before me. A lake!—a lake shining like crystal. Was I certain I saw it? Could it be the mirage? No. Its outlines were too sharply defined. It had not that filmy, whitish appearance which distinguishes the latter phenomenon. No. It was not the mirage. It was water!

I involuntarily pressed the spur against the side of my horse; but he needed not that. He had already eyed the water, and sprang forward, inspirited with new energy. The next moment he was in it up to his flanks.

I flung myself from the saddle with a plunge. I was about to lift the water in my concave palms, when the actions of my horse attracted me. Instead of drinking greedily, he stood tossing his head with snorts of disappointment. My dog, too, refused to lap, and ran along the shore whining and howling.

I knew what this meant; but, with that common obstinacy which refuses all testimony but the evidence of the senses, I lifted some drops in my hand, and applied them to my lips. They were briny and burning. I might have known this before reaching the lake, for I had ridden through a salt incrustation that surrounded it like a belt of snow. But my brain was fevered; my reason had left me.

It was of no use remaining where I was. I climbed back into my saddle, and rode along the shore, over fields of snow-white salt. Here and there my horse's hoof rang against bleaching bones of animals, the remains of many a victim. Well was this lake named the Laguna del Muerto—the "Lake of Death!"

Reaching its southern point, I again headed westward, in hopes of striking the river.

From this time until a later period, when I found myself in a far different scene, I have no distinct memories.

I remember dismounting on a high bank. I must have travelled unconsciously for hours before, for the sun was low down on the horizon as I alighted. It was a very high bank—a precipice—and below me I saw a beautiful river sweeping onward through groves of emerald greenness. I thought there were many birds fluttering in the groves, and their voices rang in delicious melody. There was fragrance on the air, and the scene below me seemed an Elysium. I thought that around where I stood all was bleak, and barren, and parched with intolerable heat. I was tortured with a slakeless thirst that grew fiercer as I gazed on the flowing water. These were real incidents. All this was true.

I must drink. I must to the river. It is cool, sweet water. Oh! I must drink. What! A horrid cliff! No; I will not go down there. I can descend more easily here. Who are these forms? Who are you, sir? Ah! it is you, my brave Moro; and you, Alp. Come! come! Follow me! Down; down to the river! Ah! again that accursed cliff! Look at the beautiful water! It smiles. It ripples on, on, on! Let us drink. No, not yet; we cannot yet. We must go farther. Ugh! Such a height to leap from! But we must drink, one and all. Come, Gode! Come, Moro, old friend! Alp, come on! We shall reach it; we shall drink. Who is Tantalus? Ha! ha! Not I; not I! Stand back, fiends! Do not push me over! Back! Back, I say! Oh!

Part of all this was a reality; part was a dream, a dream that bore some resemblance to the horrors of a first intoxication.

Chapter Twelve.

Zoe.

I lay tracing the figures upon the curtains. They were scenes of the olden time—mailed knights, helmed and mounted, dashing at each other with couched lances, or tumbling from their horses, pierced by the spear. Other scenes there were: noble dames, sitting on Flemish palfreys, and watching the flight of the merlin hawk. There were pages in waiting, and dogs of curious and extinct breeds held in the leash. Perhaps these never existed except in the dreams of some old-fashioned artist; but my eye followed their strange shapes with a sort of half-idiotic wonder.

Metallic rods upheld the curtains; rods that shone brightly, and curved upwards, forming a canopy. My eyes ran along these rods, scanning their configuration, and admiring, as a child admires, the regularity of their curves. I was not in my own land. These things were strange to me. "Yet," thought I, "I have seen something like them before, but where? Oh! this I know, with its broad stripes and silken texture; it is a Navajo blanket! Where was I last? In New Mexico? Yes. Now I remember: the Jornada! but how came I?

"Can I untwist this? It is close woven; it is wool, fine wool. No, I cannot separate a thread from—

"My fingers! how white and thin they are! and my nails, blue, and long as the talons of a bird! I have a beard! I feel it on my chin. What gave me a beard? I never wear it; I will shave it off—ha! my moustache!"

I was wearied, and slept again.

Once more my eyes were tracing the figures upon the curtains: the knights and dames, the hounds, hawks, and horses. But my brain had become clearer, and music was flowing into it. I lay silent, and listened.

The voice was a female's. It was soft and finely modulated. Someone played upon a stringed instrument. I recognised the tones of the Spanish harp, but the song was French, a song of Normandy; and the words were in the language of that romantic land. I wondered at this, for my consciousness of late events was returning; and I knew that I was far from France.

The light was streaming over my couch; and, turning my face to the front, I saw that the curtains were drawn aside.

I was in a large room, oddly but elegantly furnished. Human figures were before me, seated and standing.

After looking steadily for a while, my vision became more distinct and reliable; and I saw that there were but three persons in the room, a man and two females.

I remained silent, not certain but that the scene before me was only some new phase of my dream. My eyes wandered from one of the living figures to another, without attracting the attention of any of them.

They were all in different attitudes, and occupied differently.

Nearest me was a woman of middle age, seated upon a low ottoman. The harp I had heard was before her, and she continued to play. She must have been, I thought, when young, a woman of extreme beauty. She was still beautiful in a certain sense. The noble features were there, though I could perceive that they had been scathed by more than ordinary suffering of the mind.

She was a Frenchwoman: an ethnologist could have told that at a glance. Those lines, the characteristics of her highly gifted race, were easily traceable. I thought there was a time when that face had witched many a heart with its smiles. There were no smiles on it now, but a deep yet intellectual expression of melancholy. This I perceived, too, in her voice, in her song, in every note that vibrated from the strings of the instrument.

My eye wandered farther. A man of more than middle age stood by the table, near the centre of the room. His face was turned towards me, and his nationality was as easily determined as that of the lady. The high, florid cheeks, the broad front, the prominent chin, the small green cap with its long peak and conical crown, the blue spectacles, were all characteristics. He was a German.

His occupation was also characteristic of his nationality. Before him were strewed over the table, and upon the floor, the objects of his study—plants and shrubs of various species. He was busy with these, classifying and carefully laying them out between the leaves of his portfolio. It was evident that the old man was a botanist.

A glance to the right, and the naturalist and his labours were no longer regarded. I was looking upon the loveliest object that ever came before my eyes, and my heart bounded within me, as I strained forward in the intensity of its admiration.

Yet it was not a woman that held my gaze captive, but a child—a girl—a maid—standing upon the threshold of womanhood, ready to cross it at the first summons of Love!

My eyes, delighted, revelled along the graceful curves that outlined the beautiful being before me. I thought I had seen the face somewhere. I had, but a moment before, while looking upon that of the elder lady. They were the same face—using a figure of speech—the type transmitted from mother to daughter: the same high front and facial angle, the same outline of the nose, straight as a ray of light, with the delicate spiral-like curve of the nostril which meets you in the Greek medallion. Their hair, too, was alike in colour, golden; though, in that of the mother, the gold showed an enamel of silver.

I will desist and spare details, which to you may be of little interest. In return, do me the favour to believe, that the being who impressed me then and for ever was beautiful, was lovely.

"Ah! it wod be ver moch kindness if madame and ma'm'selle wod play la Marseillaise, la grande Marseillaise. What say mein liebe fraulein!"

"Zoe, Zoe! take thy bandolin. Yes, doctor, we will play it for you with pleasure. You like the music. So do we. Come, Zoe!"

The young girl, who, up to this time, had been watching intently the labours of the naturalist, glided to a remote corner of the room, and taking up an instrument resembling the guitar, returned and seated herself by her mother. The bandolin was soon placed in concert with the harp, and the strings of both vibrated to the thrilling notes of the Marseillaise.

There was something exceedingly graceful in the performance. The instrumentation, as I thought, was perfect; and the voices of the players accompanied it in a sweet and spirited harmony. As I gazed upon the girl Zoe, her features animated by the thrilling thoughts of the anthem, her whole countenance radiant with light, she seemed some immortal being—a young goddess of liberty calling her children "to arms!"

The botanist had desisted from his labours, and stood listening with delighted attention. At each return of the thrilling invocation, "Aux armes, citoyens!" the old man snapped his fingers, and beat the floor with his feet, marking the time of the music. He was filled with the same spirit which at that time, over all Europe, was gathering to its crisis.

"Where am I? French faces, French music, French voices, and the conversation in French!" for the botanist addressed the females in that language, though with a strong Rhenish patois, that confirmed my first impressions of his nationality. "Where am I?"

My eye ran around the room in search of an answer. I could recognise the furniture: the cross-legged Campeachy chairs, a rebozo, the palm-leaf petate. "Ha, Alp!"

The dog lay stretched along the mattress near my couch, and sleeping.

"Alp! Alp!"

"Oh, mamma! mamma! écoutez! the stranger calls."

The dog sprang to his feet, and throwing his fore paws upon the bed, stretched his nose towards me with a joyous whimpering. I reached out my hand and patted him, at the same time giving utterance to some expressions of endearment.

"Oh, mamma! mamma! he knows him. Voilà."

The lady rose hastily, and approached the bed. The German seized me by the wrist, pushing back the Saint Bernard, which was bounding to spring upward.

"Mon Dieu! he is well. His eyes, doctor. How changed!"

"Ya, ya; moch better; ver moch better. Hush! away, tog! Keep away, mine goot tog!"

"Who? where? Tell me, where am I? Who are you?"

"Do not fear! we are friends: you have been ill!"

"Yes, yes! we are friends: you have been ill, sir. Do not fear us; we will watch you. This is the good doctor. This is mamma, and I am—"

"An angel from heaven, beautiful Zoe!"

The child looked at me with an expression of wonder, and blushed as she said—

"Hear, mamma! He knows my name!"

It was the first compliment she had ever received from the lips of love.

"It is goot, madame! he is ver moch relieft; he ver soon get over now. Keep away, mine goot Alp! Your master he get well: goot tog, down!"

"Perhaps, doctor, we should leave him. The noise—"

"No, no! if you please, stay with me. The music; will you play again?"

"Yes, the music is ver goot; ver goot for te pain."

"Oh, mamma! let us play, then."

Both mother and daughter took up their instruments, and again commenced playing.

I listened to the sweet strains, watching the fair musicians a long while. My eyes at length became heavy, and the realities before me changed into the soft outlines of a dream.

My dream was broken by the abrupt cessation of the music. I thought I heard, through my sleep, the opening of a door. When I looked to the spot lately occupied by the musicians, I saw that they were gone. The bandolin had been thrown down upon the ottoman, where it lay, but "she" was not there.

I could not, from my position, see the whole of the apartment; but I knew that someone had entered at the outer door, I heard expressions of welcome and endearment, a rustling of dresses, the words "Papa!"

"My little Zoe"; the latter uttered in the voice of a man. Then followed some explanations in a lower tone, which I could not hear.

A few minutes elapsed, and I lay silent and listening. Presently there were footsteps in the hall. A boot, with its jingling rowels, struck upon the tiled floor. The footsteps entered the room, and approached the bed. I started, as I looked up. The Scalp-hunter was before me!

Chapter Thirteen.

Seguin.

"You are better; you will soon be well again. I am glad to see that you recover."

He said this without offering his hand.

"I am indebted to you for my life. Is it not so?"

It is strange that I felt convinced of this the moment that I set my eyes upon the man. I think such an idea crossed my mind before, after awaking from my long dream. Had I encountered him in my struggles for water, or had I dreamed it?

"Oh yes!" answered he, with a smile, "but you will remember that I had something to do with your being exposed to the risk of losing it."

"Will you take this hand? Will you forgive me?"

After all, there is something selfish even in gratitude. How strangely had it changed my feelings towards this man! I was begging the hand which, but a few days before, in the pride of my morality, I had spurned from me as a loathsome thing.

But there were other thoughts that influenced me. The man before me was the husband of the lady; was the father of Zoe. His character, his horrid calling, were forgotten; and the next moment our hands were joined in the embrace of friendship.

"I have nothing to forgive. I honour the sentiment that induced you to act as you did. This declaration may seem strange to you. From what you knew of me, you acted rightly; but there may be a time, sir, when you will know me better: when the deeds which you abhor may seem not only pardonable, but justifiable. Enough of this at present. The object of my being now at your bedside is to request that what you do know of me be not uttered here."

His voice sank to a whisper as he said this, pointing at the same time towards the door of the room.

"But how," I asked, wishing to draw his attention from this unpleasant theme, "how came I into this house? It is yours, I perceive. How came I here? Where did you find me?"

"In no very safe position," answered he, with a smile. "I can scarcely claim the merit of saving you. Your noble horse you may thank for that."

"Ah, my horse! my brave Moro! I have lost him."

"Your horse is standing at the maize-trough, not ten paces from where you lie. I think you will find him in somewhat better condition than when you last saw him. Your mules are without. Your packs are safe. You will find them here," and he pointed to the foot of the bed.

"And—"

"Gode you would ask for," said he, interrupting me. "Do not be uneasy on his account. He, too, is in safety. He is absent just now, but will soon return."

"How can I thank you? This is good news indeed. My brave Moro! and Alp here! But how? you say my horse saved me. He has done so before: how can this be?"

"Simply thus: we found you many miles from this place, on a cliff that overlooks the Del Norte. You were hanging over on your lasso, that by a lucky accident had become entangled around your body. One end of it was knotted to the bit-ring, and the noble animal, thrown back upon his haunches, sustained your weight upon his neck!"

"Noble Moro! what a terrible situation!"

"Ay, you may say that! Had you fallen from it, you would have passed through a thousand feet of air before striking the rocks below. It was indeed a fearful situation."

"I must have staggered over in my search for water."

"In your delirium you walked over. You would have done so a second time had we not prevented you. When we drew you up on the cliff, you struggled hard to get back. You saw the water below, but not the precipice. Thirst is a terrible thing—an insanity of itself."

"I remember something of all this. I thought it had been a dream."

"Do not trouble your brain with these things. The doctor here admonishes me to leave you. I have an object, as I have said," (here a sad expression passed over the countenance of the speaker), "else I should not have paid you this visit. I have not many moments to spare. To-night I must be far hence. In a few days I shall return. Meanwhile, compose yourself, and get well. The doctor here will see that you want for nothing. My wife and daughter will nurse you."

"Thanks! thanks!"

"You will do well to remain where you are until your friends return from Chihuahua. They must pass not far from this place, and I will warn you when they are near. You are a student. There are books here in different languages. Amuse yourself. They will give you music. Monsieur, adieu!"

"Stay, sir, one moment! You seem to have taken a strange fancy to my horse?"

"Ah! monsieur, it was no fancy; but I will explain that at some other time. Perhaps the necessity no longer exists."

"Take him, if you will. Another will serve my purpose."

"No, monsieur. Do you think I could rob you of what you esteem so highly, and with such just reason, too? No, no! Keep the good Moro. I do not wonder at your attachment to the noble brute."

"You say that you have a long journey to-night. Then take him for the time."

"That offer I will freely accept, for indeed my own horse is somewhat jaded. I have been two days in the saddle. Well, adieu!"

Seguin pressed my hand and walked away. I heard the "chinck, chinck" of his spurs as he crossed the apartment, and the next moment the door closed behind him.

I was alone, and lay listening to every sound that reached me from without. In about half an hour after he had left me, I heard the hoof-strokes of a horse, and saw the shadow of a horseman passing outside the window. He had departed on his journey, doubtless on the performance of some red duty connected with his fearful avocation!

I lay for a while harassed in mind, thinking of this strange man. Then sweet voices interrupted my meditations; before me appeared lovely faces, and the Scalp-hunter was forgotten.

Chapter Fourteen.

Love.

I would compress the history of the ten days following into as many words. I would not weary you with the details of my love—a love that in the space of a few hours became a passion deep and ardent.

I was young at the time; at just such an age as to be impressed by the romantic incidents that surrounded me, and had thrown this beautiful being in my way; at that age when the heart, unguarded by cold calculations of the future, yields unresistingly to the electrical impressions of love. I say electrical. I believe that at this age the sympathies that spring up between heart and heart are purely of this nature.

At a later period of life that power is dissipated and divided. Reason rules it. We become conscious of the capability of transferring our affections, for they have already broken faith; and we lose that sweet confidence that comforted the loves of our youth. We are either imperious or jealous, as the advantages appear in our favour or against us. A gross alloy enters into the love of our middle life, sadly detracting from the divinity of its character.

I might call that which I then felt my first real passion. I thought I had loved before, but no, it was only a dream; the dream of the village schoolboy, who saw heaven in the bright eyes of his coy class-mate; or perhaps at the family picnic, in some romantic dell, had tasted the rosy cheek of his pretty cousin.

I grew strong, and with a rapidity that surprised the skilful man of herbs. Love fed and nourished the fire of life. The will often effects the deed, and say as you may, volition has its power upon the body. The wish to be well, to live, an object to live for, are often the speediest restoratives. They were mine.

I grew stronger, and rose from my couch. A glance at the mirror told me that my colour was returning.

Instinct teaches the bird while wooing his mate to plume his pinions to their highest gloss; and a similar feeling now rendered me solicitous about my toilet. My portmanteau was ransacked, my razors were drawn forth, the beard disappeared from my chin, and my moustache was trimmed to its wonted dimensions.

I confess all this. The world had told me I was not ill-looking, and I believed what it said. I am mortal in my vanities. Are not you?

There was a guitar in the house. I had learnt in my college days to touch the strings, and its music delighted both Zoe and her mother. I sang to them the songs of my own land—songs of love; and with a throbbing heart watched whether the burning words produced any impression upon her. More than once I have laid aside the instrument with feelings of disappointment. From day to day, strange reflections passed through my mind. Could it be that she was too young to understand the import of the word love? too young to be inspired with a passion? She was but twelve years of age, but then she was the child of a sunny clime; and I had often seen at that age, under the warm sky of Mexico, the wedded bride, the fond mother.

Day after day we were together alone. The botanist was busy with his studies, and the silent mother occupied with the duties of her household.

Love is not blind. It may be to all the world beside; but to its own object it is as watchful as Argus.

I was skilled in the use of the crayon, and I amused my companion by sketches upon scraps of paper and the blank leaves of her music. Many of these were the figures of females, in different attitudes and costumes. In one respect they resembled each other: their faces were alike.

The child, without divining the cause, had noticed this peculiarity in the drawings.

"Why is it?" she asked one day, as we sat together. "These ladies are all in different costumes, of different nations; are they not? and yet there is a resemblance in their faces! They have all the same features; indeed, exactly the same, I think."

"It is your face, Zoe; I can sketch no other."

She raised her large eyes, and bent them upon me with an expression of innocent wonder. Was she blushing? No!

"Is that like me?"

"It is, as nearly as I can make it."

"And why do you not sketch other faces?"

"Why! because I—Zoe, I fear you would not understand me."

"Oh, Enrique; do you think me so bad a scholar? Do I not understand all that you tell me of the far countries where you have been? Surely I may comprehend this as well."

"I will tell you, then, Zoe."

I bent forward, with a burning heart and trembling voice.

"It is because your face is ever before me; I can paint no other. It is, that—I love you, Zoe!"

"Oh! is that the reason? And when you love one, her face is always before you, whether she herself be present or no? Is it not so?"

"It is so," I replied, with a painful feeling of disappointment.

"And is that love, Enrique?"

"It is."

"Then must I love you; for, wherever I may be, I can see your face: how plainly before me! If I could use this pencil as you do, I am sure I could paint it, though you were not near me! What then? Do you think I love you, Enrique?"

No pen could trace my feelings at that moment. We were seated; and the sheet on which were the sketches was held jointly between us. My hand wandered over its surface, until the unresisting fingers of my companion were clasped in mine. A wilder emotion followed the electric touch: the paper fell upon the floor; and with a proud but trembling heart I drew the yielding form to mine!

Chapter Fifteen.

Light and Shade.

The house we inhabited stood in a quadrangular inclosure that sloped down to the banks of the river, the Del Norte. This inclosure was a garden or shrubbery, guarded on all sides by high, thick walls of adobe. Along the summit of these walls had been planted rows of the cactus, that threw out huge, thorny limbs, forming an impassable chevaux-de-frise. There was but one entrance to the house and garden, through a strong wicket gate, which I had noticed was always shut and barred. I had no desire to go abroad. The garden, a large one, hitherto had formed the limit of my walk; and through this I often rambled with Zoe and her mother, but oftener with Zoe alone.

There were many objects of interest about the place. It was a ruin; and the house itself bore evidences of better times. It was a large building in the Moro-Spanish style, with flat roof (azotea), and notched parapet running along the front. Here and there the little stone turrets of this parapet had fallen off, showing evidence of neglect and decay.

The walls of the garden impinged upon the river, and there ended; for the bank was steep and vertical, and the deep, still water that ran under it formed a sufficient protection on that side.

A thick grove of cotton-woods fringed the bank of the river, and under their shade had been erected a number of seats of japanned mason-work, in a style peculiar to Spanish countries. There were steps cut in the face of the bank, overhung with drooping shrubs, and leading to the water's edge. I had noticed a small skiff moored under the willows, where these steps went down to the water.

From this point only could you see beyond the limits of the inclosure. The view was magnificent, and commanded the windings of the Del Norte for a distance of miles.

Evening after evening we sought the grove of cotton-woods, and, seated upon one of the benches, together watched the glowing sunset. At this time of the day we were ever alone, I and my little companion.

One evening, as usual, we sat under the solemn shadow of the grove. We had brought with us the guitar and bandolin; but, after a few notes had been struck, the music was forgotten, and the instruments lay upon the grass at our feet. We loved to listen to the music of our own voices. We preferred the utterance of our own thoughts to the sentiments of any song, however sweet. There was music enough around us; the hum of the wild bee as it bade farewell to the closing corolla; the whoop of the gruya in the distant sedge; and the soft cooing of the doves as they sat in pairs upon the adjacent branches, like us whispering their mutual loves.

Autumn had now painted the woods, and the frondage was of every hue. The shadows of the tall trees dappled the surface of the water, as the stream rolled silently on. The sun was far down, and the spire of El Paso gleamed like a golden star under the parting kiss of his beams. Our eyes wandered, and rested upon the glittering vane.

"The church!" half soliloquised my companion; "I hardly know what it is like, it is so long since I saw it."

"How long?"

"Oh, many, many years; I was very young then."

"And you have not been beyond these walls since then?"

"Oh yes! Papa has taken us down the river in the boat, mamma and myself, often, but not lately."

"And have you no wish to go abroad through these gay woods?"

"I do not desire it; I am contented here."

"And will you always be contented here?"

"And why not, Enrique? When you are near me, why should I not be happy?"

"But when—"

A dark shadow seemed to cross her thoughts. Benighted with love, she had never reflected upon the probability of my leaving her, nor indeed had I. Her cheeks became suddenly pale; and I could see the agony gathering in her eyes, as she fixed them upon me. But the words were out—

"When I must leave you?"

She threw herself on my breast, with a short, sharp scream, as though she had been stung to the heart, and in an impassioned voice cried aloud—

"Oh! my God, my God! leave me! leave me! Oh! you will not leave me? You who have taught me to love! Oh! Enrique, why did you tell me that you loved me? Why did you teach me to love?"

"Zoe!"

"Enrique, Enrique! say you will not leave me!"

"Never! Zoe! I swear it; never, never!" I fancied at this moment I heard the stroke of an oar; but the wild tumult of my feelings prevented me from rising to look over the bank. I was raising my head when an object, appearing above the bank, caught my eye. It was a black sombrero with its golden band. I knew the wearer at a glance: Seguin! In a moment, he was beside us.

"Papa!" exclaimed Zoe, rising up and reaching forward to embrace him. The father put her to one side, at the same time tightly grasping her hand in his. For a moment he remained silent, bending his eyes upon me with an expression I cannot depict. There was in it a mixture of reproach, sorrow, and indignation. I had risen to confront him, but I quailed under that singular glance, and stood abashed and silent.

"And this is the way you have thanked me for saving your life? A brave return, good sir; what think you?"

I made no reply.

"Sir!" continued he, in a voice trembling with emotion, "you have deeply wronged me."

"I know it not; I have not wronged you."

"What call you this? Trifling with my child!"

"Trifling!" I exclaimed, roused to boldness by the accusation.

"Ay, trifling! Have you not won her affections?"

"I won them fairly."

"Pshaw, sir! This is a child, not a woman. Won them fairly! What can she know of love?"

"Papa! I do know love. I have felt it for many days. Do not be angry with Enrique, for I love him; oh, papa! in my heart I love him!"

He turned to her with a look of astonishment.

"Hear this!" he exclaimed. "Oh, heavens! my child, my child!"

His voice stung me, for it was full of sorrow.

"Listen, sir!" I cried, placing myself directly before him. "I have won the affections of your daughter. I have given mine in return. I am her equal in rank, as she is mine. What crime, then, have I committed? Wherein have I wronged you?"

He looked at me for some moments without making any reply.

"You would marry her, then?" he said, at length, with an evident change in his manner.

"Had I permitted our love thus far, without that intention, I should have merited your reproaches. I should have been 'trifling,' as you have said."

"Marry me!" exclaimed Zoe, with a look of bewilderment.

"Listen! Poor child! she knows not the meaning of the word!"

"Ay, lovely Zoe! I will; else my heart, like yours, shall be wrecked for ever! Oh, sir!"

"Come, sir, enough of this. You have won her from herself; you have yet to win her from me. I will sound the depth of your affection. I will put you to the proof."

"Put me to any proof!"

"We shall see; come! let us in. Here, Zoe!"

And, taking her by the hand, he led her towards the house. I followed close behind.

As we passed through a clump of wild orange trees, the path narrowed; and the father, letting go her hand, walked on ahead. Zoe was between us; and as we reached the middle of the grove, she turned suddenly, and laying her hand upon mine, whispered in a trembling voice, "Enrique, tell me, what is 'to marry'?"

"Dearest Zoe! not now: it is too difficult to explain; another time, I—"

"Come, Zoe! your hand, child!"

"Papa, I am coming!"

Chapter Sixteen.

An Autobiography.

I was alone with my host in the apartment I had hitherto occupied. The females had retired to another part of the house; and I noticed that Seguin, on entering, had looked to the door, turning the bolt.

What terrible proof was he going to exact of my faith, of my love? Was he about to take my life, or bind me by some fearful oath, this man of cruel deeds? Dark suspicions shot across my mind, and I sat silent, but not without emotions of fear.

A bottle of wine was placed between us, and Seguin, pouring out two glasses, asked me to drink. This courtesy assured me. "But how if the wine be poi—?" He swallowed his own glass before the thought had fairly shaped itself.

"I am wronging him," thought I. "This man, with all, is incapable of an act of treachery like that."

I drank up the wine. It made me feel more composed and tranquil.

After a moment's silence he opened the conversation with the abrupt interrogatory, "What do you know of me?"

"Your name and calling; nothing more."

"More than is guessed at here;" and he pointed significantly to the door. "Who told you thus much of me?"

"A friend, whom you saw at Santa Fé."

"Ah! Saint Vrain; a brave, bold man. I met him once in Chihuahua. Did he tell you no more of me than this?"

"No. He promised to enter into particulars concerning you, but the subject was forgotten, the caravan moved on, and we were separated."

"You heard, then, that I was Seguin the Scalp-hunter? That I was employed by the citizens of El Paso to hunt the Apache and Navajo, and that I was paid a stated sum for every Indian scalp I could hang upon their gates? You heard all this?"

"I did."

"It is true."

I remained silent.

"Now, sir," he continued, after a pause, "would you marry my daughter, the child of a wholesale murderer?"

"Your crimes are not hers. She is innocent even of the knowledge of them, as you have said. You may be a demon; she is an angel."

There was a sad expression on his countenance as I said this.

"Crimes! demon!" he muttered, half in soliloquy. "Ay, you may well think this; so judges the world. You have heard the stories of the mountain men in all their red exaggeration. You have heard that, during a treaty, I invited a village of the Apaches to a banquet, and poisoned the viands—poisoned the guests, man, woman, and child, and then scalped them! You have heard that I induced to pull upon the drag rope of a cannon two hundred savages, who know not its use; and then fired the piece, loaded with grape, mowing down the row of unsuspecting wretches! These, and other inhuman acts, you have no doubt heard of?"

"It is true. I have heard these stories among the mountain hunters; but I knew not whether to believe them."

"Monsieur, they are false; all false and unfounded."

"I am glad to hear you say this. I could not now believe you capable of such barbarities."

"And yet, if they were true in all their horrid details, they would fall far short of the cruelties that have been dealt out by the savage foe to the inhabitants of this defenceless frontier. If you knew the history of this land for the last ten years; its massacres and its murders; its tears and its burnings; its spoliations; whole provinces depopulated; villages given to the flames; men butchered on their own hearths; women, beautiful women, carried into captivity by the desert robber! Oh, God! and I too have shared wrongs that will acquit me in your eyes, perhaps in the eyes of Heaven!"

The speaker buried his face in his hands, and leant forward upon the table. He was evidently suffering from some painful recollection. After a moment he resumed—"I would have you listen to a short history of my life." I signified my assent; and after filling and drinking another glass of wine, he proceeded.

"I am not a Frenchman, as men suppose. I am a Creole, a native of New Orleans. My parents were refugees from Saint Domingo, where, after the black revolution, the bulk of their fortune was confiscated by the bloody Christophe.

"I was educated for a civil engineer; and, in this capacity, I was brought out to the mines of Mexico, by the owner of one of them, who knew my father. I was young at the time, and I spent several years employed in the mines of Zacatecas and San Luis Potosi.

"I had saved some money out of my pay, and I began to think of opening upon my own account.

"Rumours had long been current that rich veins of gold existed upon the Gila and its tributaries. The washings had been seen and gathered in these rivers; and the mother of gold, the milky quartz rock, cropped out everywhere in the desert mountains of this wild region.

"I started for this country with a select party; and, after traversing it for weeks, in the Mimbres mountains, near the head waters of the Gila, I found the precious ore in its bed. I established a mine, and in five years was a rich man.

"I remembered the companion of my youth, the gentle, the beautiful cousin who had shared my confidence, and inspired me with my first passion. With me it was first and last; it was not, as is often the case under similar circumstances, a transient thing. Through all my wanderings I had remembered and loved her. Had she been as true to me?

"I determined to assure myself; and leaving my affairs in the hands of my mayoral, I set out for my native city.

"Adèle had been true; and I returned, bringing her with me.

"I built a house in Valverde, the nearest inhabited district to my mine.

"Valverde was then a thriving place; it is now a ruin, which you may have seen in your journey down.

"In this place we lived for years, in the enjoyment of wealth and happiness. I look back upon those days as so many ages of bliss. Our love was mutual and ardent; and we were blessed with two children, both girls. The youngest resembled her mother; the other, I have been told, was more like myself. We doted, I fear, too much on these pledges. We were too happy in their possession.

"At this time a new Governor was sent to Santa Fé, a man who, by his wantonness and tyranny, has since then ruined the province. There has been no act too vile, no crime too dark, for this human monster.

"He offered fair enough at first, and was feasted in the houses of the ricos through the valley. As I was classed among these, I was honoured with his visits, and frequently. He resided principally at Albuquerque; and grand fêtes were given at his palace, to which my wife and I were invited as special guests. He in return often came to our house in Valverde, under pretence of visiting the different parts of the province.

"I discovered, at length, that his visits were solely intended for my wife, to whom he had paid some flattering attentions.

"I will not dwell on the beauty of Adèle, at this time. You may imagine that for yourself; and, monsieur, you may assist your imagination by allowing it to dwell on those graces you appear to have discovered in her daughter, for the little Zoe is a type of what her mother was.

"At the time I speak of she was still in the bloom of her beauty. The fame of that beauty was on every tongue, and had piqued the vanity of the wanton tyrant. For this reason I became the object of his friendly assiduities.

"I had divined this; but confiding in the virtue of my wife, I took no notice of his conduct. No overt act of insult as yet claimed my attention.

"Returning on one occasion from a long absence at the mines, Adèle informed me what, through delicacy, she had hitherto concealed—of insults received from his excellency at various times, but particularly in a visit he had paid her during my absence.

"This was enough for Creole blood. I repaired to Albuquerque; and on the public plaza, in presence of the multitude, I chastised the insulter.

"I was seized and thrown into a prison, where I lay for several weeks. When I was freed, and sought my home again, it was plundered and desolate. The wild Navajo had been there; my household gods were scattered and broken, and my child, oh, God! my little Adèle, was carried captive to the mountains!"

"And your wife? your other child?" I inquired, eager to know the rest.

"They had escaped. In the terrible conflict—for my poor peons battled bravely—my wife, with Zoe in her arms, had rushed out and hidden in a cave that was in the garden. I found them in the ranche of a vaquero in the woods, whither they had wandered."

"And your daughter Adèle—have you heard aught of her since?"

"Yes, yes, I will come to that in a moment.

"My mine, at the same time, was plundered and destroyed; many of the workmen were slaughtered before they could escape; and the work itself, with my fortune, became a ruin.

"With some of the miners, who had fled, and others of Valverde, who, like me, had suffered, I organised a band, and followed the savage foe; but our pursuit was vain, and we turned back, many of us broken in health and heart.

"Oh, monsieur, you cannot know what it is to have thus lost a favourite child! you cannot understand the agony of the bereaved father!"

The speaker pressed his head between his hands, and remained for a moment silent. His countenance bore the indications of heartrending sorrow.

"My story will soon be told—up to the present time. Who knows the end?

"For years I hung upon the frontiers of the Indian country, hunting for my child. I was aided by a small band, most of them unfortunates like myself, who had lost wife or daughter in a similar manner. But our means became exhausted, and despair wore us out. The sympathies of my companions grew old and cold. One after another gave up. The Governor of New Mexico offered us no aid. On the contrary, it was suspected then—it is now known—that the Governor himself was in secret league with the Navajo chiefs. He had engaged to leave them unmolested; while they, on their side, promised to plunder only his enemies!

"On learning this terrible secret, I saw the hand that had dealt me the blow. Stung by the disgrace I had put upon him, as well as by my wife's scorn, the villain was not slow to avenge himself.

"Since then his life has been twice in my power, but the taking of it would, most probably, have forfeited my own, and I had objects for which to live. I may yet find a reckoning day for him.

"I have said that my band melted away. Sick at heart, and conscious of danger in New Mexico, I left the province, and crossed the Jornada to El Paso. Here for a while I lived, grieving for my lost child.

"I was not long inactive. The frequent forays made by the Apaches into Sonora and Chihuahua had rendered the government more energetic in the defence of the frontier. The presidios were repaired and garrisoned with more efficient troops, and a band of rangers organised, whose pay was proportioned to the number of scalps they might send back to the settlements.

"I was offered the command of this strange guerilla; and in the hope that I might yet recover my child, I accepted it—I became a scalp-hunter.

"It was a terrible commission; and had revenge alone been my object, it would long since have been gratified. Many a deed of blood have we enacted; many a scene of retaliatory vengeance have we passed through.

"I knew that my captive daughter was in the hands of the Navajoes. I had heard so at various times from prisoners whom I had taken; but I was always crippled for want of strength in men and means. Revolution after revolution kept the states in poverty and civil warfare, and our interests were neglected or forgotten. With all my exertions, I could never raise a force sufficient to penetrate that desert country north of the Gila, in which lie the towns of the savage Navajoes."

"And you think—"

"Patience! I shall soon finish. My band is now stronger than ever. I have received certain information, by one just escaped from a captivity among the Navajoes, that the warriors of both tribes are about to proceed southward. They are mustering all their strength, with the intention of making a grand foray; even, as we have heard, to the gates of Durango. It is my design, then, to enter their country while they are absent, and search for my daughter."

"And you think she still lives?"

"I know it. The same man who brought me this news, and who, poor fellow, has left his scalp and ears behind him, saw her often. She is grown up, and is, he says, a sort of queen among them, possessed of strange powers and privileges. Yes, she still lives; and if it be my fortune to recover her, then will this tragic scene be at an end. I will go far hence."

I had listened with deep attention to the strange recital. All the disgust with which my previous knowledge of this man's character had inspired me vanished from my mind, and I felt for him compassion—ay, admiration. He had suffered much. Suffering atones for crime, and in my sight he was justified. Perhaps I was too lenient in my judgment. It was natural I should be so.

When the revelation was ended, I was filled with emotions of pleasure. I felt a vivid joy to know that she was not the offspring of the demon I had deemed him.

He seemed to divine my thoughts; for there was a smile of satisfaction, I might say triumph, on his countenance, as he leaned across the table to refill the wine.

"Monsieur, my story must have wearied you. Drink!"

There was a moment's silence as we emptied the glasses.

"And now, sir, you know the father of your betrothed, at least somewhat better than before. Are you still in the mind to marry her?"

"Oh, sir! she is now, more than ever, to me a sacred object."

"But you must win her, as I have said, from me."

"Then, sir, tell me how. I am ready for any sacrifice that may be within my power to make."

"You must help me to recover her sister."

"Willingly."

"You must go with me to the desert."

"I will."

"Enough. We start to-morrow." And he rose, and began to pace the room.

"At an early hour?" I inquired, half fearing that I was about to be denied an interview with her whom I now more than ever longed to embrace.

"By daybreak," he replied, not seeming to heed my anxious manner.

"I must look to my horse and arms," said I, rising, and going towards the door, in hopes of meeting her without.

"They have been attended to; Gode is there. Come, boy! She is not in the hall. Stay where you are. I will get the arms you want. Adèle! Zoe! Oh, doctor, you are returned with your weeds! It is well. We journey to-morrow. Adèle, some coffee, love! and then let us have some music. Your guest leaves you to-morrow."

The bright form rushed between us with a scream.

"No, no, no, no!" she exclaimed, turning from one to the other, with the wild appeal of a passionate heart.

"Come, little dove!" said the father, taking her by the hands; "do not be so easily fluttered. It is but for a short time. He will return again."

"How long, papa? How long, Enrique?"

"But a very short while. It will be longer to me than to you, Zoe."

"Oh! no, no; an hour will be a long time. How many hours do you think, Enrique?"

"Oh! we shall be gone days, I fear."

"Days! Oh, papa! Oh, Enrique! Days!"

"Come, little chit; they will soon pass. Go! Help your mamma to make the coffee."

"Oh, papa! Days; long days. They will not soon pass when I am alone."

"But you will not be alone. Your mamma will be with you."

"Ah!"

And with a sigh, and an air of abstraction, she departed to obey the command of her father. As she passed out at the door, she again sighed audibly.

The doctor was a silent and wondering spectator of this last scene; and as her figure vanished into the hall, I could hear him muttering to himself—

"Oh ja! Poor leetle fraulein! I thought as mosh."

Chapter Seventeen.

Up the Del Norte.

I will not distress you with a parting scene. We were in our saddles before the stars had died out, and riding along the sandy road.

At a short distance from the house the path angled, striking into thick, heavy timber. Here I checked my horse, allowing my companions to pass, and, standing in the stirrup, looked back. My eyes wandered along the old grey walls, and sought the azotea. Upon the very edge of the parapet, outlined against the pale light of the aurora, was the object I looked for. I could not distinguish the features, but I easily recognised the oval curvings of the figure, cut like a dark medallion against the sky.

She was standing near one of the yucca palm trees that grew up from the azotea. Her hand rested upon its trunk, and she bent forward, straining her gaze into the darkness below. Perhaps she saw the waving of a kerchief; perhaps she heard her name, and echoed the parting prayer that was sent back to her on the still breath of the morning. If so, her voice was drowned by the tread of my chafing horse, that, wheeling suddenly, bore me off into the sombre shadows of the forest.

I rode forward, turning at intervals to catch a glimpse of those lovely outlines, but from no other point was the house visible. It lay buried in the dark, majestic woods. I could only see the long bayonets of the picturesque palmillas; and our road now descending among hills, these too were soon hidden from my view.

Dropping the bridle, and leaving my horse to go at will, I fell into a train of thoughts at once pleasant and painful.

I knew that I had inspired this young creature with a passion deep and ardent as my own, perhaps more vital; for my heart had passed through other affections, while hers had never throbbed with any save the subdued solicitudes of a graceful childhood. She had never known emotion. Love was her first strong feeling, her first passion. Would it not, thus enthroned, reign over all other thoughts in her heart's kingdom? She, too, so formed for love; so like its mythic goddess!

These reflections were pleasant. But the picture darkened as I turned from looking back for the last time, and something whispered me, some demon it was, "You may never see her more!"

The suggestion, even in this hypothetical form, was enough to fill my mind with dark forebodings, and I began to cast my thoughts upon the future. I was going upon no party of pleasure, from which I might return at a fixed hour. Dangers were before me, the dangers of the desert; and I knew that these were of no ordinary character. In our plans of the previous night, Seguin had not concealed the perils of our expedition. These he had detailed before exacting my final promise to accompany him. Weeks before, I would not have regarded them—they would only have lured me on to meet them; now my feelings were different, for I believed that in my life there was another's. What, then, if the demon had whispered truly? I might never see her more! It was a painful thought; and I rode on, bent in the saddle, under the influence of its bitterness.

But I was once more upon the back of my favourite Moro, who seemed to "know his rider"; and as his elastic body heaved beneath me, my spirit answered his, and began to resume its wonted buoyancy.

After a while I took up the reins, and shortening them in my hands, spurred on after my companions. Our road lay up the river, crossing the shallow ford at intervals, and winding through the bottom-lands, that were heavily timbered. The path was difficult on account of the thick underwood; and although the trees had once been blazed for a road, there were no signs of late travel upon it, with the exception of a few solitary horse-tracks. The country appeared wild and uninhabited. This was evident from the frequency with which deer and antelope swept across our path, or sprang out of the underwood close to our horses' heads. Here and there our path trended away from the river, crossing its numerous loops. Several times we passed large tracts where the heavy timber had been felled, and clearings had existed. But this must have been long ago, for the land that had been furrowed by the plough was now covered with tangled and almost impenetrable thickets. A few broken and decaying logs, or crumbling walls of the adobe were all that remained to attest where the settlers' rancho had stood.

We passed a ruined church with its old turrets dropping by piecemeal. Piles of adobe lay around covering the ground for acres. A thriving village had stood there. Where was it now? Where were the busy gossips? A wild-cat sprang over the briar-laced walls, and made off into the forest. An owl flew sluggishly up from the crumbling cupola, and hovered around our heads, uttering its doleful "woo-hoo-a," that rendered the desolation of the scene more impressive. As we rode through the ruin, a dead stillness surrounded us, broken only by the hooting of the night-bird, and the "cranch-cranch" of our horses' feet upon the fragments of pottery that covered the deserted streets.

But where were they who had once made these walls echo with their voices? Who had knelt under the sacred shadow of that once hallowed pile? They were gone; but where? and when? and why?

I put these questions to Seguin, and was answered thus briefly—

"The Indians."

The savage it was, with his red spear and scalping-knife, his bow and his battle-axe, his brand and his poisoned arrows.

"The Navajoes?" I inquired. "Navajo and Apache."

"But do they come no more to this place?" A feeling of anxiety had suddenly entered my mind. I thought of our proximity to the mansion we had left. I thought of its unguarded walls. I waited with some impatience for an answer.

"No more," was the brief reply. "And why?" I inquired.

"This is our territory," he answered, significantly. "You are now, monsieur, in a country where live strange fellows; you shall see. Woe to the Apache or Navajo who may stray into these woods!"

As we rode forward, the country became more open, and we caught a glimpse of high bluffs trending north and south on both sides of the river. These bluffs converged till the river channel appeared to be completely barred up by a mountain. This was only an appearance. On riding farther, we found ourselves entering one of those fearful gaps, cañons, as they are called, so often met with in the table-lands of tropical America.

Through this the river foamed between two vast cliffs, a thousand feet in height, whose profiles, as you approached them, suggested the idea of angry giants, separated by some almighty hand, and thus left frowning at each other. It was with a feeling of awe that one looked up the face of these stupendous cliffs, and I felt a shuddering sensation as I neared the mighty gate between them.

"Do you see that point?" asked Seguin, indicating a rock that jutted out from the highest ledge of the chasm. I signified in the affirmative, for the question was addressed to myself.

"That is the leap you were so desirous of taking. We found you dangling against yonder rock."

"Good God!" I ejaculated, as my eyes rested upon the dizzy eminence. My brain grew giddy as I sat in my saddle gazing upward, and I was fain to ride onward.

"But for your noble horse," continued my companion, "the doctor here would have been stopping about this time to hypothecate upon your bones. Ho, Moro! beautiful Moro!"

"Oh, mein Gott! Ya, ya!" assented the botanist, looking up against the precipice, apparently with a feeling of awe such as I felt myself.

Seguin had ridden alongside me, and was patting my horse on the neck with expressions of admiration.

"But why?" I asked, the remembrance of our first interview now occurring to me, "why were you so eager to possess him?"

"A fancy."

"Can I not understand it? I think you said then that I could not?"

"Oh, yes! Quite easily, monsieur. I intended to steal my own daughter, and I wanted, for that purpose, to have the aid of your horse."

"But how?"

"It was before I had heard the news of this intended expedition of our enemy. As I had no hopes of obtaining her otherwise, it was my design to have entered their country alone, or with a tried comrade, and by stratagem to have carried her off. Their horses are swift, yet far inferior to the Arab, as you may have an opportunity of seeing. With such an animal as that, I would have been comparatively safe, unless hemmed in or surrounded, and even then I might have got off with a few scratches, I intended to have disguised myself, and entered the town as one of their own warriors. I have long been master of their language."

"It would have been a perilous enterprise."

"True! It was a *dernier ressort*, and only adopted because all other efforts had failed; after years of yearning, deep craving of the heart. I might have perished. It was a rash thought, but I, at that time, entertained it fully."

"I hope we shall succeed now."

"I have high hopes. It seems as if some overruling providence were now acting in my favour. This absence of her captors; and, besides, my band has been most opportunely strengthened by the arrival of a number of trappers from the eastern plains. The beaver-skins have fallen, according to their phraseology, to a 'plew a plug,' and they find 'red-skin' pays better. Ah! I hope this will soon be over."

And he sighed deeply as he uttered the last words.

We were now at the entrance of the gorge, and a shady clump of cotton-woods invited us to rest.

"Let us noon here," said Seguin.

We dismounted, and ran our animals out on their trail-ropes to feed. Then seating ourselves on the soft grass, we drew forth the viands that had been prepared for our journey.

Chapter Eighteen.

Geography and Geology.

We rested above an hour in the cool shade, while our horses refreshed themselves on the "grama" that grew luxuriantly around. We conversed about the singular region in which we were travelling; singular in its geography, its geology, its botany, and its history; singular in all respects.

I am a traveller, as I might say, by profession. I felt an interest in learning something of the wild countries that stretched for hundreds of miles around us; and I knew there was no man living so capable of being my informant as he with whom I then conversed.

My journey down the river had made me but little acquainted with its features. At that time, as I have already related, there was fever upon me; and my memory of objects was as though I had encountered them in some distorted dream.

My brain was now clear; and the scenes through which we were passing—here soft and south-like, there wild, barren, and picturesque—forcibly impressed my imagination.

The knowledge, too, that parts of this region had once been inhabited by the followers of Cortez, as many a ruin testified; that it had been surrendered back to its ancient and savage lords, and the inference that this surrender had been brought about by the enactment of many a tragic scene, induced a train of romantic thought, which yearned for gratification in an acquaintance with the realities that gave rise to it.

Seguin was communicative. His spirits were high. His hopes were buoyant. The prospect of again embracing his long-lost child imbued him, as it were, with new life. He had not, he said, felt so happy for many years.

"It is true," said he, in answer to a question I had put, "there is little known of this whole region, beyond the boundaries of the Mexican settlements. They who once had the opportunity of recording its geographical features have left the task undone. They were too busy in the search for gold; and their weak descendants, as you see, are too busy in robbing one another to care for aught else. They know nothing of the country beyond their own borders; and these are every day contracting upon them. All they know of it is the fact that thence come their enemies, whom they dread, as children do ghosts or wolves."

"We are now," continued Seguin, "near the centre of the continent, in the very heart of the American Sahara."

"But," said I, interrupting him, "we cannot be more than a day's ride south of New Mexico. That is not a desert; it is a cultivated country."

"New Mexico is an oasis, nothing more. The desert is around it for hundreds of miles; nay, in some directions you may travel a thousand miles from the Del Norte without seeing one fertile spot. New Mexico is an oasis which owes its existence to the irrigating waters of the Del Norte. It is the only settlement of white men from the frontiers of the Mississippi to the shores of the Pacific in California. You approached it by a desert, did you not?"

"Yes; as we ascended from the Mississippi towards the Rocky Mountains the country became gradually more sterile. For the last three hundred miles or so we could scarcely find grass or water for the sustenance of our animals. But is it thus north and south of the route we travelled?"

"North and south for more than a thousand miles, from the plains of Texas to the lakes of Canada, along the whole base of the Rocky Mountains, and half-way to the settlements on the Mississippi, it is a treeless, herbless land."

"To the west of the mountains?"

"Fifteen hundred miles of desert; that is its length, by at least half as many miles of breadth. The country to the west is of a different character. It is more broken in its outlines, more mountainous, and if possible more sterile in its aspect. The volcanic fires have been more active there; and though that may have been thousands of years ago, the igneous rocks in many places look as if freshly upheaved. No vegetation, no climatic action has sensibly changed the hues of the lava and scoriae that in some places cover the plains for miles. I say no climatic action, for there is but little of that in this central region."

"I do not understand you."

"What I mean is, that there is but little atmospheric change. It is but one uniform drought; it is seldom tempestuous or rainy. I know some districts where a drop of rain has not fallen for years."

"And can you account for that phenomenon?"

"I have my theory. It may not satisfy the learned meteorologist, but I will offer it to you."

I listened with attention, for I knew that my companion was a man of science, as of experience and observation, and subjects of the character of those about which we conversed had always possessed great interest for me. He continued—

"There can be no rain without vapour in the air. There can be no vapour in the air without water on the earth below to produce it. Here there is no great body of water.

"Nor can there be. The whole region of the desert is upheaved—an elevated table-land. We are now nearly six thousand feet above sea level. Hence its springs are few; and by hydraulic law must be fed by its own waters, or those of some region still more elevated, which does not exist on the continent.

"Could I create vast seas in this region, walled in by the lofty mountains that traverse it—and such seas existed coeval with its formation; could I create those seas without giving them an outlet, not even allowing the smallest rill to drain them, in process of time they would empty themselves into the ocean, and leave everything as it now is, a desert."

"But how? by evaporation?"

"On the contrary, the absence of evaporation would be the cause of their drainage. I believe it has been so already."

"I cannot understand that."

"It is simply thus: this region possesses, as we have said, great elevation; consequently a cool atmosphere, and a much less evaporating power than that which draws up the water of the ocean. Now, there would be an interchange of vapour between the ocean and these elevated seas, by means of winds and currents; for it is only by that means that any water can reach this interior plateau. That interchange would result in favour of the inland seas, by reason of their less evaporation, as well as from other causes. We have not time, or I could demonstrate such a result. I beg you will admit it, then, and reason it out at your leisure."

"I perceive the truth; I perceive it at once."

"What follows, then? These seas would gradually fill up to overflowing. The first little rivulet that trickled forth from their lipping fulness would be the signal of their destruction. It would cut its channel over the ridge of the lofty mountain, tiny at first, but deepening and widening with each successive shower, until, after many years—ages, centuries, cycles perhaps—a great gap such as this," (here Seguin pointed to the cañon), "and the dry plain behind it, would alone exist to puzzle the geologist."

"And you think that the plains lying among the Andes and the Rocky Mountains are the dry beds of seas?"

"I doubt it not; seas formed after the upheaval of the ridges that barred them in, formed by rains from the ocean, at first shallow, then deepening, until they had risen to the level of their mountain barriers; and, as I have described, cut their way back again to the ocean."

"But does not one of these seas still exist?"

"The Great Salt Lake? It does. It lies north-west of us. Not only one, but a system of lakes, springs, and rivers, both salt and fresh; and these have no outlet to the ocean. They are barred in by highlands and mountains, of themselves forming a complete geographical system."

"Does not that destroy your theory?"

"No. The basin in which this phenomenon exists is on a lower level than most of the desert plateaux. Its evaporating power is equal to the influx of its own rivers, and consequently neutralises their effect; that is to say, in its exchange of vapour with the ocean, it gives as much as it receives. This arises, not so much from its low elevation as from the peculiar dip of the mountains that guide the waters into its bosom. Place it in a colder position, *ceteris paribus*, and in time it would cut the canal for its own drainage. So with the Caspian Sea, the Aral, and the Dead Sea. No, my friend, the existence of the Salt Lake supports my theory. Around its shores lies a fertile country, fertile from the quick returns of its own waters moistening it with rain. It exists only to a limited extent, and cannot influence the whole region of the desert, which lies parched and sterile, on account of its great distance from the ocean."

"But does not the vapour rising from the ocean float over the desert?"

"It does, as I have said, to some extent, else there would be no rain here. Sometimes by extraordinary causes, such as high winds, it is carried into the heart of the continent in large masses. Then we have storms, and fearful ones too. But, generally, it is only the skirt of a cloud, so to speak, that reaches thus far; and that, combined with the proper evaporation of the region itself, that is, from its own springs and rivers, yields all the rain that falls upon it. Great bodies of vapour, rising from the Pacific and drifting eastward, first impinge upon the coast range, and there deposit their waters; or perhaps they are more highly-heated, and soaring above the tops of these mountains, travel farther. They will be intercepted a hundred miles farther on by the loftier ridges of the Sierra Nevada, and carried back, as it were, captive, to the ocean by the streams of the Sacramento and San Joaquim. It is only the skirt of these clouds, as I have termed it, that, soaring still higher, and escaping the attractive influence of the Nevada, floats on, and falls into the desert region. What then? No sooner has it fallen than it hurries back to the sea by the Gila and Colorado, to rise again and fertilise the slopes of the Nevada; while the fragment of some other cloud drifts its scanty supply over the arid uplands of the interior, to be spent in rain or snow upon the peaks of the Rocky Mountains. Hence the source of the rivers running east and west, and hence the oases, such as the parks that lie among these mountains. Hence the fertile valleys upon the Del Norte, and other streams that thinly meander through this central land.

"Vapour-clouds from the Atlantic undergo a similar detention in crossing the Alleghany range; or, cooling, after having circled a great distance round the globe, descend into the valleys of the Ohio and Mississippi. From all sides of this great continent, as you approach its centre, fertility declines, and only from the want of water. The soil in many places where there is scarcely a blade of grass to be seen, possesses all the elements of vegetation. So the doctor will tell you; he has analysed it."

"Ya, ya! dat ish true," quietly affirmed the doctor.

"There are many oases," continued Seguin; "and where water can be used to irrigate the soil, luxuriant vegetation is the consequence. You have observed this, no doubt, in travelling down the river; and such was the case in the old Spanish settlements on the Gila."

"But why were these abandoned?" I inquired, never having heard any reason assigned for the desertion of these once flourishing colonies.

"Why!" echoed Seguin, with a peculiar energy; "why! Unless some other race than the Iberian take possession of these lands, the Apache, the Navajo, and the Comanche, the conquered of Cortez and his conquerors, will yet drive the descendants of those very conquerors from the soil of Mexico. Look at Sonora and Chihuahua, half-depopulated! Look at New Mexico; its citizens living by suffrance: living, as it were, to till the land and feed the flocks for the support of their own enemies, who levy their blackmail by the year! But, come; the sun tells us we must on. Come!

"Mount! we can go through," continued he. "There has been no rain lately, and the water is low, otherwise we should have fifteen miles of a ride over the mountain yonder. Keep close to the rocks! Follow me!"

And with this admonition he entered the cañon, followed by myself, Gode, and the doctor.

Chapter Nineteen.

The Scalp-Hunters.

It was still early in the evening when we reached the camp—the camp of the scalp-hunters. Our arrival was scarcely noticed. A single glance at us, as we rode in amongst the men was all the recognition we received. No one rose from his seat or ceased his occupation. We were left to unsaddle our horses and dispose of them as best we might.

I was wearied with the ride, having been so long unused to the saddle. I threw my blanket on the ground, and sat down, resting my back against the stump of a tree. I could have slept, but the strangeness of everything around me excited my imagination, and, with feelings of curiosity, I looked and listened.

I should call the pencil to my aid to give you an idea of the scene, and that would but faintly illustrate it. A wilder and more picturesque *coup-d'oeil* never impressed human vision. It reminded me of pictures I had seen representing the bivouacs of brigands under the dark pines of the Abruzzi.

I paint from a recollection that looks back over many years of adventurous life. I can give only the more salient points of the picture. The *petite détail* is forgotten, although at that time the minutest objects were things new and strange to my eye, and each of them for a while fixed my attention. I afterwards grew familiar with them; and hence they are now in my memory, as a multitude of other things, indistinct from their very distinctness.

The camp was in a bend of the Del Norte, in a glade surrounded by tall cotton-woods, whose smooth trunks rose vertically out of a thick underwood of palmettoes and Spanish bayonet. A few tattered tents stood in the open ground; and there were skin lodges after the Indian fashion. But most of the hunters had made their shelter with a buffalo-robe stretched upon four upright poles. There were "lairs" among the underwood, constructed of branches, and thatched with the palmated leaves of the yucca, or with reeds brought from the adjacent river.

There were paths leading out in different directions, marked by openings in the foliage. Through one of these a green meadow was visible. Mules and mustangs, picketed on long trail-ropes, were clustered over it.

Through the camp were seen the saddles, bridles, and packs, resting upon stumps or hanging from the branches. Guns leaned against the trees, and rusted sabres hung suspended over the tents and lodges. Articles of camp furniture, such as pans, kettles, and axes, littered the ground in every direction. Log fires were burning. Around them sat clusters of men. They were not seeking warmth, for it was not cold. They were roasting ribs of venison, or smoking odd-fashioned pipes. Some were scouring their arms and accoutrements.

The accents of many languages fell upon my ear. I heard snatches of French, Spanish, English, and Indian. The exclamations were in character with the appearance of those who uttered them. "Hollo, Dick! hang it, old hoss, what are ye 'bout?" "Carambo!" "By the 'tarnal airthquake!" "Vaya! hombre, vaya!" "Carrajo!" "By Gosh!" "Santisima Maria!" "Sacr-r-ré!"

It seemed as if the different nations had sent representatives to contest the supremacy of their shibboleths.

I was struck with three groups. A particular language prevailed in each; and there was a homogeneousness about the costumes of the men composing each. That nearest me conversed in the Spanish language. They were Mexicans. I will describe the dress of one, as I remember it.

Calzoneros of green velvet. These are cut after the fashion of sailor-trousers, short waist, tight round the hips, and wide at the bottoms, where they are strengthened by black leather stamped and stitched ornamentally. The outer seams are split from hip to thigh, slashed with braid, and set with rows of silver "castletops." These seams are open, for the evening is warm, and underneath appear the calzoncillos of white muslin, hanging in white folds around the ankles. The boot is of calf-skin, tanned, but not blackened. It is reddish, rounded at the toe, and carries a spur at least a pound in weight, with a rowel three inches in diameter! The spur is curiously fashioned and fastened to the boot by straps of stamped leather. Little bells, campanulas, hang from the teeth of the rowels, and tinkle at the slightest motion of the foot! Look upward. The calzoneros are not braced, but fastened at the waist by a silken sash or scarf. It is scarlet. It is passed several times round the body, and made fast behind, where the fringed ends hang gracefully over the left hip. There is no waistcoat. A jacket of dark cloth embroidered and tightly fitting, short behind, *à la Grecque*, leaving the shirt to puff out over the scarf. The shirt itself, with its broad collar and flowered front, exhibits the triumphant skill of some dark-eyed poblana. Over all this is the broad-brimmed, shadowy sombrero; a heavy hat of black glaze, with its thick band of silver bullion. There are tags of the same metal stuck in the sides, giving it an appearance altogether unique. Over one shoulder is hanging, half-folded, the picturesque serape. A belt and pouch, an escopette upon which the hand is resting, a waist-belt with a pair of small pistols stuck under it, a long Spanish knife suspended obliquely across the left hip, complete the *tout ensemble* of him whom I have chosen to describe.

It may answer as a characteristic of the dress of many of his companions, those of the group that was nearest me. There was variety in their habiliments, yet the national costume of Mexico was traceable in all. Some wore leather calzoneros, with a spencer or jerkin of the same material, close both at front and behind. Some carried, instead of the pictured serape, the blanket of the Navajoes, with its broad black stripes. Suspended from the shoulders of others hung the beautiful and graceful manga. Some were moccasined; while a few of the inferior men wore the simple guarache, the sandal of the Aztecs.

The countenances of these men were swarth and savage-looking, their hair long, straight, and black as the wing of a crow; while both beard and moustache grew wildly over their faces. Fierce dark eyes gleamed under the broad brims of their hats. Few of them were men of high stature; yet there was a litheness in their bodies that showed them to be capable of great activity. Their frames were well knit, and inured to fatigues and hardships. They were all, or nearly all, natives of the Mexican border, frontier men, who had often closed in deadly fight with the Indian foe. They were ciboleros, vaqueros, rancheros, monteros; men who in their frequent association with the mountain men, the Gallic and Saxon hunters from the eastern plains, had acquired a degree of daring which by no means belongs to their own race. They were the chivalry of the Mexican frontier.

They smoked cigaritas, rolling them between their fingers in husks of maize. They played monte on their spread blankets, staking their tobacco. They cursed, and cried "Carrajo!" when they lost, and thanks to the "Santisima Virgin" when the cards were pulled out in their favour!

Their language was a Spanish patois; their voices were sharp and disagreeable.

At a short distance from these was the second group that attracted my attention. The individuals composing this were altogether different from the former. They were different in every essential point: in voice, dress, language, and physiognomy. Theirs was the Anglo-American face, at a glance. These were the trappers, the prairie hunters, the mountain men.

Let us again choose a type that may answer for a description of all.

He stands leaning on his long straight rifle, looking into the fire. He is six feet in his moccasins, and of a build that suggests the idea of strength and Saxon ancestry. His arms are like young oaks, and his hand, grasping the muzzle of his gun, is large, fleshless, and muscular. His cheek is broad and firm. It is partially covered by a bushy whisker that meets over the chin and fringes all around the lips. It is neither fair nor dark, but of a dull-brown colour, lighter around the mouth, where it has been bleached by the sun, "ambeer," and water. The eye is grey, or bluish grey, small, and slightly crowed at the corner. It is well set, and rarely wanders. It seems to look into you rather than at you. The hair is brown and of a medium length (cut, no doubt, on his last visit to the trading post, or the settlements); and the complexion, although dark as that of a mulatto, is only so from tan. It was once fair: a blonde. The countenance is not unprepossessing. It might be styled handsome. Its whole expression is bold, but good-humoured and generous.

The dress of the individual described is of home manufacture; that is, of his home, the prairie and the wild mountain park, where the material has been bought by a bullet from his rifle. It is the work of his own hands, unless indeed he may be one who has shared his cabin with some Indian—Sioux, Crow, or Cheyenne.

It consists of a hunting-shirt of dressed deer-skin, smoked to the softness of a glove; leggings, reaching to the waist, and moccasins of the same material; the latter soled with the parfleche of the buffalo. The shirt is belted at the waist, but open at the breast and throat, where it falls back into a graceful cape just covering the shoulders. Underneath is seen the undershirt, of finer material, the dressed skin of the antelope, or the fawn of the fallow-deer. On his head is a raccoon cap, with the face of the animal looking to the front, while the barred tail hangs like a plume drooping down to his left shoulder.

His accoutrements are, a bullet-pouch made from the undressed skin of the mountain cat, and a huge crescent-shaped horn, upon which he has carved many a strange souvenir. His arms consist of a long knife, a bowie, and a heavy pistol, carefully secured by a holster to the leathern belt around his waist. Add to this a rifle nearly five feet long, taking ninety to the pound, and so straight that the line of the barrel scarcely deflects from that of the butt.

But little attention has been paid to ornament in either his dress, arms, or equipments; and yet there is a gracefulness in the hang of his tunic-like shirt; a stylishness about the fringing of the cape and leggings; and a jauntiness in the set of that coon-skin cap that shows the wearer to be not altogether unmindful of his personal appearance. A small pouch or case, neatly embroidered with stained porcupine quills, hangs upon his breast.

At intervals he contemplates this with a pleased and complacent look. It is his pipe-holder: a love-token from some dark-eyed, dark-haired damsel, no doubt, like himself a denizen of the wild wilderness. Such is the *tout ensemble* of a mountain trapper.

There were many around him whom I have described almost similarly attired and equipped. Some wore slouch hats of greyish felt, and some catskin caps. Some had hunting-shirts bleached to a brighter hue, and broidered with gayer colours. Others looked more tattered and patched, and smoky; yet in the costume of all there was enough of character to enable you to class them. There was no possibility of mistaking the regular mountain man.

The third group that attracted my attention was at a greater distance from the spot I occupied. I was filled with curiosity, not to say astonishment, on perceiving that they were Indians.

"Can they be prisoners?" thought I. "No; they are not bound. There are no signs of captivity either in their looks or gestures, and yet they are Indians. Can they belong to the band, fighting against—?"

As I sat conjecturing, a hunter passed near me.

"Who are these Indians?" I asked, indicating the group.

"Delawares; some Shawnees."

These, then, were the celebrated Delawares, descendants of that great tribe who, on the Atlantic shores, first gave battle to the pale-faced invader. Theirs had been a wonderful history. War their school, war their worship, war their pastime, war their profession. They are now but a remnant. Their story will soon be ended.

I rose up, and approached them with a feeling of interest. Some of them were sitting around the fire, smoking out of curiously-carved pipes of the red claystone. Others strode back and forth with that majestic gait for which the forest Indian has been so much celebrated. There was a silence among them that contrasted strangely with the jabbering kept up by their Mexican allies. An occasional question put in a deep-toned, sonorous voice, a short but emphatic reply, a guttural grunt, a dignified nod, a gesture with the hand; and thus they conversed, as they filled their pipe-bowls with the kini-kin-ik, and passed the valued instruments from one to another.

I stood gazing upon these stoical sons of the forest with emotions stronger than curiosity, as one contemplates for the first time an object of which he has heard and read strange accounts. The history of their wars and their wanderings were fresh in my memory. Before me were the actors themselves, or types of them, in all their truthful reality, in all their wild picturesqueness. These were the men who, driven from their homes by the Atlantic border, yielded only to fate—to the destiny of their race. Crossing the Appalachian range, they had fought their way from home to home, down the steep sides of the Alleghany, along the wooded banks of the Ohio, into the heart of the "Bloody Ground." Still the pale-face followed on their track, and drove them onward, onward towards the setting sun. Red wars, Punic faith, broken treaties, year after year, thinned their ranks. Still, disdaining to live near their white conquerors, they pushed on, fighting their way through tribes of their own race and colour thrice their numbers! The forks of the Osage became their latest resting-place. Here the usurper promised to guarantee them a home, to be theirs to all time. The concession came too late. War and wandering had grown to be part of their natures; and with a scornful pride they disdained the peaceful tillage of the soil. The remnant of their tribe was collected on the Osage, but in one season it had disappeared. The braves and young men wandered away, leaving only the old, the women, and the worthless in their allotted home. Where have they gone? Where are they now? He who would find the Delawares must seek them on the broad prairies, in the mountain parks, in the haunts of the bear and the beaver, the big-horn and the buffalo. There he may find them, in scattered bands, leagued with their ancient enemies the whites, or alone, trapping, hunting, fighting the Yuta or Rapaho, the Crow or Cheyenne, the Navajo and the Apache.

I stood gazing upon the group with feelings of profound interest, upon their features and their picturesque habiliments. Though no two of them were dressed exactly alike, there was a similarity about the dress of all. Most of them wore hunting-shirts, not made of deer-skin like those of the whites, but of calico, printed in bright patterns. This dress, handsomely fashioned and fringed, under the accoutrements of the Indian warrior, presented a striking appearance. But that which chiefly distinguished the costumes of both the Delaware and Shawano from that of their white allies was the head-dress. This was, in fact, a turban, formed by binding the head with a scarf or kerchief of a brilliant colour, such as may be seen on the dark Creoles of Hayti. In the group before me no two of these turbans were alike, yet they were all of a similar character. The finest were those made by the chequered kerchiefs of Madras. Plumes surmounted them of coloured feathers from the wing of the war-eagle, or the blue plumage of the gruya.

For the rest of their costume they wore deer-skin leggings and moccasins, nearly similar to those of the trappers. The leggings of some were ornamented by scalp-locks along the outer seam, exhibiting a dark history of the wearer's prowess. I noticed that their moccasins were peculiar, differing altogether from those worn by the Indians of the prairies. They were seamed up the fronts, without braiding or ornament, and gathered into a double row of plaits.

The arms and equipments of these warrior men were like those of the white hunters. They have long since discarded the bow; and in the management of the rifle most of them can "draw a bead" and hit "plumb centre" with any of their mountain associates. In addition to the firelock and knife, I noticed that they still carried the ancient weapon of their race, the fearful tomahawk.

I have described three characteristic groups that struck me on glancing over the camp ground. There were individuals belonging to neither, and others partaking of the character of one or all. There were Frenchmen, Canadian voyageurs, strays of the north-west company, wearing white capotes, and chatting, dancing, and singing their boat-songs with all the *ésprit* of their race. There were pueblos, Indios manzos, clad in their ungraceful tilmas, and rather serving than associating with those around them. There were mulattoes, too, and negroes of a jetty blackness from the plantations of Louisiana, who had exchanged for this free, roving life the twisted "cow-skin" of the overseer. There were tattered uniforms showing the deserters who had wandered from some frontier post into this remote region. There were Kanakas from the Sandwich Isles, who had crossed the deserts from California. There were men apparently of every hue and clime and tongue here assembled, drawn together by the accidents of life, by the instinct of adventure—all more or less strange individuals of the strangest band it has ever been my lot to witness: the band of the Scalp-Hunters!

Chapter Twenty.

Sharp-Shooting.

I had returned to my blanket, and was about to stretch myself upon it, when the whoop of a gruya drew my attention. Looking up, I saw one of these birds flying towards the camp. It was coming through a break in the trees that opened from the river. It flew low, and tempted a shot with its broad wings, and slow, lazy flight.

A report rang upon the air. One of the Mexicans had fired his escopette; but the bird flew on, plying its wings with more energy, as if to bear itself out of reach.

There was a laugh from the trappers, and a voice cried out—

"Yur fool! D'yur think 'ee kud hit a spread blanket wi' that beetle-shaped blunderbox? Pish!"

I turned to see who had delivered this odd speech. Two men were poising their rifles, bringing them to bear upon the bird. One was the young hunter whom I have described. The other was an Indian whom I had not seen before.

The cracks were simultaneous; and the crane, dropping its long neck, came whirling down among the trees, where it caught upon a high branch, and remained.

From their position neither party knew that the other had fired. A tent was between them, and the two reports had seemed as one. A trapper cried out—

"Well done, Garey! Lord help the thing that's afore old Killbar's muzzle when you squints through her hind-sights."

The Indian just then stepped round the tent. Hearing this side speech, and perceiving the smoke still oozing from the muzzle of the young hunter's gun, he turned to the latter with the interrogation—

"Did you fire, sir?"

This was said in well-accentuated and most un-Indianlike English, which would have drawn my attention to the man had not his singularly-imposing appearance riveted me already.

"Who is he?" I inquired from one near me.

"Don't know; fresh arriv'," was the short answer.

"Do you mean that he is a stranger here?"

"Just so. He kumb in thar a while agone. Don't b'lieve anybody knows him. I guess the captain does; I seed them shake hands."

I looked at the Indian with increasing interest. He seemed a man of about thirty years of age, and not much under seven feet in height. He was proportioned like an Apollo, and, on this account, appeared smaller than he actually was. His features were of the Roman type; and his fine forehead, his aquiline nose and broad jawbone, gave him the appearance of talent, as well as firmness and energy. He was dressed in a hunting-shirt, leggings, and moccasins; but all these differed from anything worn either by the hunters or their Indian allies. The shirt itself was made out of the dressed hide of the red deer, but differently prepared from that used by the trappers. It was bleached almost to the whiteness of a kid glove. The breast, unlike theirs, was close, and beautifully embroidered with stained porcupine quills. The sleeves were similarly ornamented; and the cape and skirts were trimmed with the soft, snow-white fur of the ermine. A row of entire skins of that animal hung from the skirt border, forming a fringe both graceful and costly. But the most singular feature about this man was his hair. It fell loosely over his shoulders, and swept the ground as he walked! It could not have been less than seven feet in length. It was black, glossy, and luxuriant, and reminded me of the tails of those great Flemish horses I had seen in the funeral carriages of London.

He wore upon his head the war-eagle bonnet, with its full circle of plumes: the finest triumph of savage taste. This magnificent head-dress added to the majesty of his appearance.

A white buffalo robe hung from his shoulders, with all the graceful draping of a toga. Its silky fur corresponded to the colour of his dress, and contrasted strikingly with his own dark tresses.

There were other ornaments about his person. His arms and accoutrements were shining with metallic brightness, and the stock and butt of his rifle were richly inlaid with silver.

I have been thus minute in my description, as the first appearance of this man impressed me with a picture that can never be effaced from my memory. He was the *beau ideal* of a picturesque and romantic savage; and yet there was nothing savage either in his speech or bearing. On the contrary, the interrogation which he had just addressed to the trapper was put in the politest manner. The reply was not so courteous.

"Did I fire! Didn't ye hear a crack? Didn't ye see the thing fall? Look yonder!"

Garey, as he spoke, pointed up to the bird.

"We must have fired simultaneously."

As the Indian said this he appealed to his gun, which was still smoking at the muzzle.

"Look hyar, Injun! whether we fired symultainyously, or extraneously, or cattawampously, ain't the flappin' o' a beaver's tail to me; but I tuk sight on that bird; I hut that bird; and 'twar my bullet brought the thing down."

"I think I must have hit it too," replied the Indian, modestly.

"That's like, with that ar' spangled gimcrack!" said Garey, looking disdainfully at the other's gun, and then proudly at his own brown weather-beaten piece, which he had just wiped, and was about to reload.

"Gimcrack or no," answered the Indian, "she sends a bullet straighter and farther than any piece I have hitherto met with. I'll warrant she has sent hers through the body of the crane."

"Look hyar, mister for I s'pose we must call a gentleman 'mister' who speaks so fine an' looks so fine, tho' he be's an Injun—it's mighty easy to settle who hut the bird. That thing's a fifty or tharabouts; Killbar's a ninety. 'Taint hard to tell which has plugged the varmint. We'll soon see;" and, so saying, the hunter stepped off towards the tree on which hung the gruya, high up.

"How are you to get it down?" cried one of the men, who had stepped forward to witness the settlement of this curious dispute.

There was no reply, for everyone saw that Garey was poising his rifle for a shot. The crack followed; and the branch, shivered by his bullet, bent downward under the weight of the gruya. But the bird, caught in a double fork, still stuck fast on the broken limb.

A murmur of approbation followed the shot. These were men not accustomed to hurrah loudly at a trivial incident.

The Indian now approached, having reloaded his piece. Taking aim, he struck the branch at the shattered point, cutting it clean from the tree! The bird fell to the ground, amidst expressions of applause from the spectators, but chiefly from the Mexican and Indian hunters. It was at once picked up and examined. Two bullets had passed through its body. Either would have killed it.

A shadow of unpleasant feeling was visible on the face of the young trapper. In the presence of so many hunters of every nation, to be thus equalled, beaten in the in of his favourite weapon, and by an "Injun"; still worse by one of "them ar' gingerbread guns!" The mountain men have no faith in an ornamented stock, or a big bore. Spangled rifles, they say, are like spangled razors, made for selling to greenhorns. It was evident, however, that the strange Indian's rifle had been made to shoot as well.

It required all the strength of nerve which the trapper possessed to conceal his chagrin. Without saying a word, he commenced wiping out his gun with that stoical calmness peculiar to men of his calling. I observed that he proceeded to load with more than usual care. It was evident that he would not rest satisfied with the trial already made, but would either beat the "Injun," or be himself "whipped into shucks." So he declared in a muttered speech to his comrades.

His piece was soon loaded; and, swinging her to the hunter's carry, he turned to the crowd, now collected from all parts of the camp.

"Thar's one kind o' shootin'," said he, "that's jest as easy as fallin' off a log. Any man kin do it as kin look straight through hind-sights. But then thar's another kind that ain't so easy; it needs narve."

Here the trapper paused, and looked towards the Indian, who was also reloading.

"Look hyar, stranger!" continued he, addressing the latter, "have ye got a cummarade on the ground as knows yer shooting?"

The Indian after a moment's hesitation, answered, "Yes."

"Kin your cummarade depend on yer shot?"

"Oh! I think so. Why do you wish to know that?"

"Why, I'm a-going to show ye a shot we sometimes practise at Bent's Fort, jest to tickle the greenhorns. 'Tain't much of a shot nayther; but it tries the narves a little I reckon. Hoy! Rube!"

"What doo 'ee want?"

This was spoken in an energetic and angry-like voice, that turned all eyes to the quarter whence it proceeded. At the first glance, there seemed to be no one in that direction. In looking more carefully among the logs and stumps, an individual was discovered seated by one of the fires. It would have been difficult to tell that it was a human body, had not the arms at the moment been in motion. The back was turned toward the crowd, and the head had disappeared, sunk forward over the fire. The object, from where we were standing, looked more like the stump of a cotton-wood, dressed in dirt-coloured buckskin, than the body of a human being. On getting nearer, and round to the front of it, it was seen to be a man, though a very curious one, holding a long rib of deer-meat in both hands, which he was polishing with a very poor set of teeth.

The whole appearance of this individual was odd and striking. His dress, if dress it could be called, was simple as it was savage. It consisted of what might have once been a hunting-shirt, but which now looked more like a leathern bag with the bottom ripped open, and the sleeves sewed into the sides. It was of a dirty-brown colour, wrinkled at the hollow of the arms, patched round the armpits, and greasy all over; it was fairly caked with dirt! There was no attempt at either ornament or fringe. There had been a cape, but this had evidently been drawn upon from time to time, for patches and other uses, until scarcely a vestige of it remained. The leggings and moccasins were on a par with the shirt, and seemed to have been manufactured out of the same hide. They, too, were dirt-brown, patched, wrinkled, and greasy. They did not meet each other, but left a piece of the ankle bare, and that also was dirt-brown, like the buck-skin. There was no undershirt, waistcoat, or other garment to be seen, with the exception of a close-fitting cap, which had once been cat-skin, but the hair was all worn off it, leaving a greasy, leathery-looking surface, that corresponded well with the other parts of the dress. Cap, shirt, leggings, and moccasins looked as if they had never been stripped off since the day they were first tried on, and that might have been many a year ago. The shirt was open, displaying the naked breast and throat, and these, as well as the face, hands, and ankles, had been tanned by the sun, and smoked by the fire, to the hue of rusty copper. The whole man, clothes and all, looked as if he had been smoked on purpose!

His face bespoke a man of sixty. The features were sharp and somewhat aquiline; and the small eye was dark, quick, and piercing. His hair was black and cut short. His complexion had been naturally brunette, though there was nothing of the Frenchman or Spaniard on his physiognomy. He was more likely of the black Saxon breed.

As I looked at this man (for I had walked towards him, prompted by some instinct of curiosity), I began to fancy that there was a strangeness about him, independent of the oddness of his attire. There seemed to be something peculiar about his head, something wanting. What was it? I was not long in conjecture. When fairly in front of him, I saw what was wanting. It was his ears!

This discovery impressed me with a feeling akin to awe. There is something awful in a man without ears. It suggests some horrid drama, some terrible scene of cruel vengeance. It suggests the idea of crime committed and punishment inflicted.

These thoughts were wandering through my mind, when all at once I remembered a remark which Seguin had made on the previous night. This, then, thought I, is the person of whom he spoke. My mind was satisfied.

After making answer as above, the old fellow sat for some time with his head between his knees, chewing, mumbling, and growling, like a lean old wolf, angry at being disturbed in his meal.

"Come hyar, Rube! I want ye a bit," continued Garey, in a tone of half entreaty.

"And so 'ee will want me a bit; this child don't move a peg till he has cleaned this hyur rib; he don't, now!"

"Dog-gone it, man! make haste, then!" and the impatient trapper dropped the butt of his rifle to the ground, and stood waiting in sullen silence.

After chewing, and mumbling, and growling a few minutes longer, old Rube, for that was the name by which the leathery sinner was known, slowly erected his lean carcass; and came walking up to the crowd.

"What do 'ee want, Billee?" he inquired, going up to the trapper.

"I want ye to hold this," answered Garey, offering him a round white shell, about the size of a watch, a species of which there were many strewed over the ground.

"It's a bet, boyee?"

"No, it is not."

"Ain't wastin' yur powder, ar yur?"

"I've been beat shootin'," replied the trapper, in an undertone, "by that 'ar Injun."

The old man looked over to where the strange Indian was standing erect and majestic, in all the pride of his plumage. There was no appearance of triumph or swagger about him, as he stood leaning on his rifle, in an attitude at once calm and dignified.

It was plain, from the way old Rube surveyed him, that he had seen him before, though not in that camp. After passing his eyes over him from head to foot, and there resting them a moment, a low murmur escaped his lips, which ended abruptly in the word "Coco."

"A Coco, do ye think?" inquired the other, with an apparent interest.

"Are 'ee blind, Billee? Don't 'ee see his moccasin?"

"Yes, you're right, but I was in thar nation two years ago. I seed no such man as that."

"He w'an't there."

"Whar, then?"

"Whur thur's no great show o' redskins. He may shoot well; he did oncest on a time: plumb centre."

"You knew him, did ye?"

"O-ee-es. Oncest. Putty squaw: hansum gal. Whur do 'ee want me to go?"

I thought that Garey seemed inclined to carry the conversation further. There was an evident interest in his manner when the other mentioned the "squaw." Perhaps he had some tender recollection; but seeing the other preparing to start off, he pointed to an open glade that stretched eastward, and simply answered, "Sixty."

"Take care o' my claws, d'yur hear! Them Injuns has made 'em scarce; this child can't spare another."

The old trapper said this with a flourish of his right hand. I noticed that the little finger had been chopped off!

"Never fear, old hoss!" was the reply; and at this, the smoky carcase moved away with a slow and regular pace, that showed he was measuring the yards.

When he had stepped the sixtieth yard, he faced about, and stood erect, placing his heels together. He then extended his right arm, raising it until his hand was on a level with his shoulder, and holding the shell in his fingers, flat side to the front, shouted back—

"Now, Billee, shoot, and be hanged to yur!"

The shell was slightly concave, the concavity turned to the front. The thumb and finger reached half round the circumference, so that a part of the edge was hidden; and the surface turned towards the marksman was not larger than the dial of a common watch.

This was a fearful sight. It is one not so common among the mountain men as travellers would have you believe. The feat proves the marksman's skill; first, if successful, by showing the strength and steadiness of his nerves; secondly, by the confidence which the other reposes in it, thus declared by stronger testimony than any oath. In any case the feat of holding the mark is at least equal to that of hitting it. There are many hunters willing to risk taking the shot, but few who care to hold the shell.

It was a fearful sight, and my nerves tingled as I looked on. Many others felt as I. No one interfered. There were few present who would have dared, even had these two men been making preparations to fire at each other. Both were "men of mark" among their comrades: trappers of the first class.

Garey, drawing a long breath, planted himself firmly, the heel of his left foot opposite to, and some inches in advance of, the hollow of his right. Then, jerking up his gun, and throwing the barrel across his left palm, he cried out to his comrade—

"Steady, ole bone an' sinyer! hyar's at ye!"

The words were scarcely out when the gun was levelled. There was a moment's death-like silence, all eyes looking to the mark. Then came the crack, and the shell was seen to fly, shivered into fifty fragments! There was a cheer from the crowd. Old Rube stopped to pick up one of the pieces, and after examining it for a moment, shouted in a loud voice;—

"Plumb centre, by—!"

The young trapper had, in effect, hit the mark in the very centre, as the blue stain of the bullet testified.

Chapter Twenty One.

A Feat à la Tell.

All eyes were turned upon the strange Indian. During the scene described he has stood silent, and calmly looking on. His eye now wanders over the ground, apparently in search of an object.

A small convolvulus, known as the prairie gourd, is lying at his feet. It is globe-shaped, about the size of an orange, and not unlike one in colour. He stoops and takes it up. He seems to examine it with great care, balancing it upon his hand, as though he were calculating its weight.

What does he intend to do with this? Will he fling it up, and send his bullet through it in the air? What else?

His motions are watched in silence. Nearly all the scalp-hunters, sixty or seventy, are on the ground. Seguin only, with the doctor and a few men, is engaged some distance off, pitching a tent. Garey stands upon one side, slightly elated with his triumph, but not without feelings of apprehension that he may yet be beaten. Old Rube has gone back to the fire, and is roasting another rib.

The gourd seems to satisfy the Indian, for whatever purpose he intends it. A long piece of bone, the thigh joint of the war-eagle, hangs suspended over his breast. It is curiously carved, and pierced with holes like a musical instrument. It is one.

He places this to his lips, covering the holes, with his fingers. He sounds three notes, oddly inflected, but loud and sharp. He drops the instrument again, and stands looking eastward into the woods. The eyes of all present are bent in the same direction. The hunters, influenced by a mysterious curiosity, remain silent, or speak only in low mutterings.

Like an echo, the three notes are answered by a similar signal! It is evident that the Indian has a comrade in the woods, yet not one of the band seems to know aught of him or his comrade. Yes, one does. It is Rube.

"Look'ee hyur, boyees!" cries he, squinting over his shoulders; "I'll stake this rib against a griskin o' poor bull that 'ee'll see the puttiest gal as 'ee ever set yur eyes on."

There is no reply; we are gazing too intently for the expected arrival.

A rustling is heard, as of someone parting the bushes, the tread of a light foot, the snapping of twigs. A bright object appears among the leaves. Someone is coming through the underwood. It is a woman.

It is an Indian girl, attired in a singular and picturesque costume.

She steps out of the bushes, and comes boldly towards the crowd. All eyes are turned upon her with looks of wonder and admiration. We scan her face and figure and her striking attire.

She is dressed not unlike the Indian himself, and there is resemblance in other respects. The tunic worn by the girl is of finer materials; of fawn-skin. It is richly trimmed, and worked with split quills, stained to a variety of bright colours. It hangs to the middle of the thighs, ending in a fringe-work of shells, that tinkle as she moves.

Her limbs are wrapped in leggings of scarlet cloth, fringed like the tunic, and reaching to the ankles where they meet the flaps of her moccasins. These last are white, embroidered with stained quills, and fitting closely to her small feet.

A belt of wampum closes the tunic on her waist, exhibiting the globular developments of a full-grown bosom and the undulating outlines of a womanly person. Her headdress is similar to that worn by her companion, but smaller and lighter; and her hair, like his, hangs loosely down, reaching almost to the ground! Her neck, throat, and part of her bosom are nude, and clustered over with bead-strings of various colours.

The expression of her countenance is high and noble. Her eye is oblique. The lips meet with a double curve, and the throat is full and rounded. Her complexion is Indian; but a crimson hue, struggling through the brown upon her cheek, gives that pictured expression to her countenance which may be observed in the quadroon of the West Indies.

She is a girl, though full-grown and boldly developed: a type of health and savage beauty.

As she approaches, the men murmur their admiration. There are hearts beating under hunting-shirts that rarely deign to dream of the charms of woman.

I am struck at this moment with the appearance of the young trapper Garey. His face has fallen, the blood has forsaken his cheeks, his lips are white and compressed, and dark rings have formed round his eyes. They express anger, but there is still another meaning in them.

Is it jealousy? Yes!

He has stepped behind one of his comrades, as if he did not wish to be seen. One hand is playing involuntarily with the handle of his knife. The other grasps the barrel of his gun, as though he would crush it between his fingers!

The girl comes up. The Indian hands her the gourd, muttering some words in an unknown tongue—unknown, at least, to me. She takes it without making any reply, and walks off towards the spot where Rube had stood, which has been pointed out to her by her companion.

She reaches the tree, and halts in front of it, facing round as the trapper had done.

There was something so dramatic, so theatrical, in the whole proceeding, that up to the present time we had all stood waiting for the *dénouement* in silence. Now we knew what it was to be, and the men began to talk.

"He's a-goin' to shoot the gourd from the hand of the gal," suggested a hunter.

"No great shot, after all," added another; and indeed this was the silent opinion of most on the ground.

"Wagh! it don't beat Garey if he diz hit it," exclaimed a third.

What was our amazement at seeing the girl fling off her plumed bonnet, place the gourd upon her head, fold her arms over her bosom, and standing fronting us as calm and immobile as if she had been carved upon the tree!

There was a murmur in the crowd. The Indian was raising his rifle to take aim, when a man rushed forward to prevent him. It was Garey!

"No, yer don't! No!" cried he, clutching the levelled rifle; "she's deceived me, that's plain, but I won't see the gal that once loved me, or said she did, in the trap that a-way. No! Bill Garey ain't a-goin' to stand by and see it."

"What is this?" shouted the Indian, in a voice of thunder. "Who dares to interrupt me?"

"I dares," replied Garey. "She's yourn now, I suppose. You may take her whar ye like; and take this too," continued he, tearing off the embroidered pipe-case, and flinging it at the Indian's feet; "but ye're not a-goin' to shoot her down whiles I stand by."

"By what right do you interrupt me? My sister is not afraid, and—"

"Your sister!"

"Yes, my sister."

"And is yon gal your sister?" eagerly inquired Garey, his manner and the expression of his countenance all at once changing.

"She is. I have said she is."

"There is no risk!"

"And are you El Sol?"

"I am."

"I ask your pardon; but—"

"I pardon you. Let me proceed!"

"Oh, sir, do not. No! no! She is your sister, and I know you have the right, but thar's no needcessity. I have heerd of your shootin'. I give in; you kin beat me. For God's sake, do not risk it; as you care for her, do not!"

"There is no risk. I will show you."

"No, no! If you must, then, let me! I will hold it. Oh, let me!" stammered the hunter, in tones of entreaty.

"Hollo, Billee! What's the dratted rumpus?" cried Rube, coming up. "Hang it, man! let's see the shot. I've heern o' it afore. Don't be skeert, ye fool! he'll do it like a breeze; he will!"

And as the old trapper said this he caught his comrade by the arm, and swung him round out of the Indian's way.

The girl, during all this, had stood still, seemingly not knowing the cause of the interruption. Garey's back was turned to her, and the distance, with two years of separation, doubtless prevented her from recognising him.

Before Garey could turn to interpose himself, the rifle was at the Indian's shoulder and levelled. His finger was on the trigger, and his eyes glanced through the sights. It was too late to interfere. Any attempt at that might bring about the dreaded result. The hunter, as he turned, saw this, and halting in his tracks, stood straining and silent.

It was a moment of terrible suspense to all of us—a moment of intense emotion. The silence was profound. Every breath seemed suspended; every eye was fixed on the yellow object, not larger, I have said, than an orange. Oh, God! will the shot never come?

It came. The flash, the crack, the stream of fire, the wild hurrah, the forward rush, were all simultaneous things. We saw the shivered globe fly off. The girl was still upon her feet; she was safe!

I ran with the rest. The smoke for a moment blinded me. I heard the shrill notes of the Indian whistle. I looked before me. The girl had disappeared.

We ran to the spot where she had stood. We heard a rustling in the underwood, a departing footstep. We knew it was she; but guided by an instinct of delicacy, and a knowledge that it would be contrary to the wish of her brother, no one followed her.

We found the fragments of the calabash strewed over the ground. We found the leaden mark upon them. The bullet itself was buried in the bark of the tree, and one of the hunters commenced digging it out with the point of his bowie.

When we turned to go back we saw that the Indian had walked away, and now stood chatting easily and familiarly with Seguin.

As we re-entered the camp-ground I observed Garey stoop and pick up a shining object. It was the *gage d'amour*, which he carefully readjusted around his neck in its wonted position.

From his look and the manner in which he handled it, it was plain that he now regarded that souvenir with more reverence than ever.

Chapter Twenty Two.

A Feat à la Tail.

I had fallen into a sort of reverie. My mind was occupied with the incidents I had just witnessed, when a voice, which I recognised as that of old Rube, roused me from my abstraction.

"Look'ee hyur, boyees! Tain't of'n as ole Rube wastes lead, but I'll beat that Injun's shot, or 'ee may cut my ears off."

A loud laugh hailed this allusion of the trapper to his ears, which, as we have observed, were already gone; and so closely had they been trimmed that nothing remained for either knife or shears to accomplish.

"How will you do it, Rube?" cried one of the hunters; "shoot the mark off a yer own head?"

"I'll let 'ee see if 'ee wait," replied Rube, stalking up to a tree, and taking from its rest a long, heavy rifle, which he proceeded to wipe out with care.

The attention of all was now turned to the manoeuvres of the old trapper. Conjecture was busy as to his designs. What feat could he perform that would eclipse the one just witnessed? No one could guess.

"I'll beat it," continued he, muttering, as he loaded his piece, "or 'ee may chop the little finger off ole Rube's right paw."

Another peal of laughter followed, as all perceived that this was the finger that was wanting.

"'Ee—es," continued he, looking at the faces that were around him, "'ee may scalp me if I don't."

This last remark elicited fresh roars of laughter; for although the cat-skin was closely drawn upon his head, all present knew that old Rube was minus his scalp.

"But how are ye goin' to do it? Tell us that, old hoss!"

"'Ee see this, do 'ee?" asked the trapper, holding out a small fruit of the cactus pitahaya, which he had just plucked and cleaned of its spikelets.

"Ay, ay," cried several voices, in reply.

"'Ee do, do 'ee? Wal; 'ee see 'tain't half as big as the Injun's squash. 'Ee see that, do 'ee?"

"Oh, sartinly! Any fool can see that."

"Wal; s'pose I plug it at sixty, plump centre?"

"Wagh!" cried several, with shrugs of disappointment.

"Stick it on a pole, and any o' us can do that," said the principal speaker. "Here's Barney could knock it off wid his owld musket. Couldn't you, Barney?"

"In truth, an' I could thry," answered a very small man, leaning upon a musket, and who was dressed in a tattered uniform that had once been sky-blue. I had already noticed this individual with some curiosity, partly struck with his peculiar costume, but more particularly on account of the redness of his hair, which was the reddest I had ever seen. It bore the marks of a severe barrack discipline—that is, it had been shaved, and was now growing out of his little round head short and thick, and coarse in the grain, and of the colour of a scraped carrot. There was no possibility of mistaking Barney's nationality. In trapper phrase, any fool could have told that.

What had brought such an individual to such a place? I asked this question, and was soon enlightened. He had been a soldier in a frontier post, one of Uncle Sam's "Sky-blues." He had got tired of pork and pipe-clay, accompanied with a too liberal allowance of the hide. In a word, Barney was a deserter. What his name was, I know not, but he went under the appellation of O'Cork—Barney O'Cork.

A laugh greeted his answer to the hunter's question.

"Any o' us," continued the speaker, "could plug the persimmon that a way. But thar's a mighty heap o' diff'rence when you squints thro' hind-sights at a girl like yon."

"Ye're right, Dick," said another hunter; "it makes a fellow feel queery about the jeints."

"Holy vistment! An' wasn't she a raal beauty?" exclaimed the little Irishman, with an earnestness in his manner that set the trappers roaring again.

"Pish!" cried Rube, who had now finished loading, "yur a set o' channering fools; that's what 'ee ur. Who palavered about a post? I've got an ole squaw as well's the Injun. She'll hold the thing for this child—she will."

"Squaw! You a squaw?"

"Yes, hoss; I has a squaw I wudn't swop for two o' his'n. I'll make tracks an' fetch the old 'oman. Shet up yur heads, an' wait, will ye?"

So saying, the smoky old sinner shouldered his rifle, and walked off into the woods.

I, in common with others, late comers, who were strangers to Rube, began to think that he had an "old 'oman." There were no females to be seen about the encampment, but perhaps she was hid away in the woods. The trappers, however, who knew him, seemed to understand that the old fellow had some trick in his brain; and that, it appeared, was no new thing for him.

We were not kept long in suspense. In a few minutes Rube was seen returning, and by his side the "old 'oman," in the shape of a long, lank, bare-ribbed, high-boned mustang, that turned out on close inspection to be a mare! This, then, was Rube's squaw, and she was not at all unlike him, excepting the ears. She was long-eared, in common with all her race: the same as that upon which Quixote charged the windmill. The long ears caused her to look mulish, but it was only in appearance; she was a pure mustang when you examined her attentively. She seemed to have been at an earlier period of that dun-yellowish colour known as "clay-bank," a common colour among Mexican horses; but time and scars had somewhat metamorphosed her, and grey hairs predominated all over, particularly about the head and neck. These parts were covered with a dirty grizzle of mixed hues. She was badly wind-broken; and at stated intervals of several minutes each, her back, from the spasmodic action of the lungs, heaved up with a jerk, as though she were trying to kick with her hind legs, and couldn't. She was as thin as a rail, and carried her head below the level of her shoulders; but there was something in the twinkle of her solitary eye (for she had but one), that told you she had no intention of giving up for a long time to come. She was evidently game to the backbone.

Such was the "old 'oman" Rube had promised to fetch; and she was greeted by a loud laugh as he led her up.

"Now, look'ee hyur, boyees," said he, halting in front of the crowd. "Ee may larf, an' gabble, an' grin till yur sick in the guts—yur may! but this child's a-gwine to take the shine out o' that Injun's shot—he is, or bust a-tryin'."

Several of the bystanders remarked that that was likely enough, and that they only waited to see in what manner it was to be done. No one who knew him doubted old Rube to be, as in fact he was, one of the very best marksmen in the mountains—fully equal, perhaps, to the Indian; but it was the style and circumstances which had given such *éclat* to the shot of the latter. It was not every day that a beautiful girl could be found to stand fire as the squaw had done; and it was not every hunter who would have ventured to fire at a mark so placed. The strength of the feat lay in its newness and peculiarity. The hunters had often fired at the mark held in one another's hands. There were few who would like to carry it on their head. How, then, was Rube to "take the shine out o' that Injun's shot"? This was the question that each was asking the other, and which was at length put directly to Rube himself.

"Shet up your meat-traps," answered he, "an I'll show 'ee. In the fust place, then, 'ee all see that this hyur prickly ain't more'n hef size o' the squash?"

"Yes, sartainly," answered several voices. "That wur one sukumstance in his favour. Wa'nt it?"

"It wur! it wur!"

"Wal, hyur's another. The Injun, 'ee see, shot his mark off o' the head. Now, this child's a-gwine to knock his'n off o' the tail. Kud yur Injun do that? Eh, boyees?"

"No, no!"

"Do that beat him, or do it not, then?"

"It beats him!"

"It does!"

"Far better!"

"Hooray!" vociferated several voices, amidst yells of laughter. No one dissented, as the hunters, pleased with the joke, were anxious to see it carried through.

Rube did not detain them long. Leaving his rifle in the hands of his friend Garey, he led the old mare up towards the spot that had been occupied by the Indian girl. Reaching this, he halted.

We all expected to see him turn the animal with her side towards us, thus leaving her body out of range. It soon became evident that this was not the old fellow's intention. It would have spoiled the look of the thing, had he done so; and that idea was no doubt running in his mind.

Choosing a place where the ground chanced to be slightly hollowed out, he led the mustang forward, until her fore feet rested in the hollow. The tail was thus thrown above the body.

Having squared her hips to the camp, he whispered something at her head; and going round to the hind quarters, adjusted the pear upon the highest curve of the stump. He then came walking back.

Would the mare stand? No fear of that. She had been trained to stand in one place for a longer period than was now required of her.

The appearance which the old mare exhibited, nothing visible but her hind legs and buttocks, for the mules had stripped her tail of the hair, had by this time wound the spectators up to the risible point, and most of them were yelling.

"Stop yur giggle-goggle, wull yur!" said Rube, clutching his rifle, and taking his stand. The laughter was held in, no one wishing to disturb the shot.

"Now, old Tar-guts, don't waste your fodder!" muttered the trapper, addressing his gun, which the next moment was raised and levelled.

No one doubted but that Rube would hit the object at which he was aiming. It was a shot frequently made by western riflemen; that is, a mark of the same size at sixty yards. And no doubt Rube would have done it; but just at the moment of his pulling trigger the mare's back heaved up in one of its periodic jerks, and the pitahaya fell to the ground.

But the ball had sped; and grazing the animal's shoulder, passed through one of her ears!

The direction of the bullet was not known until afterwards, but its effect was visible at once; for the mare, stung in her tenderest part, uttered a sort of human-like scream, and wheeling about, came leaping into camp, kicking over everything that happened to lie in her way.

The yells and loud laughing of the trappers, the odd ejaculations of the Indians, the "vayas" and "vivas" of the Mexicans, the wild oaths of old Rube himself, all formed a medley of sounds that fell strangely upon the ear, and to give an idea of which is beyond the art of my pen.

Chapter Twenty Three.

The Programme.

Shortly after, I was wandering out to the caballada to look after my horse, when the sound of a bugle fell upon my ear. It was the signal for the men to assemble, and I turned back towards the camp.

As I re-entered it, Seguin was standing near his tent, with the bugle still in his hand. The hunters were gathering around him.

They were soon all assembled, and stood in groups, waiting for the chief to speak.

"Comrades!" said Seguin, "to-morrow we break up this camp for an expedition against the enemy. I have brought you together that you may know my plans and lend me your advice."

A murmur of applause followed this announcement. The breaking up of a camp is always joyous news to men whose trade is war. It seemed to have a like effect upon this motley group of guerilleros.

The chief continued—

"It is not likely that you will have much fighting. Our dangers will be those of the desert; but we will endeavour to provide against them in the best manner possible.

"I have learned, from a reliable source, that our enemies are at this very time about starting upon a grand expedition to plunder the towns of Sonora and Chihuahua.

"It is their intention, if not met by the Government troops, to extend their foray to Durango itself. Both tribes have combined in this movement; and it is believed that all the warriors will proceed southward, leaving their country unprotected behind them.

"It is my intention then, as soon as I can ascertain that they have gone out, to enter their territory, and pierce to the main town of the Navajoes."

"Bravo!" "Hooray!" "Bueno!" "Très bien!" "Good as wheat!" and numerous other exclamations, hailed this declaration.

"Some of you know my object in making this expedition. Others do not. I will declare it to you all. It is, then, to—"

"Git a grist of scalps; what else?" cried a rough, brutal-looking fellow, interrupting the chief.

"No, Kirker!" replied Seguin, bending his eye upon the man, with an expression of anger. "It is not that. We expect to meet only women. On his peril let no man touch a hair upon the head of an Indian woman. I shall pay for no scalps of women or children."

"Where, then, will be your profits? We cannot bring them prisoners? We'll have enough to do to get back ourselves, I reckon, across them deserts."

These questions seemed to express the feelings of others of the band, who muttered their assent.

"You shall lose nothing. Whatever prisoners you take shall be counted on the ground, and every man shall be paid according to his number. When we return I will make that good."

"Oh! that's fair enough, captain," cried several voices.

"Let it be understood, then, no women nor children. The plunder you shall have, it is yours by our laws, but no blood that can be spared. There is enough on our hands already. Do you all bind yourselves to this?"

"Yes, yes!" "Si!" "Oui, oui!" "Ya, ya!" "All!" "Todos, todos!" cried a multitude of voices, each man answering in his own language.

"Let those who do not agree to it speak."

A profound silence followed this proposal. All had bound themselves to the wishes of their leader.

"I am glad that you are unanimous. I will now state my purpose fully. It is but just you should know it."

"Ay, let us know that," muttered Kirker, "if tain't to raise har we're goin'."

"We go, then, to seek for our friends and relatives, who for years have been captives to our savage enemy. There are many among us who have lost kindred, wives, sisters, and daughters."

A murmur of assent, uttered chiefly by men in Mexican costume, testified to the truth of this statement.

"I myself," continued Seguin, and his voice slightly trembled as he spoke, "am among that number. Years, long years ago, I was robbed of my child by the Navajoes. I have lately learned that she is still alive, and at their head town with many other white captives. We go, then, to release and restore them to their friends and homes."

A shout of approbation broke from the crowd, mingled with exclamations of "Bravo!" "We'll fetch them back!" "Vive le capitaine!" "Viva el gefe!"

When silence was restored, Seguin continued—

"You know our purpose. You have approved it. I will now make known to you the plan I had designed for accomplishing it, and listen to your advice."

Here the chief paused a moment, while the men remained silent and waiting.

"There are three passes," continued he at length, "by which we might enter the Indian country from this side. There is, first, the route of the Western Puerco. That would lead us direct to the Navajo towns."

"And why not take that way?" asked one of the hunters, a Mexican. "I know the route well, as far as the Pecos towns."

"Because we could not pass the Pecos towns without being seen by Navajo spies. There are always some of them there. Nay, more," continued Seguin, with a look that expressed a hidden meaning, "we could not get far up the Del Norte itself before the Navajoes would be warned of our approach. We have enemies nearer home."

"Carrai! that is true," said a hunter, speaking in Spanish.

"Should they get word of our coming, even though the warriors had gone southward, you can see that we would have a journey for nothing."

"True, true!" shouted several voices.

"For the same reason, we cannot take the pass of Polvidera. Besides, at this season, there is but little prospect of game on either of these routes. We are not prepared for an expedition with our present supply. We must pass through a game-country before we can enter on the desert."

"That is true, captain; but there is as little game to be met if we go by the old mine. What other road, then, can we take?"

"There is still another route better than all, I think. We will strike southward, and then west across the Llanos to the old mission. From thence we can go north into the Apache country."

"Yes, yes; that is the best way, captain."

"We will have a longer journey, but with advantages. We will find the wild cattle or the buffaloes upon the Llanos. Moreover, we will make sure of our time, as we can 'cache' in the Pinon Hills that overlook the Apache war-trail, and see our enemies pass out. When they have gone south, we can cross the Gila, and keep up the Azul or Prieto. Having accomplished the object of our expedition, we may then return homeward by the nearest route."

"Bravo!" "Viva!" "That's jest right, captain!"

"That's clarly our best plan!" were a few among the many forms by which the hunters testified their approval of the programme. There was no dissenting voice. The word "Prieto" struck like music upon their ears. That was a magic word: the name of the far-famed river on whose waters the trapper legends had long placed the El Dorado, "the mountain of gold." Many a story of this celebrated region had been told at the hunters' camp-fire, all agreeing in one point: that there the gold lay in "lumps" upon the surface of the ground, and filled the rivers with its shining grains. Often had the trappers talked of an expedition to this unknown land; and small parties were said to have actually entered it, but none of these adventurers had ever been known to return.

The hunters saw now, for the first time, the prospect of penetrating this region with safety, and their minds were filled with fancies wild and romantic. Not a few of them had joined Seguin's band in hopes that some day this very expedition might be undertaken, and the "golden mountain" reached. What, then, were their feelings when Seguin declared his purpose of travelling by the Prieto! At the mention of it a buzz of peculiar meaning ran through the crowd, and the men turned to each other with looks of satisfaction.

"To-morrow, then, we shall march," added the chief. "Go now and make your preparations; we start by daybreak."

As Seguin ceased speaking, the hunters departed, each to look after his "traps and possibles"; a duty soon performed, as these rude rangers were but little encumbered with camp equipage.

I sat down upon a log, watching for some time the movements of my wild companions, and listening to their rude and Babel-like converse.

At length arrived sunset, or night, for they are almost synonymous in these latitudes. Fresh logs were flung upon the fires, till they blazed up. The men sat around them, cooking, eating, smoking, talking loudly, and laughing at stories that illustrated their own wild habits. The red light fell upon fierce, dark faces, now fiercer and more swarthy under the glare of the burning cotton-wood.

By its light the savage expression was strengthened on every countenance. Beards looked darker, and teeth gleamed whiter through them. Eyes appeared more sunken, and their glances more brilliant and fiend-like. Picturesque costumes met the eye: turbans, Spanish hats, plumes, and mottled garments; escopettes and rifles leaning against the trees; saddles, high-peaked, resting upon logs and stumps; bridles hanging from the branches overhead; strings of jerked meat drooping in festoons in front of the tents, and haunches of venison still smoking and dripping their half-coagulated drops!

The vermilion smeared on the foreheads of the Indian warriors gleamed in the night light as though it were blood. It was a picture at once savage and warlike—warlike, but with an aspect of ferocity at which the sensitive heart drew back. It was a picture such as may be seen only in a bivouac of guerilleros, of brigands, of man-hunters.

Chapter Twenty Four.

El Sol and La Luna.

"Come," said Seguin, touching me on the arm, "our supper is ready; I see the doctor beckoning us." I was not slow to answer the call, for the cool air of the evening had sharpened my appetite. We approached the tent, in front of which was a fire.

Over this, the doctor, assisted by Gode and a pueblo peon, was just giving the finishing touch to a savoury supper.

Part of it had already been carried inside the tent. We followed it, and took our seats upon saddles, blankets, and packs.

"Why, doctor," said Seguin, "you have proved yourself a perfect *maître de cuisine* to-night. This is a supper for a Lucullus."

"Ach! mein captain, ich have goet help; Meinherr Gode assist me most wonderful."

"Well, Mr Haller and I will do full justice to your dishes. Let us to them at once!"

"Oui, oui! bien, Monsieur Capitaine," said Gode, hurrying in with a multitude of viands. The "Canadien" was always in his element when there was plenty to cook and eat.

We were soon engaged on fresh steaks (of wild cows), roasted ribs of venison, dried buffalo tongues, tortillas, and coffee. The coffee and tortillas were the labours of the pueblo, in the preparation of which viands he was Gode's master.

But Gode had a choice dish, *un petit morceau*, in reserve, which he brought forth with a triumphant flourish.

"Voici, messieurs?" cried he, setting it before us.

"What is it, Gode?"

"Une fricassée, monsieur."

"Of what?"

"Les frog; what de Yankee call boo-frog!"

"A fricassee of bull-frogs!"

"Oui, oui, mon maître. Voulez vous?"

"No, thank you!"

"I will trouble you, Monsieur Gode," said Seguin.

"Ich, ich, mein Gode; frocks ver goot;" and the doctor held out his platter to be helped.

Gode, in wandering by the river, had encountered a pond of giant frogs, and the fricassée was the result. I had not then overcome my national antipathy to the victims of Saint Patrick's curse; and, to the voyageur's astonishment, I refused to share the dainty.

During our supper conversation I gathered some facts of the doctor's history, which, with what I had already learned, rendered the old man an object of extreme interest to me.

Up to this time, I had wondered what such a character could be doing in such company as that of the Scalp-hunters. I now learned a few details that explained all.

His name was Reichter—Friedrich Reichter. He was a Strasburgher, and in the city of bells had been a medical practitioner of some repute. The love of science, but particularly of his favourite branch, botany, had lured him away from his Rhenish home. He had wandered to the United States, then to the Far West, to classify the flora of that remote region. He had spent several years in the great valley of the Mississippi; and, falling in with one of the Saint Louis caravans, had crossed the prairies to the oasis of New Mexico. In his scientific wanderings along the Del Norte he had met with the Scalp-hunters, and, attracted by the opportunity thus afforded him of penetrating into regions hitherto unexplored by the devotees of science, he had offered to accompany the band. This offer was gladly accepted on account of his services as their medico; and for two years he had been with them, sharing their hardships and dangers.

Many a scene of peril had he passed through, many a privation had he undergone, prompted by a love of his favourite study, and perhaps, too, by the dreams of future triumph, when he would one day spread his strange flora before the *savants* of Europe. Poor Reichter! Poor Friedrich Reichter! yours was the dream of a dream; it never became a reality!

Our supper was at length finished, and washed down with a bottle of Paso wine. There was plenty of this, as well as Taos whisky in the encampment; and the roars of laughter that reached us from without proved that the hunters were imbibing freely of the latter.

The doctor drew out his great meerschaum, Gode filled a red claystone, while Seguin and I lit our husk cigarettes.

"But tell me," said I, addressing Seguin, "who is the Indian?—he who performed the wild feat of shooting the—"

"Ah! El Sol; he is a Coco."

"A Coco?"

"Yes; of the Maricopa tribe."

"But that makes me no wiser than before. I knew that much already."

"You knew it? Who told you?"

"I heard old Rube mention the fact to his comrade Garey."

"Ay, true; he should know him." Seguin remained silent.

"Well?" continued I, wishing to learn more. "Who are the Maricopas? I have never heard of them."

"It is a tribe but little known, a nation of singular men. They are foes of the Apache and Navajo; their country lies down the Gila. They came originally from the Pacific, from the shores of the Californian Sea."

"But this man is educated, or seems so. He speaks English and French as well as you or I. He appears to be talented, intelligent, polite—in short, a gentleman."

"He is all you have said."

"I cannot understand this."

"I will explain to you, my friend. That man was educated at one of the most celebrated universities in Europe. He has travelled farther and through more countries, perhaps, than either of us."

"But how did he accomplish all this? An Indian!"

"By the aid of that which has often enabled very little men (though El Sol is not one of those) to achieve very great deeds, or at least to get the credit of having done so. By gold."

"Gold! and where got he the gold? I have been told that there is very little of it in the hands of Indians. The white men have robbed them of all they once had."

"That is in general a truth; and true of the Maricopas. There was a time when they possessed gold in large quantities, and pearls too, gathered from the depths of the Vermilion Sea. It is gone. The Jesuit padres could tell whither."

"But this man? El Sol?"

"He is a chief. He has not lost all his gold. He still holds enough to serve him, and it is not likely that the padres will coax it from him for either beads or vermilion. No; he has seen the world, and has learnt the all-pervading value of that shining metal."

"But his sister?—is she, too, educated?"

"No. Poor Luna is still a savage; but he instructs her in many things. He has been absent for several years. He has returned but lately to his tribe."

"Their names are strange: 'The Sun,' 'The Moon'!"

"They were given by the Spaniards of Sonora; but they are only translations or synonyms of their Indian appellations. That is common upon the frontier."

"Why are they here?"

I put this question with hesitation, as I knew there might be some peculiar history connected with the answer.

"Partly," replied Seguin, "from gratitude, I believe, to myself. I rescued El Sol when a boy out of the hands of the Navajoes. Perhaps there is still another reason. But come," continued he, apparently wishing to give a turn to the conversation, "you shall know our Indian friends. You are to be companions for a time. He is a scholar, and will interest you. Take care of your heart with the gentle Luna. Vincente, go to the tent of the Coco chief. Ask him to come and drink a cup of Paso wine. Tell him to bring his sister with him."

The servant hurried away through the camp. While he was gone, we conversed about the feat which the Coco had performed with his rifle.

"I never knew him to fire," remarked Seguin, "without hitting his mark. There is something mysterious about that. His aim is unerring; and it seems to be on his part an act of pure volition. There may be some guiding principle in the mind, independent of either strength of nerve or sharpness of sight. He and another are the only persons I ever knew to possess this singular power."

The last part of this speech was uttered in a half soliloquy; and Seguin, after delivering it, remained for some moments silent and abstracted.

Before the conversation was resumed, El Sol and his sister entered the tent, and Seguin introduced us to each other. In a few moments we were engaged, El Sol, the doctor, Seguin, and myself, in an animated conversation. The subject was not horses, nor guns, nor scalps, nor war, nor blood, nor aught connected with the horrid calling of that camp. We were discussing a point in the pacific science of botany: the relationship of the different forms of the cactus family.

I had studied the science, and I felt that my knowledge of it was inferior to that of any of my three companions. I was struck with it then, and more when I reflected on it afterwards; the fact of such a conversation, the time, the place, and the men who carried it on.

For nearly two hours we sat smoking and talking on like subjects.

While we were thus engaged I observed upon the canvas the shadow of a man. Looking forth, as my position enabled me without rising, I recognised in the light that streamed out of the tent a hunting-shirt, with a worked pipe-holder hanging over the breast.

La Luna sat near her brother, sewing "parfleche" soles upon a pair of moccasins. I noticed that she had an abstracted air, and at short intervals glanced out from the opening of the tent. While we were engrossed with our discussion she rose silently, though not with any appearance of stealth, and went out.

After a while she returned. I could read the love-light in her eye as she resumed her occupation.

El Sol and his sister at length left us, and shortly after Seguin, the doctor, and I rolled ourselves in our serapes, and lay down to sleep.

Chapter Twenty Five.

The War-Trail.

The band was mounted by the earliest dawn, and as the notes of the bugle died away our horses plashed through the river, crossing to the other side. We soon debouched from the timber bottom, coming out upon sandy plains that stretched westward to the Mibres Mountains. We rode over these plains in a southerly direction, climbing long ridges of sand that traversed them from east to west. The drift lay in deep furrows, and our horses sank above the fetlocks as we journeyed. We were crossing the western section of the Jornada.

We travelled in Indian file. Habit has formed this disposition among Indians and hunters on the march. The tangled paths of the forest, and the narrow defiles of the mountains admit of no other. Even when passing a plain, our cavalcade was strung out for a quarter of a mile. The atajo followed in charge of the arrieros.

For the first day of our march we kept on without nooning. There was neither grass nor water on the route; and a halt under the hot sun would not have refreshed us.

Early in the afternoon a dark line became visible, stretching across the plain. As we drew nearer, a green wall rose before us, and we distinguished the groves of cotton-wood. The hunters knew it to be the timber on the Paloma. We were soon passing under the shade of its quivering canopy, and reaching the banks of a clear stream, we halted for the night.

Our camp was formed without either tents or lodges. Those used on the Del Norte had been left behind in "caché." An expedition like ours could not be cumbered with camp baggage. Each man's blanket was his house, his bed, and his cloak.

Fires were kindled, and ribs roasted; and fatigued with our journey (the first day's ride has always this effect), we were soon wrapped in our blankets and sleeping soundly.

We were summoned next morning by the call of the bugle sounding reveille. The band partook somewhat of a military organisation, and everyone understood the signals of light cavalry.

Our breakfast was soon cooked and eaten; our horses were drawn from their pickets, saddled, and mounted; and at another signal we moved forward on the route.

The incidents of our first journey were repeated, with but little variety, for several days in succession. We travelled through a desert country, here and there covered with wild sage and mezquite.

We passed on our route clumps of cacti, and thickets of creosote bushes, that emitted their foul odours as we crushed through them. On the fourth evening we camped at a spring, the Ojo de Vaca, lying on the eastern borders of the Llanos.

Over the western section of this great prairie passes the Apache war-trail, running southward into Sonora. Near the trail, and overlooking it, a high mountain rises out of the plain. It is the Pinon.

It was our design to reach this mountain, and "cacher" among the rocks, near a well-known spring, until our enemies should pass; but to effect this we would have to cross the war-trail, and our own tracks would betray us. Here was a difficulty which had not occurred to Seguin. There was no other point except the Pinon from which we could certainly see the enemy on their route and be ourselves hidden. This mountain, then, must be reached; and how were we to effect it without crossing the trail?

After our arrival at Ojo de Vaca, Seguin drew the men together to deliberate on this matter.

"Let us spread," said a hunter, "and keep wide over the paraira, till we've got clar past the Apash trail. They won't notice a single track hyar and thyar, I reckin."

"Ay, but they will, though," rejoined another. "Do ye think an Injun's a-goin' to pass a shod horse track 'ithout follerin' it up? No, siree!"

"We kin muffle the hoofs, as far as that goes," suggested the first speaker.

"Wagh! That ud only make it worse. I tried that dodge once afore, an' nearly lost my har for it. He's a blind Injun kin be fooled that away. 'Twon't do nohow."

"They're not going to be so partickler when they're on the war-trail, I warrant ye. I don't see why it shouldn't do well enough."

Most of the hunters agreed with the former speaker. The Indians would not fail to notice so many muffled tracks, and suspect there was something in the wind. The idea of "muffling" was therefore abandoned. What next? The trapper Rube, who up to this time had said nothing, now drew the attention of all by abruptly exclaiming, "Pish!"

"Well! what have you to say, old hoss?" inquired one of the hunters.

"Thet yur a set o' fools, one and all o' ee. I kud take the full o' that paraira o' hosses acrosst the 'Pash trail, 'ithout making a sign that any Injun's a-gwine to foller, particularly an Injun on the war-beat as them is now."

"How?" asked Seguin.

"I'll tell yur how, cap, ev yur'll tell me what 'ee wants to cross the trail for."

"Why, to conceal ourselves in the Pinon range; what else?"

"An' how are 'ee gwine to 'cacher' in the Peenyun 'ithout water?"

"There is a spring on the side of it, at the foot of the mountain."

"That's true as Scripter. I knows that; but at that very spring the Injuns 'll cool their lappers as they go down south'ard. How are 'ee gwine to get at it with this cavayard 'ithout makin' sign? This child don't see that very clur."

"You are right, Rube. We cannot touch the Pinon spring without leaving our marks too plainly; and it is the very place where the war-party may make a halt."

"I sees no confoundered use in the hul on us crossin' the paraira now. We kan't hunt buffler till they've passed, anyways. So it's this child's idee that a dozen o' us 'll be enough to 'cacher' in the Peenyun, and watch for the niggurs a-goin' south. A dozen mout do it safe enough, but not the hul cavayard."

"And would you have the rest to remain here?"

"Not hyur. Let 'em go north'ard from hyur, and then strike west through the Musquite Hills. Thur's a crick runs thur, about twenty mile or so this side the trail. They can git water and grass, and 'cacher' thur till we sends for 'em."

"But why not remain by this spring, where we have both in plenty?"

"Cap'n, jest because some o' the Injun party may take a notion in thur heads to kum this way themselves. I reckin we had better make blind tracks before leavin' hyur."

The force of Rube's reasoning was apparent to all, and to none more than Seguin himself. It was resolved to follow his advice at once. The vidette party was told off; and the rest of the band, with the atajo, after blinding the tracks around the spring, struck off in a north-westerly direction.

They were to travel on to the Mezquite Hills, that lay some ten or twelve miles to the north-west of the spring. There they were to "cacher" by a stream well known to several of them, and wait until warned to join us.

The vidette party, of whom I was one, moved westward across the prairie.

Rube, Garey, El Sol, and his sister, with Sanchez, a *ci-devant* bull-fighter, and half a dozen others, composed the party. Seguin himself was our head and guide.

Before leaving the Ojo de Vaca we had stripped the shoes off the horses, filling the nail-holes with clay, so that their tracks would be taken for those of wild mustangs. Such were the precautions of men who knew that their lives might be the forfeit of a single footprint.

As we approached the point where the war-trail intersected the prairie, we separated and deployed to distances of half a mile each. In this manner we rode forward to the Pinon mountain, where we came together again, and turned northward along the foot of the range.

It was sundown when we reached the spring, having ridden all day across the plain. We descried it, as we approached, close in to the mountain foot, and marked by a grove of cotton-woods and willows. We did not take our horses near the water; but, having reached a defile in the mountain, we rode into it, and "cached" them in a thicket of nut-pine. In this thicket we spent the night.

With the first light of morning we made a reconnaissance of our caché.

In front of us was a low ridge covered with loose rocks and straggling trees of the nut-pine. This ridge separated the defile from the plain; and from its top, screened by a thicket of the pines, we commanded a view of the water as well as the trail, and the Llanos stretching away to the north, south, and east. It was just the sort of hiding-place we required for our object.

In the morning it became necessary to descend for water. For this purpose we had provided ourselves with a mule-bucket and extra xuages. We visited the spring, and filled our vessels, taking care to leave no traces of out footsteps in the mud.

We kept constant watch during the first day, but no Indians appeared. Deer and antelopes, with a small gang of buffaloes, came to the spring-branch to drink, and then roamed off again over the green meadows. It was a tempting sight, for we could easily have crept within shot, but we dared not touch them. We knew that the Indian dogs would scent their slaughter.

In the evening we went again for water, making the journey twice, as our animals began to suffer from thirst. We adopted the same precautions as before.

Next day we again watched the horizon to the north with eager eyes. Seguin had a small pocket-glass, and we could see the prairie with it for a distance of nearly thirty miles; but as yet no enemy could be descried.

The third day passed with a like result; and we began to fear that the warriors had taken some other trail.

Another circumstance rendered us uneasy. We had eaten nearly the whole of our provisions, and were now chewing the raw nuts of the pinon. We dared not kindle a fire to roast them. Indians can read the smoke at a great distance.

The fourth day arrived and still no sign on the horizon to the north. Our tasajo was all eaten, and we began to hunger. The nuts did not satisfy us. The game was in plenty at the spring, and mottling the grassy plain. One proposed to lie among the willows and shoot an antelope or a black-tailed deer, of which there were troops in the neighbourhood.

"We dare not," said Seguin; "their dogs would find the blood. It might betray us."

"I can procure one without letting a drop," rejoined a Mexican hunter.

"How?" inquired several in a breath.

The man pointed to his lasso.

"But your tracks; you would make deep footmarks in the struggle?"

"We can blind them, captain," rejoined the man.

"You may try, then," assented the chief.

The Mexican unfastened the lasso from his saddle, and, taking a companion, proceeded to the spring. They crept in among the willows, and lay in wait. We watched them from the ridge.

They had not remained more than a quarter of an hour when a herd of antelopes was seen approaching from the plain. These walked directly for the spring, one following the other in Indian file. They were soon close in to the willows where the hunters had concealed themselves. Here they suddenly halted, throwing up their heads and snuffing the air. They had scented danger, but it was too late for the foremost to turn and lope off.

"Yonder goes the lasso!" cried one.

We saw the noose flying in the air and settling over his head. The herd suddenly wheeled, but the loop was around the neck of their leader; and after three or four skips, he sprang up, and falling upon his back, lay motionless.

The hunter came out from the willows, and, taking up the animal, now choked dead, carried him towards the entrance of the defile. His companion followed, blinding the tracks of both. In a few minutes they had reached us. The antelope was skinned, and eaten raw, in the blood!

Our horses grow thin with hunger and thirst. We fear to go too often to the water, though we become less cautious as the hours pass. Two more antelopes are lassoed by the expert hunter.

The night of the fourth day is clear moonlight. The Indians often march by moonlight, particularly when on the war-trail. We keep our vidette stationed during the night as in the day. On this night we look out with more hopes than usual. It is such a lovely night! a full moon, clear and calm.

We are not disappointed. Near midnight the vidette awakes us. There are dark forms on the sky away to the north. It may be buffaloes, but we see that they are approaching.

We stand, one and all, straining our eyes through the white air, and away over the silvery sward. There are glancing objects: arms it must be. "Horses! horsemen! They are Indians!"

"Oh, God! comrades, we are mad! Our horses: they may neigh!"

We bound after our leader down the hill, over the rocks, and through the trees. We run for the thicket where our animals are tied. We may be too late, for horses can hear each other miles off; and the slightest concussion vibrates afar through the elastic atmosphere of these high plateaux. We reach the caballada. What is Seguin doing? He has torn the blanket from under his saddle, and is muffling the head of his horse!

We follow his example, without exchanging a word, for we know this is the only plan to pursue.

In a few minutes we feel secure again, and return to our watch-station on the height.

We had shaved our time closely; for, on reaching the hill-top, we could hear the exclamations of Indians, the "thump, thump" of hoofs on the hard plain, and an occasional neigh, as their horses scented the water. The foremost were advancing to the spring; and we could see the long line of mounted men stretching in their deploying to the far horizon.

Closer they came, and we could distinguish the pennons and glittering points of their spears. We could see their half-naked bodies gleaming in the clear moonlight.

In a short time the foremost of them had ridden up to the bushes, halting as they came, and giving their animals to drink. Then one by one they wheeled out of the water, and trotting a short distance over the prairie, flung themselves to the ground, and commenced unharnessing their horses.

It was evidently their intention to camp for the night.

For nearly an hour they came filing forward, until two thousand warriors, with their horses, dotted the plain below us.

We stood observing their movements. We had no fear of being seen ourselves. We were lying with our bodies behind the rocks, and our faces partially screened by the foliage of the pinon trees. We could see and hear with distinctness all that was passing, for the savages were not over three hundred yards from our position.

They proceed to picket their horses in a wide circle, far out on the plain. There the grama grass is longer and more luxuriant than in the immediate neighbourhood of the spring. They strip the animals, and bring away their horse-furniture, consisting of hair bridles, buffalo robes, and skins of the grizzly bear. Few have saddles. Indians do not generally use them on a war expedition.

Each man strikes his spear into the ground, and rests against it his shield, bow, and quiver. He places his robe or skin beside it. That is his tent and bed.

The spears are soon aligned upon the prairie, forming a front of several hundred yards; and thus they have pitched their camp with a quickness and regularity far outstripping the Chasseurs of Vincennes.

They are encamped in two parties. There are two bands, the Apache and Navajo. The latter is much the smaller, and rests farther off from our position.

We hear them cutting and chopping with their tomahawks among the thickets at the foot of the mountain. We can see them carrying faggots out upon the plain, piling them together, and setting them on fire.

Many fires are soon blazing brightly. The savages squat around them, cooking their suppers. We can see the paint glittering on their faces and naked breasts. They are of many hues. Some are red, as though they were smeared with blood. Some appear of a jetty blackness. Some black on one side of the face, and red or white on the other. Some are mottled like hounds, and some striped and chequered. Their cheeks and breasts are tattooed with the forms of animals: wolves, panthers, bears, buffaloes, and other hideous devices, plainly discernible under the blaze of the pine-wood fires. Some have a red hand painted on their bosoms, and not a few exhibit as their device the death's head and cross-bones!

All these are their coats of arms, symbolical of the "medicine" of the wearer; adopted, no doubt, from like silly fancies to those which put the crest upon the carriage, on the lackey's button, or the brass seal stamp of the merchant's clerk.

There is vanity in the wilderness. In savage as in civilised life there is a "snobdom."

What do we see? Bright helmets, brazen and steel, with nodding plumes of the ostrich! These upon savages! Whence came these?

From the cuirassiers of Chihuahua. Poor devils! They were roughly handled upon one occasion by these savage lancers.

We see the red meat spluttering over the fires upon spits of willow rods. We see the Indians fling the pinon nuts into the cinders, and then draw them forth again, parched and smoking. We see them light their claystone pipes, and send forth clouds of blue vapour. We see them gesticulate as they relate their red adventures to one another. We hear them shout, and chatter, and laugh like mountebanks. How unlike the forest Indian!

For two hours we watch their movements, and listen to their voices. Then the horse-guard is detailed, and marches off to the caballada; and the Indians, one after another, spread their skins, roll themselves in their blankets, and sleep.

The fires cease to blaze; but by the moonlight we can distinguish the prostrate bodies of the savages. White objects are moving among them. They are dogs prowling after the *débris* of their supper. These run from point to point, snarling at one another, and barking at the coyotes that sneak around the skirts of the camp.

Out upon the prairie the horses are still awake and busy. We can hear them stamping their hoofs and cropping the rich pasture. Erect forms are seen standing at intervals along the line. These are the guards of the caballada.

Chapter Twenty Six.

Three Days in the Trap.

Our attention was now turned to our own situation. Dangers and difficulties suddenly presented themselves to our minds.

"What if they should stay here to hunt?"

The thought seemed to occur to all of us at the same instant, and we faced each other with looks of apprehension and dismay.

"It is not improbable," said Seguin, in a low and emphatic voice. "It is plain they have no supply of meat, and how are they to pass to the south without it? They must hunt here or elsewhere. Why not here?"

"If so, we're in a nice trap!" interrupted a hunter, pointing first to the embouchure of the defile and then to the mountain. "How are we to get out? I'd like to know that."

Our eyes followed the direction indicated by the speaker. In front of the ravine in which we were, extended the line of the Indian camp, not a hundred yards distant from the rocks that lay around its entrance. There was an Indian sentinel still nearer; but it would be impossible to pass out, even were he asleep, without encountering the dogs that prowled in numbers around the camp.

Behind us, the mountain rose vertically like a wall. It was plainly impassable. We were fairly "in the trap."

"Carrai!" exclaimed one of the men, "we will die of hunger and thirst if they stay to hunt!"

"We may die sooner," rejoined another, "if they take a notion in their heads to wander up the gully."

This was not improbable, though it was but little likely. The ravine was a sort of *cul de sac*, that entered the mountain in a slanting direction, and ended at the bottom of the cliff. There was no object to attract our enemies into it, unless indeed they might come up in search of pinon nuts. Some of their dogs, too, might wander up, hunting for food, or attracted by the scent of our horses. These were probabilities, and we trembled as each of them was suggested.

"If they do not find us," said Seguin, encouragingly, "we may live for a day or two on the pinons. When these fail us, one of our horses must be killed. How much water have we?"

"Thank our luck, captain, the gourds are nearly full."

"But our poor animals must suffer."

"There is no danger of thirst," said El Sol, looking downward, "while these last;" and he struck with his foot a large round mass that grew among the rocks. It was thc spheroidal cactus. "See!" continued he, "there are hundreds of them!"

All present knew the meaning of this, and regarded the cacti with a murmur of satisfaction.

"Comrades!" said Seguin, "it is of no use to weary ourselves. Let those sleep who can. One can keep watch yonder while another stays up here. Go, Sanchez!" and the chief pointed down the ravine to a spot that commanded a view of its mouth.

The sentinel walked off, and took his stand in silence. The rest of us descended, and after looking to the muffling of our horses, returned to the station of the vidette upon the hill. Here we rolled ourselves in our blankets, and, lying down among the rocks, slept out the night.

We were awake before dawn, and peering through the leaves with feelings of keen solicitude.

There is no movement in the Indian camp. It is a bad indication. Had they intended to travel on, they would have been stirring before this. They are always on the route before daybreak. These signs strengthen our feelings of apprehension.

The grey light begins to spread over the prairie. There is a white band along the eastern sky. There are noises in the camp. There are voices. Dark forms move about among the upright spears. Tall savages stride over the plain. Their robes of skins are wrapped around their shoulders to protect them from the raw air of the morning.

They carry faggots. They are rekindling the fires!

Our men talk in whispers, as we lie straining our eyes to catch every movement.

"It's plain they intend to make a stay of it."

"Ay! we're in for it, that's sartin! Wagh! I wonder how long thar a-goin' to squat hyar, any how."

"Three days at the least: may be four or five."

"Great gollies! we'll be froze in half the time."

"What would they be doin' here so long? I warrant ye they'll clar out as soon as they can."

"So they will; but how can they in less time?"

"They can get all the meat they want in a day. See! yonder's buffalo a plenty; look! away yonder!" and the speaker points to several black objects outlined against the brightening sky. It is a herd of buffaloes.

"That's true enough. In half a day I warrant they kin get all the meat they want: but how are they a-goin' to jirk it in less than three? That's what I want to know."

"Es verdad!" says one of the Mexicans, a cibolero; "très dias, al menos!" (It is true—three days, at the least!)

"Ay, hombre! an' with a smart chance o' sunshine at that, I guess."

This conversation is carried on by two or three of the men in a low tone, but loud enough for the rest of us to overhear it.

It reveals a new phase of our dilemma on which we have not before reflected. Should the Indians stay to "jerk" their meat, we will be in extreme danger from thirst, as well as of being discovered in our cache.

We know that the process of jerking buffalo beef takes three days, and that with a hot sun, as the hunter has intimated. This, with the first day required for hunting, will keep us four days in the ravine!

The prospect is appalling. We feel that death or the extreme torture of thirst is before us. We have no fear of hunger. Our horses are in the grove, and our knives in our belts. We can, live for weeks upon them; but will the cacti assuage the thirst of men and horses for a period of three or four days? This is a question no one can answer. It has often relieved the hunter for a short period, enabling him to crawl on to the water; but for days!

The trial will soon commence. The day has fairly broken. The Indians spring to their feet. About one-half of them draw the pickets of their horses, and lead them to the water. They adjust their bridles, pluck up their spears, snatch their bows, shoulder their quivers, and leap on horseback.

After a short consultation they gallop off to the eastward. In half an hour's time, we can see them running the buffalo far out upon the prairie: piercing them with their arrows, and impaling them on their long lances.

Those who have remained behind lead their horses down to the spring-branch, and back again to the grass. Now they chop down young trees, and carry faggots to the fires. See! they are driving long stakes into the ground, and stretching ropes from one to the other. For what purpose? We know too well.

"Ha! look yonder!" mutters one of the hunters, as this is first noticed; "yonder goes the jerking-line! Now we're caged in airnest, I reckin."

"Por todos santos, es verdad!"

"Carambo! carrajo! chingaro!" growls the cibolero, who well knows the meaning of those stakes and lines.

We watch with a fearful interest the movements of the savages.

We have now no longer any doubt of their intention to remain for several days.

The stakes are soon erected, running for a hundred yards or more along the front of the encampment. The savages await the return of their hunters. Some mount and scour off toward the scene of the buffalo battue, still going on, far out upon the plain.

We peer through the leaves with great caution, for the day is bright, and the eyes of our enemies are quick, and scan every object. We speak only in whispers, though our voices could not be heard if we conversed a little louder, but fear makes us fancy that they might. We are all concealed except our eyes. These glance through small loopholes in the foliage.

The Indian hunters have been gone about two hours. We now see them returning over the prairie in straggling parties.

They ride slowly back. Each brings his load before him on the withers of his horse. They have large masses of red flesh, freshly skinned and smoking. Some carry the sides and quarters; others the hump-ribs, the tongue, the heart, and liver—the *petits morceaux*—wrapped up in the skins of the slaughtered animals.

They arrive in camp, and fling their loads to the ground.

Now begins a scene of noise and confusion. The savages run to and fro, whooping, chattering, laughing, and dancing. They draw their long scalping-knives, and hew off broad steaks. They spit them over the blazing fires. They cut out the hump-ribs. They tear off the white fat, and stuff the boudins. They split the brown liver, eating it raw! They break the shanks with their tomahawks, and delve out the savoury marrow; and, through all these operations, they whoop, and chatter, and laugh, and dance over the ground like so many madmen.

This scene lasts for more than an hour.

Fresh parties of hunters mount and ride off. Those who remain cut the meat into long thin strips, and hang it over the lines already prepared for this purpose. It is thus left to be baked by the sun into "tasajo."

We know part of what is before us. It is a fearful prospect; but men like those who compose the band of Seguin do not despond while the shadow of a hope remains. It is a barren spot indeed, where they cannot find resources.

"We needn't holler till we're hurt," says one of the hunters.

"If yer call an empty belly a hurt," rejoins another, "I've got it already. I kud jest eat a raw jackass 'ithout skinnin' him."

"Come, fellers!" cries a third, "let's gramble for a meal o' these peenyuns."

Following this suggestion, we commence searching for the nuts of the pine. We find to our dismay that there is but a limited supply of this precious food; not enough either on the trees or the ground to sustain us for two days.

"By gosh!" exclaims one, "we'll have to draw for our critters."

"Well, and if we have to—time enough yet a bit, I guess. We'll bite our claws a while first."

The water is distributed in a small cup. There is still a little left in the xuages; but our poor horses suffer.

"Let us look to them," says Seguin; and, drawing his knife, he commences skinning one of the cacti. We follow his example.

We carefully pare off the volutes and spikelets. A cool, gummy liquid exudes from the opened vessels. We break the short stems, and lifting the green, globe-like masses, carry them to the thicket, and place them before our animals. These seize the succulent plants greedily, crunch them between their teeth, and swallow both sap and fibres. It is food and drink to them. Thank Heaven! we may yet save them!

This act is repeated several times, until they have had enough.

We keep two videttes constantly on the look-out—one upon the hill, the other commanding the mouth of the defile. The rest of us go through the ravine, along the sides of the ridge, in search of the cones of the pinon.

Thus our first day is spent.

The Indian hunters keep coming into their camp until a late hour, bringing with them their burdens of buffalo flesh. Fires blaze over the ground, and the savages sit around them, cooking and eating, nearly all the night.

On the following day they do not rouse themselves until a late hour. It is a day of lassitude and idleness; for the meat is hanging over the strings, and they can only wait upon it. They lounge around the camp, mending their bridles and lassos, or looking to their weapons; they lead their horses to the water, and then picket them on fresh ground; they cut large pieces of meat, and broil them over the fires. Hundreds of them are at all times engaged in this last occupation. They seem to eat continually.

Their dogs are busy, too, growling over the knife-stripped bones. They are not likely to leave their feast; they will not stray up the ravine while it lasts. In this thought we find consolation.

The sun is hot all the second day, and scorches us in the dry defile. It adds to our thirst; but we do not regret, this so much, knowing it will hasten the departure of the savages. Towards evening, the tasajo begins to look brown and shrivelled. Another such day and it will be ready for packing.

Our water is out, and we chew the succulent slices of the cactus. These relieve our thirst without quenching it.

Our appetite of hunger is growing stronger. We have eaten all the pinons, and nothing remains but to slaughter one of our horses.

"Let us hold out till to-morrow," suggests one. "Give the poor brutes a chance. Who knows but what they may flit in the morning?"

This proposition is voted in the affirmative. No hunter cares to risk losing his horse, especially when out upon the prairies.

Gnawed by hunger, we lie waiting for the third day.

The morning breaks at last, and we crawl forward as usual, to watch the movements of the camp. The savages sleep late, as on yesterday; but they arouse themselves at length, and after watering their animals, commence cooking. We see the crimson streaks and the juicy ribs smoking over the fires, and the savoury odours are wafted to us on the breeze. Our appetites are whetted to a painful keenness. We can endure no longer. A horse must die!

Whose? Mountain law will soon decide.

Eleven white pebbles and a black one are thrown into the water-bucket, and one by one we are blinded and led forward.

I tremble as I place my hand in the vessel. It is like throwing the die for my own life.

"Thank Heaven! my Moro is safe!"

One of the Mexicans has drawn the black.

"Thar's luck in that!" exclaims a hunter. "Good fat mustang better than poor bull any day!"

The devoted horse is in fact a well-conditioned animal; and placing our videttes again, we proceed to the thicket to slaughter him.

We set about it with great caution. We tie him to a tree, and hopple his fore and hind feet, lest he may struggle. We propose bleeding him to death.

The cibolero has unsheathed his long knife, while a man stands by, holding the bucket to catch the precious fluid: the blood. Some have cups in their hands, ready to drink it as it flows!

We were startled by an unusual sound. We look through the leaves. A large grey animal is standing by the edge of the thicket, gazing in at us. It is wolfish-looking. Is it a wolf? No. It is an Indian dog!

The knife is stayed; each man draws his own. We approach the animal, and endeavour to coax it nearer. But no; it suspects our intentions, utters a low growl, and runs away down the defile.

We follow it with our eyes. The owner of the doomed horse is the vidette. The dog must pass him to get out, and he stands with his long lance ready to receive it.

The animal sees himself intercepted, turns and runs back, and again turning, makes a desperate rush to pass the vidette. As he nears the latter, he utters a loud howl. The next moment he is impaled upon the lance!

Several of us rush up the hill to ascertain if the howling has attracted the attention of the savages. There is no unusual movement among them; they have not heard it.

The dog is divided and devoured before his quivering flesh has time to grow cold! The horse is reprieved.

Again we feed our animals on the cooling cactus. This occupies us for some time. When we return to the hill a glad sight is before us. We see the warriors seated around their fires, renewing the paint upon their bodies.

We know the meaning of this.

The tasajo is nearly black. Thanks to the hot sun, it will soon be ready for packing!

Some of the Indians are engaged in poisoning the points of their arrows. All these signs inspire us with fresh courage. They will soon march; if not to-night, by daybreak on the morrow.

We lie congratulating ourselves, and watching every movement of their camp. Our hopes continue rising as the day falls.

Ha! there is an unusual stir. Some order has been issued. "Voilà!" "Mira! mira!" "See!" "Look, look!" are the half-whispered ejaculations that break from the hunters as this is observed.

"By the livin' catamount, thar a-going to mizzle!"

We see the savages pull down the tasajo and tie it in bunches. Then every man runs out for his horse; the pickets are drawn; the animals are led in and watered; they are bridled; the robes are thrown over them and girthed. The warriors pluck up their lances, sling their quivers, seize their shields and bows, and leap lightly upon horseback. The next moment they form with the rapidity of thought, and wheeling in their tracks, ride off in single file, heading to the southward.

The larger band has passed. The smaller, the Navajoes, follow in the same trail. No! The latter has suddenly filed to the left, and is crossing the prairie towards the east, towards the spring of the Ojo de Vaca.

Chapter Twenty Seven.

The Diggers.

Our first impulse was to rush down the ravine, satisfy our thirst at the spring, and our hunger on the half-polished bones that were strewed over the prairie. Prudence, however, restrained us.

"Wait till they're clar gone," said Garey. "They'll be out o' sight in three skips o' a goat."

"Yes! stay where we are a bit," added another; "some of them may ride back; something may be forgotten."

This was not improbable; and in spite of the promptings of our appetites, we resolved to remain a while longer in the defile.

We descended straightway into the thicket to make preparations for moving—to saddle our horses and take off their mufflings, which by this time had nearly blinded them. Poor brutes! they seemed to know that relief was at hand.

While we were engaged in these operations, our vidette was kept at the top of the hill to watch both bands, and warn us when their heads should sink to the prairie level.

"I wonder why the Navajoes have gone by the Ojo de Vaca," remarked our chief, with an apparent anxiety in his manner. "It is well our comrades did not remain there."

"They'll be tired o' waitin' on us, whar they are," rejoined Garey, "unless blacktails is plentier among them Musquites than I think for."

"Vaya!" exclaimed Sanchez; "they may thank the Santisima they were not in our company! I'm spent to a skeleton. Mira! carrai!"

Our horses were at length bridled and saddled, and our lassoes coiled up. Still the vidette had not warned us. We grew every moment more impatient.

"Come!" cried one; "hang it! they're far enough now. They're not a-goin' to be gapin' back all the way. They're looking ahead, I'm bound. Golly! thar's fine shines afore them."

We could resist no longer. We called out to the vidette. He could just see the heads of the hindmost.

"That will do," cried Seguin; "come, take your horses!"

The men obeyed with alacrity, and we all moved down the ravine, leading our animals.

We pressed forward to the opening. A young man, the pueblo servant of Seguin, was ahead of the rest. He was impatient to reach the water. He had gained the mouth of the defile, when we saw him fall back with frightening looks, dragging at his horse and exclaiming—

"Mi amo! mi amo! to davia son!" (Master, master! they are here yet!)

"Who?" inquired Seguin, running forward in haste.

"The Indians, master; the Indians!"

"You are mad! Where did you see them?"

"In the camp, master. Look yonder!"

I pressed forward with Seguin to the rocks that lay along the entrance of the defile. We looked cautiously over. A singular sight met our eyes.

The camp-ground was lying as the Indians had left it. The stakes were still standing; the shaggy hides of the buffaloes, and pile of their bones, were strewn upon the plain; hundreds of coyotes were loping back and forward, snarling at one another, or pursuing one of their number which had picked up a nicer morsel than his companions. The fires were still smouldering, and the wolves galloped through the ashes, raising them in yellow clouds.

But there was a sight stranger than all this, a startling sight to me. Five or six forms, almost human, were moving about among the fires, collecting the débris of skins and bones, and quarrelling with the wolves that barked round them in troops. Five or six others, similar forms were seated around a pile of burning wood, silently gnawing at half roasted ribs. Can they be—yes, they are human beings!

I was for a moment awe-struck as I gazed at the shrivelled and dwarfish bodies, the long, ape-like arms, and huge disproportioned heads, from which fell their hair in snaky tangles, black and matted.

But one or two appeared to have any article of dress, and that was a ragged breech-clout. The others were naked as the wild beasts around them, naked from head to foot!

It was a horrid sight to look upon these fiend-like dwarfs squatted around the fires, holding up half-naked bones in their long, wrinkled arms, and tearing off the flesh with their glistening teeth. It was a horrid sight, indeed; and it was some moments before I could recover sufficiently from my amazement to inquire who or what they were. I did so at length.

"Los Yamparicos," answered the cibolero.

"Who?" I asked again.

"Los Indios Yamparicos, señor."

"The Diggers, the Diggers," said a hunter, thinking that would better explain the strange apparitions.

"Yes, they are Digger Indians," added Seguin. "Come on; we have nothing to fear from them."

"But we have somethin' to git from them," rejoined one of the hunters, with a significant look. "Digger plew good as any other; worth jest as much as 'Pash chief."

"No one must fire," said Seguin, in a firm tone. "It is too soon yet; look yonder!" and he pointed over the plain, where two or three glancing objects, the helmets of the retreating warriors, could still be seen above the grass.

"How are we goin' to get them, then, captain?" inquired the hunter. "They'll beat us to the rocks; they kin run like scared dogs."

"Better let them go, poor devils!" said Seguin, seemingly unwilling that blood should be spilled so wantonly.

"No, captain," rejoined the same speaker, "we won't fire, but we'll git them, if we kin, 'ithout it. Boys, follow me down this way."

And the man was about guiding his horse in among the loose rocks, so as to pass unperceived between the dwarfs and the mountain.

But the brutal fellow was frustrated in his design; for at that moment El Sol and his sister appeared in the opening, and their brilliant habiliments caught the eyes of the Diggers. Like startled deer they sprang to their feet, and ran, or rather flew, toward the foot of the mountain. The hunters galloped to intercept them, but they were too late. Before they could come up, the Diggers had dived into the crevices of the rocks, or were seen climbing like chamois along the cliffs, far out of reach.

One of the hunters only—Sanchez—succeeded in making a capture. His victim had reached a high ledge, and was scrambling along it, when the lasso of the bull-fighter settled round his neck. The next moment he was plucked out into the air, and fell with a "cranch" upon the rocks!

I rode forward to look at him. He was dead. He had been crushed by the fall; in fact, mangled to a shapeless mass, and exhibited a most loathsome and hideous sight.

The unfeeling hunter recked not of this. With a coarse jest he stooped over the body; and severing the scalp, stuck it, reeking and bloody, behind the waist of his calzoneros!

Chapter Twenty Eight.

Dacoma.

We all now hurried forward to the spring, and, dismounting, turned our horses' heads to the water, leaving them to drink at will. We had no fear of their running away.

Our own thirst required slaking as much as theirs; and, crowding into the branch, we poured the cold water down our throats in cupfuls. We felt as though we should never be surfeited; but another appetite, equally strong, lured us away from the spring; and we ran over the camp-ground in search of the means to gratify it. We scattered the coyotes and white wolves with our shouts, and drove them with missiles from the ground.

We were about stooping to pick up the dust-covered morsels, when a strange exclamation from one of the hunters caused us to look hastily round.

"Malaray, camarados; mira el arco!"

The Mexican who uttered these words stood pointing to an object that lay upon the ground at his feet. We ran up to ascertain what it was.

"Caspita!" again ejaculated the man. "It is a white bow!"

"A white bow, by gosh!" echoed Garey.

"A white bow!" shouted several others, eyeing the object with looks of astonishment and alarm.

"That belonged to a big warrior, I'll sartify," said Garey.

"Ay," added another, "an' one that'll ride back for it as soon as—holies! look yonder! he's coming by—!"

Our eyes rolled over the prairie together, eastward, as the speaker pointed. An object was just visible low down on the horizon, like a moving blazing star. It was not that. At a glance we all knew what it was. It was a helmet, flashing under the sunbeam, as it rose and fell to the measured gallop of a horse.

"To the willows, men! to the willows!" shouted Seguin. "Drop the bow! Leave it where it was. To your horses! Lead them! Crouch! crouch!"

We all ran to our horses, and, seizing the bridles, half-led, half-dragged them within the willow thicket. We leaped into our saddles, so as to be ready for any emergency, and sat peering through the leaves that screened us.

"Shall we fire as he comes up, captain?" asked one of the men.

"No."

"We kin take him nicely, just as he stoops for the bow."

"No; not for your lives!"

"What then, captain?"

"Let him take it, and go," was Seguin's reply.

"Why, captain? what's that for?"

"Fools! do you not see that the whole tribe would be back upon our trail before midnight? Are you mad? Let him go. He may not notice our tracks, as our horses are not shod. If so, let him go as he came, I tell you."

"But how, captain, if he squints yonder-away?"

Garey, as he said this, pointed to the rocks at the foot of the mountain.

"Sac-r–r–ré! the Digger!" exclaimed Seguin, his countenance changing expression.

The body lay on a conspicuous point, on its face, the crimson skull turned upward and outward, so that it could hardly fail to attract the eye of anyone coming in from the plain. Several coyotes had already climbed up on the slab where it lay, and were smelling around it, seemingly not caring to touch the hideous morsel.

"He's bound to see it, captain," added the hunter.

"If so, we must take him with the lance, the lasso, or alive. No gun must be fired. They might still hear it, and would be on us before we could get round the mountain. No! sling your guns! Let those who have lances and lassoes get them in readiness."

"When would you have us make the dash, captain?"

"Leave that to me. Perhaps he may dismount for the bow; or, if not, he may ride into the spring to water his horse, then we can surround him. If he see the Digger's body, he may pass up to examine it more closely. In that case we can intercept him without difficulty. Be patient! I shall give you the signal."

During all this time, the Navajo was coming up at a regular gallop. As the dialogue ended, he had got within about three hundred yards of the spring, and still pressed forward without slackening his pace. We kept our gaze fixed upon him in breathless silence, eyeing both man and horse.

It was a splendid sight. The horse was a large, coal-black mustang, with fiery eyes and red, open nostrils. He was foaming at the mouth, and the white flakes had clouted his throat, counter, and shoulders. He was wet all over, and glittered as he moved with the play of his proud flanks. The rider was naked from the waist up, excepting his helmet and plumes, and some ornaments that glistened on his neck, bosom and wrists. A tunic-like skirt, bright and embroidered, covered his hips and thighs. Below the knee his legs were naked, ending in a buskined moccasin, that fitted tightly round the ankle. Unlike the Apaches,

"Dacoma!"

there was no paint upon his body, and his bronze complexion shone with the hue of health. His features were noble and warlike, his eye bold and piercing, and his long black hair swept away behind him, mingling with the tail of his horse. He rode upon a Spanish saddle with his lance poised on the stirrup, and resting lightly against his right arm. His left was thrust through the strap of a white shield, and a quiver with its feathered shafts peeped over his shoulder.

His bow was before him.

It was a splendid sight, both horse and rider, as they rose together over the green swells of the prairie; a picture more like that of some Homeric hero than a savage of the wild west.

"Wagh!" exclaimed one of the hunters in an undertone; "how they glitter! Look at that 'ar headpiece! It's fairly a-blazin'!"

"Ay," rejoined Garey, "we may thank the piece o' brass. We'd have been in as ugly a fix as he's in now if we hadn't sighted it in time. What!" continued the trapper, his voice rising into earnestness; "Dacoma, by the Etarnal! The second chief of the Navajoes!"

I turned toward Seguin to witness the effect of this announcement. The Maricopa was leaning over to him, muttering some words in an unknown tongue, and gesticulating with energy. I recognised the name "Dacoma," and there was an expression of fierce hatred in the chief's countenance as he pointed to the advancing horseman.

"Well, then," answered Seguin, apparently assenting to the wishes of the other, "he shall not escape, whether he sees it or no. But do not use your gun; they are not ten miles off, yonder behind the swell. We can easily surround him. If not, I can overtake him on this horse, and here's another."

As Seguin uttered the last speech he pointed to Moro. "Silence!" he continued, lowering his voice. "Hish-sh!"

The silence became death-like. Each man sat pressing his horse with his knees, as if thus to hold him at rest.

The Navajo had now reached the border of the deserted camp; and inclining to the left, he galloped down the line, scattering the wolves as he went. He sat leaning to one side, his gaze searching the ground. When nearly opposite to our ambush, he descried the object of his search, and sliding his feet out of the stirrup, guided his horse so as to shave closely past it. Then, without reining in, or even slacking his pace, he bent over until his plume swept the earth, and picking up the bow, swung himself back into the saddle.

"Beautiful!" exclaimed the bull-fighter.

"By gosh! it's a pity to kill him," muttered a hunter; and a low murmur of admiration was heard among the men.

After a few more springs, the Indian suddenly wheeled, and was about to gallop back, when his eye was caught by the ensanguined object upon the rock. He reined in with a jerk, until the hips of his horse almost rested upon the prairie, and sat gazing upon the body with a look of surprise.

"Beautiful!" again exclaimed Sanchez; "carambo, beautiful!"

It was, in effect, as fine a picture as ever the eye looked upon. The horse with his tail scattered upon the ground, with crest erect and breathing nostril, quivering under the impulse of his masterly rider; the rider himself, with his glancing helmet and waving plumes, his bronze complexion, his firm and graceful seat, and his eye fixed in the gaze of wonder.

It was, as Sanchez had said, a beautiful picture—a living statue; and all of us were filled with admiration as we looked upon it. Not one of the party, with perhaps an exception, should have liked to fire the shot that would have tumbled it from its pedestal.

Horse and man remained in this attitude for some moments. Then the expression of the rider's countenance suddenly changed. His eye wandered with an inquiring and somewhat terrified look. It rested upon the water, still muddy with the trampling of our horses.

One glance was sufficient; and, with a quick, strong jerk upon the bridle, the savage horseman wheeled, and struck out for the prairie.

Our charging signal had been given at the same instant; and springing forward, we shot out of the copse-wood in a body.

We had to cross the rivulet. Seguin was some paces in advance as we rode forward to it. I saw his horse suddenly baulk, stumble over the bank, and roll headlong into the water!

The rest of us went splashing through. I did not stop to look back. I knew that now the taking of the Indian was life or death to all of us; and I struck my spur deeply, and strained forward in the pursuit.

For some time we all rode together in a dense clump. When fairly out on the plain, we saw the Indian ahead of us about a dozen lengths of his horse, and one and all felt with dismay that he was keeping his distance, if not actually increasing it.

We had forgotten the condition of our animals. They were faint with hunger, and stiff from standing so long in the ravine. Moreover, they had just drunk to a surfeit.

I soon found that I was forging ahead of my companions. The superior swiftness of Moro gave me the advantage. El Sol was still before me. I saw him circling his lasso; I saw him launch it, and suddenly jerk up; I saw the loop sliding over the hips of the flying mustang. He had missed his aim.

He was recoiling the rope as I shot past him, and I noticed his look of chagrin and disappointment.

My Arab had now warmed to the chase, and I was soon far ahead of my comrades. I perceived, too, that I was closing upon the Navajo. Every spring brought me nearer, until there were not a dozen lengths between us.

I knew not how to act. I held my rifle in my hands, and could have shot the Indian in the back; but I remembered the injunction of Seguin, and we were now closer to the enemy than ever. I did not know but that we might be in sight of them. I dared not fire.

I was still undecided whether to use my knife or endeavour to unhorse the Indian with my clubbed rifle, when he glanced over his shoulder and saw that I was alone.

Suddenly he wheeled, and throwing his lance to a charge, came galloping back. His horse seemed to work without the rein, obedient to his voice and the touch of his knees.

I had just time to throw up my rifle and parry the charge, which was a right point. I did not parry it successfully. The blade grazed my arm, tearing my flesh. The barrel of my rifle caught in the sling of the lance, and the piece was whipped out of my hands.

The wound, the shock, and the loss of my weapon, had discomposed me in the manage of my horse, and it was some time before I could

“We closed at full gallop.”

gain the bridle to turn him. My antagonist had wheeled sooner, as I knew by the “hist” of an arrow that scattered the curls over my right ear. As I faced him again, another was on the string, and the next moment it was sticking through my left arm.

I was now angry; and, drawing a pistol from the holster, I cocked it, and galloped forward. I knew it was the only chance for my life.

The Indian, at the same time, dropped his bow, and, bringing his lance to the charge, spurred on to meet me. I was determined not to fire until near and sure of hitting.

We closed at full gallop. Our horses almost touched. I levelled and pulled trigger. The cap snapped upon my pistol!

The lance-blade glittered in my eyes; its point was at my breast. Something struck me sharply in the face. It was the ring-loop of a lasso. I saw it settle over the shoulders of the Indian, falling to his elbows. It tightened as it fell. There was a wild yell, a quick jerk of my antagonist’s body, the lance flew from his hands, and the next moment he was plucked out of his saddle, and lying helpless upon the prairie.

His horse met mine with a concussion that sent both of them to the earth. We rolled and scrambled about, and rose again.

When I came to my feet, El Sol was standing over the Navajo, with his knife drawn, and his lasso looped around the arms of his captive.

“The horse! the horse! secure the horse!” shouted Seguin, as he galloped up; and the crowd dashed past me in pursuit of the mustang, which, with trailing bridle, was scouring over the prairie.

In a few minutes the animal was lassoed, and led back to the spot so near being made sacred with my grave.

Chapter Twenty Nine.

A Dinner with Two Dishes.

El Sol, I have said, was standing over the prostrate Indian. His countenance indicated the blending of two emotions, hate and triumph.

His sister at this moment galloped up, and, leaping from her horse, advanced rapidly forward.

"Behold!" said he, pointing to the Navajo chief; "behold the murderer of our mother!"

The girl uttered a short, sharp exclamation; and, drawing a knife, rushed upon the captive.

"No, Luna!" cried El Sol, putting her aside; "no; we are not assassins. That is not revenge. He shall not yet die. We will show him alive to the squaws of the Maricopa. They shall dance the mamanchic over this great chief—this warrior captured without a wound!"

El Sol uttered these words in a contemptuous tone. The effect was visible on the Navajo.

"Dog of a Coco!" cried he, making an involuntary struggle to free himself; "dog of a Coco! leagued with the pale robbers. Dog!"

"Ha! you remember me, Dacoma? It is well—"

"Dog!" again ejaculated the Navajo, interrupting him; and the words hissed through his teeth, while his eyes glared with an expression of the fiercest malignity.

"He! he!" cried Rube, at this moment galloping up; "he! he! that Injun's as savagerous as a meat axe. Lamm him! Warm his collops wi' the bull rope; he's warmed my old mar. Nick syrup him!"

"Let us look to your wound, Monsieur Haller," said Seguin, alighting from his horse, and approaching me, as I thought, with an uneasiness of manner. "How is it? through the flesh? You are safe enough; if, indeed, the arrow has not been poisoned. I fear—El Sol! here! quick, my friend! tell me if this point has been dipped."

"Let us first take it out," replied the Maricopa, coming up; "we shall lose no time by that."

The arrow was sticking through my forearm. The barb had pierced through the flesh, until about half of the shaft appeared on the opposite side.

El Sol caught the feather end in both his hands, and snapped it at the lapping. He then took hold of the barb and drew it gently out of the wound.

"Let it bleed," said he, "till I have examined the point. It does not look like a war-shaft; but the Navajoes use a very subtle poison. Fortunately I possess the means of detecting it, as well as its antidote."

As he said this, he took from his pouch a tuft of raw cotton. With this he rubbed the blood lightly from the blade. He then drew forth a small stone phial, and, pouring a few drops of liquid upon the metal, watched the result.

I waited with no slight feeling of uneasiness. Seguin, too, appeared anxious; and as I knew that he must have oftentimes witnessed the effect of a poisoned arrow, I did not feel very comfortable, seeing him watch the assaying process with so much apparent anxiety. I knew there was danger where he dreaded it.

"Monsieur Haller," said El Sol, at length, "you are in luck this time. I think I may call it luck, for your antagonist has surely some in his quiver not quite so harmless as this one.

"Let me see," he added; and, stepping up to the Navajo, he drew another arrow from the quiver that still remained slung upon the Indian's back. After subjecting the blade to a similar test, he exclaimed—

"I told you so. Look at this, green as a plantain! He fired two: where is the other? Comrades, help me to find it. Such a tell-tale as that must not be left behind us."

Several of the men leaped from their horses, and searched for the shaft that had been shot first. I pointed out the direction and probable distance as near as I could, and in a few moments it was picked up.

El Sol took it, and poured a few drops of his liquid on the blade. It turned green like the other.

"You may thank your saints, Monsieur Haller," said the Coco, "it was not this one made that hole in your arm, else it would have taken all the skill of Doctor Reichter and myself to have saved you. But what's this? Another wound! Ha! He touched you as he made his right point. Let me look at it."

"I think it is only a scratch."

"This is a strange climate, Monsieur Haller. I have seen scratches become mortal wounds when not sufficiently valued. Luna! Some cotton, sis! I shall endeavour to dress yours so that you need not fear that result. You deserve that much at my hands. But for you, sir, he would have escaped me."

"But for you, sir, he would have killed me."

"Well," replied the Coco, with a smile, "it is possible you would not have come off so well. Your weapon played you false. It is hardly just to expect a man to parry a lance-point with a clubbed rifle, though it was beautifully done. I do not wonder that you pulled trigger in the second joust. I intended doing so myself, had the lasso failed me again. But we are in luck both ways. You must sling this arm for a day or two. Luna! that scarf of yours."

"No!" said I, as the girl proceeded to unfasten a beautiful scarf which she wore around her waist; "you shall not: I will find something else."

"Here, mister; if this will do," interposed the young trapper Garey, "you are heartily welcome to it."

As Garey said this, he pulled a coloured handkerchief out of the breast of his hunting-shirt, and held it forth.

"You are very kind; thank you!" I replied, although I knew on whose account the kerchief was given; "you will be pleased to accept this in return." And I offered him one of my small revolvers—a weapon that, at that time and in that place, was worth its weight in pearls.

The mountain man knew this, and very gratefully accepted the proffered gift; but much as he might have prized it, I saw that he was still more gratified with a simple smile that he received from another quarter, and I felt certain that the scarf would soon change owners, at any rate.

I watched the countenance of El Sol to see if he had noticed or approved of this little by-play. I could perceive no unusual emotion upon it. He was busy with my wounds, which he dressed in a manner that would have done credit to a member of the R.C.S.

"Now," said he, when he had finished, "you will be ready for as much more fighting in a couple of days at the furthest. You have a bad bridle-arm, Monsieur Haller, but the best horse I ever saw. I do not wonder at your refusing to sell him."

Most of the conversation had been carried on in English; and it was spoken by the Coco chief with an accent and emphasis, to my ear, as good as I had ever heard. He spoke French, too, like a Parisian; and it was in this language that he usually conversed with Seguin. I wondered at all this.

The men had remounted, with the intention of returning to the camp. Extreme hunger was now prompting us, and we commenced riding back to partake of the repast so unceremoniously interrupted.

At a short distance from the camp we dismounted, and, picketing our horses upon the grass, walked forward to search for the stray steaks and ribs we had lately seen in plenty. A new chagrin awaited us; not a morsel of flesh remained! The coyotes had taken advantage of our absence, and we could see nothing around us but naked bones. The thighs and ribs of the buffaloes had been polished as if scraped with a knife. Even the hideous carcass of the Digger had become a shining skeleton!

"Wagh!" exclaimed one of the hunters; "wolf now or nothing: hyar goes!" and the man levelled his rifle.

"Hold!" exclaimed Seguin, seeing the act. "Are you mad, sir?"

"I reckon not, capt'n," replied the hunter, doggedly bringing down his piece. "We must eat, I s'pose. I see nothin' but them about; an' how are we goin' to get them 'ithout shootin'?"

Seguin made no reply, except by pointing to the bow which El Sol was making ready.

"Eh-ho!" added the hunter; "yer right, capt'n. I asks pardon. I had forgot that piece o' bone."

The Coco took an arrow from the quiver, and tried the head with the assaying liquid. It proved to be a hunting-shaft; and, adjusting it to the string, he sent it through the body of a white wolf, killing it instantly. He took up the shaft again, and wiping the feather, shot another, and another, until the bodies of five or six of these animals lay stretched upon the ground.

"Kill a coyote when ye're about it," shouted one of the hunters; "gentlemen like we oughter have leastwise two courses to our dinner."

The men laughed at this rough sally; and El Sol, smiling, again picked up the arrow, and sent it whizzing through the body of one of the coyotes.

"I think that will be enough for one meal, at all events," said El Sol, recovering the arrow, and putting it back into the quiver.

"Ay!" replied the wit; "if we wants more we kin go back to the larder agin. It's a kind o' meat that eats better fresh, anyhow."

"Well, it diz, hoss. Wagh! I'm in for a griskin o' the white. Hyar goes!"

The hunters, laughing at the humour of their comrades, drew their shining knives, and set about skinning the wolves. The adroitness with which this operation was performed showed that it was by no means new to them.

In a short time the animals were stripped of their hides and quarters; and each man, taking his quarter, commenced roasting it over the fire.

"Fellers! what d'ye call this anyhow? Beef or mutton?" asked one, as they began to eat.

"Wolf-mutton, I reckin," was the reply.

"It's dog-gone good eatin', I say; peels off as tender as squ'll."

"It's some'ut like goat, ain't it?"

"Mine tastes more like dog to me."

"It ain't bad at all; better than poor bull any day."

"I'd like it a heap better if I war sure the thing hadn't been up to yon varmint on the rocks." And the man who said this pointed to the skeleton of the Digger.

The idea was horrible, and under other circumstances would have acted as a sufficient emetic.

"Wagh!" exclaimed a hunter; "ye've most taken away my stammuck. I was a-goin' to try the coyoat afore ye spoke. I won't now, for I seed them smellin' about him afore we rid off."

"I say, old case, you don't mind it, do ye?"

This was addressed to Rube, who was busy on his rib and made no reply.

"He? not he," said another, answering for him. "Rube's ate a heap o' queery tit-bits in his time. Hain't ye, Rube?"

"Ay, an' afore yur be as long in the mountains as this child, 'ee'll be glad to get yur teeth over wuss chawin's than wolf-meat; see if 'ee don't, young fellur."

"Man-meat, I reckin?"

"Ay, that's what Rube means."

"Boyees!" said Rube, not heeding the remark, and apparently in good humour, now that he was satisfying his appetite, "what's the nassiest thing, leavin' out man-meat, any o' 'ees iver chawed?"

"Woman-meat, I reckin."

"'Ee chuckle-headed fool! yur needn't be so peert now, showin' yur smartness when 'tain't called for nohow."

"Wal, leaving out man-meat, as you say," remarked one of the hunters, in answer to Rube's question, "a muss-rat's the meanest thing I ever set teeth on."

"I've chawed sage-hare—raw at that," said a second, "an' I don't want to eat anything that's bitterer."

"Owl's no great eatin'," added a third.

"I've ate skunk," continued a fourth; "an' I've ate sweeter meat in my time."

"Carrajo!" exclaimed a Mexican, "what do you think of monkey? I have dined upon that down south many's the time."

"Wal, I guess monkey's but tough chawin's; but I've sharpened my teeth on dry buffler hide, and it wa'n't as tender as it mout 'a been."

"This child," said Rube, after the rest had given in their experience, "leavin' monkey to the beside, have ate all them critturs as has been named yet. Monkey he hain't, bein' as thur's none o' 'em in these parts. It may be tough, or it mayn't; it may be bitter, an' it mayn't, for what I knows to the contrairywise; but, oncest on a time, this niggur chawed a varmint that wa'n't much sweeter, if it wur as sweet."

"What was it, Rube?"

"What was it?" asked several in a breath, curious to know what the old trapper could have eaten more unpalatable than the viands already named.

"'Twur turkey-buzzart, then; that's what it wur."

"Turkey-buzzard!" echoed everyone.

"'Twa'n't any thin' else."

"Wagh? that was a stinkin' pill, an' no mistake."

"That beats me all hollow."

"And when did ye eat the buzzard, old boy?" asked one, suspecting that there might be a story connected with this feat of the earless trapper.

"Ay! tell us that, Rube; tell us!" cried several.

"Wal," commenced Rube, after a moment's silence, "'twur about six yeern ago, I wur set afoot on the Arkansaw, by the Rapahoes, leastwise two hunder mile below the Big Timmer. The cussed skunks tuk hoss, beaver, an' all. He! he!" continued the speaker with a chuckle; "he! he! they mout 'a did as well an' let ole Rube alone."

"I reckon that, too," remarked a hunter. "'Tain't like they made much out o' that speckelashun. Well—about the buzzard?"

"'Ee see, I wur cleaned out, an' left with jest a pair o' leggins, better than two hunder miles from anywhur. Bent's wur the nearest; an' I tuk up the river in that direkshun.

"I never seed varmint o' all kinds as shy. They wudn't 'a been if I'd 'a had my traps; but there wa'n't a critter, from the minners in the waters to the bufflers on the paraira, that didn't look like they knowed how this niggur were fixed. I kud git nuthin' for two days but lizard, an' scarce at that."

"Lizard's but poor eatin'," remarked one.

"'Ee may say that. This hyur thigh jeint's fat cow to it—it are."

And Rube, as he said this, made a fresh attack upon the wolf-mutton.

"I chawed up the ole leggins, till I wur as naked as Chimley Rock."

"Gollies! was it winter?"

"No. 'Twur calf-time, an' warm enuf for that matter. I didn't mind the want o' the buckskin that a way, but I kud 'a eat more o' it.

"The third day I struck a town o' sand-rats. This niggur's har wur longer then than it ur now. I made snares o' it, an' trapped a lot o' the rats; but they grew shy too, cuss 'em! an' I had to quit that speck'lashun. This wur the third day from the time I'd been set down, an' I wur getting nasty weak on it. I 'gin to think that the time wur come for this child to go under.

"'Twur a leetle arter sun-up, an' I wur sittin' on the bank, when I seed somethin' queery floatin' a-down the river. When I kim closer, I seed it wur the karkidge o' a buffler—calf at that—an' a couple o' buzzarts floppin' about on the thing, pickin' its peepers out. 'Twur far out, an' the water deep; but I'd made up my mind to fetch it ashore. I wa'n't long in strippin', I reckin."

Here the hunters interrupted Rube's story with a laugh.

"I tuk the water, an' swam out. I kud smell the thing afore I wur half-way, an' when I got near it, the birds mizzled. I wur soon clost up, an' seed at a glimp that the calf wur as rotten as punk."

"What a pity!" exclaimed one of the hunters.

"I wa'n't a-gwine to have my swim for nuthin'; so I tuk the tail in my teeth, an' swam back for the shore. I hadn't made three strokes till the tail pulled out!

"I then swum round ahint the karkidge, an' pushed it afore me till I got it landed high an' dry upon a sandbar. 'Twur like to fall to pieces, when I pulled it out o' the water. 'Twa'n't eatable nohow!"

Here Rube took a fresh mouthful of the wolf-mutton, and remained silent until he had masticated it. The men had become interested in the story, and waited with impatience. At length he proceeded—

"I seed the buzzarts still flyin' about, an' fresh ones a-comin'. I tuk a idee that I mout git my claws upon some o' 'em. So I lay down clost up agin the calf, an' played 'possum.

"I wa'n't long that a way when the birds begun to light on the sandbar, an' a big cock kim floppin' up to the karkidge. Afore he kud flop up agin, I grupped him by the legs."

"Hooraw! well done, by gollies!"

"The cussed thing wur nearly as stinkin' as t'other, but it wur die dog—buzzart or calf—so I skinned the buzzart."

"And ate it?" inquired an impatient listener. "No-o," slowly drawled Rube, apparently "miffed" at being thus interrupted. "It ate me."

The laugh that followed this retort restored the old trapper to good humour again.

"Did you go it raw, Rube?" asked one of the hunters. "How could he do otherwise? He hadn't a spark o' fire, an' nothing to make one out of."

"Yur'n etarnal fool!" exclaimed Rube, turning savagely on the last speaker. "I kud make a fire if thur wa'n't a spark anywhar!"

A yell of laughter followed this speech, and it was some minutes before the trapper recovered his temper sufficiently to resume his narration.

"The rest o' the birds," continued he at length, "seein' the ole cock rubbed out, grew shy, and kep away on t'other side o' the river. 'Twa'n't no use tryin' that dodge over agin. Jest then I spied a coyoat comin' lopin' down the bank, an' another follerin' upon his heels, an' two or three more on the same trail. I know'd it wud be no joke gruppin' one o' them by the leg, but I made up my mind to try it; an' I lay down jest as afore, close up to the calf. 'Twur no go. The cunnin' things seed the float stick, an' kep clur o' the karkidge. I wur a-gwine to cacher under some bush that wur by, an' I begun to carry it up, when all of a suddint I tuk a fresh idee in my head. I seed thur wur drift-wood a plenty on the bank, so I fotched it up, an' built a pen-trap roun' about the calf. In the twinklin' o' a goat's eye I had six varmints in the trap."

"Hooraw! Ye war safe then, old hoss."

"I tuk a lot o' stones, an' then clomb up on the pen, an' killed the hul kit on 'em. Lord, boyees! 'ee never seed sich a snappin', and snarlin', and jumpin', an' yowltin', as when I peppered them donicks down on 'em. He! he! he! Ho! ho! hoo!"

And the smoky old sinner chuckled with delight at the remembrance of his adventure.

"You reached Bent's then safe enough, I reckin?"

"'Ee—es. I skinned the critters wi' a sharp stone, an' made me a sort o' shirt an' leggins. This niggur had no mind, comin' in naked, to gi' them thur joke at the Fort. I packed enough of the wolf-meat to last me up, an' I got there in less'n a week. Bill wur thur himself, an' 'ee all know Bill Bent. He know'd me. I wa'n't in the Fort a half an hour till I were spick-span in new buckskins, wi' a new rifle; an' that rifle wur Tar-guts, now afore ye."

"Ha! you got Tear-guts thar then?"

"I got Tar-guts thur then, an' a gun she ur. He! he! he! 'Twa'n't long arter I got her till I tried her. He! he! he! Ho! ho! hoo!"

And the old trapper went off into another fit of chuckling.

"What are ye laughin' at now, Rube?" asked one of his comrades.

"He! he! he! What am I larfin' at? He! he! he! Ho! ho! That ur the crisp o' the joke. He! he! he! What am I larfin' at?"

"Yes; tell us, man!"

"It are this then I'm larfin' at," replied Rube, sobering down a little, "I wa'n't at Bent's three days when who do 'ee think shed kum to the Fort?"

"Who? Maybe the Rapahoes!"

"Them same Injuns; an' the very niggurs as set me afoot. They kum to the Fort to trade wi' Bill, an' thur I sees both my old mar an' rifle!"

"You got them back then?"

"That wur likely. Thur wur a sight o' mountainy men thur, at the time, that wa'n't the fellurs to see this child put down on the parairar for nuthin'. Yander's the critter!" and Rube pointed to the old mare. "The rifle I gin to Bill, an' kep Tar-guts instead, seeing she wur a better gun."

"So you got square with the Rapahoes?"

"That, young fellur, justs rests on what 'ee 'ud call squar. Do 'ee see these hyur nicks: them standin' sep'rate?"

And the trapper pointed to a row of small notches cut in the stock of his rifle.

"Ay, ay!" cried several men in reply. "Thur's five o' 'em, ain't thur?"

"One, two, three; yes, five."

"Them's Rapahoes!"

Rube's story was ended.

Chapter Thirty.

Blinding the Pursuer.

By this time the men had finished eating, and now began to gather around Seguin, for the purpose of deliberating on what course we should pursue. One had already been sent up to the rocks to act as a vidette, and warn us in case any of the Indians should be descried upon the prairie.

We all felt that we were still in a dilemma. The Navajo was our captive, and his men would come to seek for him. He was too important a personage (second chief of the nation) to be abandoned without a search, and his own followers, nearly half of the tribe, would certainly be back to the spring. Not finding him there, should they not discover our tracks, they would return upon the war-trail to their country.

This, we all saw, would render our expedition impracticable, as Dacoma's band alone outnumbered us; and should we meet them in their mountain fastnesses, we should have no chance of escape.

For some time Seguin remained silent, with his eyes fixed on the ground. He was evidently tracing out in his mind some plan of action. None of the hunters chose to interrupt him.

"Comrades!" said he at length, "this is an unfortunate *coup*, but it could not be avoided. It is well it is no worse. As it is, we must alter our plans. They will be sure to return on his track, and follow their own trail back to the Navajo towns. What then? Our band cannot either come on to the Pinon or cross the war-trail at any point. They would discover our tracks to a certainty."

"Why, can't we go straight up to whar the rest's cached, and then take round by the old mine? That won't interfere with the war-trail nohow." This was proposed by one of the hunters. "Vaya!" rejoined a Mexican; "we should meet the Navajoes just when we had got to their town! Carrai! that would never do, amigo. There wouldn't many, of us get back again. Santisima! No."

"We ain't obleeged to meet them," argued the first speaker. "They're not a-goin' to stop at thur town when they find the nigger hain't been back."

"It is true," said Seguin, "they will not remain there. They will doubtless return on the war-trail again; but I know the country by the mine."

"So do I! So do I!" cried several voices. "There is no game," continued Seguin. "We have no provisions; it is therefore impossible for us to go that way."

"We couldn't go it, nohow."

"We should starve before we had got through the Mimbres."

"Thar's no water that way."

"No, by gosh! not enough to make a drink for a sand-rat."

"We must take our chances, then," said Seguin. Here he paused thoughtfully, and with a gloomy expression of countenance.

"We must cross the trail," he continued, "and go by the Prieto, or abandon the expedition."

The word "Prieto," in opposition to the phrase "abandon the expedition," put the hunters to their wits' end for invention, and plan after plan was proposed; all, however, ending in the probability—in fact, certainty—that if adopted, our trail would be discovered by the enemy, and followed up before we could escape back to the Del Norte. They were, therefore, one after another rejected.

During all this discussion, old Rube had not said a word. The earless trapper was sitting upon the prairie, squat on his hams, tracing out some lines with his bow, and apparently laying out the plan of a fortification.

"What are ye doin', old hoss?" inquired one of his comrades.

"My hearin' ain't as good as 'twur afore I kim into this cussed country; but I thought I heerd some o' 'ees say, jest now, we cudn't cross the 'Pash trail 'ithout bein' followed in two days. That's a dod-rotted lie. It are."

"How are ye goin' to prove it, hoss?"

"Chut, man! yur tongue wags like a beaver's tail in flood-time."

"Can you suggest any way in which it can be done, Rube? I confess I see none."

As Seguin made this appeal, all eyes were turned upon the trapper.

"Why, cap, I kin surgest my own notion o' the thing. It may be right, an' it mayn't be right; but if it wur follered out, there'll be neither 'Pash nor Navagh that'll smell where we go for a week. If they diz, 'ee may cut my ears off."

This was a favourite joke with Rube, and the hunters only laughed. Seguin himself could not restrain a smile, as he requested the speaker to proceed.

"Fust an' fo'most, then," said Rube, "thur not a-gwine to come arter that nigger in less than two days."

"How can you tell that?"

"This way: 'Ee see he's only second chief, an' they kin go on well enough 'ithout him. But that ain't it. The Injun forgot his bow; white at that. Now 'ee all knows as well as this child, that that's a big disgrace in the eyes o' Injuns."

"You're right about that, hoss," remarked one.

"Wal, so the ole 'coon thinks. Now, 'ee see, it's as plain as Pike's Peak that he kim away back 'ithout tellin' any o' the rest a syllabub about it. He'd not let 'em know if he kud help it."

"That is not improbable," said Seguin. "Proceed, Rube!"

"More'n that," continued the trapper, "I'll stake high thet he ordered them not to foller him, afeerd thet some on 'em mout see what he kim for. If he'd a-thought they knew or suspected, he'd 'a sent some other, an' not kum himself; that's what he'd 'a done."

This was all probable enough; and with the knowledge which the scalp-hunters possessed of the Navajo character, they one and all believed it to be so.

"I'm sartin they'll kum back," continued Rube; "that ur, his half o' the tribe, anyways; but it'll be three days clur, an' well up till another, afore they drinks Peenyun water."

"But they would strike our trail the day after."

"If we were green fools enough to let 'em, they wud."

"How can we prevent that?" asked Seguin.

"Easy as fallin' off a log."

"How? how?" inquired several at once.

“By puttin’ them on another scent, do ’ee see?”

“Yes! but in what way can we effect that?” inquired Seguin.

“Why, cap, yur tumble has surely dumfoundered ye. I wud think less o’ these other dummies not seein’ at a glimp how we kin do it.”

“I confess, Rube,” replied Seguin, with a smile, “I do not perceive how we can mislead them.”

“Wal, then,” continued the trapper, with a chuckle of satisfaction at his own superior prairie-craft, “this child’s a-gwyne to tell ’ee how ’ee kin put them on a different track.”

“Hooraw for you, old hoss!”

“’Ee see a quiver on that Injun’s back?”

“Ay, ay!” cried several voices.

“It’s full o’ arrows, or pretty near it, I reckin.”

“It is. Well?”

“Wal, then, let some o’ us ride the Injun’s mustang: any other critter thet’s got the same track ’ll do; away down the ’Pash trail, an’ stick them things pointin’ south’art; an’ if the Navagh don’t travel that a way till they comes up with the ’Pashes, ’ee may have this child’s har for a plug o’ the wust Kaintucky terbaccer.”

“Viva!”

“He’s right, he’s right!”

“Hooraw for old Rube!” and various exclamations, were uttered by the hunters.

“’Tain’t needcessary for them to know why he shud ’a tuk that track. They’ll know his arrows; that’s enuf. By the time they gits back, with their fingers in thur meat-traps, we’ll hev start enough to carry us to Hackensack.”

“Ay, that we will, by gollies!”

“The band,” continued Rube, “needn’t come to the Peenyun spring no howsomever. They kin cross the war-trail higher up to to’rst the Heely, an’ meet us on t’other side o’ the mountain, whur thur’s a grist o’ game, both cattle an’ buffler. A plenty o’ both on the ole mission lands, I’ll be boun’. We’d hev to go thur anyways. Thur’s no hopes o’ meetin’ the buffler this side, arter the splurry them Injuns has gin them.”

“That is true enough,” said Seguin. “We must go round the mountain before we can expect to fall in with the buffalo. The Indian hunt has chased them clean off from the Llanos. Come, then! Let us set about our work at once. We have yet two hours before sunset. What would you do first, Rube? You have given the plan: I will trust to you for the details.”

“Why, in my opeenyun, cap, the fust thing to be did are to send a man as straight as he can gallip to whur the band’s cached. Let him fotch them acrost the trail.”

“Where should they cross, do you think?”

“About twenty mile north o’ hyur thur’s a dry ridge, an’ a good grist o’ loose donicks. If they cross as they oughter, they needn’t make much sign. I kud take a train o’ Bent’s waggons over, that ’ud puzzle deaf Smith to foller ’em. I kud.”

“I will send a man off instantly. Here, Sanchez! you have a good horse, and know the ground. It is not over twenty miles to where they are cached. Bring them along the ridge, and with caution, as you have heard. You will find us around the north point of the mountain. You can travel all night, and be up with us early in the morning. Away!”

The torero, without making any answer, drew his horse from the picket, leaped into the saddle, and rode off at a gallop towards the north-west.

“It is fortunate,” said Seguin, looking after him for some moments, “that they have trampled the ground about here, else the tracks made in our last encounter would certainly have told tales upon us.”

“Thur’s no danger about that,” rejoined Rube; “but when we rides from hyur, cap’n, we mustn’t foller their trail. They’d soon sight our back tracks. We had best keep up yander among the loose donicks.” Rube pointed to the shingle that stretched north and south along the foot of the mountain.

“Yes, that shall be our course. We can leave this without leaving any tracks. What next?”

“The next idee ur, to get rid o’ yon piece o’ machin’ry,” and the trapper, as he spoke, nodded in the direction of the skeleton.

“True! I had forgotten it. What shall we do with it?”

“Bury it,” advised one.

“Wagh! no. Burn it!” cried another.

“Ay, that’s best,” said a third.

The latter suggestion was adopted.

The skeleton was brought down; the stains of the blood were carefully rubbed from the rocks; the skull was shivered with a tomahawk, and the joints were broken in pieces. The whole mass was then flung upon the fire, and pounded down among numerous bones of the buffalo, already simmering in the cinders. An anatomist only could have detected the presence of a human skeleton.

“Now, Rube; the arrows?”

“If ’ee’ll leave that to me an’ Bill Garey, I think them two niggurs kin fix ’em so as to bamfoozle any Injuns thur is in these parts. We’ll hev to go three mile or tharabout; but we’ll git back by the time ’ee hev filled yur gourds, an’ got yur traps ready for skeetin’.”

“Very well! take the arrows.”

"Four's gobs for us," said Rube, taking that number from the quiver. "Keep the rest. 'Ee'll want more wolf-meat afore we start. Thur's not a tail o' anythin' else till we git clur roun' the mountain yander. Billee! throw your ugly props over that Navagh mustang. Putty hoss too; but I wudn't giv my old mar for a hul cavayard o' him. Gi's a sprig o' the black feather."

Here the old trapper drew one of the ostrich feathers out of the helmet of the Navajo chief, and continued—

"Boyees! take care o' the ole mar till I kum back, an don't let her stampede, do 'ee hear. I wants a blanket. Don't all speak at oncest!"

"Here, Rube, here!" cried several, holding out their blankets.

"E'er a one 'll do. We needs three: Bill's an' mine an' another'n. Hyur, Billee! take these afore ye. Now ride down the 'Pash trail three hunred yards, or tharabout, an' then pull up. Don't take the beaten pad, but keep alongside, an' make big tracks. Gallop!"

The young hunter laid his quirt to the flanks of the mustang, and started at full gallop along the Apache trail.

When he had ridden a distance of three hundred yards or so, he halted to wait for further directions from his comrade.

Old Rube, at the same time, took an arrow; and, fastening a piece of ostrich feather to the barb, adjusted it on one of the upright poles which the Indians had left standing on the camp-ground. It was placed in such a manner that the head pointed southward in the direction of the Apache trail, and was so conspicuous with the black feather that no one coming in from the Llanos could fail to see it.

This done, he followed his companion on foot, keeping wide out from the trail, and making his tracks with great caution. On coming up with Garey, he stuck a second arrow in the ground: its point also inclined to the south, and so that it could be seen from the former one.

Garey then galloped forward, keeping on the trail, while Rube struck out again to the open prairie, and advanced in a line parallel to it.

Having ridden a distance of two or three miles, Garey slackened his pace, and put the mustang to a slow walk. A little farther on he again halted, and held his horse at rest, in the beaten path.

Rube now came up, and spread the three blankets lengthwise along the ground, and leading westward from the trail. Garey dismounted, and led the animal gently on the blankets.

As its feet rested on two at a time, each, as it became the rearmost, was taken up, and spread again in front; and this was repeated until they had got the mustang some fifty lengths of himself out into the prairie. The movement was executed with an adroitness equal to that which characterised the feat of Sir Walter Raleigh.

Garey now took up the blankets, and, remounting, commenced riding slowly back by the foot of the mountain; while Rube returned to the trail, and placed a third arrow at the point where the mustang had parted from it. He then proceeded south as before. One more was yet needed to make doubly sure.

When he had gone about half a mile, we saw him stoop over the trail, rise up again, cross toward the mountain foot, and follow the path taken by his companion. The work was done; the finger-posts were set; the ruse was complete!

El Sol, meanwhile, had been busy. Several wolves were killed and skinned, and the meat was packed in their skins. The gourds were filled, our captive was tied on a mule, and we stood waiting the return of the trappers.

Seguin had resolved to leave two men at the spring as videttes. They were to keep their horses by the rocks, and supply them with the mule-bucket, so as to make no fresh tracks at the water. One was to remain constantly on an eminence, and watch the prairie with the glass. They could thus descry the returning Navajoes in time to escape unobserved themselves along the foot of the mountain. They were then to halt at a place ten miles to the north, where they could still have a view of the plain. There they were to remain until they had ascertained what direction the Indians should take after leaving the spring, when they were to hurry forward and join the band with their tidings.

All these arrangements having been completed as Rube and Garey came up, we mounted our horses and rode by a circuitous route for the mountain foot. When close in, we found the path strewed with loose cut-rock, upon which the hoofs of our animals left no track. Over this we rode forward, heading to the north, and keeping in a line nearly parallel to the "war-trail."

Chapter Thirty One.

A Buffalo "Surround."

A march of twenty miles brought us to the place where we expected to be joined by the band. We found a small stream heading in the Pinon Range, and running westward to the San Pedro. It was fringed with cotton-trees and willows, and with grass in abundance for our horses. Here we encamped, kindled a fire in the thicket, cooked our wolf-mutton, ate it, and went to sleep.

The band came up in the morning, having travelled all night. Their provisions were spent as well as ours, and instead of resting our wearied animals, we pushed on through a pass in the sierra in hopes of finding game on the other side.

About noon we debouched through the mountain pass into a country of openings—small prairies, bounded by jungly forests, and interspersed with timber islands. These prairies were covered with tall grass, and buffalo signs appeared as we rode into them. We saw their "roads," "chips," and "wallows."

We saw, moreover, the *bois de vache* of the wild cattle. We would soon meet with one or the other.

We were still on the stream by which we had camped the night before, and we made a noon halt to refresh our animals.

The full-grown forms of the cacti were around us, bearing red and yellow fruit in abundance. We plucked the pears of the pitahaya, and ate them greedily; we found service-berries, yampo, and roots of the "pomme blanche." We dined on fruits and vegetables of various sorts, indigenous only to this wild region.

But the stomachs of the hunters longed for their favourite food, the hump ribs and boudins of the buffalo; and after a halt of two hours, we moved forward through the openings.

We had ridden about an hour among chapparal, when Rube, who was some paces in advance, acting as guide, turned in his saddle and pointed downward.

"What's there, Rube?" asked Seguin, in a low voice.

"Fresh track, cap'n; buffler!"

"What number; can you guess?"

"A gang o' fifty or tharabout. They've tuk through the thicket yander-away. I kin sight the sky. Thur's clur ground not fur from us; and I'd stak a plew thur in it. I think it's a small parairia, cap."

"Halt here, men!" said Seguin; "halt and keep silent. Ride forward, Rube. Come, Monsieur Haller, you're fond of hunting; come along with us!"

I followed the guide and Seguin through the bushes; like them, riding slowly and silently.

In a few minutes we reached the edge of a prairie covered with long grass. Peering cautiously through the leaves of the prosopis, we had a full view of the open ground. The buffaloes were on the plain!

It was, as Rube had rightly conjectured, a small prairie about a mile and a half in width, closed in on all sides by a thick chapparal. Near the centre was a motte of heavy timber, growing up from a leafy underwood. A spur of willows running out from the timber indicated the presence of water.

"Thur's a spring yander," muttered Rube. "They've jest been a-coolin' their noses at it."

This was evident enough, for some of the animals were at the moment walking out of the willows; and we could see the wet clay glistening upon their flanks, and the saliva glancing down from their jaws.

"How will we get at them, Rube?" asked Seguin; "can we approach them, do you think?"

"I doubt not, cap. The grass 'ud hardly kiver us, an thur a-gwine out o' range o' the bushes."

"How then? We cannot run them; there's not room. They would be into the thicket at the first dash. We would lose every hoof of them."

"Sartin as Scripter."

"What is to be done?"

"This niggur sees but one other plan as kin be used jest at this time."

"What is it?"

"Surround."

"Right; if we can do that. How is the wind?"

"Dead as an Injun wi' his head cut off," replied the trapper, taking a small feather out of his cap and tossing it in the air. "See, cap, it falls plump!"

"It does, truly."

"We kin easily git roun' them bufflers afore they wind us; an' we hev men enough to make a picket fence about them. We can hardly set about it too soon, cap. Thur a movin' torst the edge yander."

"Let us divide the men, then," said Seguin, turning his horse; "you can guide one-half of them to their stands. I will go with the other. Monsieur Haller, you had better remain where you are. It is as good a stand as you can get. Have patience. It may be an hour before all are placed. When you hear the bugle, you may gallop forward and do your best. If we succeed, you shall have sport and a good supper, which I suppose you feel the need of by this time."

So saying, Seguin left me, and rode back to the men, followed by old Rube.

It was their purpose to separate the band into two parties, each taking an opposite direction, and to drop men here and there at regular intervals around the prairie. They would keep in the thicket while on the march, and only discover themselves at a given signal. In this way, should the buffaloes allow time for the execution of the movement, we should be almost certain of securing the whole gang.

As soon as Seguin had left me, I looked to my rifle and pistols, putting on a fresh set of caps. After that, having nothing else to occupy me, I remained seated in my saddle, eyeing the animals as they fed unconscious of danger. I was full of anxiety lest some clumsy fellow might discover himself too soon, and thus spoil our anticipated sport.

After a while I could see the birds flying up from the thicket, and the screaming of the blue jay indicated to me the progress of the "surround."

Now and then, an old bull, on the skirts of the herd, would toss up his shaggy mane, snuff the wind, and strike the ground fiercely with his hoof, evidently labouring under a suspicion that all was not right.

The others did not seem to heed these demonstrations, but kept on quietly cropping the luxuriant grama.

I was thinking how nicely we were going to have them in the trap, when an object caught my eye, just emerging from the motte. It was a buffalo calf, and I saw that it was proceeding to join the gang. I thought it somewhat strange that it should be separated from the rest, for the calves, trained by their mothers to know the wolf, usually keep up with the herd.

"It has stayed behind at the spring," thought I. "Perhaps the others pushed it from the water, and it could not drink until they were gone."

I fancied that it moved clumsily, as if wounded; but it was passing through the long grass, and I could not get a good view of it.

There was a pack of coyotes (there always is) sneaking after the herd. These, perceiving the calf, as it came out of the timber, made an instant and simultaneous attack upon it. I could see them skipping around it, and fancied I could hear their fierce snarling; but the calf appeared to fight its way through the thick of them; and after a short while, I saw it close in to its companions, where I lost sight of it among the others.

"A game young bull," soliloquised I, and again I ran my eye around the skirting of the chapparal to watch how the hunters were getting forward with the "surround." I could perceive the flashing of brilliant wings over the bramble, and hear the shrill voices of the jay-birds. Judging by these, I concluded that the men were moving slowly enough. It was half an hour since Seguin had left me, and I could perceive that they were not half-way round as yet.

I began to make calculations as to how long I would have to wait, soliloquising as follows:—

"Diameter of the prairie, a mile and a half. It is a circle three times that: four miles and a half. Phew! I shall not hear the signal in much less than an hour. I must be patient then, and—what! The brutes are lying down! Good! There is no danger now of their making off. We shall have rare sport! One, two, three, six of them down! It must be the heat and the water. They have drunk too much. There goes another. Lucky devils! They have nothing else to do but eat and sleep, while I—no! eight down! Well! I hope soon to eat, too. What an odd way they have of coming to the ground! How different from anything of the bovine tribe I have yet observed! I have never seen buffaloes quieting down before. One would think they were falling as if shot! Two more alongside the rest! They will soon be all upon the turf. So much the better. We can gallop up before they get to their feet again. Oh, that I could hear that horn!"

And thus I went on rambling from thought to thought, and listening for the signal, although I knew that it could not be given for some time yet.

The buffaloes kept moving slowly onward, browsing as they went, and continuing to lie down one after another. I thought it strange, their stretching themselves thus successively; but I had observed farm cattle do the same, and I was at that time but little acquainted with the habits of the buffalo. Some of them appeared to toss about on the ground and kick violently. I had heard of a peculiarity of these animals termed "wallowing."

"They are at it," thought I. I wished much to have a clearer view of this curious exercise, but the high grass prevented me. I could only see their shaggy shoulders, and occasionally their hoofs kicking up over the sward.

I watched their movements with great interest, now feeling secure that the "surround" would be complete before they would think of rising.

At length the last one of the gang followed the example of his companions, and dropped over.

They were all now upon their sides, half-buried in the bunch grass. I thought I noticed the calf still upon its feet; but at that moment the bugle sounded, and a simultaneous cheer broke from all sides of the prairie.

I pressed the spur to my horse's flank, and dashed out into the open plain. Fifty others had done the same, yelling as they shot out of the thicket.

With my reins resting on my left fingers, and my rifle thrown crosswise, I galloped forward, filled with the wild excitement that such an adventure imparts. I was cocked and ready, resolved upon having the first shot.

It was but a short distance from where I had started to the nearest buffalo. I was soon within range, my horse flying like an arrow.

"Is the animal asleep? I am within ten paces of him, and still he stirs not! I will fire at him as he lies."

I raised my rifle, levelled it, and was about to pull the trigger, when something red gleamed before my eyes. It was blood!

I lowered the piece with a feeling of terror, and commenced dragging upon the rein; but, before I could pull up, I was carried into the midst of the prostrate herd. Here my horse suddenly stopped, and I sat in my saddle as if spell-bound. I was under the influence of a superstitious awe. Blood was before me and around me. Turn which way I would, my eye rested upon blood!

My comrades closed in, yelling as they came; but their yelling suddenly ceased, and one by one reined up, as I had done, with looks of consternation and wonder.

It was not strange, at such a sight. Before us lay the bodies of the buffaloes. They were all dead, or quivering in the last throes. Each bad a wound above the brisket, and from this the red stream gurled out, and trickled down their still panting sides. Blood welled from their mouths and out of their nostrils. Pools of it were filtering through the prairie turf; and clotted gouts, flung out by the struggling hoof, sprinkled the grass around them!

"Oh, heavens! what could it mean?"

"Wagh! Santisima! Sacré Dieu!" were the exclamations of the hunters.

"Surely no mortal hand has done this?"

"It wa'n't nuthin' else," cried a well-known voice, "ef yur call an Injun a mortal. 'Twur a red-skin, and this child—look 'ee-e!"

I heard the click of a rifle along with this abrupt exclamation. I turned suddenly. Rube was in the act of levelling his piece. My eye involuntarily followed the direction of the barrel. There was an object moving in the long grass.

"A buffalo that still kicks," thought I, as I saw the

"The ball had sped."

mass of dark-brown hair; "he is going to finish him; it is the calf!"

I had scarcely made the observation when the animal reared up on its hind legs, uttering a wild human scream; the shaggy hide was flung off; and a naked savage appeared, holding out his arms in an attitude of supplication.

I could not have saved him. The rifle had cracked, the ball had sped. I saw it piercing his brown breast, as a drop of sleet strikes upon the pane of glass; the red spout gushed forth, and the victim fell forward upon the body of one of the animals.

"Wagh! Rube!" exclaimed one of the men; "why didn't ye give him time to skin the meat? He mout as well 'a done that when he war about it;" and the man laughed at his savage jest.

"Look 'ee hyur, boyees!" said Rube, pointing to the motte; "if 'ee look sharp, yur mout scare up another calf yander away! I'm a-gwine to see arter this Injun's har; I am."

The hunters, at the suggestion, galloped off to surround the motte.

I felt a degree of irresolution and disgust at this cool shedding of blood. I drew my rein almost involuntarily, and moved forward to the spot where the savage had fallen. He lay back uppermost. He was naked to the breech-clout. There was the debouchure of a bullet below the left shoulder, and the black-red stream was trickling down his ribs. The limbs still quivered, but it was in the last spasms of parting life.

The hide in which he had disguised himself lay piled up where it had been flung. Beside it were a bow and several arrows. The latter were crimsoned to the notch, the feathers steeped in blood and clinging to the shafts. They had pierced the huge bodies of the animals, passing through and through. Each arrow had taken many lives! The old trapper rode up to the corpse, and leisurely dismounted from his mare.

"Fifty dollar a plew!" he muttered, unsheathing his knife and stooping over the body. "It's more'n I got for my own. It beats beaver all hollow. Cuss beaver, say this child. Plew a plug—ain't worth trappin' if the varmint wur as thick as grass-jumpers in calf-time. 'Ee up, niggur," he continued, grasping the long hair of the savage, and holding the face upward; "let's get a squint of your phisog. Hooraw! Coyote 'Pash! Hooraw!"

And a gleam of triumph lit up the countenance of the old man as he uttered these wild exclamations.

"Apash, is he?" asked one of the hunters, who had remained near the spot.

"That he are, Coyote 'Pash, the very niggurs that bobtailed this child's ears. I kin swar to thur ugly picters anywhur I get my peepers upon 'em. Wouwough—ole woofy! got 'ee at last, has he! Yur a beauty, an' no mistake."

So saying, he gathered the long crown locks in his left hand, and with two slashes of his knife, held quarte and tierce, he cut a circle around the top of the head, as perfect as if it had been traced by compasses. He then took a turn of the hair over his wrist, giving it a quick jerk outward. At the same instant, the keen blade passed under the skin, and the scalp was taken!

"Counts six," he continued, muttering to himself while placing the scalp in his belt; "six at fifty—three hunder shiners for 'Pash har; cuss beaver trappin'! says I."

Having secured the bleeding trophy, he wiped his knife upon the hair of one of the buffaloes, and proceeded to cut a small notch in the woodwork of his gun, alongside five others that had been carved there already. These six notches stood for Apaches only; for as my eye wandered along the outlines of the piece, I saw that there were many other columns in that terrible register!

Chapter Thirty Two.

Another "Coup."

A shot ringing in my ears caused me to withdraw my attention from the proceedings of the earless trapper. As I turned I saw a blue cloud floating away over the prairie, but I could not tell at what the shot had been fired. Thirty or forty of the hunters had surrounded the motte, and, halted, were sitting in their saddles in a kind of irregular circle. They were still at some distance from the timber, as if keeping out of arrow-range. They held their guns crosswise, and were shouting to one another.

It was improbable that the savage was alone; doubtless there were some of his companions in the thicket. There could not be many, however, for the underwood was not large enough to conceal more than a dozen bodies, and the keen eyes of the hunters were piercing it in every direction.

They reminded me of so many huntsmen in a gorse waiting the game to be sprung; but here, the game was human.

It was a terrible spectacle. I looked towards Seguin, thinking that he might interfere to prevent the barbarous battue. He noticed my inquiring glance, and turned his face from me. I fancied that he felt ashamed of the work in which his followers were engaged; but the killing, or capture, of whatever Indians might be in the motte had now become a necessary measure, and I knew that any remonstrance of mine would be disregarded. As for the men themselves, they would have laughed at it. This was their pastime, their profession, and I am certain that, at that moment, their feelings were not very different from those which would have actuated them had they been driving a bear from his den. They were, perhaps, a trifle more intense; certainly not more inclined towards mercy.

I reined up my horse, and awaited with painful emotions the *dénouement* of this savage drama.

"Vaya, Irlandes! What did you see?" inquired one of the Mexicans, appealing to Barney. I saw by this that it was the Irishman who had fired the shot.

"A rid-skin, by japers!" replied the latter.

"Warn't it yer own shadder ye sighted in the water?" cried a hunter, jeeringly.

"Maybe it was the divil, Barney?"

"In trath, frinds, I saw a somethin' that looked mighty like him, and I kilt it too."

"Ha! ha! Barney has killed the devil. Ha! ha!"

"Wagh!" exclaimed a trapper, spurring his horse toward the thicket; "the fool saw nothin'. I'll chance it, anyhow."

"Stop, comrade!" cried the hunter Garey; "let's take a safer plan. Redhead's right. Thar's Injuns in them bushes, whether he seen it or not; that skunk warn't by himself, I reckin; try this a way!"

The young trapper dismounted, and turned his horse broadside to the bushes. Keeping on the outside, he commenced walking the animal in a spiral ring that gradually closed in upon the clump. In this way his body was screened; and his head only could be seen above the pommel of his saddle, over which he rested his rifle, cocked and ready.

Several others, observing this movement on the part of Garey, dismounted, and followed his example.

A deep silence prevailed as they narrowed the diameters of their circling courses.

In a short time they were close in to the motte, yet still no arrow whizzed out. Was there no one there? So it seemed; and the men pushed fearlessly into the thicket.

I watched all this with excited feelings. I began to hope there was no one in the bushes. I listened to every sound; I heard the snapping of the twigs and the muttering of the men. There was a moment's silence as they pushed eagerly forward.

Then I heard a sudden exclamation, and a voice calling out—

"Dead red-skin! Hurrah for Barney!"

"Barney's bullet through him, by the holies!" cried another. "Hollo, old sky-blue! Come hyar and see what ye've done!"

The rest of the hunters, along with the *ci-devant* soldier, now rode forward to the copse. I moved slowly after. On coming up, I saw them dragging the body of an Indian into the open ground: a naked savage, like the other. He was dead, and they were preparing to scalp him.

"Come now, Barney!" cried one of the men in a joking manner, "the har's your'n. Why don't ye off wid it, man?"

"It's moine, dev yez say?" asked Barney, appealing to the speaker.

"Sartinly; you killed him. It's your'n by right."

"An' it is raaly worth fifty dollars?"

"Good as wheat for that."

"Would yez be so frindly, thin, as to cut it aff for me?"

"Oh! sartinly, wid all the plizyer of life," replied the hunter, imitating Barney's accent, at the same time severing the scalp, and handing it to him.

Barney took the hideous trophy, and I fancy that he did not feel very proud of it. Poor Celt! he may have been guilty of many a breach in the laws of garrison discipline, but it was evident that this was his first lesson in the letting of human blood.

The hunters now dismounted, and commenced trampling the thicket through and through. The search was most minute, for there was still a mystery. An extra bow—that is to say, a third—had been found, with its quiver of arrows. Where was the owner? Could he have escaped from the thicket while the men were engaged around the fallen buffaloes? He might, though it was barely probable; but the hunters knew that these savages run more like wild animals, like hares, than human beings, and he might have escaped to the chapparal.

"If that Injun has got clar," said Garey, "we've no time to lose in skinnin' them bufflers. Thar's plenty o' his tribe not twenty miles from hyar, I calc'late."

"Look down among the willows there!" cried the voice of the chief; "close down to the water."

There was a pool. It was turbid and trampled around the edges with buffalo tracks. On one side it was deep. Here willows dropped over and hung into the water. Several men pressed into this side, and commenced sounding the bottom with their lances and the butts of their rifles.

Old Rube had come up among the rest, and was drawing the stopper of his powder-horn with his teeth, apparently with the intention of reloading. His small dark eyes were scintillating every way at once: above, around him, and into the water.

A sudden thought seemed to enter his head. I saw him push back the plug, grasp the Irishman, who was nearest him, by the arm, and mutter, in a low and hurried voice, "Paddy! Barney! gi' us yur gun; quick, man, quick!"

Barney, at this earnest solicitation, immediately surrendered his piece, taking the empty rifle that was thrust into his hand by the trapper.

Rube eagerly grasped the musket, and stood for a moment as if he was about to fire at some object in the pond. Suddenly he jerked his body round, and, poising the gun upward, fired into the thick foliage.

A shrill scream followed; a heavy body came crashing through the branches, and struck the ground at my feet. Warm drops sparkled into my eyes, causing me to wince. It was blood! I was blinded with it; I rubbed my eyes to clear them. I heard men rushing from all parts of the thicket. When I could see again, a naked savage was just disappearing through the leaves.

"Missed him!" cried the trapper. "Away wi' yur sodger gun!" he added, flinging down the musket, and rushing after the savage with his drawn knife.

I followed among the rest. I heard several shots as we scrambled through the brushwood.

When I had got to the outer edge I could see the Indian still on his feet, and running with the speed of an antelope. He did not keep in a direct line, but zigzag, leaping from side to side, in order to baffle the aim of his pursuers, whose rifles were all the time ringing behind him. As yet none of their bullets had taken effect, at least so as to cripple him. There was a streak of blood visible on his brown body, but the wound, wherever it was did not seem to hinder him in his flight.

I thought there could be no chance of his escape, and I had no intention of emptying my gun at such a mark. I remained, therefore, among the bushes, screening myself behind the leaves and watching the chase.

Some of the hunters continued to follow him on foot, while the more cunning ones rushed back for their horses. These happened to be all on the opposite side of the thicket, with one exception, and that was the mare of the trapper Rube. She was browsing where Rube had dismounted, out among the slaughtered buffaloes, and directly in the line of the chase.

As the savage approached her, a sudden thought seemed to strike him, and diverging slightly from his course, he plucked up the picket-pin, coiled the lasso with the dexterity of a gaucho, and sprang upon the animal's back.

It was a well-conceived idea, but unfortunate for the Indian. He had scarcely touched the saddle when a peculiar shout was heard above all other sounds. It was a call uttered in the voice of the earless trapper. The mustang recognised it; and instead of running forward, obedient to the guidance of her rider, she wheeled suddenly and came galloping back. At this moment a shot fired at the savage scorched her hip, and, setting back her ears, she commenced squealing and kicking so violently that all her feet seemed to be in the air at the same time.

The Indian now endeavoured to fling himself from the saddle; but the alternate plunging of the fore and hind quarters kept him for some moments tossing in a sort of balance. He was at length pitched outward, and fell to the ground upon his back. Before he could recover himself a Mexican had ridden up, and with his long lance pinned him to the earth.

A scene followed in which Rube played the principal character; in fact, had "the stage to himself."

"Sodger guns" were sent to perdition; and as the old trapper was angry about the wound which his mare had received, "crook-eyed greenhorns" came in for a share of his anathemas. The mustang, however, had sustained no serious damage; and after this was ascertained, the emphatic ebullitions of her master's anger subsided into a low growling, and then ceased altogether.

As there appeared no sign that there were other savages in the neighbourhood, the next concern of the hunters was to satisfy their hunger. Fires were soon kindled, and a plenteous repast of buffalo meat produced the desired effect.

After the meal was ended, a consultation was held. It was agreed that we should move forward to the old mission, which was known to be not over ten miles distant. We could there defend ourselves in case of an attack from the tribe of Coyoteros, to which the three savages belonged. It was feared by all that these might strike our trail, and come up with us before we could take our departure from the ruin.

The buffaloes were speedily skinned and packed, and taking a westerly course, we journeyed on to the mission.

Chapter Thirty Three.

A Bitter Trap.

We reached the ruin a little after sunset. We frightened the owl and the wolf, and made our bivouac among the crumbling walls. Our horses were picketed upon the deserted lawns, and in the long-neglected orchards, where the ripe fruit was raining down its ungathered showers. Fires were kindled, lighting the grey pile with their cheerful blazing; and joints of meat were taken out of the hide-packs and roasted for supper.

There was water in abundance. A branch of the San Pedro swept past the walls of the mission. There were yams in the spoliated gardens; there were grapes, and pomegranates, and quinces, and melons, and pears, and peaches, and apples; and with all these was our repast garnished.

It was soon over, and videttes were thrown out on the tracks that led to the ruin. The men were weak and weary with their late fasting, and in a short while stretched themselves by their saddles and slept.

So much for our first night at the mission of San Pedro.

We were to remain for three days, or until the buffalo meat should be dried for packing.

They were irksome days to me. Idleness displayed the bad qualities of my half-savage associates. The ribald jest and fearful oath rang continually in my ears, until I was fain to wander off to the woods with the old botanist, who, during these three days, revelled in the happy excitement of discovery.

I found companionship also in the Maricopa. This strange man had studied science deeply, and was conversant with almost every noted author. He was reserved only when I wished him to talk of himself.

Seguin during these days was taciturn and lonely. He took but little heed of what was going on around him. He seemed to be suffering from impatience, as every now and then he paid a visit to the tasajo. He passed many hours upon the adjacent heights, looking anxiously towards the east: that point whence our spies would come in from the Pinon.

There was an azotea on the ruin. I was in the habit of seeking this place at evening after the sun had grown less fervid. It afforded a fine prospect of the valley; but its chief attraction to me lay in the retirement I could there obtain. The hunters rarely climbed up to it, and their wild and licenced converse was unheard for the time. I used to spread my blanket among the crumbling parapets, and stretched upon it, deliver myself up to the sweet retrospect, or to still sweeter dreams that my fancy outlined upon the future. There was one object on my memory: upon that object only did my hopes dwell.

I need not make this declaration; at least to those who have truly loved.

In the programme placed before me by Seguin, I had not bargained for such wanton cruelties as I was now compelled to witness. It was not the time to look back, but forward, and perhaps, over other scenes of blood and brutality, to that happier hour, when I should have redeemed my promise, and won the prize, beautiful Zoe.

My reverie was interrupted. I heard voices and footsteps; they were approaching the spot where I lay. I could see that there were two men engaged in an earnest conversation. They did not notice me, as I was behind some fragments of the broken parapet, and in the shadow. As they drew nearer, I recognised the patois of my Canadian follower, and that of his companion was not to be mistaken. The brogue was Barney's, beyond a doubt.

These worthies, I had lately noticed, had become "as thick as two thieves," and were much in each other's company. Some act of kindness had endeared the "infantry" to his more astute and experienced associate, who had taken him under his patronage and protection.

I was vexed at the intrusion; but prompted by some impulse of curiosity, I lay still and listened.

Barney was speaking as they approached.

"In trath, Misther Gowdey, an' it's meself 'ud go far this blissed night for a dhrap o' the crayter. I noticed the little kig afore; but divil resave me av I thought it was anythin' barrin' cowld water. Vistment! only think o' the owld Dutch sinner bringin' a whole kig wid 'im, an' keepin' it all to himself. Yez are sure now it's the stuff?"

"Oui! oui! C'est liqueur! aguardiente."

"Agwardenty, ye say, div ye?"

"Oui! c'est vrai, Monsieur Barney. I have him smell, ver many time. It is of stink très fort: strong! good!"

"But why cudn't ye stale it yerself? Yez know exactly where the doctor keeps it, an' ye might get at it a hape handier than I can."

"Pourquoi, Barney? pecause, mon ami, I help pack les possibles of Monsieur le docteur. Pardieu! he would me suspect."

"I don't see the raison clear. He may suspect ye at all evints. How thin?"

"Ah! then, n'importe. I sall make von grand swear. No! I sall have ver clear conscience then."

"Be the powers! we must get the licker anyhow; av you won't, Misther Gowdey, I will; that's said, isn't it?"

"Oui! Très bien!"

"Well, thin, now or niver's the time. The ould fellow's just walked out, for I saw him meself. This is a nate place to drink it in. Come an' show me where he keeps it; and, by Saint Patrick! I'm yer man to hook it."

"Très bien! allons! Monsieur Barney, allons!"

Unintelligible as this conversation may appear, I understood every word of it. The naturalist had brought among his packs a small keg of aguardiente, mezcal spirits, for the purpose of preserving any new species of the lizard or snake tribe he should chance to fall in with. What I heard, then, was neither more or less than a plot to steal the keg and its contents!

My first impulse was to leap up and stop them in their design, as well as administer a salutary rebuke to my voyageur and his red-haired companion; but a moment's reflection convinced me that they could be better punished in another way. I would leave them to punish themselves.

I remembered that some days previous to our reaching the Ojo de Vaca, the doctor had captured a snake of the adder kind, two or three species of lizards, and a hideous-looking animal, called, in hunter phraseology, the horned frog: the *agama cornuta* of Texas and Mexico. These he had immersed in the spirit for preservation. I had observed him do so, and it was evident that neither my Frenchman nor the Irishman had any idea of this. I adopted the resolution, therefore, to let them drink a full bumper of the "pickle" before I should interfere.

Knowing that they would soon return, I remained where I was.

I had not long to wait upon them. In a few minutes they came up, Barney carrying what I knew to be the devoted keg.

They sat down close to where I lay, and prising out the bung, filled the liquor into their tin cups, and commenced imbibing.

A drouthier pair of mortals could not have been found anywhere; and at the first draught, each emptied his cup to the bottom!

"It has a quare taste, hasn't it?" said Barney, after he had taken the vessel from his lips.

"Oui! c'est vrai, monsieur!"

"What dev ye think it is?"

"Je ne sais quoi. It smells like one—one—"

"Is it fish, ye mane?"

"Oui! like one feesh: un bouquet très bizarre Fichtro!"

"I suppose it's something that the Mexicans have drapped in to give the agwardenty a flayver. It's mighty strong anyhow. It's nothing the worse av that; but it 'ud be sorry drinkin' alongside a nate dimmyjan of Irish patyeen. Och! mother av Moses! but that's the raal bayvaridge!"

Here the Irishman shook his head to express with more emphasis his admiration of the native whisky.

"Well, Misther Gowdey," continued he, "whisky's whisky at any rate; and if we can't get the butther, it's no raison we should refuse the brid; so I'll thank ye for another small thrifle out of the kig," and the speaker held out his tin vessel to be replenished.

Gode lifted the keg, and emptied more of its contents into their cups.

"Mon Dieu! what is dis in my cops?" exclaimed he, after a draught.

"Fwhat is it? Let me see. That! Be me sowl! that's a quare-looking crayter anyhow."

"Sac–r–r–ré! it is von Texan! von fr–r–og! Dat is de feesh we smell stink. Owah—ah—ah!"

"Oh! holy mother! if here isn't another in moine! By jabers! it's a scorpion lizard! Hoach—wach—wach!"

"Ow—ah—ah—ack—ack! Mon Dieu! Oach—ach—! Sac-r! O—ach—ach—o—oa—a—ach!"

"Tare-an-ages! He—ach! the owld doctor has—oach—ack—ack! Blessed Vargin! Ha—he—hoh—ack! Poison! poison!"

And the brace of revellers went staggering over the azotea, delivering their stomachs, and ejaculating in extreme terror as the thought struck them that there might be poison in the pickle.

I had risen to my feet, and was enjoying the joke in loud laughter. This and the exclamations of the men brought a crowd of hunters up to the roof, who, as soon as they perceived what had happened, joined in, and made the ruin ring with their wild peals.

The doctor, who had come up among the rest, was not so well satisfied with the occurrence. After a short search, however, the lizards were found and returned to the keg, which still contained enough of the spirit for his purposes. It was not likely to be disturbed again, even by the thirstiest hunter in the band.

Chapter Thirty Four.

The Phantom City.

On the morning of the fourth day our spies came in, and reported that the Navajoes had taken the southern trail.

They had returned to the spring on the second day after our leaving it, and thence had followed the guiding of the arrows. It was Dacoma's band, in all about three hundred warriors.

Nothing remained for us now but to pack up as quickly as possible, and pursue our march to the north.

In an hour we were in our saddles, and following the rocky banks of the San Pedro.

A long day's journey brought us to the desolate valley of the Gila, upon whose waters we encamped for the night. We slept near the celebrated ruins, the second resting-place of the migrating Aztecs.

With the exception of the botanist, the Coco chief, myself, and perhaps Seguin, no one in the band seemed to trouble himself about these interesting antiquities. The sign of grizzly bears, that was discovered upon the mud bottom, gave the hunters far more concern than the broken pottery and its painted hieroglyphics. Two of these animals were discovered near the camp, and a fierce battle ensued, in which one of the Mexicans nearly lost his life, escaping only after most of the skin had been clawed from his head and neck. The bears themselves were killed, and made part of our suppers.

Our next day's march lay up the Gila, to the mouth of the San Carlos river, where we again halted for the night. The San Carlos runs in from the north; and Seguin had resolved to travel up this stream for a hundred miles or so, and afterwards strike eastward to the country of the Navajoes.

When this determination was made known, a spirit of discontent showed itself among the men, and mutinous whisperings were heard on all sides.

Shortly after we halted, however, several of them strayed up the banks of the stream, and gathered some grains of gold out of its bed. Indications of the precious metal, the quixa, known among the Mexicans as the "gold mother," were also found among the rocks. There were miners in the band, who knew it well, and this served to satisfy them. There was no more talk of keeping on to the Prieto. Perhaps the San Carlos might prove equally rich. Rumour had also given it the title of a "golden river"; at all events, the expedition must cross the head waters of the Prieto in its journey eastward; and this prospect had the effect of quieting the mutineers, at least for the time.

There was another influence: the character of Seguin. There was no single individual in the band who cared to cross him on slight grounds. They knew him too well for that; and though few of these men set high value on their lives, when they believe themselves, according to "mountain law," in the right, yet they knew that to delay the expedition for the purpose of gathering gold was neither according to their compact with him nor agreeable to his wishes. Not a few of the band, moreover, were actuated by motives similar to those felt by Seguin himself, and these were equally desirous of pushing on to the Navajo towns.

Still another consideration had its influence upon the majority. The party of Dacoma would be on our track as soon as they had returned from the Apache trail. We had, therefore, no time to waste in gold-hunting, and the simplest of the scalp-hunters knew this.

By daybreak we were again on the march, and riding up the banks of the San Carlos.

We had now entered the great desert which stretches northward from the Gila away to the head waters of the Colorado. We entered it without a guide, for not one of the band had ever traversed these unknown regions. Even Rube knew nothing about this part of the country. We were without compass, too, but this we heeded not. There were few in the band who could not point to the north or the south within the variation of a degree: few of them but could, night or day, tell by the heavens within ten minutes of the true time. Give them but a clear sky, with the signs of the trees and rocks, and they needed neither compass nor chronometer. A life spent beneath the blue heavens of the prairie uplands and the mountain parks, where a roof rarely obstructed their view of the azure vaults, had made astronomers of these reckless rovers.

Of such accomplishments was their education, drawn from many a perilous experience. To me their knowledge of such things seemed instinct.

But we had a guide as to our direction, unerring as the magnetic needle: we were traversing the region of the "polar plant," the planes of whose leaves, at almost every step, pointed out our meridian. It grew upon our track, and was crushed under the hoofs of our horses as we rode onward.

We travelled northward through a country of strange-looking mountains, whose tops shot heavenward in fantastic forms and groupings. At one time we saw semi-globular shapes like the domes of churches; at another, Gothic turrets rose before us; and the next opening brought in view sharp needle-pointed peaks, shooting upward into the blue sky. We saw columnar forms supporting others that lay horizontally: vast boulders of trap-rock, suggesting the idea of some antediluvian ruin, some temple of gigantic Druids!

Along with singularity of formation was the most brilliant colouring. There were stratified rocks, red, white, green, and yellow, as vivid in their hues as if freshly touched from the palette of the painter.

No smoke had tarnished them since they had been flung up from their subterranean beds. No cloud draped their naked outlines. It was not a land of clouds, for as we journeyed amongst them we saw not a speck in the heavens; nothing above us but the blue and limitless ether.

I remembered the remarks of Seguin.

There was something inspiriting in the sight of these bright mountains; something life-like, that prevented us from feeling the extreme and real desolation by which we were surrounded. At times we could not help fancying that we were in a thickly-populated country—a country of vast wealth and civilisation, as appeared from its architectural grandeur. Yet in reality we were journeying through the wildest of earth's dominions, where no human foot ever trod excepting such as wear the moccasin; the region of the "wolf" Apache and the wretched Yamparico.

We travelled up the banks of the river, and here and there, at our halting-places, searching for the shining metal. It could be found only in small quantities, and the hunters began to talk loudly of the Prieto. There, according to them, the yellow gold lay in lumps.

On the fourth day after leaving the Gila, we came to a place where the San Carlos cañoned through a high sierra. Here we halted for the night. When morning came, we found we could follow the river no farther without climbing over the mountain; and Seguin announced his intention of leaving it and striking eastward. The hunters responded to this declaration with a joyous hurrah. The golden vision was again before them.

We remained at the San Carlos until after the noon heat, recruiting our horses by the stream; then mounting, we rode forward into the plain. It was our intention to travel all night, or until we reached water, as we knew that without this, halting would be useless.

We had not ridden far until we saw that a fearful Jornada was before us—one of those dreaded stretches without grass, wood, or water. Ahead of us we could see a low range of mountains, trending from north to south, and beyond these, another range still higher than the first. On the farther range there were snowy summits. We saw that they were distinct chains, and that the more distant was of great elevation. This we knew from the appearance upon its peaks of the eternal snow.

We knew, moreover, that at the foot of the snowy range we should find water, perhaps the river we were in search of; but the distance was immense. If we did not find it at the nearer sierra, we should have an adventure: the danger of perishing from thirst. Such was the prospect.

We rode on over the arid soil; over plains of lava and cut-rock that wounded the hoofs of our horses, laming many. There was no vegetation around us except the sickly green of the artemisia, or the fetid foliage of the creosote plant. There was no living thing to be seen save the brown and hideous lizard, the rattlesnake, and the desert crickets that crawled in myriads along the parched ground, and were crunched under the hoofs of our animals. "Water!" was the word that began to be uttered in several languages.

"Water!" cried the choking trapper.

"L'eau!" ejaculated the Canadian.

"Agua! agua!" shouted the Mexican.

We were not twenty miles from the San Carlos before our gourd canteens were as dry as a shingle. The dust of the plains and the hot atmosphere had created unusual thirst, and we had soon emptied them.

We had started late in the afternoon. At sundown the mountains ahead of us did not seem a single mile nearer. We travelled all night, and when the sun rose again we were still a good distance from them. Such is the illusory character of this elevated and crystal atmosphere.

The men mumbled as they talked. They held in their mouths leaden bullets and pebbles of obsidian, which they chewed with a desperate fierceness.

It was some time after sunrise when we arrived at the mountain foot. To our consternation no water could be found!

The mountains were a range of dry rocks, so parched-like and barren that even the creosote bush could not find nourishment along their sides. They were as naked of vegetation as when the volcanic fires first heaved them into the light.

Parties scattered in all directions, and went up the ravines; but after a long while spent in fruitless wandering, we abandoned the search in despair.

There was a pass that appeared to lead through the range; and entering this, we rode forward in silence and with gloomy thoughts.

We soon debouched on the other side, when a scene of singular character burst upon our view.

A plain lay before us, hemmed in on all sides by high mountains. On its farther edge was the snowy ridge, with stupendous cliffs rising vertically from the plain, towering thousands of feet in height. Dark rocks seemed piled upon each other, higher and higher, until they became buried under robes of the spotless snow.

But that which appeared most singular was the surface of the plain. It was covered with a mantle of virgin whiteness, apparently of snow; and yet the more elevated spot from which we viewed it was naked, with a hot sun shining upon it. What we saw in the valley, then, could not be snow.

As I gazed over the monotonous surface of this plain, and then looked upon the chaotic mountains that walled it in, my mind became impressed with ideas of coldness and desolation. It seemed as if everything was dead around us, and Nature was laid out in her winding-sheet. I saw that my companions experienced similar feelings, but no one spoke; and we commenced riding down the pass that led into this singular valley.

As far as we could see, there was no prospect of water on the plain; but what else could we do than cross it? On its most distant border, along the base of the snowy mountains, we thought we could distinguish a black line, like that of timber, and for this point we directed our march.

On reaching the plain, what had appeared like snow proved to be soda. A deep incrustation of this lay upon the ground, enough to satisfy the wants of the whole human race; yet there it lay, and no hand had ever stooped to gather it.

Three or four rocky buttes were in our way, near the debouchure of the pass. As we rounded them, getting farther out into the plain, a wide gap began to unfold itself, opening through the mountains beyond. Through this gap the sun's rays were streaming in, throwing a band of yellow light across one end of the valley. In this the crystals of the soda, stirred up by the breeze, appeared floating in myriads.

As we descended, I observed that objects began to assume a very different aspect from what they had exhibited from above. As if by enchantment, the cold snowy surface all at once disappeared. Green fields lay before us, and tall trees sprang up, covered with a thick and verdant frondage!

"Cotton-woods!" cried a hunter, as his eye rested on these still distant groves.

"Tall saplins at that—wagh!" ejaculated another.

"Water thar, fellers, I reckin!" remarked a third.

"Yes, siree! Yer don't see such sprouts as them growin' out o' a dry paraira. Look! Hollo!"

"By gollies, yonder's a house!"

"A house? One, two, three! A house? Thar's a whole town, if thar's a single shanty. Gee! Jim, look yonder! Wagh!"

I was riding in front with Seguin, the rest of the band strung out behind us. I had been for some time gazing upon the ground, in a sort of abstraction, looking: at the snow-white efflorescence, and listening to the crunching of my horse's hoofs through its icy incrustation. These exclamatory phrases caused me to raise my eyes. The sight that met them was one that made me rein up with a sudden jerk. Seguin had done the same, and I saw that the whole band had halted with a similar impulse.

We had just cleared one of the buttes that had hitherto obstructed our view of the great gap. This was now directly in front of us; and along its base, on the southern side, rose the walls and battlements of a city—a vast city, judging from its distance and the colossal appearance of its architecture. We could trace the columns of temples, and doors, and gates, and windows, and balconies, and parapets, and spires. There were many towers rising high over the roofs, and in the middle was a temple-like structure, with its massive dome towering far above all the others.

I looked upon this sudden apparition with a feeling of incredulity. It was a dream, an imagination, a mirage. Ha! it was the mirage!

No! The mirage could not effect such a complete picture. There were the roofs, and chimneys, and walls, and windows. There were the parapets of fortified houses, with their regular notches and embrasures. It was a reality. It was a city!

Was it the Cibolo of the Spanish padre? Was it that city of golden gates and burnished towers? After all, was the story of the wandering priest true? Who had proved it a fable? Who had ever penetrated this region, the very country in which the ecclesiastic represented the golden city of Cibolo to exist?

I saw that Seguin was puzzled, dismayed, as well as myself. He knew nothing of this land. He had never witnessed a mirage like that.

For some time we sat in our saddles, influenced by strange emotions. Shall we go forward? Yes! We must reach water. We are dying of thirst; and, impelled by this, we spur onward.

We had ridden only a few paces farther when the hunters uttered a sudden and simultaneous cry. A new object—an object of terror—was before us. Along the mountain foot appeared a string of dark forms. They were mounted men!

We dragged our horses to their haunches, our whole line halting as one man.

"Injuns!" was the exclamation of several.

"Indians they must be," muttered Seguin. "There are no others here. Indians! No! There never were such as them. See! they are not men! Look! their huge horses, their long guns; they are giants! By Heaven!" continued he, after a moment's pause, "they are bodiless! They are phantoms!"

There were exclamations of terror from the hunters behind.

Were these the inhabitants of the city? There was a striking proportion in the colossal size of the horses and the horsemen.

For a moment I was awe-struck like the rest. Only a moment. A sudden memory flashed upon me. I thought of the Hartz Mountains and their demons. I knew that the phenomenon before us could be no other; an optical delusion; a creation of the mirage.

I raised my hand above my head. The foremost of the giants imitated the motion.

I put spurs to my horse and galloped forward. So did he, as if to meet me. After a few springs I had passed the refracting angle, and, like a thought, the shadowy giants vanished into the air.

The men had ridden forward after me, and having also passed the angle of refraction saw no more of the phantom host.

The city, too, had disappeared; but we could trace the outlines of many a singular formation in the trap-rock strata that traversed the edge of the valley.

The tall groves were no longer to be seen; but a low belt of green willows, real willows, could be distinguished along the foot of the mountain within the gap. Under their foliage there was something that sparkled in the sun like sheets of silver. It was water! It was a branch of the Prieto.

Our horses neighed at the sight; and, shortly after, we had alighted upon its banks, and were kneeling before the sweet spirit of the stream.

Chapter Thirty Five.

The Mountain of Gold.

After so fatiguing a march, it was necessary to make a longer halt than usual. We stayed by the arroyo all that day and the following night. But the hunters longed to drink from the Prieto itself; and the next morning we drew our pickets, and rode in the direction of that river. By noon we were upon its banks.

A singular stream it was, running through a region of bleak, barren, and desolate mountains. Through these the stream had forged its way by numerous cañons, and rushed along a channel at most places inaccessible. It was a black and gloomy river. Where were its sands of gold?

After riding for some distance along its banks, we halted at a point where its bed could be reached. The hunters, disregarding all else, clambered eagerly over the steep bluffs, and descended to the water. They hardly stayed to drink. They crawled through narrow interstices, between detached masses of rock that had fallen from above. They lifted the mud in their hands, and washed it in their cups; they hammered the quartz rock with their tomahawks, and pounded it between great stones. Not a particle of the precious metal could be found. They must either have struck the river too high up, or else the El Dorado lay still farther to the north.

Wet, weary, angry, uttering oaths and expressions of disappointment, they obeyed the signal to march forward.

We rode up the stream, halting for the night at another place where the water was accessible to our animals.

Here the hunters again searched for gold, and again found it not. Mutinous murmurs were now spoken aloud. "The gold country lay below them; they had no doubt of it. The chief took them by the San Carlos on purpose to disappoint them. He knew this would prevent delay. He cared not for them. His own ends were all he wanted to accomplish. They might go back as poor as they had come, for aught he cared. They would never have so good a chance again."

Such were their mutterings, embellished with many an oath.

Seguin either heard not or did not heed them. He was one of those characters who can patiently bear until a proper cue for action may offer itself. He was fiery by nature, like all Creoles; but time and trials had tempered him to that calmness and coolness that befitted the leader of such a band. When roused to action, he became what is styled in western phraseology a "dangerous man"; and the scalp-hunters knew it. He heeded not their murmurings.

Long before daybreak, we were once more in our saddles, and moving onward, still up the Prieto. We had observed fires at a distance during the night, and we knew that they were at the villages of the "Club" Apache. We wished to pass their country without being seen; and it was our intention, when daylight appeared, to "cacher" among the rocks until the following night.

As dawn advanced, we halted in a concealed ravine, whilst several of us climbed the hill to reconnoitre. We could see the smoke rising over the distant villages; but we had passed them in the darkness, and instead of remaining in caché, we continued on through a wide plain covered with sage and cactus plants. Mountains towered up on every side of us as we advanced. They rose directly from the plains, exhibiting the fantastic shapes which characterise them in those regions. Their stupendous precipices overlooked the bleak, barren tables frowning upon them in sublime silence. The plains themselves ran into the very bases of these, cliffs. Water had surely washed them. These plateaux had once been the bed of an ancient ocean. I remembered Seguin's theory of the inland seas.

Shortly after sunrise, the trail we were following led us to an Indian crossing. Here we forded the stream with the intention of leaving it and heading eastward.

We halted our horses in the water, permitting them to drink freely. Some of the hunters, moving ahead of the rest, had climbed the high banks. We were attracted by their unusual exclamations. On looking upward, we perceived several of them standing on the top of a hill, and pointing to the north in an earnest and excited manner. Could it be Indians?

"What is it?" shouted Seguin, as we pushed forward.

"A gold mountain! a gold mountain!" was the reply.

We spurred our horses hurriedly up the hill. On reaching its top, a strange sight met our gaze. Away to the north, and as far as the eye could see, an object glistened in the sun. It was a mountain, and along its sides, from base to summit, the rocks glittered with the bright semblance of gold! A thousand jets danced in the sunbeams, dazzling the eye as it looked upon them. Was it a mountain of gold?

The men were in a frenzy of delight. This was the mountain so often discussed over the bivouac fires. Who of them had not heard of it, whether credulous or not? It was no fable, then. There it was before them, in all its burning splendour.

I turned to look at Seguin. His brow was bent. There was the expression of anxiety on his countenance. He understood the illusion; so did the Maricopa; so did Reichter. I knew it too. At a glance I had recognised the sparkling scales of the selenite.

Seguin saw that there was a difficulty before us. This dazzling hallucination lay far out of our course; but it was evident that neither commands nor persuasion would be heeded now. The men were resolved upon reaching it. Some of them had already turned their horses' heads and were moving in that direction.

Seguin ordered them back. A stormy altercation ensued; in short, a mutiny.

In vain Seguin urged the necessity of our hastening forward to the town. In vain he represented the danger we were in of being overtaken by Dacoma's party, who by this time were upon our trail. In vain the Coco chief, the doctor, and myself, assured our uneducated companions that what they saw was but the glancing surface of a worthless rock. The men were obstinate. The sight, operating upon long-cherished hopes, had intoxicated them. They had lost all reason. They were mad.

"On, then!" cried Seguin, making a desperate effort to restrain his passion. "On, madmen, and satisfy yourselves—our lives may answer for your folly!" and, so saying, he turned his horse, and headed him for the shining beacon.

The men rode after, uttering loud and joyful acclamations.

At the end of a long day's ride we reached the base of the mountain. The hunters leaped from their horses, and clambered up to the glittering rocks. They reached them. They broke them with their tomahawks and pistol-butts, and cleft them with their knives. They tore off the plates of mica and glassy selenite. They flung them at their feet, abashed and mortified; and, one after another, came back to the plain with looks of disappointment and chagrin. Not one of them said a word, as they climbed into their saddles, and rode sullenly after the chief.

We had lost a day by this bootless journey; but our consolation lay in the belief that our Indian pursuers, following upon our trail, would make the same détour.

Our course now lay to the south-west; but finding a spring not far from the foot of the mountain, we remained by it for the night.

After another day's march in a south-easterly course, Rube recognised the profiles of the mountains. We were nearing the great town of the Navajoes.

That night we encamped on a running water, a branch of the Prieto that headed to the eastward. A vast chasm between two cliffs marked the course of the stream above us. The guide pointed into the gap, as we rode forward to our halting-place.

"What is it, Rube?" inquired Seguin.

"'Ee see that gully ahead o' us?"

"Yes; what of it?"

"The town's thur."

Chapter Thirty Six.

Navajoa.

It was near evening of the next day when we arrived at the foot of the sierra, at the debouchure of the cañon. We could not follow the stream any farther, as there was no path by the channel. It would be necessary to pass over the ridge that formed the southern jaw of the chasm. There was a plain trail among scrubby pines; and, following our guide, we commenced riding up the mountain.

After ascending for an hour or so, by a fearful road along the very brink of the precipice, we climbed the crest of the ridge, and looked eastward. We had reached the goal of our journey. The town of the Navajoes was before us.

"Voilà!"

"Mira el pueblo!"

"Thar's the town!"

"Hurrah!" were the exclamations that broke from the hunters.

"Oh, God! at last it is!" muttered Seguin, with a singular expression of countenance. "Oh, God be praised! Halt, comrades! halt!"

Our reins were tightened, and we sat on our weary horses looking over the plain. A magnificent panorama, magnificent under any circumstances, lay before us; but its interest was heightened by the peculiar circumstances under which we viewed it.

We are at the western extremity of an oblong valley, looking up it lengthwise. It is not a valley, though so called in the language of Spanish America, but a plain walled in on all sides by mountains. It is elliptical in form, the diameter of its foci being ten or twelve miles in length. Its shortest diameter is five or six miles. It has the surface of a green meadow, and its perfect level is unbroken by brake, bush, or hillock. It looks like some quiet lake transformed into an emerald.

It is bisected by a line of silvery brightness that curves gracefully through its whole extent, marking the windings of a crystal stream.

But the mountains! What wild-looking mountains, particularly those on the north side of the valley! They are granite upheaved. Nature must have warred at the birth of these; the very sight of them suggests the throes of a troubled planet. Huge rocks hang over, only half resting upon fearful precipices; vast boulders that seem as though the touch of a feather would cause them to topple down. Grim chasms open into deep, dark defiles, that lie silent, and solemn, and frowning. Here and there, stunted trees, the cedar and pinon, hang horizontally out, clinging along the cliffs. The unsightly limbs of the cactus, and the gloomy foliage of the creosote bush, grow together in seams of the rocks, heightening their character of ruggedness and gloom. Such is the southern barrier of the valley.

Look upon the northern sierra! Here is a contrast, a new geology. Not a rock of granite meets the eye; but there are others piled as high, and glistening with the whiteness of snow. These are mountains of the milky quartz. They exhibit a variety of peaks, naked and shining; crags that hang over deep, treeless ravines, and needle-shaped summits aspiring to the sky. They too have their vegetation, a vegetation that suggests ideas of the desert and desolation.

The two sierras appear to converge at the eastern end of the valley. We are upon a transverse ridge that shuts it in upon the west, and from this point we view the picture.

Where the valley ends eastwardly, we perceive a dark background lying up against the mountains. We know it is a pine-forest, but we are at too great a distance to distinguish the trees. Out of this forest the stream appears to issue; and upon its banks, near the border of the woods, we perceive a collection of strange pyramidal structures. They are houses. It is the town of Navajoa! Our eyes were directed upon it with eager gaze. We could trace the outlines of the houses, though they stood nearly ten miles distant. They suggested images of a strange architecture. There were some standing apart from the rest, with terraced roofs, and we could see there were banners waving over them. One, larger than the rest, presented the appearance of a temple. It was out on the open plain, and by the glass we could detect numerous forms clustered upon its top—the forms of human beings. There were others upon the roofs and parapets of the smaller houses; and many more moving upon the plain nearer us, driving before them flocks of animals, mules, and mustangs. Some were down upon the banks of the river, and others we could see plunging about in the water.

Several droves of horses, whose mottled flanks showed their breed, were quietly browsing on the open prairie. Flocks of wild swans, geese, and gruyas winged their way up and down the meandering current of the stream.

The sun was setting. The mountains were tinged with an amber-coloured light; and the quartzose crystals sparkled on the peaks of the southern sierra.

It was a scene of silent beauty. How long, thought I, ere its silence would be broken by the sounds of ravage and ruin!

We remained for some time gazing up the valley, without anyone uttering his thoughts. It was the silence that precedes resolve. In the minds of my companions there were varied emotions at play, varied in kind as they differed in intensity.

Some were holy. Men sat straining their eyes over the long reach of meadow, thinking, or fancying, that in the distance they might distinguish a loved object—a wife, a sister, a daughter, or perhaps the object of a still dearer and deeper affection. No; the last could not be. None could have been more deeply affected than he who was seeking for his child. A father's love was the strongest passion there.

Alas! there were other emotions in the bosoms of those around me, passions dark and sinful. Fierce looks were bent upon the town. Some of these betokened fierce feelings of revenge; others indicated the desire of plunder; and others still spoke, fiend-like, of murder! There had been mutterings of this from day to day as we journeyed. Men disappointed in their golden dreams had been heard to talk about the price of scalps!

By a command from Seguin the hunters drew back among the trees, and entered into a hurried council. How was the town to be taken? We could not approach it in the open light. The inhabitants would see us before we could ride up, and make their escape to the forest beyond. This would defeat the whole purpose of our expedition.

Could not a party get round to the eastern end of the valley and prevent this? Not through the plain itself, for the mountains rested upon its surface, without either foothills or paths along their sides. In some places vast cliffs rose to the height of a thousand feet, stepping directly upon the level plain. This idea was given up.

Could we not turn the southern sierra, and come in through the forest itself? This would bring us close to the houses under cover. The guide was questioned, and answered in the affirmative. But that could only be accomplished by making a détour of nearly fifty miles. We had no time for such a journey, and the thought was abandoned.

The town, then, must be approached in the night. This was the only plan practicable; at least, the most likely to succeed. It was adopted.

It was not Seguin's intention to make a night attack, but only to surround the buildings, keeping at some distance out, and remain in ambush till the morning. All retreat would thus be cut off, and we should make sure of taking our captives under the light of day.

The men threw themselves to the ground, and, holding their bridles, waited the going down of the sun.

Chapter Thirty Seven.

The Night Ambuscade.

A short hour passes. The bright orb sinks behind us, and the quartz rock saddens into a sombre hue. The straggling rays of twilight hover but a moment over the chalky cliffs, and then vanish away. It is night.

Descending the hills in a long string, we arrive upon the plain. We turn to the left, and keep round the mountain foot. The rocks guide us.

We proceed with caution, and exchange our words only in whispers. We crawl around and among loose boulders that have fallen from above. We turn many spurs that shoot out into the plain. Occasionally we halt and hold council.

After a journey of ten or twelve miles, we find ourselves opposite the Indian town. We are not over a mile from it. We can see the fires burning on the plain, and hear the voices of those who move around them.

At this point the band is divided. A small party remains making its caché in a defile among the rocks. These guard the captive chief and the antajo of mules. The rest move forward, guided by Rube, who carries them round the edge of the forest, here and there dropping a picket of several men as he proceeds.

These parties conceal themselves at their respective stations, remain silent, and wait for the signal from the bugle, which is to be given at the hour of daybreak.

The night passes slowly and silently. The fires one by one go out, until the plain is wrapt in the gloom of a moonless midnight. Dark clouds travel over the sky, portending rain: a rare phenomenon in these regions. The swan utters its wild note, the gruya whoops over the stream, and the wolf howls upon the skirts of the sleeping village. The voice of the bull-bat wails through the air. You hear the "flap, flap" of his long wings as he dashes down among the cocuyos. You hear the hoof-stroke on the hard plain, the "crop" of the browsing steed, and the tinkling of the bit-ring, for the horses eat bridled.

At intervals, a drowsy hunter mutters through his sleep, battling in dreams with some terrible foe. Thus goes the night. These are its voices.

They cease as daybreak approaches. The wolf howls no longer; the swan and the blue crane are silent; the night-hawk has filled his ravenous maw, and perches on the mountain pine; the fire-flies disappear, chased by the colder hours; and the horses, having eaten what grew within their reach, stand in lounging attitudes, asleep.

A grey light begins to steal into the valley. It flickers along the white cliffs of the quartz mountain. It brings with it a raw, cold air that awakens the hunters.

One by one they arouse themselves. They shiver as they stand up, and carry their blankets wrapped about their shoulders. They feel weary, and look pale and haggard. The grey dawn lends a ghastly hue to their dusty beards and unwashed faces.

After a short while they coil up their trail-ropes and fasten them to the rings. They look to their flints and priming, and tighten the buckles of their belts. They draw forth from their haversacks pieces of dry tasajo, eating it raw. They stand by their horses, ready to mount. It is not yet time.

The light is gathering into the valley. The blue mist that hung over the river during the night is rising upward. We can see the town. We can trace the odd outlines of the houses. What strange structures they are!

Some of them are higher than others: one, two, four stories in height. They are each in form like a pyramid without its apex. Each upper story is smaller than that below it, the roofs of the lower ones serving as terraces for those above. They are of a whitish yellow, the colour of the clay out of which they are built. They are without windows, but doors lead into each story from the outside; and ladders stretch from terrace to terrace, leaning against the walls. On the tops of some there are poles carrying bannerets. These are the residences of the principal war-chiefs and great warriors of the nation.

We can see the temple distinctly. It is like the houses in shape, but higher and of larger dimensions. There is a tall shaft rising out of its roof, and a banner with a strange device floating at its peak.

Near the houses we see corrals filled with mules and mustangs, the live-stock of the village.

The light grows stronger. Forms appear upon the roofs and move along the terraces. They are human forms enveloped in hanging garments, robe-like and striped. We recognise the Navajo blanket, with its alternate bands of black and white.

With the glass we can see these forms more distinctly; we can tell their sex.

Their hair hangs loosely upon their shoulders, and far down their backs. Most of them are females, girls and women. There are many children, too. There are men, white-haired and old. A few other men appear, but they are not warriors. The warriors are absent.

They come down the ladders, descending from terrace to terrace. They go out upon the plain, and rekindle the fires. Some carry earthen vessels, ollas, upon their heads, and pass down to the river. They go in for water. These are nearly naked. We can see their brown bodies and uncovered breasts. They are slaves.

See! the old men are climbing to the top of the temple. They are followed by women and children, some in white, others in bright-coloured costumes. These are girls and young lads, the children of the chiefs.

Over a hundred have climbed up. They have reached the highest root. There is an altar near the staff. A smoke rolls up—a blaze: they have kindled a fire upon the altar.

Listen! the chant of voices, and the beat of an Indian drum!

The sounds cease, and they all stand motionless and apparently silent, facing to the east.

"What does it mean?"

"They are waiting for the sun to appear. These people worship him."

The hunters, interested and curious, strain their eyes, watching the ceremony.

The topmost pinnacle of the quartz mountain is on fire. It is the first flash of the sun!

The peak is yellowing downward. Other points catch the brilliant beams. They have struck the faces of the devotees. See! there are white faces! One—two—many white faces, both of women and girls.

"Oh, God! grant that it may be!" cries Seguin, hurriedly putting up the glass, and raising the bugle to his lips.

A few wild notes peal over the valley. The horsemen hear the signal. They debouche from the woods and the defiles of the mountains. They gallop over the plain, deploying as they go.

In a few minutes we have formed the arc of a circle, concave to the town. Our horses' heads are turned inwards, and we ride forward, closing upon the walls.

We have left the atajo in the defile; the captive chief, too, guarded by a few of the men. The notes of the bugle have summoned the attention of the inhabitants. They stand for a while in amazement, and without motion. They behold the deploying of the line. They see the horsemen ride inward.

Could it be a mock surprise of some friendly tribe? No. That strange voice, the bugle, is new to Indian ears; yet some of them have heard it before. They know it to be the war-trumpet of the pale-faces!

For awhile their consternation hinders them from action. They stand looking on until we are near. Then they behold pale-faces, strange armour, and horses singularly caparisoned. It is the white enemy!

They run from point to point, from street to street. Those who carry water dash down their ollas, and rush screaming to the houses. They climb to the roofs, drawing the ladders after them. Shouts are exchanged, and exclamations uttered in the voices of men, women, and children. Terror is on every face; terror displays itself in every movement.

Meanwhile our line has approached, until we are within two hundred yards of the walls. We halt for a moment. Twenty men are left as an outer guard. The rest of us, thrown into a body, ride forward, following our leader.

Chapter Thirty Eight.

Adèle.

We direct ourselves to the great building, and, surrounding it, again halt. The old men are still upon the roof, standing along the parapet. They are frightened, and tremble like children.

"Do not fear; we are friends!" cried Seguin, speaking in a strange language, and making signs to them.

His voice is not heard amidst the shrieks and shouting that still continue.

The words are repeated, and the sign given in a more emphatic manner.

The old men crowd along the edge of the parapet. There is one among them who differs from the rest. His snow-white hair reaches below his waist. There are bright ornaments hanging from, his ears and over his breast. He is attired in white robes. He appears to be a chief; for the rest obey him. He makes a signal with his hands, and the screaming subsides. He stands forward on the parapet, as if to speak to us.

"Amigos, amigos!" (friends!) cries he, speaking in Spanish.

"Yes, yes; we are friends," replies Seguin, in the same language. "Do not fear us! We came not to harm you."

"Why harm us? We are at peace with the white pueblos to the east. We are the children of Montezuma; we are Navajoes. What want you with us?"

"We come for our relatives, your white captives. They are our wives and daughters."

"White captives! You mistake us. We have no captives. Those you seek are among the nations of the Apache, away far to the south."

"No; they are with you," replies Seguin. "I have certain information that they are here. Delay us not, then! We have come a far journey for them, and will not go without them."

The old man turns to his companions. They converse in a low voice, and exchange signs. Again he faces round to Seguin.

"Believe me, señor chief," says he, speaking with emphasis, "you have been wrongly informed. We have no white captives."

"Pish! 'Ee dod-rotted ole liar!" cries Rube, pushing out of the crowd, and raising his cat-skin cap as he speaks. "'Ee know this child, do 'ee?"

The skinless head is discovered to the gaze of the Indians. A murmur, indicative of alarm, is heard among them. The white-haired chief seems disconcerted. He knows the history of that scalp!

A murmur, too, runs through the ranks of the hunters. They had seen white faces as they rode up. The lie exasperates them, and the ominous click of rifles being cocked is heard on all sides.

"You have spoken falsely, old man," cries Seguin. "We know you have white captives. Bring them forth, then, if you would save your own lives!"

"Quick!" shouts Garey, raising his rifle in a threatening manner; "quick! or I'll dye the flax on yer old skull."

"Patience, amigo! you shall see our white people; but they are not captives. They are our daughters, the children of Montezuma."

The Indian descends to the third story of the temple. He enters a door, and presently returns, bringing with him five females dressed in the Navajo costume. They are women and girls, and, as anyone could tell at a glance, of the Hispano-Mexican race.

But there are those present who know them still better. Three of them are recognised by as many hunters, and recognise them in turn. The girls rush out to the parapet, stretch forth their arms, and utter exclamations of joy. The hunters call to them—

"Pepe!" "Rafaela!" "Jesusita!" coupling their names with expressions of endearment. They shout to them to come down, pointing to the ladders.

"Bajan, niñas, bajan! aprisa, aprisa!" (Come down, dear girls! quickly, quickly!)

The ladders rest upon the upper terraces. The girls cannot move them. Their late masters stand beside them, frowning and silent.

"Lay holt thar!" cries Garey, again threatening with his piece; "lay holt, and help the gals down, or I'll fetch some o' yerselves a-tumblin' over!"

"Lay holt! lay holt!" shouted several others in a breath.

The Indians place the ladders. The girls descend, and the next moment leap into the arms of their friends.

Two of them remain above; only three have come down. Seguin has dismounted, and passes these three with a glance. None of them is the object of his solicitude!

He rushes up the ladder, followed by several of the men. He springs from terrace to terrace, up to the third. He presses forward to the spot where stand the two captive girls. His looks are wild, and his manner that of one frantic. They shrink back at his approach, mistaking his intentions. They scream with terror!

He pierces them with his look. The instincts of the father are busy: they are baffled. One of the females is old, too old; the other is slave-like and coarse.

"Mon Dieu! it cannot be!" he exclaims, with a sigh. "There was a mark; but no, no, no! it cannot be!"

He leans forward, seizing the girl, though not ungently, by the wrist. Her sleeve is torn open, and the arm laid bare to the shoulder.

"No, no!" he again exclaims; "it is not there. It is not she."

He turns from them. He rushes forward to the old Indian, who falls back frightened at the glare of his fiery eye.

"These are not all!" cries he, in a voice of thunder; "there are others. Bring them forth, old man, or I will hurl you to the earth!"

"There are no other white squaws," replied the Indian, with a sullen and determined air.

"A lie! a lie! your life shall answer. Here! confront him, Rube!"

"'Ee dratted old skunk! That white har o' yourn ain't a-gwine to stay thur much longer ev you don't bring her out. Whur is she? the young queen?"

"Al sur," and the Indian points to the south.

"Oh! mon Dieu! mon Dieu!" cries Seguin, in his native tongue, and with an accentuation that expresses his complete wretchedness.

"Don't believe him, cap! I've seed a heap o' Injun in my time; an' a lyiner old varmint than this'n I never seed yet. Ye heerd him jest now 'bout the other gals?"

"Yes, true; he lied directly; but she—she might have gone—"

"Not a bit o' it. Lyin's his trade. He's thur great medicine, an' humbugs the hul kit o' them. The gal is what they call Mystery Queen. She knows a heap, an' helps ole whitey hyur in his tricks an' sacrifiches. He don't want to lose her. She's hyur somewhur, I'll be boun'; but she ur cached: that's sartin."

"Men!" cries Seguin, rushing forward to the parapet, "take ladders! Search every house! Bring all forth, old and young. Bring them to the open plain. Leave not a corner unsearched. Bring me my child!"

The hunters rush for the ladders. They seize those of the great building, and soon possess themselves of others. They run from house to house, and drag out the screaming inmates.

There are Indian men in some of the houses—lagging braves, boys, and "dandies." Some of these resist. They are slaughtered, scalped, and flung over the parapets.

Crowds arrive, guarded, in front of the temple: girls and women of all ages.

Seguin's eye is busy; his heart is yearning. At the arrival of each new group, he scans their faces. In vain! Many of them are young and pretty, but brown as the fallen leaf. She is not yet brought up.

I see the three captive Mexicans standing with their friends. They should know where she may be found.

"Question them," I whisper to the chief.

"Ha! you are right. I did not think of that. Come, come!"

We run together down the ladders, and approach the delivered captives. Seguin hurriedly describes the object of his search.

"It must be the Mystery Queen," says one.

"Yes, yes!" cries Seguin, in trembling anxiety; "it is; she is the Mystery Queen."

"She is in the town, then," adds another.

"Where? where?" ejaculates the halt-frantic father.

"Where? where?" echo the girls, questioning one another.

"I saw her this morning, a short time ago, just before you came up."

"I saw him hurry her off," adds a second, pointing upward to the old Indian. "He has hidden her."

"Caval!" cries another, "perhaps in the estufa!"

"The estufa! what is it?"

"Where the sacred fire burns; where he makes his medicine."

"Where is it? lead me to it!"

"Ay de mi! we know not the way. It is a sacred place where they burn people! Ay de mi!"

"But, señor, it is in this temple; somewhere under the ground. He knows. None but he is permitted to enter it. Carrai! The estufa is a fearful place. So say the people."

An indefinite idea that his daughter may be in danger crosses the mind of Seguin. Perhaps she is dead already, or dying by some horrid means. He is struck, so are we, with the expression of sullen malice that displays itself upon the countenance of the medicine chief. It is altogether an Indian expression—that of dogged determination to die rather than yield what he has made up his mind to keep. It is a look of demoniac cunning, characteristic of men of his peculiar calling among the tribes.

Haunted by this thought, Seguin runs to the ladder, and again springs upward to the root, followed by several of the band. He rushes upon the lying priest, clutching him by the long hair.

"Lead me to her!" he cries, in a voice of thunder; "lead me to this queen, this Mystery Queen! She is my daughter."

"Your daughter! the Mystery Queen!" replies the Indian, trembling with fear for his life, yet still resisting the appeal. "No, white man; she is not. The queen is ours. She is the daughter of the Sun. She is the child of a Navajo chief."

"Tempt me no longer, old man! No longer, I say. Look forth! If a hair of her head has been harmed, all these shall suffer. I will not leave a living thing in your town. Lead on! Bring me to the estufa!"

"To the estufa! to the estufa!" shout several voices.

Strong hands grasp the garments of the Indian, and are twined into his loose hair. Knives, already red and reeking, are brandished before his eyes. He is forced from the roof, and hurried down the ladders.

He ceases to resist, for he sees that resistance is death; and half-dragged, half-leading, he conducts them to the ground-floor of the building.

He enters by a passage covered with the shaggy hides of the buffalo. Seguin follows, keeping his eye and hand upon him. We crowd after, close upon the heels of both.

We pass through dark ways, descending, as we go, through an intricate labyrinth. We arrive in a large room, dimly lighted. Ghastly images are before us and around us, the mystic symbols of a horrid religion! The walls are hung with hideous shapes and skins of wild beasts. We can see the fierce visages of the grizzly bear, of the white buffalo, of the carcajou, of the panther, and the ravenous wolf. We can recognise the horns and frontlets of the elk, the cimmaron, and the grim bison. Here and there are idol figures, of grotesque and monster forms, carved from wood and the red claystone of the desert.

A lamp is flickering with a feeble glare; and on a brazero, near the centre of the room, burns a small bluish flame. It is the sacred fire—the fire that for centuries has blazed to the god Quetzalcoatl!

We do not stay to examine these objects. The fumes of the charcoal almost suffocate us. We run in every direction, overturning the idols and dragging down the sacred skins.

There are huge serpents gliding over the floor, and hissing around our feet. They have been disturbed and frightened by the unwonted intrusion. We, too, are frightened, for we hear the dreaded rattle of the crotalus!

The men leap from the ground, and strike at them with the butts of their rifles. They crush many of them on the stone pavement.

There are shouts and confusion. We suffer from the exhalations of the charcoal. We shall be stifled. Where is Seguin? Where has he gone?

Hark! There are screams! It is a female voice! There are voices of men, too!

We rush towards the spot where they are heard. We dash aside the walls of pendant skins. We see the chief. He has a female in his arms—a girl, a beautiful girl, robed in gold and bright plumes.

She is screaming as we enter, and struggling to escape him. He holds her firmly, and has torn open the fawn-skin sleeve of her tunic. He is gazing on her left arm, which is bared to the bosom!

"It is she! it is she!" he cries, in a voice trembling with emotion. "Oh, God! it is she! Adèle! Adèle! do you not know me? Me—your father?"

Her screams continue. She pushes him off, stretching out her arms to the Indian, and calling upon him to protect her!

The father entreats her in wild and pathetic words. She heeds him not. She turns her face from him, and crouches down, hugging the knees of the priest!

"She knows me not! Oh, God! my child! my child!"

Again Seguin speaks in the Indian tongue, and with imploring accents—

"Adèle! Adèle! I am your father!"

"You! Who are you? The white men; our foes! Touch me not! Away, white men! away!"

"Dear, dearest Adèle! do not repel me—me, your father! You remember—"

"My father! My father was a great chief. He is dead. This is my father now. The Sun is my father. I am a daughter of Montezuma! I am a queen of the Navajoes!"

As she utters these words, a change seems to come over her spirit. She crouches no longer. She rises to her feet. Her screaming has ended, and she stands in an attitude of pride and indignation.

"Oh, Adèle!" continues Seguin, more earnest than ever, "look at me! look! Do you not remember? Look in my face! Oh, Heaven! Here, see! Here is your mother, Adèle! See! this is her picture: your angel mother. Look at it! Look, oh, Adèle!"

Seguin, while he is speaking, draws a miniature from his bosom, and holds it before the eyes of the girl. It arrests her attention. She looks upon it, but without any signs of recognition. It is to her only a curious object.

She seems struck with his manner, frantic but intreating. She seems to regard him with wonder. Still she repels him. It is evident she knows him not. She has lost every recollection of him and his. She has forgotten the language of her childhood; she has forgotten her father, her mother: she has forgotten all!

I could not restrain my tears as I looked upon the face of my friend, for I had grown to consider him such. Like one who has received a mortal wound, yet still lives, he stood in the centre of the group, silent and crushed. His head had fallen upon his breast, his cheek was blanched and bloodless; and his eye wandered with an expression of imbecility painful to behold. I could imagine the terrible conflict that was raging within.

He made no further efforts to intreat the girl. He no longer offered to approach her; but stood for some moments in the same attitude without speaking a word.

"Bring her away!" he muttered, at length, in a voice husky and broken; "bring her away! Perhaps, in God's mercy, she may yet remember."

Chapter Thirty Nine.

The White Scalp.

We repassed the horrid chamber, and emerged upon the lowermost terrace of the temple. As I walked forward to the parapet, there was a scene below that filled me with apprehension. A cloud seemed to fall over my heart.

In front of the temple were the women of the village—girls, women, and children; in all, about two hundred. They were variously attired: some were wrapped in their striped blankets; some wore tilmas, and tunics of embroidered fawn-skin, plumed and painted with dyes of vivid colour; some were dressed in the garb of civilised life—in rich satins, that had been worn by the dames of the Del Norte; in flounces that had fluttered in the dance around the ankles of some gay maja.

Not a few in the crowd were entirely nude. They were all Indians, but of lighter and darker shades; differing in colour as in expression of face. Some were old, wrinkled, and coarse; but there were many of them young, noble-like, and altogether beautiful.

They were grouped together in various attitudes. They had ceased their screaming, but murmured among themselves in low and plaintive exclamations.

As I looked, I saw blood running from their ears! It had dappled their throats and spurted over their garments.

A glance satisfied me as to the cause of this. They had been rudely robbed of their golden hangings.

Near and around them stood the scalp-hunters, in groups and afoot. They were talking in whispers and low mutterings. There were objects about their persons that attracted my eye. Curious articles of ornament or use peeped out from their pouches and haversacks—bead-strings and pieces of shining metal—gold it was—hung around their necks and over their breasts. These were the plundered bijouterie of the savage maidens.

There were other objects upon which my eye rested with feelings of deeper pain. Stuck behind the belts of many were scalps, fresh and reeking. Their knife-hilts and fingers were red; there was blood upon their hands; there was gloom in their glances.

The picture was appalling; and, adding to its awful impression, black clouds were at the moment rolling over the valley, and swathing the mountains in their opaque masses. The lightning jetted from peak to peak, followed by short claps of close and deafening thunder.

"Bring up the atajo!" shouted Seguin, as he descended the ladder with his daughter.

A signal was given; and shortly after the mules, in charge of the arrieros, came stringing across the plain.

"Collect all the dry meat that can be found. Let it be packed as speedily as possible."

In front of most of the houses there were strings of tasajo hanging against the walls. There were also dried fruits and vegetables, chile, roots of the kamas, and skin-bags filled with pinons and choke-berries.

The meat was soon brought together, and several of the men assisted the arrieros in packing it.

"There will be barely enough," said Seguin. "Here, Rube," continued he, calling to the old trapper; "pick out your prisoners. Twenty will be as many as we can take. You know them: chose those most likely to tempt an exchange."

So saying, the chief turned off towards the atajo, leading his daughter with the intention of mounting her on one of the mules.

Rube proceeded to obey the orders given him. In a short time he had collected a number of unresisting captives, and had put them aside from the rest. They were principally girls and young lads, whose dress and features bespoke them of the noblesse of the nation, the children of chiefs and warriors.

This movement was not regarded in silence. The men had drawn together, and commenced talking in loud and mutinous language.

"Wagh!" exclaimed Kirker, a fellow of brutal aspect; "thar are wives apiece, boys: why not every man help himself? Why not?"

"Kirker's right," Rejoined another; "and I've made up my mind to have one, or bust."

"But how are ye goin' to feed 'em on the road? We ha'n't meat if we take one apiece."

"Meat be hanged!" ejaculated the second speaker; "we kin reach the Del Norte in four days or less. What do we want with so much meat?"

"There's meat a-plenty," rejoined Kirker. "That's all the captain's palaver. If it runs out we kin drop the weemen, and take what o' them's handiest to carry."

This was said with a significant gesture, and a ferocity of expression revolting to behold.

"Now, boys! what say ye?"

"I freeze to Kirker."

"And I."

"And I."

"I'm not goin' to advise anybody," added the brute. "Ye may all do as ye please about it; but this niggur's not a-goin' to starve in the midst o' plenty."

"Right, comrade! right, I say."

"Wal. First spoke first pick, I reckin. That's mountain law; so, old gal, I cottons to you. Come along, will yer?"

Saying this, he seized one of the Indians, a large, fine-looking woman, roughly by the wrist, and commenced dragging her towards the atajo.

The woman screamed and resisted, frightened, not at what had been said, for she did not understand it, but terrified by the ruffian expression that was plainly legible in the countenance of the man.

"Shut up yer meat-trap, will ye?" cried he, still pulling her towards the mules; "I'm not goin' to eat ye. Wagh! Don't be so skeert. Come! mount hyar. Gee yup!"

And with this exclamation he lifted the woman upon one of the mules.

"If ye don't sit still, I'll tie ye; mind that!" and he held up the lasso, making signs of his determination.

A horrid scene now ensued.

A number of the scalp-hunters followed the example of their ruffian comrade. Each one chose the girl or woman he had fancied, and commenced hurrying her off to the atajo. The women shrieked. The men shouted and swore. Several scrambled for the same prize—a girl more beautiful than her companions. A quarrel was the consequence. Oaths and ejaculations rang out; knives were drawn and pistols cocked.

"Toss up for her!" cried one.

"Ay, that's fair; toss up! toss up!" shouted several.

The hint was adopted; the lots were cast; and the savage belle became the property of the winner.

In the space of a few minutes nearly every mule in the atajo carried an Indian damsel.

Some of the hunters had taken no part in this Sabine proceeding. Some disapproved of it (for all were not bad) from motives of humanity. Others did not care for being "hampered with a squaw," but stood apart, savagely laughing at the scene.

During all this time Seguin was on the other side of the building with his daughter. He had mounted her upon one of the mules, and covered her shoulders with his serape. He was making such preparations for her journey as the tender solicitudes of the father suggested.

The noise at length attracted him; and, leaving her in charge of his servants, he hurried round to the front.

"Comrades!" cried he, glancing at the mounted captives, and comprehending all that had occurred, "there are too many here. Are these whom you have chosen?" This question was directed to the trapper Rube.

"No," replied the latter, "them's 'em," and he pointed to the party he had picked out.

"Dismount these, then, and place those you have selected upon the mules. We have a desert to cross, and it will be as much as we can do to pass it with that number."

And without appearing to notice the scowling looks of his followers, he proceeded, in company with Rube and several others, to execute the command he had given.

The indignation of the hunters now showed itself in open mutiny. Fierce looks were exchanged, and threats uttered aloud.

"By Heaven!" cried one, "I'll have my gal along, or her scalp."

"Vaya!" exclaimed another, in Spanish; "why take any of them? They're not worth the trouble, after all. There's not one of them worth the price of her own hair."

"Take the har then, and leave the niggurs!" suggested a third.

"I say so too."

"And I."

"I vote with you, hoss."

"Comrades!" said Seguin, turning to the mutineers, and speaking in a tone of extreme mildness, "remember your promise. Count the prisoners, as we agreed. I will answer for the payment of all."

"Can ye pay for them now?" asked a voice.

"You know that that would be impossible."

"Pay for them now! Pay for them now!" shouted several.

"Cash or scalps, says I."

"Carrajo! where is the captain to get the money when we reach El Paso more than here? He's neither a Jew nor a banker; and it's news to me if he's grown so rich. Where, then, is all the money to some from?"

"Not from the Cabildo, unless the scalps are forthcoming; I'll warrant that."

"True, José! They'll give no money to him, more than to us; and we can get it ourselves if we show the skins for it. That we can."

"Wagh! what cares he for us, now that he has got what he wanted?"

"Not a niggur's scalp. He wouldn't let us go by the Prieto, when we kud 'a gathered the shining stuff in chunks."

"Now he wants us to throw away this chance too. We'd be green fools to do it, I say."

It struck me at this moment that I might interfere, with success. Money seemed to be what the mutineers wanted; at least it was their alleged grievance; and rather than witness the fearful drama which appeared to be on the eve of enactment, I would have sacrificed my fortune.

"Men!" cried I, speaking so that I could be heard above the din, "if you deem my word worth listening to, it is this: I have sent a cargo to Chihuahua with the last caravan. By the time we get back to El Paso the traders will have returned, and I shall be placed in possession of funds double what you demand. If you will accept my promise, I shall see that you be paid."

"Wagh! that talk's all very well, but what do we know of you or yer cargo?"

"Vaya! A bird in the hand's worth two in the bush."

"He's a trader. Who's goin' to take his word?"

"Rot his cargo! Scalps or cash, cash or scalps! that's this niggur's advice; an' if ye don't take it, boys, ye may leave it! but it's all the pay ye'll ever crook yer claws on."

The men had tasted blood, and like the tiger, they thirsted for more. There were glaring eyes on all sides, and the countenances of some exhibited an animal ferociousness hideous to look upon. The half-robber discipline that hitherto ruled in the band seemed to have completely departed, and the authority of the chief to be set at defiance.

On the other side stood the females, clinging and huddling together. They could not understand the mutinous language, but they saw threatening attitudes and angry faces. They saw knives drawn, and heard the cocking of guns and pistols. They knew there was danger, and they crouched together, whimpering with fear.

Up to this moment Seguin had stood giving directions for the mounting of his captives. His manner was strangely abstracted, as it had been ever since the scene of meeting with his daughter. That greater care, gnawing at his heart, seemed to render him insensible to what was passing. He was not so.

As Kirker ended (for he was the last speaker) a change came over Sequin's manner, quick as a flash of lightning. Suddenly rousing himself from his attitude of indifference, he stepped forward in front of the mutineers.

"Dare!" shouted he, in a voice of thunder, "dare to dishonour your oaths! By heavens! the first man who raises knife or rifle shall die on the instant!"

There was a pause, and a moment of deep silence.

"I had made a vow," continued he, "that should it please God to restore me my child, this hand should be stained with no more blood. Let any man force me to break that vow, and, by Heaven, his blood shall be the first to stain it!"

A vengeful murmur ran through the crowd, but no one replied.

"You are but a cowardly brute, with all your bluster," he continued, turning round to Kirker, and looking him in the eye. "Up with that knife! quick! or I will send this bullet through your ruffian heart!"

Seguin had drawn his pistol, and stood in an attitude that told he would execute the threat. His form seemed to have grown larger; his eye dilated, flashing as it rolled, and the man shrank before its glance. He saw death in it if he disobeyed, and with a surly murmur he fumbled mechanically at his belt, and thrust the blade back into its sheath.

But the mutiny was not yet quelled. These were men not so easily conquered. Fierce exclamations still continued, and the mutineers again began to encourage one another with shouts.

I had thrown myself alongside the chief, with my revolvers cocked and ready, resolved to stand by him to the death. Several others had done the same, among whom were Rube, Garey, Sanchez the bull-fighter, and the Maricopa.

The opposing parties were nearly equal, and a fearful conflict would have followed had we fought; but at this moment an object appeared that stifled the resentment of all. It was the common enemy!

Away on the western border of the valley we could see dark objects, hundreds of them, coming over the plain. They were still at a great distance, but the practised eyes of the hunters knew them at a glance. They were horsemen; they were Indians; they were our pursuers, the Navajoes!

They were riding at full gallop, and strung over the prairie like hounds upon a run. In a twinkling they would be on us.

"Yonder!" cried Seguin, "yonder are scalps enough to satisfy you; but let us see to our own. Come! to your horses! On with the atajo! I will keep my word with you at the pass. Mount! my brave fellows, mount!"

The last speech was uttered in a tone of reconciliation; but it needed not that to quicken the movements of the hunters. They knew too well their own danger. They could have sustained the attack among the houses, but it would only have been until the return of the main tribe, when they knew that every life would be taken. To make a stand at the town would be madness, and was not thought of. In a moment we were in our saddles; and the atajo, strung out with the captives and provisions, was hurrying off toward the woods. We purposed passing the defile that opened eastward, as our retreat by the other route was now cut off by the advancing horsemen.

Seguin had thrown himself at the head, leading the mule upon which his daughter was mounted. The rest followed, straggling over the plain without rank or order.

I was among the last to leave the town. I had lingered behind purposely, fearing some outrage, and determined, if possible, to prevent it.

"At length," thought I, "they have all gone!" and putting spurs to my horse, I galloped after.

When I had ridden about a hundred yards from the walls, a loud yell rang behind me; and, reining in my horse, I turned in the saddle and looked back. Another yell, wild and savage, directed me to the point whence the former had come.

On the highest roof of the temple two men were struggling. I knew them at a glance; and I knew, too, it was a death-struggle. One was the medicine chief, as I could tell by the flowing, white hair. The scanty skirt and leggings, the naked ankles, the close-fitting skull-cap, enabled me easily to distinguish his antagonist. It was the earless trapper!

The conflict was a short one. I had not seen the beginning of it, but I soon witnessed the dénouement. As I turned, the trapper had forced his adversary against the parapet, and with his long, muscular arm was bending him over its edge. In the other hand, uplifted, he brandished his knife!

I saw a quick flash as the blade was plunged; a red gush spurted over the garments of the Indian; his arms dropped, his body doubled over the wall, balanced a moment, and then fell with a dull, sodden sound upon the terrace below!

The same wild whoop again rang in my ears, and the hunter disappeared from the root.

I turned to ride on. I knew it was the settling of some old account, the winding up of some terrible revenge.

The clattering of hoofs sounded behind me, and a horseman rode up alongside. I knew, without turning my head, that it was the trapper.

"Fair swop, they say, ain't no stealin'. Putty har, too, it ur. Wagh! It won't neyther match nor patch mine; but it makes one's feelin's easier."

Puzzled at this speech, I turned to ascertain its meaning. I was answered by the sight that met my eye. An object was hanging from the old man's belt, like a streak of snow-white flax. But it was not that. It was hair. It was a scalp!

There were drops of blood struggling down the silvery strands as they shook, and across them, near the middle, was a broad red band. It was the track of the trapper's knife where he had wiped it!

Chapter Forty.

The Fight in the Pass.

We entered the woods, and followed the Indian trail up stream. We hurried forward as fast as the atajo could be driven. A scramble of five miles brought us to the eastern end of the valley. Here the sierras impinged upon the river, forming a cañon. It was a grim gap, similar to that we had passed on entering from the west, but still more fearful in its features. Unlike the former, there was no road over the mountains on either side. The valley was headed in by precipitous cliffs, and the trail lay through the cañon, up the bed of the stream. The latter was shallow. During freshets it became a torrent; and then the valley was inaccessible from the east, but that was a rare occurrence in these rainless regions.

We entered the cañon without halting, and galloped over the detritus, and round huge boulders that lay in its bed. Far above us rose the frowning cliffs, thousands of feet overhead. Great rocks scarped out, abutting over the stream; shaggy pines hung top downward, clinging in their seams; shapeless bunches of cacti and mezcals crawled along the cliffs, their picturesque but gloomy foliage adding to the wildness of the scene.

It was dark within the pass, from the shadow of the jutting masses; but now darker than usual, for black storm-clouds were swathing the cliffs overhead. Through these, at short intervals, the lightning forked and flashed, glancing in the water at our feet. The thunder, in quick, sharp percussions, broke over the ravine; but as yet it rained not.

We plunged hurriedly through the shallow stream, following the guide. There were places not without danger, where the water swept around angles of the cliff with an impetuosity that almost lifted our horses from their feet; but we had no choice, and we scrambled on, urging our animals with voice and spur.

After riding for a distance of several hundred yards, we reached the head of the cañon and climbed out on the bank.

"Now, cap'n," cried the guide, reining up, and pointing to the entrance, "hyur's yur place to make stand. We kin keep them back till thur sick i' the guts; that's what we kin do."

"You are sure there is no pass that leads out but this one?"

"Ne'er a crack that a cat kud get out at; that ur, 'ceptin' they go back by the other eend; an' that'll take them a round-about o' two days, I reckin."

"We will defend this, then. Dismount, men! Throw yourselves behind the rocks!"

“If ’ee take my advice, cap, I’d let the mules and weemen keep for’ard, with a lot o’ the men to look arter ’em; them that’s ridin’ the meanest critters. It’ll be nose an’ tail when we do go; and if they starts now, yur see wa kin easy catch up with ’em t’other side o’ the parairar.”

“You are right, Rube! We cannot stay long here. Our provisions will give out. They must move ahead. Is that mountain near the line of our course, think you?”

As Seguin spoke, he pointed to a snow-crowned peak that towered over the plain, far off to the eastward.

“The trail we oughter take for the ole mine passes clost by it, cap’n. To the south’art o’ yon snowy, thur’s a pass; it’s the way I got clur myself.”

“Very well; the party can take the mountain for their guide. I will despatch them at once.”

About twenty men, who rode the poorest horses, were selected from the band. These, guarding the atajo and captives, immediately set out and rode off in the direction of the snowy mountain. El Sol went with this party, in charge of Dacoma and the daughter of our chief. The rest of us prepared to defend the pass.

Our horses were tied in a defile; and we took our stands where we could command the embouchure of the cañon with our rifles.

We waited in silence for the approaching foe. As yet no war-whoop had reached us; but we knew that our pursuers could not be far off; and we knelt behind the rocks, straining our eyes down the dark ravine.

It is difficult to give an idea of our position by the pen. The ground we had selected as the point of defence was unique in its formation, and not easily described; yet it is necessary you should know something of its peculiar character in order to comprehend what followed.

The stream, after meandering over a shallow, shingly channel, entered the cañon through a vast gate-like gap, between two giant portals. One of these was the abrupt ending of the granite ridge, the other a detached mass of stratified rock. Below this gate the channel widened for a hundred yards or so, where its bed was covered with loose boulders and logs of drift timber. Still farther down, the cliffs approached each other, so near that only two horsemen could ride between them abreast; and beyond this the channel again widened, and the bed of the stream was filled with rocks, huge fragments that had fallen from the mountain.

The place we occupied was among the rocks and drift, within the cañon, and below the great gap which formed its mouth. We had chosen the position from necessity, at at this point the bank shelved out and offered a way to the open country, by which our pursuers could outflank us, should we allow them to get so far up. It was necessary, therefore, to prevent this; and we placed ourselves to defend the lower or second narrowing of the channel. We knew that below that point beetling cliffs walled in the stream on both sides, so that it would be impossible for them to ascend out of its bed. If we could restrain them from making a rush at the shelving bank, we would have them penned up from any farther advance. They could only flank our position by returning to the valley, and going about by the western end, a distance of fifty miles at the least. At all events, we should hold them in check until the atajo had got a long start; and then, trusting to our horses, we intended to follow it in the night. We knew that in the end we should have to abandon the defence, as the want of provisions would not allow us to hold out for any length of time.

At the command of our leader we had thrown ourselves among the rocks. The thunder was now pealing over our heads, and reverberating through the cañon. Black clouds rolled along the cliffs, split and torn by brilliant jets. Big drops, still falling thinly, slapped down upon the stones.

As Seguin had told me, rain, thunder, and lightning are rare phenomena in these regions; but when they do occur, it is with that violence which characterises the storms of the tropics. The elements, escaping from their wonted continence, rage in fiercer war. The long-gathering electricity, suddenly displaced from its equilibrium, seems to revel in havoc, rending asunder the harmonies of nature.

The eye of the geognosist, in scanning the features of this plateau land, could not be mistaken in the character of its atmosphere. The dread cañons, the deep barrancas, the broken banks of streams, and the clay-cut channels of the arroyos, all testified that we were in a land of sudden floods.

Away to the east, towards the head waters of the river, we could see that the storm was raging in its full fury. The mountains in that direction were no longer visible. Thick rain-clouds were descending upon them, and we could hear the sough of the falling water. We knew that it would soon be upon us.

“What’s keepin’ them anyhow?” inquired a voice.

Our pursuers had time to have been up. The delay was unexpected.

“The Lord only knows!” answered another. “I s’pose thar puttin’ on a fresh coat o’ paint at the town.”

“They’ll get their paint washed off, I reckin. Look to yer primin’, hosses! that’s my advice.”

“By gosh! it’s a-goin’ to come down in spouts.”

“That’s the game, boyees! hooray for that!” cried old Rube.

“Why? Do you want to git soaked, old case?”

“That’s adzactly what this child wants.”

“Well, it’s more ’n I do. I’d like to know what ye want to git wet for. Do ye wish to put your old carcass into an agey?”

“If it rains two hours, do ’ee see,” continued Rube, without paying attention to the last interrogatory, “we needn’t stay hyur, do ’ee see?”

“Why not, Rube?” inquired Seguin, with interest.

“Why, cap,” replied the guide, “I’ve seed a skift o’ a shower make this hyur crick that ’ee wudn’t care to wade it. Hooray! it ur a-comin’, sure enuf! Hooray!”

As the trapper uttered these exclamations, a vast black cloud came rolling down from the east, until its giant winds canopied the defile. It was filled with rumbling thunder, breaking at intervals into louder percussions, as the red bolts passed hissing through it. From this cloud the rain fell, not in drops, but, as the hunter had predicted, in “spouts.”

The men, hastily throwing the skirts of their hunting shirts over their gun-locks, remained silent under the pelting of the storm.

Another sound, heard between the peals, now called our attention. It resembled the continuous noise of a train of waggons passing along a gravelly road. It was the sound of hoof-strokes on the shingly bed of the cañon. It was the horse-tread of the approaching Navajoes!

Suddenly it ceased. They had halted. For what purpose? Perhaps to reconnoitre.

This conjecture proved to be correct; for in a few moments a small red object appeared over a distant rock. It was the forehead of an Indian with its vermilion paint. It was too distant for the range of a rifle, and the hunters watched it without moving.

Soon another appeared, and another, and then a number of dark forms were seen lurking from rock to rock, as they advanced up the cañon. Our pursuers had dismounted, and were approaching us on foot.

Our faces were concealed by the "wrack" that covered the stones; and the Indians had not yet discovered us. They were evidently in doubt as to whether we had gone on, and this was their vanguard making the necessary reconnaissance.

In a short time the foremost, by starts and runs, had got close up to the narrow part of the cañon. There was a boulder below this point, and the upper part of the Indian's head showed itself for an instant over the rock. At the same instant half a dozen rifles cracked; the head disappeared; and, the moment after, an object was seen down upon the pebbles, at the base of the boulder. It was the brown arm of the savage, lying palm upward. We knew that the leaden messengers had done their work.

The pursuers, though at the expense of one of their number, had now ascertained the fact of our presence, as well as our position; and the advanced party were seen retreating as they had approached.

The men who had fired reloaded their pieces, and, kneeling down as before, watched with sharp eyes and cocked rifles.

It was a long time before we heard anything more of the enemy; but we knew that they were deliberating on some plan of attack.

There was but one way by which they could defeat us: by charging up the cañon, and fighting us hand-to-hand. By an attack of this kind their main loss would be in the first volley. They might ride upon us before we could reload; and, far outnumbering us, would soon decide the day with their long lances. We knew all this; but we knew, too, that a first volley, when well delivered, invariably staggers an Indian charge, and we relied on such a hope for our safety.

We had arranged to fire by platoons, and thus have the advantage of a second discharge, should the Indians not retreat at the first.

For nearly an hour the hunters crouched under the drenching rain, looking only to keep dry the locks of their pieces. The water, in muddy rivulets, began to trickle through the shingle, and eddying around the rocks, covered the wide channel in which we now stood, ankle-deep.

"Several got fairly through."

Both above and below us, the stream, gathered up by the narrowing of the channel, was running with considerable velocity.

The sun had set, at least it seemed so, in the dismal ravine where we were. We were growing impatient for the appearance of our enemy.

"Perhaps they have gone round," suggested one.

"No; thar a-waitin' till night. They'll try it then."

"Let 'em wait, then," muttered Rube, "ef thur green enuf. A half an hour more'll do; or this child don't understan' weather signs."

"Hist! hist!" cried several voices together. "See; they are coming!"

All eyes were bent down the pass. A crowd of dark objects appeared in the distance, filling up the bed of the stream. They were the Indians, and on horseback. We knew from this that they were about to make a dash. Their movements, too, confirmed it. They had formed two deep, and held their bows ready to deliver a flight of arrows as they galloped up.

"Look out, boyees!" cried Rube; "thur a-comin' now in airnest. Look to yur sights, and give 'em gos; do 'ee hear?"

As the trapper spoke, two hundred voices broke into a simultaneous yell. It was the war-cry of the Navajoes!

As its vengeful notes rang upon the cañon, they were answered by loud cheers from the hunters, mingled with the wild whoops of their Delaware and Shawano allies.

The Indians halted for a moment beyond the narrowing of the cañon, until those who were rearmost should close up. Then, uttering another cry, they dashed forward into the gap.

So sudden was their charge that several of them had got fairly through before a shot was fired. Then came the reports of the guns; the crack—crack—crack of rifles; the louder detonations of the Spanish pieces, mingled with the whizzing sound of Indian arrows. Shouts of encouragement and defiance were given on both sides; and groans were heard, as the grooved bullet or the poisoned barb tore up the yielding flesh.

Several of the Indians had fallen at the first volley. A number had ridden forward to the spot of our ambush, and fired their arrows in our faces. But our rifles had not all been emptied; and these daring savages were seen to drop from their saddles at the straggling and successive reports.

The main body wheeled behind the rocks, and were now forming for a second charge. This was the moment of danger. Our guns were idle, and we could not prevent them from passing the gap, and getting through to the open country.

I saw Seguin draw his pistol, and rush forward, calling upon those who were similarly armed to follow his example. We ran after our leader down to the very jaws of the cañon, and stood waiting the charge.

It was soon to come; for the enemy, exasperated by many circumstances, were determined on our destruction, cost what it might. Again we heard their fierce war-cry, and amidst its wild echoes the savages came galloping into the gap.

"Now's yur time," cried a voice; "fire! Hooray!"

The cracks of fifty pistols were almost simultaneous. The foremost horses reared up and fell back, kicking and sprawling in the gap. They fell, as it were, in a body, completely choking up the channel. Those who came on behind urged their animals forward. Some stumbled on the heap of fallen bodies. Their horses rose and fell again, trampling both dead and living among their feet. Some struggled over and fought us with their lances. We struck back with our clubbed guns, and closed upon them with our knives and tomahawks.

The stream rose and foamed against the rocks, pent back by the prostrate animals. We fought thigh-deep in the gathering flood. The thunder roared overhead, and the lightning flashed in our faces, as though the elements took part in the conflict!

The yelling continued wild and vengeful as ever. The hunters answered it with fierce shouts. Oaths flew from foaming lips, and men grappled in the embrace that ended only in death!

And now the water, gathered into a deep dam, lifted the bodies of the animals that had hitherto obstructed it, and swept them out of the gap. The whole force of the enemy would be upon us. Good heavens! they are crowding up, and our guns are empty!

At this moment a new sound echoed in our ears. It was not the shouts of men, nor the detonation of guns, nor the pealing of the thunder. It was the hoarse roaring: of the torrent!

A warning cry was heard behind us. A voice called out: "Run for your lives! To the bank! to the bank!"

I turned, and beheld my companions rushing for the slope, uttering words of terror and caution. At the same instant my eye became fixed upon an approaching object. Not twenty yards above where I stood, and just entering the cañon, came a brown and foaming mass. It was water, bearing on its crested front huge logs of drift and the torn branches of trees. It seemed as though the sluice of some great dam had been suddenly carried away, and this was the first gush of the escaping flood!

As I looked it struck the portals of the cañon with a concussion like thunder, and then, rearing back, piled up to a height of twenty feet. The next moment it came surging through the gap.

I heard their terrified cry as the Indians wheeled their horses and fled. I ran for the bank, followed by my companions. I was impeded by the water, which already reached to my thighs; but with desperate energy I plunged and weltered through it, till I had gained a point of safety.

I had hardly climbed out when the torrent rolled past with a hissing, seething sound. I stood to observe it. From where I was I could see down the ravine for a long reach. The Indians were already in full gallop, and I saw the tails of their hindmost horses just disappearing round the rocks.

The bodies of the dead and wounded were still lying in the channel. There were hunters as well as Indians. The wounded screamed as they saw the coming flood. Those who had been our comrades called to us for help; we could do nothing to save them. Their cries had hardly reached us when they were lifted upon the crest of the whirling current, like so many feathers, and carried off with the velocity of projectiles!

"Thar's three good fellows gone under! Wagh!"

"Who are they?" asked Seguin, and the men turned round with inquiring looks.

"Thar's one Delaware, and big Jim Harris, and—"

"Who is the third man that's missing? Can anyone tell?"

"I think, captain, it's Kirker."

"It is Kirker, by the 'tarnal! I seed him down. Wagh! They'll lift his har to a sartinty."

"Ay, they'll fish him out below. That's a sure case."

"They'll fish out a good haul o' thur own, I reckin. It'll be a tight race, anyhow. I've heern o' a horse runnin' agin a thunder shower; but them niggurs 'll make good time, if thur tails ain't wet afore they git t'other eend—they will."

As the trapper spoke, the floating and still struggling bodies of his comrades were carried to a bend in the cañon, and whirled out of sight. The channel was now filled with the foaming yellow flood that frothed against the rocks as it forged onward.

Our danger was over for the time. The cañon had become impassable; and, after gazing for a while upon the torrent, most of us with feelings of awe, we turned away, and walked toward the spot where we had left our horses.

Chapter Forty One.

The Barranca.

We staked our horses upon the open plain, and, returning to the thicket, cut down wood and kindled fires. We felt secure. Our pursuers, even had they escaped back to the valley, could not now reach us, except by turning the mountains or waiting for the falling of the flood.

We knew that that would be as sudden as its rise, should the rain cease; but the storm still raged with unabated fury.

We could soon overtake the atajo; but we determined to remain for some time at the cañon, until men and horses had refreshed themselves by eating. Both were in need of food, as the hurried events of the preceding days had given no opportunity for a regular bivouac.

The fires were soon blazing under shelter of the overhanging rocks; and the dried meat was broiled for our suppers, and eaten with sufficient relish. Supper ended, we sat, with smoking garments, around the red embers. Several of the men had received wounds. These were rudely dressed by their comrades, the doctor having gone forward with the atajo.

We remained for several hours by the cañon. The tempest still played around us, and the water rose higher and higher. This was exactly what we wished for; and we had the satisfaction of seeing the flood increase to such a height that, as Rube assured us, it could not subside for hours. It was then resolved that we should continue our journey.

It was near midnight when we drew our pickets and rode off. The rain had partially blinded the trail made by El Sol and his party, but the men who now followed it were not much used to guide-posts, and Rube, acting as leader, lifted it at a trot. At intervals the flashes of lightning showed the mule tracks in the mud, and the white peak that beckoned us in the distance.

We travelled all night. An hour after sunrise we overtook the atajo, near the base of the snow mountain. We halted in the mountain pass; and, after a short while spent in cooking and eating breakfast, continued our journey across the sierra. The road led through a dry ravine, into an open plain that stretched east and south beyond the reach of our vision. It was a desert.

I will not detail the events that occurred to us in the passage of that terrible jornada. They were similar to those we experienced in the deserts to the west. We suffered from thirst, making one stretch of sixty miles without water. We passed over sage-covered plains, without a living object to break the death-like monotony that extended around us. We cooked our meals over the blaze of the artemisia. But our provisions gave out; and the pack mules, one by one, fell under the knives of the hungry hunters. By night we camped without fires; we dared not kindle them; for though, as yet, no pursuers had appeared, we knew they must be on our trail. We had travelled with such speed that they had not been able to come up with us.

For three days we headed towards the south-east. On the evening of the third we descried the Mimbres Mountains towering up on the eastern border of the desert. The peaks of these were well known to the hunters, and became our guides as we journeyed on.

We approached the Mimbres in a diagonal direction, as it was our purpose to pass through the sierra by the route of the old mine, once the prosperous property of our chief. To him every feature of the landscape was a familiar object. I observed that his spirits rose as we proceeded onward.

At sundown we reached the head of the Barranca del Oro, a vast cleft that traversed the plain leading down to the deserted mine. This chasm, like a fissure caused by some terrible earthquake, extended for a distance of twenty miles. On either side was a trail; for on both the table-plain ran in horizontally to the very lips of the abyss. About midway to the mine, on the left brow, the guide knew of a spring, and we proceeded towards this with the intention of camping by the water.

We dragged wearily along. It was near midnight when we arrived at the spring. Our horses were unsaddled and staked on the open plain.

Here Seguin had resolved that we should rest longer than usual. A feeling of security had come over him as he approached these well-remembered scenes.

There was a thicket of young cotton-trees and willows fringing the spring, and in the heart of this a fire was kindled. Another mule was sacrificed to the manes of hunger; and the hunters, after devouring the tough steaks, flung themselves upon the ground and slept. The horse-guard only, out by the caballada, stood leaning upon his rifle, silent and watchful.

Resting my head in the hollow of my saddle, I lay down by the fire. Seguin was near me with his daughter. The Mexican girls and the Indian captives lay clustered over the ground, wrapped in their tilmas and striped blankets. They were all asleep, or seemed so.

I was as wearied as the rest, but my thoughts kept me awake. My mind was busy with the bright future. "Soon," thought I, "shall I escape from these horrid scenes; soon shall I breathe a purer atmosphere in the sweet companionship of my beloved Zoe. Beautiful Zoe! before two days have passed I shall again be with you, press your impassioned lips, call you my loved: my own! Again shall we wander through the silent garden by the river groves; again shall we sit upon the moss-grown seats in the still evening hours; again shall we utter those wild words that caused our hearts to vibrate with mutual happiness! Zoe, pure and innocent as the angels." The child-like simplicity of that question, "Enrique, what is to marry?" Ah! sweet Zoe! you shall soon learn. Ere long I shall teach you. Ere long wilt thou be mine; for ever mine!

"Zoe! Zoe! are you awake? Do you lie sleepless on your soft couch? or am I present in your dreams? Do you long for my return, as I to hasten it? Oh, that the night were past! I cannot wait for rest. I could ride on sleepless—tireless—on—on!"

My eye rested upon the features of Adèle, upturned and shining in the blaze of the fire. I traced the outlines of her sister's face: the high, noble front, the arched eyebrow, and the curving nostril. But the brightness of complexion was not there; the smile of angelic innocence was not there. The hair was dark, the skin browned; and there was a wildness in the expression of the eye, stamped, no doubt, by the experience of many a savage scene. Still was she beautiful, but it was beauty of a far less spiritual order than that of my betrothed.

Her bosom rose and fell in short, irregular pulsations. Once or twice, while I was gazing, she half awoke, and muttered some words in the Indian tongue. Her sleep was troubled and broken.

During the journey, Seguin had waited upon her with all the tender solicitude of a father; but she had received his attentions with indifference, or at most regarded them with a cold thankfulness. It was difficult to analyse the feelings that actuated her. Most of the time she remained silent and sullen.

The father endeavoured, once or twice, to resuscitate the memories of her childhood, but without success; and with sorrow at his heart he had each time relinquished the attempt.

I thought he was asleep. I was mistaken. On looking more attentively in his face, I saw that he was regarding her with deep interest, and listening to the broken phrases that fell from her lips. There was a picture of sorrow and anxiety in his look that touched me to the heart.

As I watched him, the girl murmured some words, to me unintelligible, but among them I recognised the name "Dacoma."

I saw that Seguin started as he heard it.

"Poor child!" said he, seeing that I was awake; "she is dreaming, and a troubled dream it is. I have half a mind to wake her out of it."

"She needs rest," I replied.

"Ay, if that be rest. Listen! again 'Dacoma.'"

"It is the name of the captive chief."

"Ay; they were to have been married according to their laws."

"But how did you learn this?"

"From Rube: he heard it while he was a prisoner at the town."

"And did she love him, do you think?"

"No. It appears not. She had been adopted as the daughter of the medicine chief, and Dacoma claimed her for a wife. On certain conditions she was to have been given to him; but she feared, not loved him, as her words now testify. Poor child! a wayward fate has been hers."

"In two journeys more her sufferings will be over. She will be restored to her home, to her mother."

"Ah! if she should remain thus it will break the heart of my poor Adèle."

"Fear not, my friend. Time will restore her memory. I think I have heard of a parallel circumstance among the frontier settlements of the Mississippi."

"Oh! true, there have been many. We will hope for the best."

"Once in her home the objects that surrounded her in her younger days may strike a chord in her recollection. She may yet remember all. May she not?"

"Hope! Hope!"

"At all events, the companionship of her mother and sister will soon win her from the thoughts of savage life. Fear not! She will be your daughter again."

I urged these ideas for the purpose of giving consolation. Seguin made no reply; but I saw that the painful and anxious expression still remained clouding his features.

My own heart was not without its heaviness. A dark foreboding began to creep into it from some undefined cause. Were his thoughts in communion with mine?

"How long," I asked, "before we can reach your house on the Del Norte?"

I scarce knew why I was prompted to put this question. Some fear that we were still in peril from the pursuing foe?

"The day after to-morrow," he replied, "by the evening. Heaven grant we may find them safe!"

I started as the words issued from his lips. They had brought pain in an instant. This was the true cause of my undefined forebodings.

"You have fears?" I inquired, hastily.

"I have."

"Of what? of whom?"

"The Navajoes."

"The Navajoes!"

"Yes. My mind has not been easy since I saw them go eastward from the Pinon. I cannot understand why they did so, unless they meditated an attack on some settlements that lie on the old Llanos' trail. If not that, my fears are that they have made a descent on the valley of El Paso, perhaps on the town itself. One thing may have prevented them from attacking the town: the separation of Dacoma's party, which would leave them too weak for that; but still the more danger to the small settlements both north and south of it."

The uneasiness I had hitherto felt arose from an expression which Seguin had dropped at the Pinon spring. My mind had dwelt upon it, from time to time, during our desert journeyings; but as he did not speak of it afterwards, I thought that he had not attached so much importance to it. I had reasoned wrongly.

"It is just probable," continued the chief, "that the Passenos may defend themselves. They have done so heretofore with more spirit than any of the other settlements, and hence their long exemption from being plundered. Partly that, and partly because our band has protected their neighbourhood for a length of time, which the savages well know. It is to be hoped that the fear of meeting with us will prevent them from coming into the Jornada north of the town. If so, ours have escaped."

"God grant," I faltered, "that it may be thus!"

"Let us sleep," added Seguin. "Perhaps our apprehensions are idle, and they can benefit nothing. To-morrow we shall march forward without halt, if our animals can bear it. Go to rest, my friend; you have not much time."

So saying, he laid his head in his saddle, and composed himself to sleep. In a short while, as if by an act of volition, he appeared to be in a profound slumber.

With me it was different. Sleep was banished from my eyes, and I tossed about, with a throbbing pulse and a brain filled with fearful fancies. The very reaction from the bright dreams in which I had just been indulging rendered my apprehensions painfully active. I began to imagine scenes that might be enacting at that very moment: my betrothed struggling in the arms of some savage; for these southern Indians, I knew, possessed none of the chivalrous delicacy that characterise the red men of the "forest."

I fancied her carried into a rude captivity; becoming the squaw of some brutal brave; and with the agony of the thought I rose to my feet and rushed out upon the prairie.

Half-frantic, I wandered, not heeding whither I went. I must have walked for hours, but I took no note of the time.

I strayed back upon the edge of the barranca. The moon was shining brightly, but the grim chasm, yawning away into the earth at my feet, lay buried in silence and darkness. My eye could not pierce its fathomless gloom.

I saw the camp and the caballada far above me on the bank; but my strength was exhausted, and, giving way to my weariness, I sank down upon the very brink of the abyss. The keen torture that had hitherto sustained me was followed by a feeling of utter lassitude. Sleep conquered agony, and I slept.

Chapter Forty Two.

The Foe.

I must have slept an hour or more. Had my dreams been realities, they would have filled the measure of an age.

At length the raw air of the morning chilled and awoke me. The moon had gone down, for I remembered that she was close to the horizon when I last saw her. Still it was far from being dark, for I could see to a considerable distance through the fog.

"Perhaps the day is breaking," thought I, and I turned my face to the east. It was as I had guessed: the eastern sky was streaked with light; it was morning.

I knew it was the intention of Seguin to start early, and I was about summoning resolution to raise myself when voices broke on my ear. There were short, exclamatory phrases, and hoof-strokes upon the prairie turf.

"They are up, and preparing to start." With this thought, I leaped to my feet, and commenced hurrying towards the camp.

I had not walked ten paces when I became conscious that the voices were behind me!

I stopped and listened. Yes; beyond a doubt I was going from them.

"I have mistaken the way to the camp!" and I stepped forward to the edge of the barranca for the purpose of assuring myself. What was my astonishment to find that I had been going in the right direction, and that the sounds were coming from the opposite quarter.

My first thought was that the band had passed me, and were moving on the route.

"But no; Seguin would not. Oh! he has sent of a party to search for me: it is they."

I called out "Hollo!" to let them know where I was. There was no answer; and I shouted again, louder than before. All at once the sounds ceased. I knew the horsemen were listening, and I called once more at the top of my voice. There was a moment's silence! Then I could hear a muttering of many voices and the trampling of horses as they galloped towards me.

I wondered that none of them had yet answered my signal; but my wonder was changed into consternation when I perceived that the approaching party were on the other side of the barranca!

Before I could recover from my surprise, they were opposite me and reining up on the bank of the chasm. They were still three hundred yards distant, the width of the gulf; but I could see them plainly through the thin and filmy fog. There appeared in all about a hundred horsemen; and their long spears, their plumed heads, and half-naked bodies, told me at a glance they were Indians!

I stayed to inquire no further, but ran with all my speed for the camp. I could see the horsemen on the opposite cliff keeping pace with me at a slow gallop.

On reaching the spring I found the hunters in surprise, and vaulting into their saddles. Seguin and a few others had gone out on the extreme edge, and were looking over. They had not thought of an immediate retreat, as the enemy, having the advantage of the light, had already discovered the strength of our party.

Though only a distance of three hundred yards separated the hostile bands, twenty miles would have to be passed before they could meet in battle. On this account Seguin and the hunters felt secure for the time; and it was hastily resolved to remain where we were, until we had examined who and what were our opponents.

They had halted on the opposite bank, and sat in their saddles, gazing across. They seemed puzzled at our appearance. It was still too dark for them to distinguish our complexions. Soon, however, it grew clearer; our peculiar dress and equipments were recognised; and a wild yell, the Navajo war-cry, came pealing over the abyss!

"It's Dacoma's party!" cried a voice, "they have taken the wrong side o' the gully."

"No," exclaimed another, "thar's too few o' them for Dacoma's men. Thar ain't over a hundred."

"Maybe the flood tuk the rest," suggested the first speaker.

"Wagh! how could they 'a missed our trail, that's as plain as a waggon track? 'Tain't them nohow."

"Who then? It's Navagh. I kud tell thar yelp if I wur sleepin'."

"Them's head chief's niggurs," said Rube, at this moment riding forward. "Looke! yonder's the old skunk hisself, on the spotted hoss!"

"You think it is they, Rube?" inquired Seguin.

"Sure as shootin', cap."

"But where are the rest of his band? These are not all."

"They ain't far off, I'll be boun'. Hish-sh! I hear them a-comin'."

"Yonder's a crowd! Look, boys! look!"

Through the fog, now floating away, a dark body of mounted men were seen coming up the opposite side. They advanced with shouts and ejaculations, as though they were driving cattle. It was so. As the fog rose up, we could see a drove of horses, horned cattle, and sheep, covering the plain to a great distance. Behind these rode mounted Indians, who galloped to and fro, goading the animals with their spears, and pushing them forward.

"Lord, what a plunder!" exclaimed one of the hunters.

"Ay, them's the fellows have made something by thar expedition. We are comin' back empty as we went. Wagh!"

I had been engaged in saddling my horse, and at this moment came forward. It was not upon the Indians that my eye rested, nor upon the plundered cattle. Another object attracted my gaze, and sent the blood curdling to my heart.

Away in the rear of the advancing drove I saw a small party, distinct from the rest. Their light dresses fluttering in the wind told me that they were not Indians. They were women; they were captives!

There appeared to be about twenty in all; but my feelings were such that I took little heed of their number. I saw that they were mounted, and that each was guarded by an Indian, who rode by her side.

With a palpitating heart I passed my eye over the group from one to the other; but the distance was too great to distinguish the features of any of them. I turned towards the chief. He was standing with the glass to his eye. I saw him start; his cheek suddenly blanched; his lips quivered convulsively, and the instrument fell from his fingers to the ground! With a wild look he staggered back, crying out—

"Mon Dieu! Mon Dieu! Oh, God! Thou hast stricken me now!"

I snatched up the telescope to assure myself. But it needed not that. As I was raising it, an object running along the opposite side caught my eye. It was the dog Alp! I levelled the glass, and the next moment was gazing through it on the face of my betrothed!

So close did she seem that I could hardly restrain myself from calling to her. I could distinguish her pale, beautiful features. Her cheek was wan with weeping, and her rich golden hair hung dishevelled from her shoulders, reaching to the withers of her horse. She was covered with a serape, and a young Indian rode beside her, mounted upon a showy horse, and dressed in the habiliments of a Mexican hussar!

I looked at none of the others, though a glance showed me her mother in the string of captives that came after.

The drove of horses and cattle soon passed up, and the females with their guards arrived opposite us. The captives were left back on the prairie, while the warriors rode forward to where their comrades had halted by the brow of the barranca.

It was now bright day; the fog had cleared away, and across the impassable gulf the hostile bands stood gazing at each other!

Chapter Forty Three.

New Misery.

It was a most singular rencontre. Here were two parties of men, heart-foes to one another, each returning from the country of the other, loaded with plunder and carrying a train of captives! They had met midway, and stood within musket range, gazing at each other with feelings of the most bitter hostility, and yet a conflict was as impossible as though twenty miles of the earth's surface lay between them.

On one side were the Navajoes, with consternation in their looks, for the warriors had recognised their children. On the other stood the scalp-hunters, not a few of whom, in the captive train of their enemies, could distinguish the features of a wife, a sister, or a daughter.

Each gazed upon the other with hostile hearts and glances of revenge. Had they met thus on the open prairie they would have fought to the death. It seemed as though the hand of God had interposed to prevent the ruthless shedding of blood, which, but for the gulf that lay between these foemen, would certainly have ensued.

I cannot describe how I felt at the moment. I remember that, all at once, I was inspired with a new vigour both of mind and body. Hitherto I had been little more than a passive spectator of the events of our expedition. I had been acting without any stimulating heart-motive; now I had one that roused me to, a desperate energy.

A thought occurred to me, and I ran up to communicate it. Seguin was beginning to recover from the terrible blow. The men had learnt the cause of his strange behaviour, and stood around him, some of them endeavouring to console him. Few of them knew aught of the family affairs of their chief, but they had heard of his earlier misfortunes: the loss of his mine, the ruin of his property, the captivity of his child. Now, when it became known that among the prisoners of the enemy were his wife and daughter, even the rude hearts of the hunters were touched with pity at his more than common sufferings. Compassionate exclamations were heard from them, mingled with expressions of their determination to restore the captives or die in the attempt.

It was with the intention of exciting such a feeling that I had come forward. It was my design, out of my small stock of world's wealth, to set a premium on devotedness and valour, but I saw that nobler motives had anticipated me, and I remained silent.

Seguin seemed pleased at the loyalty of his comrades, and began to exhibit his wonted energy. Hope again had possession of him. The men clustered round him to offer their advice and listen to his directions.

"We can fight them, capt'n, even-handed," said the trapper Garey. "Thar ain't over two hundred."

"Jest a hundred and ninety-six," interposed a hunter, "without the weemen. I've counted them; that's thar number."

"Wal," continued Garey, "thar's some difference atween us in point o' pluck, I reckin; and what's wantin' in number we'll make up wi' our rifles. I never valleys two to one wi' Injuns, an' a trifle throw'd in, if ye like."

"Look at the ground, Bill! It's all plain. Whar would we be after a volley? They'd have the advantage wi' their bows and lances. Wagh! they could spear us to pieces thar!"

"I didn't say we could take them on the paraira. We kin foller them till they're in the mountains, an' git them among the rocks. That's what I advise."

"Ay. They can't run away from us with that drove. That's sartin."

"They have no notion of running away. They will most likely attack us."

"That's jest what we want," said Garey. "We kin go yonder, and fight them till they've had a bellyful."

The trapper, as he spoke, pointed to the foot of the Mimbres, that lay about ten miles off to the eastward.

"Maybe they'll wait till more comes up. There's more of head chief's party than these; there were nearly four hundred when they passed the Pinon."

"Rube, where can the rest of them be?" demanded Seguin; "I can see down to the mine, and they are not upon the plain."

"Ain't a-gwine to be, cap. Some luck in that, I reckin. The ole fool has sent a party by t'other trail. On the wrong scent—them is."

"Why do you think they have gone by the other trail?"

"Why, cap, it stans for raison. If they wur a-comin' ahint, some o' them niggurs on t'other side wud 'a gone back afore this to hurry 'em up, do 'ee see? Thur hain't gone ne'er a one, as I seed."

"You are right, Rube," replied Seguin, encouraged by the probability of what the other had asserted. "What do you advise us?" continued he, appealing to the old trapper, whose counsel he was in the habit of seeking in all cases of similar difficulty.

"Wal, cap, it's a twistified piece o' business as it stans; an' I hain't figured it out to my satersfaction jest yet. If 'ee'll gi' me a kupple o' minutes, I'll answer ye to the best o' my possibilities."

"Very well; we will wait for you. Men! look to your arms, and see that they are all in readiness."

During this consultation, which had occupied but a few seconds of time, we could see that the enemy was similarly employed on the other side. They had drawn around their chief, and from their gesticulations it was plain they were deliberating how they should act.

Our appearance, with the children of their principal men as captives, had filled them with consternation at what they saw, and apprehensions of a fearful kind for what they saw not. Returning from a successful foray, laden with spoil, and big with the prospect of feasting and triumph, they suddenly perceived themselves out-generalled at their own game. They knew we had been to their town. They conjectured that we had plundered and burnt their houses, and massacred their women and children. They fancied no less; for this was the very work in which they had themselves been engaged, and their judgment was drawn from their own conduct.

They saw, moreover, that we were a large party, able to defend what we had taken, at least against them; for they knew well that with their firearms the scalp-hunters were an over-match for them, when there was anything like an equality of numbers.

With these ideas, then, it required deliberation on their part, as well as with us; and we knew that it would be some time before they would act. They, too, were in a dilemma.

The hunters obeyed the injunctions of Seguin, and remained silent, waiting upon Rube to deliver his advice.

The old trapper stood apart, half-resting upon his rifle, which he clutched with both hands near the muzzle. He had taken out the "stopper," and was looking into the barrel, as if he were consulting some oracular spirit that he kept bottled up within it. It was one of Rube's peculiar "ways," and those who knew this were seen to smile as they watched him.

After a few minutes spent in this silent entreaty, the oracle seemed to have sent forth its response; and Rube, returning the stopper to its place, came walking forward to the chief.

"Billee's right, cap. If them Injuns must be fit, it's got to be did whur thur's rocks or timmer. They'd whip us to shucks on the paraira. That's settled. Wal, thur's two things: they'll eyther come at us; if so be, yander's our ground," (here the speaker pointed to a spur of the Mimbres); "or we'll be obleeged to foller them. If so be, we can do it as easy as fallin' off a log. They ain't over leg-free."

"But how should we do for provisions, in that case? We could never cross the desert without them."

"Why, cap, thur's no diffeeculty 'bout that. Wi' the parairas as dry as they are, I kud stampede that hul cavayard as easy as a gang o' bufflers; and we'd come in for a share o' them, I reckin. Thur's a wus thing than that, this child smells."

"What?"

"I'm afeerd we mout fall in wi' Dacoma's niggurs on the back track; that's what I'm afeerd on."

"True; it is most probable."

"It ur, unless they got overtuk in the kenyon; an I don't think it. They understan' that crik too well."

The probability of Dacoma's band soon joining those of the head chief was apparent to all, and cast a shadow of despondency over every face. They were, no doubt, still in pursuit of us, and would soon arrive on the ground.

"Now, cap," continued the trapper, "I've gi'n ye my notion o' things, if so be we're boun' to fight; but I have my behopes we kin get back the weemen 'ithout wastin' our gun-fodder."

"How? how?" eagerly inquired the chief and others.

"Why, jest this a-way," replied the trapper, almost irritating me with the prolixity of his style. "'Ee see them Injuns on t'other side o' the gulley?"

"Yes, yes," hastily replied Seguin.

"Wal; 'ee see these hyur?" and the speaker pointed to our captives.

"Yes, yes!"

"Wal; 'ee see them over yander, though thur hides be a coppery colour, has feelin's for thur childer like white Christyuns. They eat 'em by times, that's true; but thur's a releegius raison for that, not many hyur understands, I reckin."

"And what would you have us do?"

"Why, jest heist a bit o' a white rag an' offer to swop pris'ners. They'll understan' it, and come to tarms, I'll be boun'. That putty leetle gal with the long har's head chief's darter, an' the rest belongs to main men o' the tribe: I picked 'em for that. Besides, thur's Dacoma an' the young queen. They'll bite thur nails off about them. 'Ee kin give up the chief, and trade them out o' the queen best way ye kin."

"I will follow your advice," cried Seguin, his eye brightening with the anticipation of a happy result.

"Thur's no time to be wasted, then, cap; if Dacoma's men makes thur appearance, all I've been a-sayin' won't be worth the skin o' a sand-rat."

"Not a moment shall be lost;" and Seguin gave orders to make ready the flag of peace.

"It 'ud be better, cap, fust to gi' them a good sight o' what we've got. They hain't seed Dacoma yet, nor the queen. Thur in the bushes."

"Right!" answered Seguin. "Comrades! bring forward the captives to the edge of the barranca. Bring the Navajo chief. Bring the—my daughter!"

The men hurried to obey the command; and in a few minutes the captive children, with Dacoma and the Mystery Queen, were led forward to the very brink of the chasm. The serapes that had shrouded them were removed, and they stood exposed in their usual costumes before the eyes of the Indians. Dacoma still wore his helmet, and the queen was conspicuous in the rich, plume-embroidered tunic. They were at once recognised!

A cry of singular import burst from the Navajoes as they beheld these new proofs of their discomfiture. The warriors unslung their lances, and thrust them into the earth with impotent indignation. Some of them drew scalps from their belts, stuck them on the points of their spears, and shook them at us over the brow of the abyss. They believed that Dacoma's band had been destroyed, as well as their women and children; and they threatened us with shouts and gestures.

In the midst of all this, we noticed a movement among the more staid warriors. A consultation was going on.

It ended. A party were seen to gallop toward the captive women, who had been left far back upon the plain.

"Great heavens!" cried I, struck with a horrid idea, "they are going to butcher them! Quick with the flag!"

But before the banner could be attached to its staff, the Mexican women were dismounted, their rebozos pulled off, and they were led forward to the precipice.

It was only meant for a counter-vaunt, the retaliation of a pang for it was evident the savages knew that among their captives were the wife and daughter of our chief. These were placed conspicuously in front, upon the very brow of the barranca.

Chapter Forty Four.

The Flag of Truce.

They might have spared themselves the pains. That agony was already felt; but, indeed, a scene followed—that caused us to suffer afresh.

Up to this moment we had not been recognised by those near and dear to us. The distance had been too great for the naked eye, and our browned faces and travel-stained habiliments were of themselves a disguise.

But the instincts of love are quick and keen, and the eyes of my betrothed were upon me. I saw her start forward; I heard the agonised scream; a pair of snow-white arms were extended, and she sank, fainting, upon the cliff.

At the same instant Madame Seguin had recognised the chief, and had called him by name. Seguin shouted to her in reply, and cautioned her in tones of intreaty to remain patient and silent.

Several of the other females, all young and handsome, had recognised their lovers and brothers, and a scene followed that was painful to witness.

But my eyes were fixed upon her I saw that she recovered from her swoon. I saw the savage in hussar trappings dismount, and, lifting her in his arms, carry her back upon the prairie.

I followed them with impotent gaze. I saw that he was paying her kind attentions; and I almost thanked him, though I knew it was but the selfish gallantry of the lover.

In a short while she rose to her feet again, and rushed back toward the barranca. I heard my name uttered across the ravine. Hers was echoed back; but at the moment both mother and daughter were surrounded by their guards, and carried back.

Meanwhile, the white flag had been got ready, and Seguin, holding it aloft, stood out in front. We remained silent, watching with eager glances for the answer.

There was a movement among the clustered Indians. We heard their voices in earnest talk, and saw that something was going on in their midst.

Presently, a tall, fine-looking man came out from the crowd, holding an object in his left hand of a white colour. It was a bleached fawn-skin. In his right hand he carried a lance.

We saw him place the fawn-skin on the blade of the lance, and stand forward holding it aloft. Our signal of peace was answered.

"Silence, men!" cried Seguin, speaking to the hunters; and then, raising his voice, he called aloud in the Indian language—

"Navajoes! you know whom we are. We have passed through your country, and visited your head town. Our object was to search for our dear relatives, who we knew were captives in your land. Some we have recovered, but there are many others we could not find. That these might be restored to us in time, we have taken hostages, as you see. We might have brought away many more, but these we considered enough. We have not burned your town; we have not harmed your wives, your daughters, nor your children. With the exception of these, our prisoners, you will find all as you left them."

A murmur ran through the ranks of the Indians. It was a murmur of satisfaction. They had been under the full belief that their town was destroyed and their women massacred; and the words of Seguin, therefore produced a singular effect. We could hear joyful exclamations and phrases interchanged among the warriors. Silence was again restored, and Seguin continued—

"We see that you have been in our country. You have made captives as well as we. You are red men. Red men can feel for their kindred as well as white men. We know this; and for that reason have I raised the banner of peace, that each may restore to the other his own. It will please the Great Spirit, and will give satisfaction to both of us; for that which you hold is of most value to us, and that which we have is dear only to you. Navajoes! I have spoken. I await your answer."

When Seguin had ended, the warriors gathered around the head chief, and we could see that an earnest debate was going on amongst them. It was plain there were dissenting voices; but the debate was soon over, and the head chief, stepping forward, gave some instructions to the man who held the flag. The latter in a loud voice replied to Seguin's speech as follows—

"White chief! you have spoken well, and your words have been weighed by our warriors. You ask nothing more than what is just and fair. It would please the Great Spirit and satisfy us to exchange our captives; but how can we tell that your words are true? You say that you have not burned our town nor harmed our women and children. How can we know that this is true? Our town is far off; so are our women, if they be still alive. We cannot ask them. We have only your word. It is not enough."

Seguin had already anticipated this difficulty, and had ordered one of our captives, an intelligent lad, to be brought forward.

The boy at this moment appeared by his side.

"Question him!" shouted he, pointing to the captive lad.

"And why may we not question our brother, the chief Dacoma? The lad is young. He may not understand us. The chief could assure us better."

"Dacoma was not with us at the town. He knows not what was done there."

"Let Dacoma answer that."

"Brother!" replied Seguin, "you are wrongly suspicious, but you shall have his answer," and he addressed some words to the Navajo chief, who sat near him upon the ground.

The question was then put directly to Dacoma by the speaker on the other side. The proud Indian, who seemed exasperated with the humiliating situation in which he was placed, with an angry wave of his hand and a short ejaculation, answered in the negative.

"Now, brother," proceeded Seguin, "you see I have spoken truly. Ask the lad what you first proposed."

The boy was then interrogated as to whether we had burnt the town or harmed the women and children. To these two questions he also returned a negative answer.

"Well, brother," said Seguin, "are you satisfied?"

For a long time there was no reply. The warriors were again gathered in council, and gesticulating with earnestness and energy. We could see that there was a party opposed to pacific measures, who were evidently counselling, the others to try the fortunes of a battle. These were the younger braves; and I observed that he in the hussar costume, who, as Rube informed us, was the son of the head chief, appeared to be the leader of this party.

Had not the head chief been so deeply interested in the result, the counsels of these might have carried; for the warriors well knew the scorn that would await them among neighbouring tribes should they return without captives. Besides, there were numbers who felt another sort of interest in detaining them. They had looked upon the daughters of the Del Norte, and "saw that they were fair."

But the counsels of the older men at length prevailed, and the spokesman replied—

"The Navajo warriors have considered what they have heard. They believe that the white chief has spoken the truth, and they agree to exchange their prisoners. That this may be done in a proper and becoming manner, they propose that twenty warriors be chosen on each side; that these warriors shall lay down their arms on the prairie in presence of all; that they shall then conduct their captives to the crossing of the barranca by the mine, and there settle the terms of their exchange; that all the others on both sides shall remain where they now are, until the unarmed warriors have got back with the exchanged prisoners; that the white banners shall then be struck, and both sides be freed from the treaty. These are the words of the Navajo warriors."

It was some time before Seguin could reply to this proposal. It seemed fair enough; but yet there was a manner about it that led us to suspect some design, and we paused a moment to consider it. The concluding terms intimated an intention on the part of the enemy of making an attempt to retake their captives; but we cared little for this, provided we could once get them on our side of the barranca.

It was very proper that the prisoners should be conducted to the place of exchange by unarmed men, and twenty was a proper number; but Seguin well knew how the Navajoes would interpret the word "unarmed"; and several of the hunters were cautioned in an undertone to "stray" into the bushes, and conceal their knives and pistols under the flaps of their hunting-shirts. We thought that we observed a similar manoeuvre going on upon the opposite bank with the tomahawks of our adversaries.

We could make but little objection to the terms proposed; and as Seguin knew that time saved was an important object, he hastened to accept them.

As soon as this was announced to the Navajoes, twenty men—already chosen, no doubt—stepped out into the open prairie, and striking their lances into the ground, rested against them their bows, quivers, and shields. We saw no tomahawks, and we knew that every Navajo carries this weapon. They all had the means of concealing them about their persons; for most of them were dressed in the garb of civilised life, in the plundered habiliments of the rancho and hacienda. We cared little, as we, too, were sufficiently armed. We saw that the party selected were men of powerful strength; in fact, they were the picked warriors of the tribe.

Ours were similarly chosen. Among them were El Sol and Garey, Rube, and the bull-fighter Sanchez. Seguin and I were of the number. Most of the trappers, with a few Delaware Indians, completed the complement.

The twenty were soon selected; and, stepping out on the open ground, as the Navajoes had done, we piled our rifles in the presence of the enemy.

Our captives were then mounted and made ready for starting. The queen and the Mexican girls were brought forward among the rest.

This last was a piece of strategy on the part of Seguin. He knew that we had captives enough to exchange one for one, without these; but he saw, as we all did, that to leave the queen behind would interrupt the negotiation, and perhaps put an end to it altogether. He had resolved, therefore, on taking her along, trusting that he could better negotiate for her on the ground. Failing this, there would be but one appeal—to arms; and he knew that our party was well prepared for that alternative.

Both sides were at length ready, and, at a signal, commenced riding down the barranca, in the direction of the mine. The rest of the two bands remained eyeing each other across the gulf, with glances of mistrust and hatred. Neither party could move without the other seeing it; for the plains in which they were, though on opposite sides of the barranca, were but segments of the same horizontal plateau. A horseman proceeding from either party could have been seen by the others to a distance of many miles.

The flags of truce were still waving, their spears stuck into the ground; but each of the hostile bands held their horses saddled and bridled, ready to mount at the first movement of the other.

Chapter Forty Five.

A Vexed Treaty.

Within the barranca was the mine. The shafts, rude diggings, pierced the cliffs on both sides, like so many caves. The bottom between the cliffs was bisected by a rivulet that murmured among loose rocks.

On the banks of this rivulet stood the old smelting-houses and ruined ranches of the miners. Most of them were roofless and crumbling to decay. The ground about them was shaggy and choked up. There were briars, mezcal plants, and cacti—all luxuriant, hirsute, and thorny.

Approaching this point, the road on each side of the barranca suddenly dips, the trails converging downward, and meeting among the ruins.

When in view of these, both parties halted and signalled each other across the ravine. After a short parley, it was proposed by the Navajoes that the captives and horses should remain on the top of the hill, each train to be guarded by two men. The rest, eighteen on each side, should descend to the bottom of the barranca, meet among the houses, and, having smoked the calumet, arrange the terms of the exchange.

Neither Seguin nor I liked this proposal. We saw that, in the event of a rupture in the negotiation (a thing we more than half anticipated), even should our party overpower the other, we could gain nothing. Before we could reach the Navajo captives, up the steep hill, the two guards would hurry them off; or (we dreaded to think of it) butcher them on the ground! It was a fearful thought, but there was nothing improbable in it.

We knew, moreover, that smoking the peace-pipe would be another waste of time; and we were on thorns about the approach of Dacoma's party.

But the proposal had come from the enemy, and they were obstinate. We could urge no objections to it without betraying our designs; and we were compelled, though loth, to accept it.

We dismounted, leaving our horses in charge of the guard, and descending into the ravine, stood face to face with the warriors of Navajo.

They were eighteen picked men; tall, broad-shouldered, and muscular. The expression of their faces was savage, subtle, and grim. There was not a smile to be seen, and the lip that at that moment had betrayed one would have lied. There was hate in their hearts and vengeance in their looks.

For a moment both parties stood scanning each other in silence. These were no common foes; it was no common hostility that for years had nerved them against each other; and it was no common cause that had now, for the first time, brought them face to face without arms in their hands. A mutual want had forced them to their present attitude of peace, though it was more like a truce between the lion and tiger which have met in an avenue of the jungly forest, and stand eyeing one another.

Though by agreement without arms, both were sufficiently armed, and they knew that of each other.

The handles of tomahawks, the hafts of knives, and the shining butts of pistols, peeped carelessly out from the dresses both of hunters and Indians. There was little effort made to conceal these dangerous toys, and they were on all sides visible.

At length our mutual reconnaissance came to a period, and we proceeded to business.

There happened to be no breadth of ground clear of weeds and thorny rubbish, where we could seat ourselves lor the "smoke." Seguin pointed to one of the houses, an adobe structure in a tolerable state of preservation, and several entered to examine it. The building had been used as a smelting-house, and broken trucks and other implements were lying over the floor. There was but one apartment, not a large one either, and near its centre stood a brazero covered with cold slag and ashes.

Two men were appointed to kindle a fire upon the brazero, and the rest, entering, took their seats upon the trucks and masses of quartz rock ore that lay around the room!

As I was about seating myself, an object leaped against me from behind, uttering a low whine that ended in a bark. I turned, and beheld the dog Alp. The animal, frenzied with delight, rushed upon me repeatedly; and it was some time before I could quiet him and take my place.

At length we all were seated upon opposite sides of the fire, each party forming the arc of a circle, concave to the other.

There was a heavy door still hanging upon its hinge; and as there were no windows in the house, this was suffered to remain open. It opened to the inside.

The fire was soon kindled, and the clay-stone calumet filled with "kini-kinik." It was then lighted, and passed from mouth to mouth in profound silence.

We noticed that each of the Indians, contrary to their usual custom of taking a whiff or two, smoked long and slowly. We knew it was a ruse to protract the ceremony and gain time; while we—I answer for Seguin and myself—were chafing at the delay.

When the pipe came round to the hunters, it passed in quicker time.

The unsocial smoke was at length ended, and the negotiation began.

At the very commencement of the "talk," I saw that we were going to have a difficulty. The Navajoes, particularly the younger warriors, assumed a bullying and exacting attitude that the hunters were not likely to brook; nor would they have submitted to it for a moment but for the peculiar position in which their chief was placed. For his sake they held in as well as they could; but the tinder was apparent, and would not bear many sparks before it blazed up.

The first question was in relation to the number of the prisoners. The enemy had nineteen, while we, without including the queen or the Mexican girls, numbered twenty-one. This was in our favour; but, to our surprise, the Indians insisted that their captives were grown women, that most of ours were children, and that two of the latter should be exchanged for one of the former!

To this absurdity Seguin replied that we could not agree; but, as he did not wish to keep any of their prisoners, he would exchange the twenty-one for the nineteen.

"Twenty-one!" exclaimed a brave; "why, you have twenty-seven. We counted them on the bank."

"Six of those you counted are our own people. They are whites and Mexicans."

"Six whites!" retorted the savage; "there are but five. Who is the sixth?"

"Perhaps it is our queen; she is light in colour. Perhaps the pale chief has mistaken her for a white!"

"Ha! ha! ha!" roared the savages, in a taunting laugh. "Our queen a white! Ha! ha! ha!"

"Your queen," said Seguin, in a solemn voice; "your queen, as you call her, is my daughter."

"Ha! ha! ha!" again howled they, in scornful chorus; "your daughter! Ha! ha! ha!" and the room rang with their demoniac laughter.

"Yes!" repeated he, in a loud but faltering voice, for he now saw the turn that things were taking. "Yes, she is my daughter."

"How can that be?" demanded one of the braves, an orator of the tribe. "You have a daughter among our captives; we know that. She is white as the snow upon the mountain-top. Her hair is yellow as the gold upon these armlets. The queen is dark in complexion; among our tribes there are many as light as she, and her hair is like the wing of the black vulture. How is that? Our children are like one another. Are not yours the same? If the queen be your daughter, then the golden-haired maiden is not. You cannot be the father of both. But no!" continued the subtle savage, elevating his voice, "the queen is not your daughter. She is of our race—a child of Montezuma—a queen of the Navajoes!"

"The queen must be returned to us!" exclaimed several braves; "she is ours; we must have her!"

In vain Seguin reiterated his paternal claim. In vain he detailed the time and circumstances of her capture by the Navajoes themselves. The braves again cried out—

"She is our queen; we must have her!"

Seguin, in an eloquent speech, appealed to the feelings of the old chief, whose daughter was in similar circumstances; but it was evident that the latter lacked the power, if he had the will, to stay the storm that was rising. The younger warriors answered with shouts of derision, one of them crying out that "the white chief was raving."

They continued for some time to gesticulate, at intervals declaring loudly that on no terms would they agree to an exchange unless the queen were given up. It was evident that some mysterious tie bound them to such extreme loyalty. Even the exchange of Dacoma was less desired by them.

Their demands were urged in so insulting a manner that we felt satisfied it was their intention, in the end, to bring us to a fight. The rifles, so much dreaded by them, were absent; and they felt certain of obtaining a victory over us.

The hunters were equally willing to be at it, and equally sure of a conquest.

They only waited the signal from their leader.

A signal was given; but, to their surprise and chagrin, it was one of peace!

Seguin, turning to them and looking down—for he was upon his feet—cautioned them in a low voice to be patient and silent. Then covering his eyes with his hand, he stood for some moments in an attitude of meditation.

The hunters had full confidence in the talents as well as bravery of their chief. They knew that he was devising some plan of action, and they patiently awaited the result.

On the other side, the Indians showed no signs of impatience. They cared not how much time was consumed, for they hoped that by this time Dacoma's party would be on their trail. They sat still, exchanging their thoughts in grunts and short phrases, while many of them filled up the intervals with laughter. They felt quite easy, and seemed not in the least to dread the alternative of a fight with us. Indeed, to look at both parties, one should have said that, man to man, we would have been no match for them. They were all, with one or two exceptions, men of six feet—most of them over it—in height; while many of the hunters were small-bodied men. But among these there was not one "white feather."

The Navajoes knew that they themselves were well armed for close conflict. They knew, too, that we were armed. Ha! they little dreamt how we were armed. They saw that the hunters carried knives and pistols; but they thought that, after the first volley, uncertain and ill-directed, the knives would be no match for their terrible tomahawks. They knew not that from the belts of several of us—El Sol, Seguin, Garey, and myself—hung a fearful weapon, the most fearful of all others in close combat: the Colt revolver. It was then but a new patent, and no Navajo had ever heard its continuous and death-dealing detonations.

"Brothers!" said Seguin, again placing himself in an attitude to speak, "you deny that I am the father of the girl. Two of your captives, whom you know to be my wife and daughter, are her mother and sister. This you deny. If you be sincere, then, you cannot object to the proposal I am about to make. Let them be brought before us; let her be brought. If she fail to recognise and acknowledge her kindred, then shall I yield my claim, and the maiden be free to return with the warriors of Navajo."

The hunters heard this proposition with surprise. They knew that Seguin's efforts to awaken any recollection of himself in the mind of the girl had been unsuccessful. What likelihood was there that she would remember her mother? But Seguin himself had little hope of this, and a moment's reflection convinced us that his proposal was based upon some hidden idea.

He saw that the exchange of the queen was a *sine qua non* with the Indians; and without this being granted, the negotiations would terminate abruptly, leaving his wife and younger daughter still in the hands of our enemies. He reflected on the harsh lot which would await them in their captivity, while she returned but to receive homage and kindness. They must be saved at every sacrifice; she must be yielded up to redeem them.

But Seguin had still another design. It was a strategic manoeuvre, a desperate and *dernier ressort* on his part. It was this: he saw that, if he could once get the captives, his wife and daughter, down among the houses, there would be a possibility, in the event of a fight, of carrying them off. The queen, too, might thus be rescued as well. It was the alternative suggested by despair.

In a hurried whisper he communicated this to those of his comrades nearest him, in order to insure their prudence and patience.

As soon as the proposal was made, the Navajoes rose from their seats, and clustered together in a corner of the room to deliberate. They spoke in low tones. We could not, of course, understand what was said; but from the expression of their faces, and their gesticulations, we could tell that they seemed disposed to accept it. They knew that the queen had not recognised Seguin as her father. They had watched her closely as she rode down the opposite side of the barranca; in fact, conversed by signals with her, before we could interfere to prevent it. No doubt she had informed them of what happened at the cañon with Dacoma's warriors, and the probability of their approach. They had little fear, then, that she would remember her mother. Her long absence, her age when made captive, her after-life, and the more than kind treatment she had received at their hands, had long since blotted out every recollection of her childhood and its associations. The subtle savages well knew this; and at length, after a discussion which lasted for nearly an hour, they resumed their seats, and signified their assent to the proposal.

Two men, one from each party, were now sent for the three captives, and we sat waiting their arrival.

In a short time they were led in.

I find a difficulty in describing the scene that followed. The meeting of Seguin with his wife and daughter; my own short embrace and hurried kiss; the sobs and swooning of my betrothed; the mother's recognition of her long-lost child; the anguish that ensued as her yearning heart made its appeals in vain; the half-indignant, half-pitying looks of the hunters; the triumphant gestures and ejaculations of the Indians: all formed points in a picture that lives with painful vividness in my memory, though I am not sufficiently master of the author's art to paint it.

In a few minutes the captives were led out of the house, guarded by two men, while the rest of us remained to complete the negotiation.

Chapter Forty Six.

A Conflict with Closed Doors.

The occurrence did not improve the temper of either party, particularly that of the hunters. The Indians were triumphant, but not a whit the less inclined to obstinacy and exaction. They now returned to their former offer. For those of our captives that were woman-grown they would exchange one for one, and for their chief Dacoma they offered to give two; for the rest they insisted on receiving two for one.

By this arrangement, we could ransom only about twelve of the Mexican women; but finding them determined, Seguin at length assented to these terms, provided they would allow us the privilege of choosing the twelve to be exchanged.

To our surprise and indignation this was refused!

We no longer doubted what was to be the winding up of the negotiation. The air was filled with the electricity of anger. Hate kindled hate, and vengeance was burning in every eye.

The Indians scowled on us, glancing malignantly out of their oblique eyes. There was triumph, too, in their looks, for, they believed themselves far stronger than we.

On the other side sat the hunters quivering under a double indignation. I say double. I can hardly explain what I mean. They had never before been so braved by Indians. They had, all their lives, been accustomed, partly out of bravado and partly from actual experience, to consider the red men their inferiors in subtilty and courage; and to be thus bearded by them, filled the hunters, as I have said, with a double indignation. It was like the bitter anger which the superior feels towards his resisting inferior, the lord to his rebellious serf, the master to his lashed slave who has turned and struck him. It was thus the hunters felt.

I glanced along their line. I never saw faces with such expressions as I saw there and then. Their lips were white, and drawn tightly over their teeth; their cheeks were set and colourless; and their eyes, protruding forward, seemed glued in their sockets. There was no motion to be detected in the features of any, save the twitching of angry muscles. Their right hands were buried in the bosoms of their half-open shirts, each, I knew, grasping a weapon; and they appeared not to sit, but to crouch forward, like panthers quivering upon the spring.

There was a long interval of silence on both sides.

It was broken by a cry from without—the scream of the war-eagle!

We should not have noticed this, knowing that these birds were common in the Mimbres, and one might have flown over the ravine; but we thought, or fancied, that it had made an impression upon our adversaries. They were men not apt to show any sudden emotion; but it appeared to us that, all at once, their glances grew bolder, and more triumphant. Could it have been a signal?

We listened for a minute. The scream was repeated; and although it was exactly after the manner of a bird well known to us—the white-headed eagle—we sat with unsatisfied and tearful apprehensions.

The young chief, he in the hussar dress, was upon his feet. He had been the most turbulent and exacting of our opponents. He was a man of most villainous and licentious character, so Rube had told us, but nevertheless holding great power among the braves. It was he who had spoken in refusal of Seguin's offer, and he was now about to assign his reasons. We knew them without that.

"Why," said he, looking at Seguin as he spoke, "why is it that the white chief is so desirous of choosing among our captives? Is it that he wishes to get back the yellow-haired maiden?"

He paused a moment, as if for a reply; but Seguin made none.

"If the white chief believes our queen to be his daughter, would not he wish that her sister should be her companion, and return with her to our land?"

Again he paused; but, as before, Seguin remained silent.

The speaker proceeded.

"Why not let the yellow-haired maiden return with us, and become my wife? Who am I that ask this? A chief of the Navajoes, the descendants of the great Montezuma; the son of their king!"

"He never finished the sentence."

The savage looked around him with a vaunting air as he uttered these words.

"Who is she," he continued, "that I am thus begging for a bride? The daughter of one who is not even respected among his own people: the daughter of a culatta!"

I looked at Seguin. I saw his form dilating. I saw the big veins swelling along his throat. I saw gathering in his eyes that wild expression I had once before noticed. I knew that the crisis was near.

Again the eagle screamed!

"But," proceeded the savage, seeming to draw new boldness from the signal, "I shall beg no more. I love the white maiden. She must be mine; and this very night shall she sleep—"

He never finished the sentence. Seguin's bullet had sped, piercing the centre of his forehead. I caught a glimpse of the red round hole, with its circle of blue powder, as the victim tell forward on his face!

All together we sprang to our feet. As one man rose hunters and Indians. As if from one throat, pealed the double shout of defiance; and, as if by one hand, knives, pistols, and tomahawks were drawn together. The next moment we closed and battled!

Oh! it was a fearful strife, as the pistols cracked, the long knives glittered, and the tomahawks swept the air; a fearful, fearful strife!

You would suppose that the first shock would have prostrated both ranks. It was not so. The early blows of a struggle like this are wild, and well parried, and human life is hard to take. What were the lives of men like these?

A few fell. Some recoiled from the collision, wounded and bleeding, but still to battle again. Some fought hand to hand; while several pairs had clutched, and were striving to fling each other in the desperate wrestle of death!

Some rushed for the door, intending to fight outside. A few got out; but the crowd pressed against it, the door closed, dead bodies fell behind it; we fought in darkness.

We had light enough for our purpose. The pistols flashed at quick intervals, displaying the horrid picture. The light gleamed upon fiend-like faces, upon red and waving weapons, upon prostrate forms of men, upon others struggling in every attitude of deadly conflict!

The yells of the Indians, and the not less savage shouts of their white foemen, had continued from the first; but the voices grew hoarser, and the shouts were changed to groans, and oaths, and short, earnest exclamations. At intervals were heard the quick percussions of blows, and the dull, sodden sound of falling bodies.

The room became filled with smoke and dust, and choking sulphur; and the combatants were half-stifled as they fought.

At the first break of the battle I had drawn my revolver, and fired it in the face of the closing foemen. I had fired shot after shot, some at random, others directed upon a victim. I had not counted the reports, until the cock "checking" on the steel nipple told me I had gone the round of the six chambers.

This had occupied but as many seconds of time. Mechanically I stuck the empty weapon behind my belt, and, guided by an impulse, made for the door. Before I could reach it, it was closed, and I saw that to get out was impossible.

I turned to search for an antagonist; I was not long in finding one. By the flash of a pistol I saw one of the Indians rushing upon me with upraised hatchet. Up to this time something had hindered me from drawing my knife. I was now too late; and, holding out my arms to catch the blow, I ducked my head towards the savage.

I felt the keen blade cutting the flesh as it glanced along my shoulder. I was but slightly wounded. He had missed his aim from my stooping so suddenly; but the impetus brought our bodies together, and the next moment we grappled.

We stumbled over a heap of rock, and for some moments struggled together upon the ground, neither able to use his weapon. Again we rose, still locked in the angry embrace; again we were falling with terrible force. Something caught us in our descent. It shook; it gave way with a crashing sound, and we fell headlong into the broad and brilliant light!

I was dazzled and blinded. I heard behind me a strange rumbling like the noise made by falling timbers; but I heeded not that: I was too busy to speculate upon causes.

The sudden shock had separated us, and both rose at the same instant, again to grapple, and again to come together to the earth. We twisted and wriggled over the ground, among weeds and thorny cacti. I was every moment growing weaker, while the sinewy savage, used to such combats, seemed to be gaining fresh nerve and breath. Thrice he had thrown me under; but each time I had clutched his right arm, and prevented the descending blow. I had succeeded in drawing my knife as we fell through the wall; but my arm was also held fast, and I was unable to use it.

As we came to the ground for the fourth time, my antagonist fell under me. A cry of agony passed from his lips; his head "coggled" over among the weeds; and he lay in my arms without struggling.

I felt his grasp gradually relaxing. I looked in his face. His eyes were glassy and upturned. Blood was gurgling through his teeth. I saw that he was dead.

To my astonishment I saw this, for I knew I had not struck him as yet. I was drawing my arm from under him to do so, when I noticed that he ceased to resist. But the knife now caught my eye. It was red, blade and haft, and so was the hand that clasped it.

As we fell I had accidentally held it point upward. My antagonist had fallen upon the blade!

I now thought of my betrothed, and, untwining myself from the lithe and nerveless limbs of the savage, I rose to my feet. The ranche was in flames!

The roof had fallen in upon the brazero, and the dry shingles had caught the blaze. Men were crawling out from the burning ruin, but not to run away. No! Under its lurking flames, amidst the hot smoke, they still battled fierce, and foaming, and frenzied.

I did not stay to recognise whom they were, these tireless combatants. I ran forward, looking on all sides for the objects of my solicitude. The wave of female dresses caught my eye, far up the cliff, on the road leading to the Navajo captives. It was they! The three were climbing the steep path, each urged onward by a savage.

My first impulse was to rush after; but at that moment fifty horsemen made their appearance upon the hill, and came galloping downward.

I saw the madness of attempting to follow them, and turned to retreat towards the other side, where we had left our captives and horses. As I ran across the bottom, shots rang in my ear, proceeding from our side of the barranca. Looking up, I descried the mounted hunters coming down at a gallop, pursued by a cloud of savage horsemen. It was the band of Dacoma!

Uncertain what to do, I stood for a moment where I was, and watched the pursuit.

The hunters, on reaching the ranches, did not halt, but galloped on down the valley, firing as they went. A body of Indians swept on after them, while another body pulled up, clustered around the blazing ruin, and commenced searching among the walls.

I was yet screened in the thicket of cacti; but I saw that my hiding-place would soon be pierced by the eyes of the subtle savages; and dropping upon my hands and knees, I crept into the cliff. On reaching it, I found myself close to the mouth of a cave, a small shaft of the mine, and into this I at once betook myself.

Chapter Forty Seven.

A Queer Encounter in a Cave.

The place into which I had crawled was of irregular outlines. Rocks jutted along the sides, and between these, small lateral shafts had been dug, where the miners had followed the ramifications of the "quixa." The cave was not a deep one; the vein had not proved profitable, and had been abandoned for some other.

I kept up it till I was fairly "in the dark"; and then groping against one side, I found a recess, in which I ensconced myself. By peeping round the rock, I could see out of the cave and some distance over the bottom of the barranca, where the bushes grew thin and straggling.

I had hardly seated myself when my attention was called to a scene that was passing outside. Two men on their hands and knees were crawling through the cactus plants in front of the cave. Beyond them half a dozen savages on horseback were beating the thicket, but had not yet seen the men. These I recognised easily. They were Gode and the doctor. The latter was nearer me; and as he scrambled on over the shingle something started out of the rocks within reach of his hand. I noticed that it was a small animal of the armadillo kind. I saw him stretch forward, clutch it, and with a pleased look deposit it in a bag that was by his side. All this time the Indians were whooping and yelling behind him, and not fifty yards distant.

Doubtless the animal was of some new species, but the zealous naturalist never gave it to the world. He had scarcely drawn forth his hand again when a cry from the savages announced that he and Gode were discovered, and the next moment both lay upon the ground pierced with lances, and to all appearance dead!

Their pursuers now dismounted with the intention of scalping them. Poor Reichter! his cap was pulled off; the bleeding trophy followed, and he lay with the red skull towards the cave—a hideous spectacle!

Another Indian had alighted, and stood over the Canadian with his long knife in his hand. Although pitying my poor follower, and altogether in no humour for mirth, knowing what I did, I could not help watching the proceedings with some curiosity.

The savage stood for a moment, admiring the beautiful curls that embellished the head of his victim. He was no doubt thinking what handsome fringes they would make for his leggings. He appeared to be in ecstasies of delight; and from the flourishes which he made with his knife, I could see that it was his intention to skin the whole head!

After cutting several capers around it, he stooped and grasped a fistful of curls; but, before he had touched the scalp with his blade, the hair lifted off, displaying the white and marble-like skull!

With a cry of terror, the savage dropped the wig, and, running backward, fell over the body of the doctor. The cry attracted his, comrades; and several of them, dismounting, approached the strange object with looks of astonishment. One, more courageous than the rest, picked up the wig, which they all proceeded to examine with curious minuteness.

Then, one after another went up to the shining skull and passed his fingers over its smooth surface, all the while uttering exclamations of surprise. They tried on the wig, took it off, and put it on again, turning it in various ways. At length, he who claimed it as his property pulled off his plumed head-dress and, adjusting the wig upon his own head, front backward, stalked proudly around, with the long curls dangling over his face.

It was altogether a curious scene, and, under other circumstances, might have amused me. There was something irresistibly comic in the puzzled looks of the actors; but I had been too deeply affected by the tragedy to laugh at the farce. There was too much of horror around me. Seguin perhaps dead; she gone for ever, the slave of the brutal savage. My own peril, too, at the moment; for I knew not how soon I might be discovered and dragged forth. This affected me least of all. My life was now of little value to me, and so I regarded it.

But there is an instinct, so-called, of self-preservation, even when the will ceases to act. Hopes soon began to shape themselves in my mind, and along with these the wish to live. Thoughts came. I might organise a powerful band; I might yet rescue her. Yes! even though years might intervene, I would accomplish this. She would still be true! She would never forget!

Poor Seguin! what a life of hope withered in an hour! he himself sealing the sacrifice with his blood!

But I would not despair, even with his fate for a warning. I would take up the drama where he had ended. The curtain should rise upon new scenes, and I would not abandon the stage until I had accomplished a more joyous finale; or, failing this, had reached the dénouement of death or vengeance.

Poor Seguin! No wonder he had been a scalp-hunter. I could now understand how holy was his hate for the ruthless red man. I, too, had imbibed the passion.

With such reflections passing hastily—for the scene I have described, and the sequent thoughts, did not occupy much time—I turned my eyes inwards to examine whether I was sufficiently concealed in my niche. They might take it into their heads to search the shaft.

As I endeavoured to penetrate the gloom that extended inwards, my gaze became riveted on an object that caused me to shrink back with a cold shudder. Notwithstanding the scenes I had just passed through, this was the cause of still another agony.

In the thick of the darkness I could distinguish two small spots, round and shining. They did not scintillate, but rather glistened with a steady greenish lustre. I knew that they were eyes!

I was in the cave with a panther, or with a still more terrible companion, the grizzly bear!

My first impulse was to press back into the recess where I had hidden myself. This I did, until my back leaned against the rocks. I had no thoughts of attempting to escape out. That would have been from the frying-pan into the fire, for the Indians were still in front of the cave. Moreover, any attempt to retreat would only draw on the animal, perhaps at that moment straining to spring.

I cowered closely, groping along my belt for the handle of my knife. I clasped this at length, and drawing it forth, waited in a crouching attitude.

During all this time my eyes had remained fixed on the lustrous orbs before me.

I saw that they were fixed upon mine, and watched me without as much as winking.

Mine seemed to be possessed of abstract volition. I could not take them off. They were held by some terrible fascination; and I felt, or fancied, that the moment this should be broken, the animal would spring upon me.

I had heard of fierce brutes being conquered by the glance of the human eye, and I endeavoured to look back my *vis-à-vis* with interest.

We sat for some time, neither of us moving an inch. I could see nothing of the animal's body; nothing but the green gleaming circles that seemed set in a ground of ebony.

As they had remained motionless so long, I conjectured that the owner of them was still lying in his lair, and would not make his attack until something disturbed him; perhaps until the Indians had gone away.

The thought now occurred to me that I might better arm myself. I knew that a knife would be of little avail against a grizzly bear. My pistol was still in my belt, but it was empty. Would the animal permit me to load it? I resolved to make the attempt.

Still leaving my eyes to fulfil their office, I felt for my flask and pistol, and finding both ready, I commenced loading. I proceeded with silence and caution, for I knew that these animals could see in the dark, and that in this respect my *vis-à-vis* had the advantage of me. I felt the powder in with my finger, and pushing the ball on top of it, rolled the cylinder to the right notch, and cocked.

As the spring "clicked," I saw the eyes start. "It will be on me now!"

Quick as the thought, I placed my finger to the trigger but before I could level, a voice, with a well-known accent, restrained me.

"Hold on thur!" cried the voice. "Why didn't 'ee say yur hide wur white? I thought 'twur some sneaking Injun. Who are 'ee, anyhow? 'Tain't Bill Garey? No, Billee, 'tain't you, ole fellur."

"No," said I, recovering from my surprise; "it's not Bill."

"I mout 'a guessed that. Bill wud 'a know'd me sooner. He wud 'a know'd the glint o' this niggur's eyes as I wud his'n. Ah! poor Billee! I's afeerd that trapper's rubbed out; an' thur ain't many more o' his sort in the mountains. No, that thur ain't.

"Rot it!" continued the voice, with a fierce emphasis; "this comes o' layin' one's rifle ahint them. Ef I'd 'a had Tar-guts wi' me, I wudn't 'a been hidin' hyur like a scared 'possum. But she are gone; that leetle gun are gone; an' the mar too; an' hyur I am 'ithout eyther beast or weepun; cuss the luck!"

And the last words were uttered with an angry hiss, that echoed through every part of the cave.

"Yur the young fellur, the capt'n's friend, ain't 'ee?" inquired the speaker, with a sudden change of tone.

"Yes," I replied.

"I didn't see yur a-comin' in, or I mout 'a spoke sooner. I've got a smart lick across the arm, an' I wur just a-tyin' it up as ye tumbled in thur. Who did 'ee think this child wur?"

"I did not think you were anyone. I took you for a grizzly bear."

"Ha! ha! ha! He! he! he! I thort so, when I heard the click o' your pistol. He! he! he! If ever I sets my peepers on Bill Garey agin, I'll make that niggur larf till his guts ache. Ole Rube tuk for a grizzly! If that ain't— Ha! ha! ha! ha! He! he! he! Ho! ho! hoo!"

And the old trapper chuckled at the conceit, as if he had just been witnessing some scene of amusement, and there was not an enemy within a hundred miles of him.

"Did you see anything of Seguin?" I asked, wishing to learn whether there was any probability that my friend still lived.

"Did I? I did; an' a sight that wur. Did 'ee iver see a catamount riz?"

"I believe I have," said I.

"Wal, that wur him. He wur in the shanty when it felled. So were I m'self; but I wa'n't there long arter. I creeped out some'rs about the door; an' jest then I seed the cap, hand to hand wi' an Injun in a stan'-up tussle: but it didn't last long. The cap gi'n him a sockdolloger some'rs about the ribs, an' the niggur went under; he did."

"But what of Seguin? Did you see him afterwards?"

"Did I see him arterwards? No; I didn't."

"I fear he is killed."

"That ain't likely, young fellur. He knows these diggin's better'n any o' us; an' he oughter know whur to cacher, I reckin. He's did that, I'll be boun'."

"Ay, if he would," said I, thinking that Seguin might have followed the captives, and thrown away his life recklessly.

"Don't be skeert about him, young fellur. The cap ain't a-gwine to put his fingers into a bee's nest whur thur's no honey; he ain't."

"But where could he have gone, when you did not see him afterwards?"

"Whur could he 'a gone? Fifty ways he kud 'a gone through the brush. I didn't think o' lookin' arter him. He left the Injun whur he had throw'd him, 'ithout raisin' the har; so I stooped down to git it; an' when I riz agin, he wa'n't thur no how. But that Injun wur. Lor'! that Injun are some punkins; he are."

"What Indian do you mean?"

"Him as jined us on the Del Norte—the Coco."

"El Sol! What of him? is he killed?"

"Wal, he ain't, I reckin; nor can't a-be: that's this child's opeenyun o' it. He kim from under the ranche, arter it tumbled; an' his fine dress looked as spick as ef it had been jest tuk out o' a bandy-box. Thur wur two at him, an', Lor'! how he fit them! I tackled on to one o' them ahint, an' gin him a settler in the hump ribs; but the way he finished the other wur a caution to Crockett. 'Twur the puttiest lick I ever seed in these hyur mountains, an' I've seed a good few, I reckin."

"How was it?"

"'Ee know, the Injun—that are, the Coco—fit wi' a hatchet?"

"Yes."

"Wal, then; that ur's a desprit weepun, for them as knows how to use it; an' he diz; that Injun diz. T'other had a hatchet, too, but he didn't keep it long. 'Twur clinked out o' his hands in a minnit, an' then the Coco got a down blow at him. Wagh! it wur a down blow, an' it wa'n't nuthin' else. It split the niggur's head clur down to the thrapple. 'Twus sep'rated into two halves as ef 't had been clove wi' a broad-axe! Ef 'ee had 'a seed the varmint when he kim to the ground, 'ee'd 'a thort he wur double-headed. Jest then I spied the Injuns a-comin' down both sides o' the bluff; an' havin' neyther beast nor weepun, exceptin' a knife, this child tuk a notion 'twa'n't safe to be thur any longer, an' cached; he did."

Chapter Forty Eight.

Smoked Out.

Our conversation had been carried on in a low tone, for the Indians still remained in front of the cave. Many others had arrived, and were examining the skull of the Canadian with the same looks of curiosity and wonderment that had been exhibited by their comrades.

Rube and I sat for some time in silence, watching them. The trapper had flitted near me, so that he could see out and talk in whispers.

I was still apprehensive that the savages might search the cave.

"'Tain't likely," said my companion. "They mout ef thur hadn't 'a been so many o' these diggins, do 'ee see? Thur's a grist o' 'em—more'n a hundred—on t'other side; an' most o' the men who got clur tuk furrer down. It's my notion the Injuns seed that, an' won't disturb— Ef thur ain't that dog!"

I well understood the meaning of the emphasis with which these last words were repeated. My eyes, simultaneously with those of the speaker, had fallen upon the dog Alp. He was running about in front of the cave. I saw at a glance he was searching for me.

The next moment he had struck the trail where I had crawled through the cacti, and came running down in the direction of the cave.

On reaching the body of the Canadian, which lay directly in his track, he stopped for a moment and appeared to examine it. Then, uttering a short yelp, he passed on to that of the doctor, where he made a similar demonstration. He ran several times from one to the other, but at length left them; and, with his nose once more to the ground, disappeared out of our view.

His strange actions had attracted the attention of the savages, who, one and all, stood watching him.

My companion and I were beginning to hope that he had lost me, when, to our dismay, he appeared a second time, coming down the trail as before. This time he leaped over the bodies, and the next moment sprang into the mouth of the cave.

A yell from without told us that we were lost.

We endeavoured to drive the dog out again, and succeeded, Rube having wounded him with his knife; but the wound itself, and the behaviour of the animal outside, convinced our enemies that someone was within the shaft.

In a few seconds the entrance was darkened by a crowd of savages, shouting and yelling.

"Now show yur shootin', young fellur!" said my companion. "It's the new kind o' pistol 'ee hev got. Load every ber'l o' it."

"Shall I have time to load them?"

"Plenty o' time. They ain't a-gwine to come in 'ithout a light. Thur gone for a torch to the shanty. Quick wi' yur! Slap in the fodder!"

Without waiting to reply, I caught hold of my flask, and loaded the remaining five chambers of the revolver. I had scarcely finished when one of the Indians appeared in front with a flaming brand, and was about stooping into the mouth of the cavern.

"Now's yur time," cried Rube. "Fetch the niggur out o' his boots! Fetch him!"

I fired, and the savage, dropping the torch, fell dead upon the top of it!

An angry yell from without followed the report, and the Indians disappeared from the front. Shortly after, an arm was seen reaching in, and the dead body was drawn back out of the entrance.

"What will they do next, think you?" I inquired of my companion.

"I can't tell adzactly yit; but thur sick o' that game, I reckin. Load that ber'l agin. I guess we'll git a lot o' 'm afore we gins in. Cuss the luck! that gun, Tar-guts! Ef I only had that leetle piece hyur! 'Ee've got six shots, have 'ee? Good! 'Ee mout chock up the cave wi' their karkidges afore they kin reach us. It ur a great weepun, an' no mistakes. I seed the cap use it. Lor'! how he made it tell on them niggers i' the shanty! Thur ain't many o' them about, I reckin. Load sure, young fellur! Thur's plenty o' time. They knows what you've got thur."

During all this dialogue none of the Indians made their appearance, but we could hear them on both sides of the shaft without. We knew they were deliberating on what plan they would take to get at us.

As Rube suggested, they seemed to be aware that the shot had come from a revolver. Doubtless some of the survivors of the late fight had informed them of the fearful havoc that had been made among them with our pistols, and they dreaded to face them. What other plan would they adopt? Starve us out?

"They mout," said Rube, in answer to my question, "an' kin if they try. Thur ain't a big show o' vittlin' hyur, 'ceptin' we chaw donnicks. But thur's another way, ef they only hev the gumshin to go about it, that'll git us sooner than starvin'. Ha!" ejaculated the speaker, with emphasis. "I thort so. Thur a-gwine to smoke us. Look 'ee yander!"

I looked forth. At a distance I saw several Indians coming in the direction of the cave, carrying large bundles of brushwood. Their intention was evident.

"But can they do this?" I inquired, doubting the possibility of our enemies being able to effect their purpose in that way; "can we not bear the smoke?"

"Bar it! Yur green, young fellur. Do 'ee know what sort o' brush thur a-toatin' yander?"

"No," said I; "what is it?"

"It ur the stink-plant, then; an' the stinkinest plant 'ee ever smelt, I reckin. The smoke o' it ud choke a skunk out o' a persimmon log. I tell 'ee, young 'un, we'll eyther be smoked out or smothered whur we are; an' this child hain't fit Injun for thirty yeern or better, to go under that a way. When it gets to its wurst I'm a-gwine to make a rush. That's what I'm a-gwine ter do, young fellur."

"But how?" I asked, hurriedly; "how shall we act then?"

"How? Yur game to the toes, ain't 'ee?"

"I am willing to fight to the last."

"Wal, than, hyur's how, an' the only how: when they've raised the smoke so that they can't see us a-comin', we'll streak it out among 'em. You hev the pistol, an' kin go fo'most. Shoot every niggur that clutches at ye, an' run like blazes! I'll foller clost on yur heels. If we kin oncest git through the thick o' 'em, we mout make the brush, an' creep under it to the big caves on t'other side. Them caves jines one another, an' we mout dodge them thur. I seed the time this 'coon kud 'a run a bit, but these hyur jeints ain't as soople as they wur oncest. We kin try neverthemless; an' mind, young fellur, it's our only chance: do 'ee hear?"

I promised to follow the directions that my never-despairing companion had given me.

"They won't get old Rube's scalp yit, they won't. He! he! he!"

I turned towards him. The man was actually laughing at this wild and strangely-timed jest. It was awful to hear him.

Several armfuls of brush were now thrown into the mouth of the cave. I saw that it was the creosote plant, the ideodondo.

It was thrown upon the still blazing torch, and soon caught, sending up a thick, black smoke. More was piled on; and the fetid vapour, impelled by some influence from without, began to reach our nostrils and lungs, causing an almost instantaneous feeling of sickness and suffocation. I could not have borne it long. I did not stay to try how long, for at that moment I heard Rube crying out—

"Now's your time, young fellur! Out, and gi' them fits!"

With a feeling of desperate resolve, I clutched my pistol and dashed through the smoking brushwood. I heard a wild and deafening shout. I saw a crowd of men—of fiends. I saw spears, and tomahawks, and red knives raised, and—

Chapter Forty Nine.

A Novel Mode of Equitation.

When consciousness returned, I found that I was lying on the ground, and my dog, the innocent cause of my captivity, was licking my face. I could not have been long senseless, for the savages were still gesticulating violently around me. One was waving them back. I recognised him. It was Dacoma!

The chief uttered a short harangue that seemed to quiet the warriors. I could not tell what he said, but I heard him use frequently the word Quetzalcoatl. I knew that this was the name of their god, but I did not understand, at the time, what the saving of my life could have to do with him.

I thought that Dacoma was protecting me from some feeling of pity or gratitude, and I endeavoured to recollect whether I had shown him any special act of kindness during his captivity. I had sadly mistaken the motives of that splendid savage.

My head felt sore. Had they scalped me? With the thought I raised my hand, passing it over my crown. No. My favourite brown curls were still there; but there was a deep cut along the back of my head—the dent of a tomahawk. I had been struck from behind as I came out, and before I could fire a single bullet.

Where was Rube? I raised myself a little and looked around. He was not to be seen anywhere.

Had he escaped, as he intended? No; it would have been impossible for any man, with only a knife, to have fought his way through so many. Moreover, I did not observe any commotion among the savages, as if an enemy had escaped them. None seemed to have gone off from the spot. What then had—? Ha! I now understood, in its proper sense, Rube's jest about his scalp. It was not a *double-entendre*, but a *mot* of triple ambiguity.

The trapper, instead of following me, had remained quietly in his den, where, no doubt, he was at that moment watching me, his scapegoat, and chuckling at his own escape.

The Indians, never dreaming that there were two of us in the cave, and satisfied that it was now empty, made no further attempts to smoke it.

I was not likely to undeceive them. I knew that Rube's death or capture could not have benefited me; but I could not help reflecting on the strange stratagem by which the old fox had saved himself.

I was not allowed much time for reflection. Two of the savages, seizing me by the arms, dragged me up to the still blazing ruin. On, heavens! was it for this Dacoma had saved me from their tomahawks? for this, the most cruel of deaths!

They proceeded to tie me hand and foot. Several others were around, submitting to the same treatment. I recognised Sanchez the bull-fighter, and the red-haired Irishman. There were three others of the band, whose names I had never learnt.

We were in an open space in front of the burning ranche. We could see all that was going on.

The Indians were clearing it of the fallen and charred timbers to get at the bodies of their friends. I watched their proceeding's with less interest, as I now knew that Seguin was not there.

It was a horrid spectacle when the rubbish was cleared away, laying bare the floor of the ruin. More than a dozen bodies lay upon it, half-baked, half-roasted! Their dresses were burned off; but by the parts that remained still intact from the fire, we could easily recognise to what party each had belonged. The greater number of them were Navajoes. There were also the bodies of hunters smoking inside their cindery shirts. I thought of Garey; but, as far as I could judge, he was not among them.

There were no scalps for the Indians to take. The fire had been before them, and had not left a hair upon the heads of their dead foemen.

Seemingly mortified at this, they lifted the bodies of the hunters, and tossed them once more into the flames that were still blazing up from the piled rafters. They gathered the knives, pistols, and tomahawks that lay among the ashes; and carrying what remained of their own people out of the ruin, placed them in front. They then stood around them in a circle, and with loud voices chanted a chorus of vengeance.

During all this proceeding we lay where we had been thrown, guarded by a dozen savages. We were filled with fearful apprehensions. We saw the fire still blazing, and we saw that the bodies of our late comrades had been thrown upon it. We dreaded a similar fate for our own.

But we soon found that we were reserved for some other purpose. Six mules were brought up, and upon these we were mounted in a novel fashion. We were first set astride on the bare backs, with our faces turned tailwards. Our feet were then drawn under the necks of the animals, where our ankles were closely corded together. We were next compelled to bend down our bodies until we lay along the backs of the mules, our chins resting on their rumps. In this position our arms were drawn down until our hands met underneath, where they were tied tightly by the wrists.

The attitude was painful; and to add to this, our mules, not used to be thus packed, kicked and plunged over the ground, to the great mirth of our captors.

This cruel sport was kept up even after the mules themselves had got tired of it, by the savages pricking the animals with their spears, and placing branches of the cactus under their tails. We were fainting when it ended.

Our captors now divided themselves into two parties, and started up the barranca, taking opposite sides. One went with the Mexican captives and the girls and children of the tribe. The larger party, under Dacoma—now head chief, for the other had been killed in the conflict—guarded us.

We were carried up that side on which was the spring, and, arriving at the water, were halted for the night. We were taken off the mules and securely tied to one another, our guard watching us without intermission till morning. We were then packed as before and carried westward across the desert.

Chapter Fifty.

A Fast Dye.

After a four days' journey, painful even to be remembered, we re-entered the valley of Navajoa. The other captives, along with the great caballada, had arrived before us; and we saw the plundered cattle scattered over the plain.

As we approached the town, we were met by crowds of women and children, far more than we had seen on our former visit. These were guests, who had come in from other villages of the Navajoes that lay farther to the north. They were there to witness the triumphant return of the warriors, and partake of the great feast that always follows a successful foray.

I noticed many white faces among them, with features of the Iberian race. They had been captives; they were now the wives of warriors. They were dressed like the others, and seemed to participate in the general joy. They, like Seguin's daughter, had been Indianised.

There were many Mestizoes, half-bloods, the descendants of Indians and their Mexican captives, the offspring of many a Sabine wedding.

We were carried through the streets, and out to the western side of the village. The crowd followed us with mingled exclamations of triumph, hatred, and curiosity. At the distance of a hundred yards or so from the houses, and close to the river bank, our guards drew up.

I had turned my eyes on all sides as we passed through, as well as my awkward position would permit I could see nothing of her, or any of the female captives. Where could they be? Perhaps in the temple.

This building stood on the opposite side of the town, and the houses prevented me from seeing it. Its top only was visible from the spot where we had been halted.

We were untied and taken down. We were happy at being relieved from the painful attitude in which we had ridden all the way. We congratulated ourselves that we should now be allowed to sit upright. Our self-congratulation was brief. We soon found that the change was "from the frying-pan into the fire." We were only to be "turned." We had hitherto lain upon our bellies; we were now to be laid upon our backs.

In a few moments the change was accomplished, our captors handling us as unceremoniously as though we had been inanimate things. Indeed we were nearly so.

We were spread upon the green turf on our backs. Around each man four long pins were driven into the ground, in the form of a parallelogram. Our arms and legs were stretched out to their widest, and raw-hide thongs were looped about our wrists and ankles. These were passed over the pins, and drawn so tightly that our joints cracked with the cruel tension. Thus we lay, faces upturned, like so many hides spread out to be sun-dried.

We were placed in two ranks, "endways," in such a manner that the heads of the front-rank men rested between the feet of their respective "rears." As there were six of us in all, we formed three files, with short intervals between.

Our attitudes and fastenings left us without the power of moving a limb. The only member over which we had any control was the head; and this, thanks to the flexibility of our necks, we could turn about, so as to see what was going on in front or on either side of us.

As soon as we were fairly staked down, I had the curiosity to raise my head and look around me. I found that I was “rear rank, right file,” and that my file leader was the *ci-devant* soldier O’Cork.

The Indian guards, after having stripped us of most of our clothing, left us; and the girls and squaws now began to crowd around. I noticed that they were gathering in front of my position, and forming a dense circle around the Irishman. I was struck with their ludicrous gestures, their strange exclamations, and the puzzled expression of their countenances.

“Ta—yah! Ta—yah!” cried they, and the whole crowd burst into shrill screams of laughter.

What could it mean? Barney was evidently the subject of their mirth; but what was there about him to cause it, more than about any of the rest of us?

I raised my head to ascertain: the riddle was solved at once. One of the Indians, in going off, had taken the Irishman’s cap with him, and the little, round, red head was exposed to view. It lay midway between my feet, like a luminous ball, and I saw that it was the object of diversion.

By degrees, the squaws drew nearer, until they were huddled up in a thick crowd around the body of our comrade. At length one of them stooped and touched the head, drawing back her fingers with a start and a gesture, as though she had burned them.

This elicited fresh peals of laughter, and very soon all the women of the village were around the Irishman, “scroodging” one another to get a closer view. None of the rest of us were heeded, except to be liberally trampled upon; and half a dozen big, heavy squaws were standing upon my limbs, the better to see over one another’s shoulders.

As there was no great stock of clothing to curtain the view, I could see the Irishman’s head gleaming like a meteor through the forest of ankles.

After a while the squaws grew less delicate in their touch; and catching hold of the short, stiff bristles, endeavoured to pluck them out, all the while screaming with laughter.

I was neither in the state of mind nor the attitude to enjoy a joke; but there was a language in the back of Barney’s head, an expression of patient endurance, that would have drawn smiles from a gravedigger; and Sanchez and the others were laughing aloud.

For a long time our comrade endured the infliction, and remained silent; but at length it became too painful for his patience, and he began to speak out.

“Arrah, now, girls,” said he, in a tone of good-humoured intreaty, “will yez be aizy? Did yez niver see rid hair afore?”

The squaws, on hearing the appeal, which of course they understood not, only showed their white teeth in loud laughter.

“In trath, an’ iv I had yez on the sod, at the owld Cove o’ Cark beyant, I cud show yez as much av it as ’ud contint ye for yer lives. Arrah, now, keep aff me! Be the powers, ye’re trampin’ the toes aff me feet! Ach! don’t rug me! Holy Mother! will yez let me alone? Divil resave ye for a set of—”

The tone in which the last words were uttered showed that O’Cork had at length lost his temper; but this only increased the assiduity of his tormentors, whose mirth now broke beyond bounds. They plucked him harder than ever, yelling all the while; so that, although he continued to scold, I could only hear him at intervals ejaculating: “Mother av Moses!” “Tare-an-ages!” “Holy vistment!” and a variety of similar exclamations.

This scene continued for several minutes; and then, all at once, there was a lull, and a consultation among the women, that told us they were devising some scheme.

Several girls were sent off to the houses. These presently returned, bringing a large olla, and another vessel of smaller dimensions. What did they intend to do with these? We soon learned.

The olla was filled with water from the adjacent stream, and carried up, and the smaller vessel was set down beside Barney’s head. We saw that it contained the yucca soap of the Northern Mexicans. They were going to wash out the red!

The Irishman’s hand-stays were now loosened, so that he could sit upright; and a copious coat of the “soft-soap” was laid on his head, completely covering his hair. A couple of sinewy squaws then took hold of him by the shoulders, and with bunches of bark fibres applied the water, and scrubbed it in lustily.

The application seemed to be anything but pleasant to Barney, who roared out, ducking his head on all sides to avoid it. But this did not serve him. One of the squaws seized the head between her hands, and held it steady, while the other set to it afresh and rubbed harder than ever.

The Indians yelled and danced around; but in the midst of all I could hear Barney sneezing, and shouting in a smothered voice—

“Holy Mother!—htch-tch! Yez may rub—tch-itch!—till yez fetch-tch the skin aff—atch-ich-ich! an’ it won’t—tscztsh!—come out. I tell yez—itch-ch! it’s in the grain—itch-itch! It won’t come out—itch-itch!—be me sowl it won’t—atch-itch-hitch!”

But the poor fellow’s expostulations were in vain. The scrubbing continued, with fresh applications of the yucca, for ten minutes or more; and then the great olla was lifted, and its contents dashed upon his head and shoulders.

What was the astonishment of the women to find that instead of modifying the red colour, it only showed forth, if possible, more vivid than ever!

Another olla of water was lifted, and soused about the Irishman’s ears, but with no better effect.

Barney had not had such a washing for many a day; at least, not since he had been under the hands of the regimental barber.

When the squaws saw that, in spite of all their efforts, the dye still stuck fast, they desisted, and our comrade was again staked down. His bed was not so dry as before; neither was mine, for the water had saturated the ground about us, and we lay in mud. But this was a small vexation, compared with many others we were forced to put up with.

For a long time the Indian women and children clustered around us, each in turn minutely examining the head of our comrade. We, too, came in for a share of their curiosity; but O'Cork was "the elephant."

They had seen hair like ours oftentimes upon their Mexican captives; but, beyond a doubt, Barney's was the first red poll that had ever been scratched in the valley of Navajoa.

Darkness came on at length, and the squaws returned to the village, leaving us in charge of the guards, who all the night sat watchfully beside.

Chapter Fifty One.

Astonishing the Natives.

Up to this time we had no knowledge of the fate that was designed for us; but, from all that we had ever heard of these savages, as well as from our own experience of them, we anticipated that it would be a cruel one.

Sanchez, however, who knew something of their language, left us no room to doubt such a result. He had gathered from the conversation of the women what was before us. After these had gone away, he unfolded the programme as he had heard it.

"To-morrow," said he, "they will dance the mamanchic—the great dance of Montezuma. That is a fête among the girls and women. Next day will be a grand tournament, in which the warriors will exhibit their skill in shooting with the bow, in wrestling, and feats of horsemanship. If they would let me join them, I could show them how."

Sancho, besides being an accomplished torero, had spent his earlier years in the circus, and was, as we all knew, a most splendid horseman.

"On the third day," continued he, "we are to 'run amuck,' if you know what that is."

We had all heard of it.

"And on the fourth—"

"Well? upon the fourth?"

"They will roast us!"

We might have been more startled at this abrupt declaration had the idea been new to us, but it was not. The probability of such an end had been in our thoughts ever since our capture. We knew that they did not save us at the mine for the purpose of giving us an easier death; and we knew, too, that these savages never made men prisoners to keep them alive. Rube was an exception; but his story was a peculiar one, and he escaped only by his extreme cunning. "Their god," continued Sanchez, "is the same as that of the Mexican Aztecs; for these people are of that race, it is believed. I don't know much about that, though I've heard men talk of it. He is called by a queer, hard name. Carrai! I don't remember it."

"Quetzalcoatl?"

"Caval! that's the word. Pues, señores; he is a fire-god, and fond of human flesh; prefers it roasted, so they say. That's the use we'll be put to. They'll roast us to please him, and at the same time to satisfy themselves. Dos pajaros al un golpe!" (Two birds with one stone.)

That this was to be our fate was no longer probable, but certain; and we slept upon the knowledge of it the best way we could.

In the morning we observed dressing and painting among the Indians. After that began dancing, the dance of the mamanchic.

This ceremony took place upon the prairie, at some distance out in front of the temple.

As it was about commencing, we were taken from our spread positions and dragged up near it, in order that we might witness the "glory of the nation."

We were still tied, however, but allowed to sit upright. This was some relief, and we enjoyed the change of posture much more than the spectacle.

I could not describe the dance even if I had watched it, which I did not. As Sanchez had said, it was carried on only by the women of the tribe. Processions of young girls, gaily and fantastically attired, and carrying garlands of flowers, circled and leaped through a variety of figures. There was a raised platform, upon which a warrior and maiden represented Montezuma and his queen, and around these the girls danced and chanted. The ceremony ended by the dancers kneeling in front, in a grand semicircle. I saw that the occupants of the throne were Dacoma and Adèle. I fancied that the girl looked sad.

"Poor Seguin!" thought I: "there is none to protect her now. Even the false father, the medicine chief, might have been her friend. He, too, is out of the way, and—"

But I did not occupy much time with thoughts of her; there was a far more painful apprehension than that. My mind, as well as my eyes, had dwelt upon the temple during the ceremony. We could see it from the spot where we had been thrown down; but it was too distant for me to distinguish the faces of the white females that were clustered along its terraces. She no doubt was among them, but I was unable to make her out. Perhaps it was better I was not near enough. I thought so at the time.

I saw Indian men among the captives; and I had observed Dacoma, previous to the commencement of the dance, proudly standing before them in all the paraphernalia of his regal robes.

Rube had given me the character of this chief: brave, but brutal. My heart was oppressed with a painful heaviness as we were hurried back to our former places.

Most of the next night was spent by the Indians in feasting. Not so with us. We were rarely and scantily fed; and we suffered, too, from thirst, our savage guards scarcely deigning to supply us with water, though a river Was running at our feet.

Another morning, and the feasting recommenced. More sheep and cattle were slaughtered, and the fires steamed anew with the red joints that were suspended over them.

At an early hour the warriors arrayed themselves, though not in war attire, and the tournament commenced. We were again dragged forward to witness their savage sports, but placed still farther out on the prairie.

I could distinguish, upon the terrace of the temple, the whitish dresses of the captives. The temple was their place of abode.

Sanchez had told me this. He had heard it from the Indians as they conversed one with another. The girls were to remain there until the fifth day, that after our sacrifice. Then the chief would choose one of the number for his own household, and the warriors would "gamble" for the rest! Oh, these were fearful hours!

Sometimes I wished that I could see her again once before I died. And then reflection whispered me, it was better not. The knowledge of my fate would only add fresh bitterness to hers. Oh, these were fearful hours!

I looked at the savage tournament. There were feats of arms and feats of equitation. Men rode at a gallop, with one foot only to be seen over the horse, and in this attitude threw the javelin or shot the unerring shaft. Others vaulted from horse to horse, as they swept over the prairie at racing speed. Some leaped to their saddles, while their horses were running at a gallop, and some exhibited feats with the lasso. Then there was a mock encounter, in which the warriors unhorsed each other, as knights of the olden time.

It was, in fact, a magnificent spectacle—a grand hippodrome of the desert; but I had no eyes for it.

It had more attraction for Sanchez. I saw that he was observing every new feat with interested attention. All at once he became restless. There was a strange expression on his face; some thought, some sudden resolve, had taken possession of him.

Say to your bravos," said he, speaking to one of our guards in the Navajo tongue; "say that I can beat the best of them at that. I could teach them to ride a horse."

The savage reported what his prisoner had said, and shortly after several mounted warriors rode up, and replied to the taunt.

"You! a poor white slave, ride with the warriors of Navajo! Ha! ha! ha!"

"Can you ride upon your head?" inquired the torero.

"On our heads? How?"

"Standing upon your head while your horse is in a gallop."

"No; nor you, nor anyone. We are the best riders on the plains; we cannot do that."

"I can," affirmed the bull-fighter, with emphasis.

"He is boasting! he is a fool," shouted several.

"Let us see!" cried one. "Give him a horse; there is no danger."

"Give me my own horse, and I will show you."

"Which is your horse?"

"None of them now, I suppose; but bring me that spotted mustang, and clear me a hundred lengths of him on the prairie, and I shall teach you a trick."

As I looked to ascertain what horse Sanchez meant, I saw the mustang which he had ridden from the Del Norte. I noticed my own favourite, too, browsing with the rest.

After a short consultation among themselves, the torero's request was acceded to. The horse he had pointed out was lassoed out of the caballada and brought up, and our comrade's thongs were taken off. The Indians had no fear of his escaping. They knew that they could soon overtake such a steed as the spotted mustang; moreover, there was a picket constantly kept at each entrance of the valley. Even could he beat them across the plains, it would be impossible for him to get out to the open country. The valley itself was a prison.

Sanchez was not long in making his preparations. He strapped a buffalo-skin tightly on the back of his horse, and then led him round for some time in a circle, keeping him in the same track.

After practising thus for a while, he dropped the bridle and uttered a peculiar cry, on hearing which the animal fell into a slow gallop around the circle. When the horse had accomplished two or three rounds, the torero leaped upon his back, and performed the well-known feat of riding on his head.

Although a common one among professional equestrians, it was new to the Navajoes, who looked on with shouts of wonder and admiration. They caused the torero to repeat it again and again, until the spotted mustang had become all of one colour.

Sanchez, however, did not leave off until he had given his spectators the full programme of the "ring," and had fairly "astonished the natives."

When the tournament was ended, and we were hauled back to the river-side, the torero was not with us. Fortunate Sanchez! He had won his life! Henceforth he was to be riding-master to the Navajo nation!

Chapter Fifty Two.

Running Amuck.

Another day came: our day for action. We saw our enemies making their preparations; we saw them go off to the woods, and return bringing clubs freshly cut from the trees; we saw them dress as for ball-play or running.

At an early hour we were taken forward to the front of the temple. On arriving there, I cast my eyes upward to the terrace. My betrothed was above me; I was recognised.

There was mud upon my scanty garments, and spots of blood; there was dust on my hair; there were scars upon my arms; my face and throat were stained with powder, blotches of black, burnt powder: in spite of all, I was recognised. The eyes of love saw through all!

I find no scene in all my experience so difficult to describe as this. Why? There was none so terrible; none in which so many wild emotions were crowded into a moment. A love like ours, tantalised by proximity, almost within reach of each other's embrace, yet separated by relentless fate, and that for ever; the knowledge of each other's situation; the certainty of my death: these and a hundred kindred thoughts rushed into our hearts together. They could not be detailed; they cannot be described; words will not express them. You may summon fancy to your aid.

I heard her screams, her wild words and wilder weeping. I saw her snowy cheek and streaming hair, as, frantic, she rushed forward on the parapet as if to spring out. I witnessed her struggles as she was drawn back by her fellow-captives, and then, all at once, she was quiet in their arms. She had fainted, and was borne out of my sight.

I was tied by the wrists and ankles. During the scene I had twice risen to my feet, forced up by my emotions, but only to fall down again.

I made no further effort, but lay upon the ground in the agony of impotence.

It was but a short moment; but, oh! the feelings that passed over my soul in that moment! It was the compressed misery of a life-time.

For a period of perhaps half an hour I regarded not what was going on around me. My mind was not abstracted, but paralysed: absolutely dead. I had no thoughts about anything.

I awoke at length from this stupor. I saw that the savages had completed their preparations for the cruel sport.

Two rows of men extended across the plain to a distance of several hundred yards. They were armed with clubs, and stood facing each other with an interval of three or four paces between their ranks. Down the interval we were to run, receiving blows from everyone who could give them as we passed. Should any of us succeed in running through the whole line, and reach the mountain foot before we could be overtaken, the promise was that our lives should be spared!

"Is this true, Sanchez?" I whispered to the torero, who was standing near me.

"No," was the reply, given also in a whisper. "It is only a trick to make you run the better and show them the more sport. You are to die all the same. I heard them say so."

Indeed, it would have been slight grace had they given us our lives on such conditions; for it would have been impossible for the strongest and swiftest man to have passed through between their lines.

"Sanchez!" I said again, addressing the torero, "Seguin was your friend. You will do all you can for her?"

Sanchez well knew whom I meant.

"I will! I will!" he replied, seeming deeply affected.

"Brave Sanchez! tell her how I felt for her. No, no, you need not tell her that."

I scarce knew what I was saying.

"Sanchez!" I again whispered—a thought that had been in my mind now returning—"could you not—a knife, a weapon—anything—could you not drop one when I am set loose?"

"It would be of no use. You could not escape if you had fifty."

"It may be that I could not. I would try. At the worst, I can but die; and better die with a weapon in my hands!"

"It would be better," muttered the torero in reply. "I will try to help you to a weapon, but my life may be—"

He paused. "If you look behind you," he continued, in a significant manner, while he appeared to examine the tops of the distant mountains, "you may see a tomahawk. I think it is held carelessly. It might be snatched."

I understood his meaning, and stole a glance around. Dacoma was at a few paces' distance, superintending the start. I saw the weapon in his belt. It was loosely stuck. It might be snatched!

I possess extreme tenacity of life, with energy to preserve it. I have not illustrated this energy in the adventures through which we have passed; for, up to a late period, I was merely a passive spectator of the scenes enacted, and in general disgusted with their enactment. But at other times I have proved the existence of those traits in my character. In the field of battle, to my knowledge, I have saved my life three times by the quick perception of danger and the promptness to ward it off. Either less or more brave, I should have lost it. This may seem an enigma; it appears a puzzle; it is an experience.

In my earlier life I was addicted to what are termed "manly sports." In running and leaping I never met my superior; and my feats in such exercises are still recorded in the memories of my college companions.

Do not wrong me, and think that I am boasting of these peculiarities. The first is but an accident in my mental character; and others are only rude accomplishments, which now, in my more matured life, I see but little reason to be proud of. I mention them only to illustrate what follows.

Ever since the hour of my capture I had busied my mind with plans of escape. Not the slightest opportunity had as yet offered. All along the journey we had been guarded with the most zealous vigilance.

During this last night a new plan had occupied me. It had been suggested by seeing Sanchez upon his horse.

I had matured it all, except getting possession of a weapon; and I had hopes of escape, although I had neither time nor opportunity to detail them to the torero. It would have served no purpose to have told him them.

I knew that I might escape, even without the weapon; but I needed it, in case there might be in the tribe a faster runner than myself. I might be killed in the attempt; that was likely enough; but I knew that death could not come in a worse shape than that in which I was to meet it on the morrow. Weapon or no weapon, I was resolved to escape, or die in attempting it.

I saw them untying O'Cork. He was to run first.

There was a circle of savages around the starting-point; old men and idlers of the village, who stood there only to witness the sport.

There was no apprehension of our escaping; that was never thought of: an inclosed valley, with guards at each entrance; plenty of horses standing close by, that could be mounted in a few minutes. It would be impossible for any of us to get away from the ground. At least, so thought they.

O'Cork started.

Poor Barney! His race was not a long one. He had not run ten paces down the living avenue when he was knocked over, and carried back, bleeding and senseless, amidst the yells of the delighted crowd.

Another of the men shared a similar fate, and another; and then they unbound me.

I rose to my feet, and, during the short interval allowed me, stretched my limbs, imbuing my soul and body with all the energy that my desperate circumstances enabled me to concentrate within them.

The signal was again given for the Indians to be ready, and they were soon in their places, brandishing their long clubs, and impatiently waiting for me to make the start.

Dacoma was behind me. With a side glance I had marked well where he stood; and backing towards him, under pretence of getting a fairer "break," I came close up to the savage. Then suddenly wheeling, with the spring of a cat and the dexterity of a thief, I caught the tomahawk and jerked it from his belt.

I aimed a blow, but in my hurry missed him. I had no time for another. I turned and ran. He was so taken by surprise that I was out of his reach before he could make a motion to follow me.

I ran, not for the open avenue, but to one side of the circle of spectators, where were the old men and idlers.

These had drawn their hand weapons, and were closing towards me in a thick rank. Instead of endeavouring to break through them, which I doubted my ability to accomplish, I threw all my energy into the spring, and leaped clear over their shoulders. Two or three stragglers struck at me as I passed them, but missed their aim; and the next moment I was out upon the open plain, with the whole village yelling at my heels.

I well knew for what I was running. Had it not been for that, I should never have made the start. I was running for the caballada.

I was running, too, for my life, and I required no encouragement to induce me to make the best of it.

I soon distanced those who had been nearest me at starting; but the swiftest of the Indians were the young men who had formed the lines, and I saw that these were now forging ahead of the others.

Still they were not gaining upon me. My school training stood me in service now.

After a mile's chase, I saw that I was within less than half that distance of the caballada, and at least three hundred yards ahead of my pursuers; but to my horror, as I glanced back, I saw mounted men! They were still far behind, but I knew they would soon come up. Was it possible he could hear me?

I knew that in these elevated regions sounds are heard twice the ordinary distance; and I shouted, at the top of my voice, "Moro! Moro!"

I did not halt, but ran on, calling as I went.

I saw a sudden commotion among the horses. Their heads were tossed up, and then one dashed out from the drove and came galloping towards me. I knew the broad black chest and red muzzle. I knew them at a glance. It was my brave steed, my Moro!

The rest followed, trooping after; but before they were up to trample me, I had met my horse, and flung myself, panting, upon his back!

I had no rein; but my favourite was used to the guidance of my voice, hands, and knees; and directing him through the herd, I headed for the western end of the valley. I heard the yells of the mounted savages as I cleared the caballada; and looking back, I saw a string of twenty or more coming after me as fast as their horses could gallop.

But I had no fear of them now. I knew my Moro too well; and after I had cleared the ten miles of valley, and was springing up the steep front of the sierra, I saw my pursuers still back upon the plain.

Chapter Fifty Three.

A Conflict upon a Cliff.

My horse, idle for days, had recovered his full action, and bore me up the rocky path with proud, springy step. My nerves drew vigour from his, and the strength of my body was fast returning. It was well. I would soon be called upon to use it. The picket was still to be passed.

While escaping from the town, in the excitement of the more proximate peril I had not thought of this ulterior one. I now remembered it. It flashed upon me of a sudden, and I commenced gathering my resolution to meet it.

I knew there was a picket upon the mountain! Sanchez had said so; he had heard them say so. What number of men composed it? Sanchez had said two, but he was not certain of this. Two would be enough, more than enough for me, still weak, and armed as I was with a weapon in the use of which I had little skill.

How would they be armed? Doubtless with bows, lances, tomahawks, and knives. The odds were all against me.

At what point should I find them? They were videttes. Their chief duty was to watch the plains without. They would be at some station, then, commanding a view of these.

I remembered the road well—the same by which we had first entered the valley. There was a platform near the western brow of the sierra. I recollected it, for we had halted upon it while our guide went forward to reconnoitre. A cliff overhung this platform. I remembered that too; for during the absence of the guide, Seguin and I had dismounted and climbed it. It commanded a view of the whole outside country to the south and west. No doubt, then, on that very cliff would the videttes be stationed.

Would they be on its top? If so, it might be best to make a dash, and pass them before they could descend to the road, running the risk of their missiles, their arrows and lances. Make a dash! No; that would be impossible. I remembered that the path at both ends of the platform narrowed to a width of only a few feet, with the cliff rising above it and the cañon yawning below. It was, in fact, only a ledge of the precipice, along which it was dangerous to pass even at a walk. Moreover, I had re-shod my horse at the mission. The iron was worn smooth; and I knew that the rock was as slippery as glass.

All these thoughts passed through my mind as I neared the summit of the sierra. The prospect was appalling. The peril before me was extreme, and under other circumstances I would have hesitated to encounter it. But I knew that that which threatened from behind was not less desperate. There was no alternative; and with only half-formed resolutions as to how I should act, I pushed forward.

I rode with caution, directing my horse as well as I could upon the softer parts of the trail, so that his hoof-strokes might not be heard. At every turn I halted, and scanned the profile of each new prospect; but I did not halt longer than I could help. I knew that I had no time to waste.

The road ascended through a thin wood of cedars and dwarf pinons. It would zigzag up the face of the mountain. Near the crest of the sierra it turned sharply to the right, and trended in to the brow of the cañon. There the ledge already mentioned became the path, and the road followed its narrow terrace along the very face of the precipice.

On reaching this point I caught view of the cliff where I expected to see the vidette. I had guessed correctly—he was there, and, to my agreeable surprise, there was only one: a single savage.

He was seated upon the very topmost rock of the sierra, and his large brown body was distinctly visible, outlined against the pale blue sky. He was not more than three hundred yards from me, and about a third of that distance above the level of the ledge along which I had to pass.

I halted the moment I caught sight of him, and sat making a hurried reconnaissance. As yet he had neither seen nor heard me. His back was to me, and he appeared to be gazing intently towards the west. Beside the rock on which he was, his spear was sticking in the ground, and his shield, bow, and quiver were leaning against it. I could see upon his person the sparkle of a knife and tomahawk.

I have said my reconnaissance was a hurried one. I was conscious of the value of every moment, and almost at a glance I formed my resolution. That was, to "run the gauntlet," and attempt passing before the Indian could descend to intercept me. Obedient to this impulse, I gave my animal the signal to move forward.

I rode slowly and cautiously, for two reasons: because my horse dared not go otherwise; and I thought that, by riding quietly, I might get beyond the vidette without attracting his notice. The torrent was hissing below. Its roar ascended to the cliff; it might drown the sound of the hoof-strokes.

With this hope I stole onward. My eye passed rapidly from one to the other; from the savage on the cliff to the perilous path along which my horse crawled, shivering with affright.

When I had advanced about six lengths upon the ledge, the platform came in view, and with it a group of objects that caused me to reach suddenly forward and grasp the forelock of my Moro—a sign by which, in the absence of a bit, I could always halt him. He came at once to a stand, and I surveyed the objects before me with a feeling of despair.

They were two horses, mustangs; and a man, an Indian. The mustangs, bridled and saddled, were standing quietly out upon the platform; and a lasso, tied to the bit-ring of one of them, was coiled around the wrist of the Indian. The latter was sitting upon his hams, close up to the cliff, so that his back touched the rock. His arms lay horizontally across his knees, and upon these his head rested. I saw that he was asleep. Beside him were his bow and quiver, his lance and shield, all leaning against the cliff.

My situation was a terrible one. I knew that I could not pass him without being heard, and I knew that pass him I must. In fact, I could not have gone back had I wished it; for I had already entered upon the ledge, and was riding along a narrow shelf where my horse could not possibly have turned himself.

All at once, the idea entered my mind that I might slip to the ground, steal forward, and with my tomahawk—

It was a cruel thought, but it was the impulse of instinct, the instinct of self-preservation.

It was not decreed that I should adopt so fearful an alternative. Moro, impatient at being delayed in the perilous position, snorted and struck the rock with his hoof. The clink of the iron was enough for the sharp ears of the Spanish horses. They neighed on the instant. The savages sprang to their feet, and their simultaneous yell told me that both had discovered me.

I saw the vidette upon the cliff pluck up his spear, and commence hurrying downward; but my attention was soon exclusively occupied with his comrade.

The latter, on seeing me, had leaped to his feet, seized his bow, and vaulted, as if mechanically, upon the back of his mustang. Then, uttering a wild shout, he trotted over the platform, and advanced along the ledge to meet me.

An arrow whizzed past my head as he came up; but in his hurry he had aimed badly.

Our horses' heads met. They stood muzzle to muzzle

"He disappeared over the cliff"

with eyes dilated, their red nostrils steaming into each other. Both snorted fiercely, as if each was imbued with the wrath of his rider. They seemed to know that a death-strife was between us.

They seemed conscious, too, of their own danger. They had met at the very narrowest part of the ledge. Neither could have turned or backed off again. One or other must go over the cliff—must fall through a depth of a thousand feet into the stony channel of the torrent!

I sat with a feeling of utter helplessness. I had no weapon with which I could reach my antagonist; no missile. He had his bow, and I saw him adjusting a second arrow to the string.

At this crisis three thoughts passed through my mind; not as I detail them here, but following each other like quick flashes of lightning. My first impulse was to urge my horse forward, trusting to his superior weight to precipitate the lighter animal from the ledge. Had I been worth a bridle and spurs, I should have adopted this plan; but I had neither, and the chances were too desperate without them. I abandoned it for another. I would hurl my tomahawk at the head of my antagonist. No! The third thought! I will dismount, and use my weapon upon the mustang.

This last was clearly the best; and, obedient to its impulse, I slipped down between Moro and the cliff. As I did so, I heard the "hist" of another arrow passing my cheek. It had missed me from the suddenness of my movements.

In an instant I squeezed past the flanks of my horse, and glided forward upon the ledge, directly in front of my adversary.

The animal, seeming to guess my intentions, snorted with affright and reared up, but was compelled to drop again into the same tracks.

The Indian was fixing another shaft. Its notch never reached the string. As the hoofs of the mustang came down upon the rock, I aimed my blow. I struck the animal over the eye. I felt the skull yielding before my hatchet, and the next moment horse and rider, the latter screaming and struggling to clear himself of the saddle, disappeared over the cliff.

There was a moment's silence, a long moment, in which I knew they were falling—falling—down that fearful depth. Then came a loud splash, the concussion of their united bodies on the water below!

I had no curiosity to look over, and as little time. When I regained my upright attitude (for I had come to my knees in giving the blow), I saw the vidette just leaping upon the platform. He did not halt a moment, but advanced at a run, holding his spear at the charge.

I saw that I should be impaled unless I could parry the thrust. I struck wildly, but with success. The lance-blade glinted from the head of my weapon. Its shaft passed me; and our bodies met with a shock that caused us both to reel upon the very edge of the cliff.

As soon as I had recovered my balance, I followed up my blows, keeping close to my antagonist, so that he could not again use his lance. Seeing this, he dropped the weapon and drew his tomahawk. We now fought hand to hand, hatchet to hatchet!

Backward and forward along the ledge we drove each other, as the advantage of the blows told in favour of either, or against him.

Several times we grappled, and would have pushed each other over; but the fear that each felt of being dragged after mutually restrained us, and we let go, and trusted again to our tomahawks.

Not a word passed between us. We had nothing to say, even could we have understood each other. But we had no boast to make, no taunt to urge, nothing before our minds but the fixed dark purpose of murdering one another!

After the first onset the Indian had ceased yelling, and we both fought in the intense earnestness of silence.

There were sounds, though: an occasional sharp exclamation, our quick, high breathing, the clinking of our tomahawks, the neighing of our horses, and the continuous roar of the torrent. These were the symphonies of our conflict.

For some minutes we battled upon the ledge. We were both cut and bruised in several places, but neither of us had as yet received or inflicted a mortal wound.

At length, after a continuous shower of blows, I succeeded in beating my adversary back, until we found ourselves out upon the platform. There we had ample room to wind our weapons, and we struck with more energy than ever. After a few strokes, our tomahawks met, with a violent concussion, that sent them flying from our hands.

Neither dared stoop to regain his weapon; and we rushed upon each other with naked arms, clutched, wrestled a moment, and then fell together to the earth. I thought my antagonist had a knife. I must have been mistaken, otherwise he would have used it; but without it, I soon found that in this species of encounter he was my master. His muscular arms encircled me until my ribs cracked under the embrace. We rolled along the ground, over and over each other. Oh, God! we were nearing the edge of the precipice.

I could not free myself from his grasp. His sinewy fingers were across my throat. They clasped me tightly around the trachea, stopping my breath. He was strangling me.

I grew weak and nerveless. I could resist no longer. I felt my hold relax. I grew weaker and weaker. I was dying. I was—I—Oh, Heaven! pard—on. Oh—!

I could not have been long insensible; for when consciousness returned I was still warm, sweating from the effects of the struggle, and my wounds were bleeding freshly and freely. I felt that I yet lived. I saw that I was still upon the platform; but where was my antagonist? Why had not he finished me? Why had not he flung me over the cliff?

I rose upon my elbow and looked around. I could see no living things but my own horse and that of the Indian galloping over the platform, kicking and plunging at each other.

But I heard sounds, sounds of fearful import, like the hoarse, angry worrying of dogs, mingling with the cries of a human voice—a voice uttered in agony!

What could it mean? I saw that there was a break in the platform, a deep cut in the rock; and out of this the sounds appeared to issue.

I rose to my feet, and, tottering towards the spot, looked in. It was an awful sight to look upon. The gully was some ten feet in depth; and at its bottom, among the weeds and cacti, a huge dog was engaged in tearing something that screamed and struggled. It was a man, an Indian. All was explained at a glance. The dog was Alp; the man was my late antagonist!

As I came upon the edge, the dog was on the top of his adversary, and kept himself uppermost by desperate bounds from side to side, still dashing the other back as he attempted to rise to his feet. The savage was crying in despair. I thought I saw the teeth of the animal fast in his throat, but I watched the struggle no longer. Voices from behind caused me to turn round. My pursuers had reached the cañon, and were urging their animals along the ledge.

I staggered to my horse, and, springing upon his back, once more directed him to the terrace—that part which led outward. In a few minutes I had cleared the cliff and was hurrying down the mountain. As I approached its foot I heard a rustling in the bushes that on both sides lined the path. Then an object sprang out a short distance behind me. It was the Saint Bernard.

As he came alongside he uttered a low whimper and once or twice wagged his tail. I knew not how he could have escaped, for he must have waited until the Indians reached the platform; but the fresh blood that stained his jaws, and clotted the shaggy hair upon his breast, showed that he had left one with but little power to detain him.

On reaching the plain I looked back. I saw my pursuers coming down the face of the sierra; but I had still nearly half a mile of start, and, taking the snowy mountain for my guide, I struck out into the open prairie.

Chapter Fifty Four.

An Unexpected Rencontre.

As I rode off from the mountain foot, the white peak glistened at a distance of thirty miles. There was not a hillock between: not a brake or bush, excepting the low shrubs of the artemisia.

It was not yet noon. Could I reach the snowy mountain before sunset? If so, I trusted in being able to follow our old trail to the mine. Thence, I might keep on to the Del Norte, by striking a branch of the Paloma or some other lateral stream. Such were my plans, undefined as I rode forth.

I knew that I should be pursued almost to the gates of El Paso; and, when I had ridden forward about a mile, a glance to the rear showed me that the Indians had just reached the plain, and were striking out after me.

It was no longer a question of speed. I knew that I had the heels of their whole cavalcade. Did my horse possess the "bottom"?

I knew the tireless, wiry nature of the Spanish mustang; and their animals were of that race. I knew they could gallop for a long day without breaking down, and this led me to fear for the result.

Speed was nothing now, and I made no attempt to keep it up. I was determined to economise the strength of my steed. I could not be overtaken so long as he lasted; and I galloped slowly forward, watching the movements of my pursuers, and keeping a regular distance ahead of them.

At times I dismounted to relieve my horse, and ran alongside of him. My dog followed, occasionally looking up in my face, and seemingly conscious why I was making such a hurried journey.

During all the day I was never out of sight of the Indians; in fact, I could have distinguished their arms and counted their numbers at any time. There were in all about a score of horsemen. The stragglers had gone back, and only the well-mounted men now continued the pursuit.

As I neared the foot of the snowy peak, I remembered there was water at our old camping-ground in the pass; and I pushed my horse faster, in order to gain time to refresh both him and myself. I intended to make a short halt, and allow the noble brute to breathe himself and snatch a bite of the bunch-grass that grew around the spring. There was nothing to fear so long as his strength held out, and I knew that this was the plan to sustain it.

It was near sundown as I entered the defile. Before riding in among the rocks I looked back. During the last hour I had gained upon my pursuers. They were still at least three miles out upon the plain, and I saw that they were toiling on wearily.

I fell into a train of reflection as I rode down the ravine. I was now upon a known trail. My spirits rose; my hopes, so long clouded over, began to assume a brightness and buoyancy, greater from the very influence of reaction. I should still be able to rescue my betrothed. My whole energies, my fortune, my life, would be devoted to this one object. I would raise a band stronger than ever Seguin had commanded. I should get followers among the returning employés of the caravan; teamsters whose term of service had expired. I would search the posts and mountain rendezvous for trappers and hunters. I would apply to the Mexican Government for aid, in money—in troops. I would appeal to the citizens of El Paso, of Chihuahua, of Durango.

"Ge-hosaphat! Hyur's a fellur ridin' 'ithout eyther saddle or bridle!"

Five or six men with rifles sprang out from the rocks, surrounding me.

"May an Injun eat me ef 'tain't the young fellur as tuk me for a grizzly! Billee! look hyur! hyur he is! the very fellur! He! he! he! He! he! he!"

"Rube! Garey!"

"What! By Jove, it's my friend Haller! Hurrah! Old fellow, don't you know me?"

"Saint Vrain!"

"That it is. Don't I look like him? It would have been a harder task to identify you but for what the old trapper has been telling us about you. But come! how have you got out of the hands of the Philistines?"

"First tell me who you all are. What are you doing here?"

"Oh, we're a picket! The army is below."

"The army?"

"Why, we call it so. There's six hundred of us; and that's about as big an army as usually travels in these parts."

"But who? What are they?"

"They are of all sorts and colours. There's the Chihuahuanos and Passenos, and niggurs, and hunters, and trappers, and teamsters. Your humble servant commands these last-named gentry. And then there's the band of your friend Seguin—"

"Seguin! Is he—"

"What? He's at the head of all. But come! they're camped down by the spring. Let us go down. You don't look overfed; and, old fellow, there's a drop of the best Paso in my saddle-bags. Come!"

"Stop a moment! I am pursued."

"Pursued!" echoed the hunters, simultaneously raising their rifles, and looking up the ravine.

"How many?"

"About twenty."

"Are they close upon you?"

"No."

"How long before we may expect them?"

"They are three miles back, with tired horses, as you may suppose."

"Three-quarters—halt an hour at any rate. Come! we'll have time to go down and make arrangements for their reception. Rube! you with the rest can remain here. We shall join you before they get forward. Come, Haller!—come!"

Following my faithful and warm-hearted friend, I rode on to the spring. Around it I found "the army"; and it had somewhat of that appearance, for two or three hundred of the men were in uniform. These were the volunteer guards of Chihuahua and El Paso.

The late raid of the Indians had exasperated the inhabitants, and this unusually strong muster was the consequence. Seguin, with the remnant of his band, had met them at El Paso, and hurried them forward on the Navajo trail. It was from him Saint Vrain had heard of my capture; and in hopes of rescuing me had joined the expedition with about forty or fifty employés of the caravan.

Most of Seguin's band had escaped after the fight in the barranca, and among the rest, I was rejoiced to hear, El Sol and La Luna. They were now on their return with Seguin, and I found them at his tent.

Seguin welcomed me as the bearer of joyful news. They were still safe. That was all I could tell him, and all he asked for during our hurried congratulation.

We had no time for idle talk. A hundred men immediately mounted and rode up the ravine. On reaching the ground occupied by the picket, they led their horses behind the rocks, and formed an ambuscade. The order was, that all the Indians must be killed or taken.

The plan hastily agreed upon was, to let them pass the ambushed men, and ride on until they had got in sight of the main body; then both divisions were to close upon them.

It was a dry ravine above the spring, and the horses had made no tracks upon its rocky bed. Moreover, the Indians, ardent in their pursuit of me, would not be on the outlook for any sign before reaching the water. Should they pass the ambuscade, then not a man of them would escape, as the defile on both sides was walled in by a precipice.

After the others had gone, about a hundred men at the spring leaped into their saddles, and sat with their eyes bent up the pass.

They were not long kept waiting. A few minutes after the ambuscade had been placed, an Indian showed himself round an angle of the rock, about two hundred yards above the spring. He was the foremost of the warriors, and must have passed the ambushed horsemen; but as yet the latter lay still. Seeing a body of men, the savage halted with a quick jerk; and then, uttering a cry, wheeled and rode back upon his comrades. These, imitating his example, wheeled also; but before they had fairly turned themselves in the ravine, the "cached" horsemen sprang out in a body from the rocks and came galloping down.

The Indians, now seeing that they were completely in the trap, with overpowering numbers on both sides of them, threw down their spears and begged for mercy.

In a few minutes they were all captured. The whole affair did not occupy half an hour; and, with our prisoners securely tied, we returned to the spring.

The leading men now gathered around Seguin to settle on some plan for attacking the town. Should we move on to it that night?

I was asked for my advice, and of course answered, "Yes! the sooner the better, for the safety of the captives."

My feelings, as well as those of Seguin, could not brook delay. Besides, several of our late comrades were to die on the morrow. We might still be in time to save them.

How were we to approach the valley?

This was the next point to be discussed.

The enemy would now be certain to have their videttes at both ends, and it promised to be clear moonlight until morning. They could easily see such a large body approaching from the open plain. Here then was a difficulty.

"Let us divide," said one of Seguin's old band; "let a party go in at each end. That'll git 'em in the trap."

"Wagh!" replied another, "that would never do. Thar's ten miles o' rough wood thar. If we raised the niggurs by such a show as this, they'd take to them, gals and all, an' that's the last we'd see o' them."

This speaker was clearly in the right. It would never do to make our attack openly. Stratagem must again be used.

A head was now called into the council that soon mastered the difficulty, as it had many another. That was the skinless, earless head of the trapper Rube.

"Cap," said he, after a short delay, "'ee needn't show yur crowd till we've first took the luk-outs by the eend o' the kenyun."

"How can we take them?" inquired Seguin.

"Strip them twenty niggurs," replied Rube, pointing to our captives, "an' let twenty o' us put on their duds. Then we kin take the young fellur—him hyur as tuk me for the grizzly! He! he! he! Ole Rube tuk for a grizzly! We kin take him back a pris'ner. Now, cap, do 'ee see how?"

"You would have these twenty to keep far in the advance then, capture the videttes, and wait till the main body comes up?"

"Sartinly; thet's my idee adzactly."

"It is the best, the only one. We shall follow it." And Seguin immediately ordered the Indians to be stripped of their dresses. These consisted mostly of garments that had been plundered from the people of the Mexican towns, and were of all cuts and colours.

"I'd recommend 'ee, cap," suggested Rube, seeing that Seguin was looking out to choose the men for his advance party, "I'd recommend 'ee to take a smart sprinklin' of the Delawars. Them Navaghs is mighty 'cute and not easily bamfoozled. They mout sight white skin by moonlight. Them o' us that must go along 'll have to paint Injun, or we'll be fooled arter all; we will."

Seguin, taking this hint, selected for the advance most of the Delaware and Shawano Indians; and these were now dressed in the clothes of the Navajoes. He himself, with Rube, Garey, and a few other whites, made up the required number. I, of course, was to go along and play the role of a prisoner.

The whites of the party soon accomplished their change of dress, and "painted Injun," a trick of the prairie toilet well known to all of them.

Rube had but little change to make. His hue was already of sufficient deepness for the disguise, and he was not going to trouble himself by throwing off the old shirt or leggings. That could hardly have been done without cutting both open, and Rube was not likely to make such a sacrifice of his favourite buckskins. He proceeded to draw the other garments over them, and in a short time was habited in a pair of slashing calzoneros, with bright buttons from the hip to the ankle. These, with a smart, tight-fitting jacket that had fallen to his share, and a jaunty sombrero cocked upon his head, gave him the air of a most comical dandy. The men fairly yelled at seeing him thus metamorphosed, and old Rube himself grinned heartily at the odd feelings which the dress occasioned him.

Before the sun had set, everything was in readiness, and the advance started off. The main body, under Saint Vrain, was to follow an hour after. A few men, Mexicans, remained by the spring, in charge of the Navajo prisoners.

Chapter Fifty Five.

The Rescue.

We struck directly across the plain for the eastern entrance of the valley. We reached the cañon about two hours before day. Everything turned out as we had anticipated. There was an outpost of five Indians at the end of the pass, but we had stolen upon them unawares, and they were captured without the necessity of our firing a shot.

The main body came up soon after, and preceded by our party as before, passed through the cañon. Arriving at the border of the woods nearest the town, we halted, and concealed ourselves among the trees.

The town was glistening in the clear moonlight, and deep silence was over the valley. There were none stirring at so early an hour, but we could descry two or three dark objects down by the river. We knew them to be the sentinels that stood over our captive comrades. The sight was gratifying, for it told us they still lived. They little dreamed, poor fellows! how near was the hour of their deliverance. For the same reasons that had influenced us on a former occasion, the attack was not to be made until daybreak; and we waited as before, but with a very different prospect. There were now six hundred warriors in the town—about our own number; and we knew that a desperate engagement was before us. We had no fear as to the result; but we feared that the vengeful savages might take it into their heads to despatch their captives while we fought. They knew that to recover these was our main object, and, if themselves defeated, that would give them the satisfaction of a terrible vengeance.

All this we knew was far from improbable; but to guard against the possibility of such an event, every precaution was to be taken.

We were satisfied that the captive women were still in the temple. Rube assured us that it was their universal custom to keep new prisoners there for several days after their arrival, until they were finally distributed among the warriors. The queen, too, dwelt in this building.

It was resolved, then, that the disguised party should ride forward, conducting me, as their prisoner, by the first light; and that they should surround the temple, and by a clever *coup* secure the white captives. A signal then given on the bugle, or the first shot fired, was to bring the main body forward at a gallop.

This was plainly the best plan, and having fully arranged its details, we waited the approach of the dawn.

It was not long in coming. The moonlight became mixed with the faint rays of the aurora, and objects were seen more distinctly. As the milky quartz caught the hues of morning, we rode out of our cover, and forward over the plain. I was apparently tied upon my horse, and guarded between two of the Delawares.

On approaching the town we saw several men upon the roofs. They ran to and fro, summoning others out, and large groups began to appear along the terraces. As we came nearer we were greeted with shouts of congratulation.

Avoiding the streets, we pushed directly for the temple at a brisk trot. On arriving at its base we suddenly halted, flung ourselves from our horses, and climbed the ladders. There were many women upon the parapets of the building. Among these Seguin recognised his daughter, the queen. She was at once secured and forced into the inside. The next moment I held my betrothed in my arms, while her mother was by our side. The other captives were there; and, without waiting to offer any explanation, we hurried them all within the rooms, and guarded the doors with our pistols.

The whole manoeuvre had not occupied two minutes but before its completion a wild cry announced that the ruse was detected. Vengeful yells rang over the town; and the warriors, leaping down from their houses, ran towards the temple.

Arrows began to hurtle around us; but above all other sounds pealed the notes of the bugle, summoning our comrades to the attack.

Quick upon the signal they were seen debouching from the woods and coming down at a gallop.

When within two hundred yards of the houses, the charging horsemen divided into two columns, and wheeled round the town, with the intention of attacking it on both sides.

The Indians hastened to defend the skirts of the village; but in spite of their arrow-flights, which dismounted several, the horsemen closed in, and, flinging themselves from their horses, fought hand to hand among the walls. The shouts of defiance, the sharp ringing of rifles, and the louder reports of the escopettes, soon announced that the battle had fairly begun.

A large party, headed by El Sol and Saint Vrain, had ridden up to the temple. Seeing that we had secured the captives, these too dismounted, and commenced an attack upon that part of the town; clambering up to the houses, and driving out the braves who defended them.

The fight now became general. Shouts and sounds of shots rent the air. Men were seen upon high roofs, face to face in deadly and desperate conflict. Crowds of women, screaming and terrified, rushed along the terraces, or ran out upon the plain, making for the woods. Frightened horses, snorting and neighing, galloped through the streets, and off over the open prairie, with trailing bridles; while others, inclosed in corrals, plunged and broke over the walls. It was a wild scene—a terrific picture!

Through all, I was only a spectator. I was guarding a door of the temple in which were our own friends. My elevated position gave me a view of the whole village, and I could trace the progress of the battle from house to house. I saw that many were falling on both sides, for the savages fought with the courage of despair. I had no fears for the result. The whites, too, had wrongs to redress, and by the remembrance of these were equally nerved for the struggle. In this kind of encounter they had the advantage in arms. It was only on the plains that their savage foes were feared, when charging with their long and death-dealing lances.

As I continued to gaze over the azoteas a terrific scene riveted my attention, and I forgot all others. Upon a high roof two men were engaged in combat fierce and deadly. Their brilliant dresses had attracted me, and I soon recognised the combatants. They were Dacoma and the Maricopa!

The Navajo fought with a spear, and I saw that the other held his rifle clubbed and empty.

When my eye first rested upon them, the latter had just parried a thrust, and was aiming a blow at his antagonist. It fell without effect; and Dacoma, turning quickly, brought his lance again to the charge. Before El Sol could ward it off, the thrust was given, and the weapon appeared to pass through his body!

I involuntarily uttered a cry, as I expected to see the noble Indian fall. What was my astonishment at seeing him brandish his tomahawk over his head, and with a crashing blow stretch the Navajo at his feet!

Drawn down by the impaling shaft, he fell over the body, but in a moment struggled up again, drew the long lance from his flesh, and tottering forward to the parapet, shouted out—

“Here, Luna! Our mother is avenged!”

I saw the girl spring upon the roof, followed by Garey; and the next moment the wounded man sank fainting in the arms of the trapper.

Rube, Saint Vrain, and several others now climbed to the roof, and commenced examining the wound. I watched them with feelings of painful suspense, for the character of this most singular man had inspired me with friendship. Presently Saint Vrain joined me, and I was assured that the wound was not mortal. The Maricopa would live.

The battle was now ended. The warriors who survived had fled to the forest. Shots were heard only at intervals; an occasional shout, the shriek of some savage discovered lurking among the walls.

Many white captives had been found in the town, and were brought in front of the temple, guarded by the Mexicans. The Indian women had escaped to the woods during the engagement. It was well; for the hunters and volunteer soldiery, exasperated by wounds and heated by the conflict, now raged around like furies. Smoke ascended from many of the houses; flames followed; and the greater part of the town was soon reduced to a smouldering ruin.

We stayed all that day by the Navajo village, to recruit our animals and prepare for our homeward journey across the desert. The plundered cattle were collected. Some were slaughtered for immediate use, and the rest placed in charge of vaqueros, to be driven on the hoof. Most of the Indian horses were lassoed and brought in, some to be ridden by the rescued captives, others as the booty of the conquerors. But it was not safe to remain long in the valley. There were other tribes of the Navajoes to the north, who would soon be down upon us. There were their allies, the great nations of the Apaches to the south, and the Nijoras to the west; and we knew that all these would unite and follow on our trail. The object of the expedition was attained, at least as far as its leader had designed it. A great number of captives were recovered, whose friends had long since mourned them as lost for ever. It would be some time before they would renew those savage forays in which they had annually desolated the pueblos of the frontier.

By sunrise of the next day we had repassed the cañon, and were riding towards the snowy mountain.

Chapter Fifty Six.

El Paso Del Norte.

I will not describe the recrossing of the desert plains, nor will I detail the incidents of our homeward journey. With all its hardships and weariness, to me it was a pleasant one. It is a pleasure to attend upon her we love, and that along the route was my chief duty. The smiles I received far more than repaid me for the labour I underwent in its discharge. But it was not labour. It was no labour to fill her xuages with fresh water at every spring or runlet, to spread the blanket softly over her saddle, to weave her a *quitasol* out of the broad leaves of the palmilla, to assist her in mounting and dismounting. No; that was not labour to me.

We were happy as we journeyed. I was happy, for I knew that I had fulfilled my contract and won my bride; and the very remembrance of the perils through which we had so lately passed heightened the happiness of both. But one thing cast an occasional gloom over our thoughts—the queen, Adèle.

She was returning to the home of her childhood, not voluntarily, but as a captive—captive to her own kindred, her father and mother!

Throughout the journey both these waited upon her with tender assiduity, almost constantly gazing at her with sad and silent looks. There was woe in their hearts.

We were not pursued; or, if so, our pursuers never came up. Perhaps we were not followed at all. The foe had been crippled and cowed by the terrible chastisement, and we knew it would be some time before they could muster force enough to take our trail. Still we lost not a moment, but travelled as fast as the ganados could be pushed forward.

In five days we reached the Barranca del Oro, and passed the old mine, the scene of our bloody conflict. During our halt among the ruined ranches, I strayed away from the rest, impelled by a painful curiosity to see if aught remained of my late follower or his fellow-victim. I went to the spot where I had last seen their bodies. Yes; two skeletons lay in front of the shaft, as cleanly picked by the wolves as if they had been dressed for the studio of an anatomist. It was all that remained of the unfortunate men.

After leaving the Barranca del Oro, we struck the head waters of the Rio Mimbres; and, keeping on the banks of that stream, followed it down to the Del Norte. Next day we entered the pueblo of El Paso.

A scene of singular interest greeted us on our arrival. As we neared the town, the whole population flocked out to meet us. Some had come forth from curiosity, some to welcome us and take part in the ceremony that hailed our triumphant return, but not a few impelled by far different motives. We had brought with us a large number of rescued captives—nearly fifty in all—and these were soon surrounded by a crowd of citizens. In that crowd were yearning mothers and fond sisters, lovers newly awakened from despair, and husbands who had not yet ceased to mourn. There were hurried inquiries, and quick glances, that betokened keen anxiety. There were "scenes" and shouts of joy, as each one recognised some long-lost object of a dear affection. But there were other scenes of a diverse character, scenes of woe and wailing; for of many of those who had gone forth, but a few days before, in the pride of health and the panoply of war, many came not back.

I was particularly struck with one episode—a painful one to witness. Two women of the poblana class had laid hold upon one of the captives, a girl of, I should think, about ten years of age. Each claimed the girl for her daughter, and each of them held one of her arms, not rudely, but to hinder the other from carrying her off. A crowd had encircled them, and both the women were urging their claims in loud and plaintive voice.

One stated the age of the girl, hastily narrated the history of her capture by the savages, and pointed to certain marks upon her person, to which she declared she was ready at any moment to make *juramento*. The other appealed to the spectators to look at the colour of the child's hair and eyes, which slightly differed from that of the other claimant, and called upon them to note the resemblance she bore to another, who stood by, and who, she alleged, was the child's eldest sister. Both talked at the same time, and kissed the girl repeatedly as they talked.

The little wild captive stood between the two, receiving their alternate embraces with a wondering and puzzled expression. She was, in truth, a most interesting child, habited in the Indian costume, and browned by the sun of the desert. Whichever might have been the mother, it was evident she had no remembrance of either of them; for here there was no mother! In her infancy she had been carried off to the desert, and, like the daughter of Seguin, had forgotten the scenes of her childhood. She had forgotten father—mother—all!

It was, as I have said, a scene painful to witness; the women's looks of anguish, their passionate appeals, their wild but affectionate embraces lavished upon the girl, their plaintive cries mingled with sobs and weeping. It was indeed a painful scene.

It was soon brought to a close, at least as far as I witnessed it. The alcalde came upon the ground; and the girl was given in charge to the policia, until the true mother should bring forward more definite proofs of maternity. I never heard the finale of this little romance.

The return of the expedition to El Paso was celebrated by a triumphant ovation. Cannon boomed, bells rang, fireworks hissed and sputtered, masses were sung, and music filled the streets. Feasting and merriment followed, and the night was turned into a blazing illumination of wax candles, and *un gran funcion de balle*—a fandango.

Next morning, Seguin, with his wife and daughters, made preparations to journey on to the old hacienda on the Del Norte. The house was still standing; so we had heard. It had not been plundered. The savages, on taking possession of it, had been closely pressed by a body of Pasenos, and had hurried off with their captives, leaving everything else as they had found it.

Saint Vrain and I were to accompany the party to their home.

The chief had plans for the future, in which both I and my friend were interested. There we were to mature them.

I found the returns of my trading speculation even greater than Saint Vrain had promised. My ten thousand dollars had been trebled. Saint Vrain, too, was master of a large amount; and we were enabled to bestow our bounty on those of our late comrades who had proved themselves worthy.

But most of them had received "bounty" from another source. As we rode out from El Paso, I chanced to look back. There was a long string of dark objects waving over the gates. There was no mistaking what they were, for they were unlike anything else. They were scalps!

Chapter Fifty Seven.

Touching the Chords of Memory.

It is the second evening after our arrival at the old house on the Del Norte. We have gone up to the azotea—Seguin, Saint Vrain, and myself; I know not why, but guided thither by our host. Perhaps he wishes to look once more over that wild land, the theatre of so many scenes in his eventful life; once more, for upon the morrow he leaves it for ever. Our plans have been formed; we journey upon the morrow; we are going over the broad plains to the waters of the Mississippi. They go with us.

It is a lovely evening, and warm. The atmosphere is elastic; such an atmosphere as you can find only on the high tables of the western world. It seems to act upon all animated nature, judging from its voices. There is joy in the songs of the birds, in the humming of the homeward bees. There is a softness, too, in those sounds that reach us from the farther forest; those sounds usually harsh; the voices of the wilder and fiercer creatures of the wilderness. All seem attuned to peace and love.

The song of the arriero is joyous; for many of these are below, packing for our departure.

I, too, am joyous. I have been so for days; but the light atmosphere around, and the bright prospect before me, have heightened the pulsations of my happiness.

Not so my companions on the azotea. Both seem sad.

Seguin is silent. I thought he had climbed up here to take a last look of the fair valley. Not so. He paces backward and forward with folded arms, his eyes fixed upon the cemented roof. They see no farther; they see not at all. The eye of his mind only is active, and that is looking inward. His air is abstracted; his brow is clouded; his thoughts are gloomy and painful. I know the cause of all this. She is still a stranger!

But Saint Vrain—the witty, the buoyant, the sparkling Saint Vrain—what misfortune has befallen him? What cloud is crossing the rose-coloured field of his horoscope? What reptile is gnawing at his heart, that not even the sparkling wine of El Paso can drown? Saint Vrain is speechless; Saint Vrain is sighing; Saint Vrain is sad! I half divine the cause. Saint Vrain is—

The tread of light feet upon the stone stairway—the rustling of female dresses!

They are ascending. They are Madame Seguin, Adèle, Zoe.

I look at the mother—at her features. They, too, are shaded by a melancholy expression. Why is not she happy? Why not joyous, having recovered her long-lost, much-loved child? Ah! she has not yet recovered her!

I turn my eyes on the daughter—the elder one—the queen. That is the strangest expression of all.

Have you seen the captive ocelot? Have you seen the wild bird that refuses to be tamed, but against the bars of its cage-prison still beats its bleeding wings? If so, it may help you to fancy that expression. I cannot depict it.

She is no longer in the Indian costume. That has been put aside. She wears the dress of civilised life, but she wears it reluctantly. She has shown this, for the skirt is torn in several places, and the bodice, plucked open, displays her bosom, half-nude, heaving under the wild thoughts which agitate it.

She accompanies them, but not us a companion. She has the air of a prisoner, the air of the eagle whose wings have been clipped. She regards neither mother nor sister. Their constant kindness has failed to impress her.

The mother has led her to the azotea, and let go her hand. She walks no longer with them, but crouching, and in starts, from place to place, obedient to the impulse of strong emotions.

She has reached the western wing of the azotea, and stands close up against the parapet, gazing over—gazing upon the Mimbres. She knows them well, those peaks of sparkling selenite, those watch-towers of the desert land: she knows them well. Her heart is with her eyes.

We stand watching her, all of us. She is the object of common solicitude. She it is who keeps between all hearts and the light. The father looks sadly on; the mother looks sadly on; Zoe looks sadly on; Saint Vrain, too. No! that is a different expression. His gaze is the gaze of—

She has turned suddenly. She perceives that we are all regarding her with attention. Her eyes wander from one to the other. They are fixed upon the glance of Saint Vrain!

A change comes over her countenance—a sudden change, from dark to bright, like the cloud passing from the sun. Her eye is fired by a new expression. I know it well. I have seen it before; not in her eyes, but in those that resemble them: the eyes of her sister. I know it well. It is the light of love!

Saint Vrain! His, too, are lit by a similar emotion! Happy Saint Vrain! Happy that it is mutual. As yet he knows not that, but I do. I could bless him with a single word.

Moments pass. Their eyes mingle in fiery communion. They gaze into each other. Neither can avert their glance. A god rules them: the god of love!

The proud and energetic attitude of the girl gradually forsakes her; her features relax; her eye swims with a softer expression; and her whole bearing seems to have undergone a change.

She sinks down upon a bench. She leans against the parapet. She no longer turns to the west. She no longer gazes upon the Mimbres. Her heart is no longer in the desert land!

No; it is with her eyes, and these rest almost continuously on Saint Vrain. They wander at intervals over the stones of the azotea; then her thoughts do not go with them; but they ever return to the same object, to gaze upon it tenderly, more tenderly at each new glance.

The anguish of captivity is over. She no longer desires to escape. There is no prison where he dwells. It is now a paradise. Henceforth the doors may be thrown freely open. That little bird will make no further effort to fly from its cage. It is tamed.

What memory, friendship, entreaties, had tailed to effect, love had accomplished in a single instant. Love, mysterious power, in one pulsation had transformed that wild heart; had drawn it from the desert.

I fancied that Seguin had noticed all this, for he was observing her movements with attention. I fancied that such thoughts were passing in his mind, and that they were not unpleasing to him, for he looked less afflicted than before. But I did not continue to watch the scene. A deeper interest summoned me aside; and, obedient to the sweet impulse, I strayed towards the southern angle of the azotea.

I was not alone. My betrothed was by my side; and our hands, like our hearts, were locked in each other.

There was no secrecy about our love; with Zoe there never had been.

Nature had prompted the passion. She knew not the conventionalities of the world, of society, of circles refined, soi-disant. She knew not that love was a passion for one to be ashamed of.

Hitherto no presence had restrained her in its expression—not even that, to lovers of less pure design, awe-inspiring above all others—the presence of the parents. Alone or in their company, there was no difference in her conduct. She knew not the hypocrisies of artificial natures; the restraints, the intrigues, the agonies of atoms that act.

She knew not the terror of guilty minds. She obeyed only the impulse her Creator had kindled within her.

With me it was otherwise. I had shouldered society; though not much then, enough to make me less proud of love's purity—enough to render me slightly sceptical of its sincerity. But through her I had now escaped from that scepticism. I had become a faithful believer in the nobility of the passion.

Our love was sanctioned by those who alone possessed the right to sanction it. It was sanctified by its own purity.

We are gazing upon a fair scene: fairer now, at the sunset hour. The sun is no longer upon the stream, but his rays slant through the foliage of the cotton-wood trees that fringe it, and here and there a yellow beam is flung transversely on the water. The forest is dappled by the high tints of autumn. There are green leaves and red ones; some of a golden colour and others of dark maroon. Under this bright mosaic the river winds away like a giant serpent, hiding its head in the darker woods around El Paso.

We command a view of all this, for we are above the landscape. We see the brown houses of the village, with the shining vane of its church. Our eyes have often rested upon that vane in happy hours, but none happier than now, for our hearts are full of happiness.

We talk of the past as well as the present; for Zoe has now seen something of life, its darker pictures it is true; but these are often the most pleasant to be remembered; and her desert experience has furnished her with many a new thought—the cue to many an inquiry.

The future becomes the subject of our converse. It is all bright, though a long and even perilous journey is before us. We think not of that. We look beyond it to that promised hour when I am to teach, and she is to learn, what is "to marry."

Someone is touching the strings of a bandolin. We look around. Madame Seguin is seated upon a bench, holding the instrument in her hands. She is tuning it. As yet she has not played. There has been no music since our return.

It is by Seguin's request that the instrument has been brought up, with the music, to chase away heavy memories; or, perhaps, from a hope that it may soothe those savage ones still dwelling in the bosom of his child.

Madame Seguin is about to play, and my companion and I go nearer to listen.

Seguin and Saint Vrain are conversing apart. Adèle is still seated where we left her, silent and abstracted.

The music commences. It is a merry air—a fandango: one of those to which the Andalusian foot delights to keep time.

Seguin and Saint Vrain have turned. We all stand looking in the face of Adèle. We endeavour to read its expression.

The first notes have startled her from her attitude of abstraction. Her eyes wander from one to the other, from the instrument to the player, with looks of wonder—of inquiry.

The music continues. The girl has risen, and, as it mechanically, approaches the bench where her mother is seated. She crouches down by the feet of the latter, places her ear close up to the instrument, and listens attentively. There is a singular expression upon her face.

I look at Seguin. That upon his is not less singular. His eye is fixed upon the girl's, gazing with intensity. His lips are apart, yet he seems not to breathe. His arms hang neglected, and he is leaning forward as if to read the thoughts that are passing within her.

He starts erect again, as though under the impulse of some sudden resolution.

"Oh, Adèle! Adèle!" he cries, hurriedly addressing his wife; "oh, sing that song; that sweet hymn, you remember; you used to sing it to her—often, often. You remember it, Adèle! Look at her. Quick! quick! O God! Perhaps she may—"

He is interrupted by the music. The mother has caught his meaning, and with the adroitness of a practised player, suddenly changes the tune to one of a far different character. I recognise the beautiful Spanish hymn, "La madre a su hija" (The mother to her child). She sings it, accompanying her voice with the bandolin. She throws all her energy into the song until the strain seems inspired. She gives the words with full and passionate effect—

"Tu duermes, cara niña!
Tu duertnes en la paz.
Los angeles del cielo—
Los angeles guardan, guardan,
Niña mia!—Ca—ra—mi—"

The song was interrupted by a cry—a cry of singular import—uttered by the girl. The first words of the hymn had caused her to start, and then to listen, if possible, more attentively than ever. As the song proceeded, the singular expression we had noted seemed to become every moment more marked and intense. When the voice had reached the burden of the melody, a strange exclamation escaped her lips; and, springing to her feet, she stood gazing wildly in the face of the singer. Only for a moment. The next moment she cried in loud, passionate accents, "Mamma! mamma!" and fell forward upon the bosom of her mother!

Seguin spoke truly when he said, "Perhaps in God's mercy she may yet remember." She had remembered—not only her mother, but in a short time she remembered him. The chords of memory had been touched, its gates thrown open. She remembered the history of her childhood. She remembered all!

I will not essay to describe the scene that followed. I will not attempt to picture the expression of the actors; to speak of their joyous exclamations, mingled with sobs and tears; but they were tears of joy.

All of us were happy—happy to exultation; but for Seguin himself, I knew it was the hour of his life.

C ***The End.***

CPSIA information can be obtained at www.ICGtesting.com
Printed in the USA
LVOW09s1459011115
460636LV00024B/607/P